Praise for
the EPIC STORY of EVERY LIVING THING

A *Kirkus Reviews* Best Young Adult Book of the Year
A *BookPage* Best Young Adult Book of the Year
A *Booklist* Editors' Choice
A Chicago Public Library Best Book of the Year
A Bank Street College of Education Best Children's Book of the Year

★ "This **gorgeous coming-of-age novel thoughtfully examines questions of identity, family, kindness, and a longing for connection**. . . . Also deftly and empathetically engages head-on with anxiety." —*Kirkus Reviews*, starred review

★ "Caletti's bighearted novel, which endorses the wonders of being present . . . uses two seemingly perpendicular voyages to **expertly navigate themes of belonging, connection, family, and identity.**" —*Publishers Weekly*, starred review

★ "Through this novel about overcoming fear and expectations, **Caletti examines what makes a person—is it their DNA,** their lived experiences, or the family who raised them?" —*School Library Journal*, starred review

★ "[A] heartwarming and authentic story that's packed with a collage of well-researched detail, people, and themes. . . . **Will find itself right at home in collections with strong contemporary YA.**" —*Booklist*, starred review

★ "Caletti's **sophisticated, intricate storytelling** brings complexity and richness. . . . Both deeply introspective and profoundly engaged with the world." —*BookPage*, starred review

"**A rich, contemplative story** about looking beneath the (literal and figurative) surface to find love, purpose, and joy." —*The Horn Book*

True LIFE in UNCANNY Valley

Also by
DEB CALETTI

True
LIFE
in
UNCANNY
Valley

DEB CALETTI

LR LABYRINTH ROAD | NEW YORK

Labyrinth Road
An imprint of Random House Children's Books
A division of Penguin Random House LLC
1745 Broadway, New York, NY 10019
penguinrandomhouse.com
GetUnderlined.com

Text copyright © 2025 by Deb Caletti
Jacket art copyright © 2025 by Maeve Norton

Editor: Liesa Abrams
Cover Designer: Angela Carlino
Interior Designer: Megan Shortt
Production Editors: Barbara Bakowski and Clare Perret
Managing Editor: Rebecca Vitkus
Production Manager: Natalia Dextre

Library of Congress Cataloging-in-Publication Data is available upon request.
ISBN 978-0-593-70861-3 (trade) — ISBN 978-0-593-70863-7 (ebook)

The text of this book is set in 11.25-point font Adobe Garamond Pro.

Manufactured in the United States of America
10 9 8 7 6 5 4 3 2 1
The authorized representative in the EU for product safety and compliance is
Penguin Random House Ireland, Morrison Chambers, 32 Nassau Street, Dublin
D02 YH68, Ireland, https://eu-contact.penguin.ie.

For
RILEY JADE

chapter
One

SO, I'M SITTING IN MOM'S OLD FORD TAURUS, STARING right inside his house. I don't even need my binoculars—it's night, and the rooms are lit up. Even in the day you can spy pretty easily because the place is all glass. If you were as famous as he is, you'd think you'd want privacy, but nope. It's like everyone sees him, but he wants to be seen more, more, more. I mean, he lives in the biggest fishbowl ever. Huge, you can't even imagine. *Bowl* isn't really the right word—it's more of a long architectural mishmash of off-kilter squares and rectangles, set on three hundred spectacular feet of Lake Washington waterfront. That's practically a direct quote from every article ever written about the place, and, trust me, I've read them a hundred times.

Picture the extravagant, glinting lair of a titan in Gotham or Metropolis or Coast City. Yeah, the one that belongs to the brilliant, charismatic scientist of the comics, who's also a conniving billionaire. He's got headquarters downtown, too, in a building that towers over all the others, featuring a beam of neon shooting from the top. The doors spill workers with intellectual-outsider vibes.

He's either the criminal mastermind or the real hero. That's what I'm here to find out. Who is he? Who is he *really*?

Wait. I see him. Do I see him? No, it's only a trick of the light. My heart hammers anyway, battering away in my chest. Hearts get confused about what's real, and sneaking around to discover the truth is a scary business. I try to breathe deeply. If he's the brilliant scientist, then I can only be one person. Okay, she'd never be this nervous, and she'd never be wearing these crappy old yellow leggings and the Oregon Caves T-shirt we got on the one major vacation that Mom and me and my sister, Rosalind, ever took. But that's exactly why I need her. She's my inspiration and my secret power. In that car I close my eyes, ever so briefly.

Pretend you're opening an old comic book, the kind with really cool lettering and bold images colored in cyan and magenta, yellow and black. That's what I do right then. It's the Golden Age of Comics, so usually you only see chiseled superhero dudes, but not this time. This one features a woman. A woman you wish you could be. She's so brave, and stylish, and sexy, and living an amazing life of heroes and villains. Bad guys, good guys, it's all so clear. And, God, she's totally gorgeous in that tight blue-black suit, strong and physical, not afraid of anyone or anything. No one is looking at her and judging, or not seeing her at all and judging. She's just a *force*.

The comic book I envision opening is always the same one: *Miss Fury, Summer Issue, No. 2,* from 1942. On the cover, Miss Fury (in her regular life, Marla Drake) descends into a room with her cape flying. She kicks the shit out of some Nazis, and looks spectacular while doing it. How can you *not* be swept up? This is the *first* female superhero ever drawn by one of the *first* female cartoonists, June Tarpé Mills. Double inspiration, triple. Miss Fury herself, plus her creator, both of them up in a fight against sinister motivations and impossible odds, and then . . . that *art*. Man, I wish I could draw like that. One day I will. Fiction is so great, you know. It saves you. It holds your hand and gives you a kick in the butt. It's there for you, even while you sit in a Ford Taurus outside a billionaire's house.

I open my eyes. The hammering in my heart has slowed. Hey, it's still here, the house made of 2,019 framed panes of glass. I'm still here, too, even if he doesn't—can't, won't—see me.

Get it? *Frame?* 2019? Yep, *that* Frame, the very first, splashiest, most innovative AI art generator ever, released that very year by the splashiest, most innovative tech dude ever, Mr. Charisma himself, Mr. Wild Card, Mr. What Shocking Thing Will I Do Next? Mr. Sexiest Man Alive (gross). Mr. This Billionaire Is Just a Regular Guy (a *GQ* article headline about him). Mr. I Created

That App Where People Rate Each Other, Then I Created Frame. Mr. I'm Making Something New and Life-Altering Right This Minute, But It's a Secret.

Well, now you know whose house I'm staring into. I'm hoping (badly hoping, it's sad how much I'm hoping) to spot the great Hugo Harrison himself; or maybe his young, glamorous wife, Aurora; or their little two-year-old tot, Arlo. Or even their dog, Boolean. Boolean is a computer programming term, apparently. It's one of those things you have to keep looking up because it just won't stick in your brain. Boolean: a data result that has only one of two possible values, true or false. No idea. A lot of the stuff in Hugo Harrison's life, same. AI, artificial intelligence, too—my mind can't grasp the facts. What is it, actually? It's nothing and everything. It's hard to tell what's real about it. It reminds me of when we were little and Rosalind insisted on reading the rules of every board game aloud. I'd stick my fingers in my ears and sing, *Can't hear you!* and she'd yell for Mom to make me stop because *it's important, Eleanor!* I just wanted to play. The game was cool, and we'd figure it out.

This is probably hard to understand, but the same thing goes for him. I don't want to hear the rules; I just want to play. The game is *so* cool. I mean, just *creating* stuff like that. Ingenious, artistic, world-changing stuff, wow. Being a creator—it seems like the highest calling, you know. It's a connection we have, too: He invented this whole app to make art, and I want to be an artist. If he's either the criminal mastermind or the real hero in my personal comic book, I am seriously wishing for hero. The thing is—you can memorize every rule in an instruction book, but you won't actually know a thing about the game until you're playing.

I gaze in at the white living room, and I just wait for someone to enter the stage. It's one way that Hugo Harrison and I are different, for sure, because being seen usually makes me deeply uncomfortable. He's on magazine covers, and I turn red when I get called on in class. Once, in PE, a kid passed me the basketball during a game and I froze, and my teammates started yelling. After that I made sure to always run around and look busy, far from any actual ball. Private moments of excess attention can be even worse. Like that time my mom and sister decided I needed a makeover, and I had to parade out of my room wearing ripped jeans and a crop top featuring the word *Amore* in glitter. Oh geez. They were trying to be nice, but my insides curl up even thinking about it.

My sister said, *Relax! Loosen up!* and my mom said, *You look great!* but I felt like the baking-soda–and–vinegar volcano that never volcanoed. I could hear all the exclamation points they were using, ringing false. They both just looked at me for a moment, and then Rosalind sighed and said, *Oh, Eleanor,* and my mom laughed.

There's a part of me that hopes that Hugo Harrison and I are more similar than different. A big part. At home I'm always the third wheel.

Wait, wait! There's a flash of movement, for sure this time. I grab my binoculars. In the car right then, I'm not *Oh, Eleanor.* I'm Miss Fury, in my own frame, concealed in sleek black-blue. Unseen by choice, peering into the windows of my archnemesis, the gold-digging Baroness von Kampf. Another great thing about fiction? It states what it is and isn't right up front. Not the truth, but speaking truth. Doing its best to convince you it's real, but with your full knowledge and permission. People shouldn't try to trick us about that, about what isn't real, though of course they do it all the time.

Is it a staff member? The Harrison family likes to keep its household employees to a minimum, in a constant goal to live as "normal" as possible, something that gets mentioned repeatedly in interviews. Normal, meaning not wealthy, which isn't something normal people ever wish for. I'm pretty familiar with the regulars—the chef, Jak DeLario, former head chef of that chic restaurant The Block. Also the landscapers, and an older woman who's the housekeeper, I'm pretty sure. There's Hugo's executive assistant, Mathew, too, and a few different nannies, who don't seem to stay long. I focus, twist the dials for clarity; wouldn't that be an awesome feature in real life?

Ah, the flash isn't even a person. It's just Boolean. He's one of those huge, beautiful Bernese mountain dogs, the kind that always manage to look tired and hot and overburdened even when it's a cold day. I watch him make his way down the Harrisons' third-floor hall and collapse on the floor, as if it's all suddenly too much to bear. I've had that exact same feeling a thousand times.

I touched him once, Boolean. He felt so good! The Harrisons had a dog walker for a while, this lady named Sahara or Sierra or something like that. I heard Aurora calling out a greeting to her once. An outdoor name that suggested adventure in the vast world when she pretty much just walked around Laurelhurst with rich people's dogs. Remind me if I ever have a baby not to name the poor kid something that she has to measure up to. Sahara or Sierra was the kind of dog walker you'd see in a romantic comedy where she's always getting the leashes twisted up and almost tripping because she's trying to talk on her phone at the same time. In her case, though, she only had Boolean. The point is, she was distracted enough that I could drive down the block, whip out of Mom's car, and pretend I was just walking along from the other direction. Tra-la-la—oh, what a surprise! A gorgeous giant dog! I wanted to start up a conversation, you know, see if I could maybe get some little piece of information.

Those bits of information . . . It sounds pathetic, but they mean so much. They really do. I can relish a tiny detail same as a chocolate, savoring it as it slowly fades. Like that time a kid in my class bragged that he saw Hugo Harrison at Whole Foods, buying only a mango and a bar of avocado soap. This is embarrassing to admit, but I even went to Whole Foods and looked at the avocado soap to try to guess which kind. I mean, there were, like, six varieties, which is one of those things people from the pioneer days would find unbelievable. I find it pretty unbelievable now, to be honest. But I even picked them up, the white box with the artistic image of the avocado, the green box with no avocado, the cream box with the avocado line drawing, the box-less avocado soap stacked on the table with all the other scents, vanilla and papaya and mint, sitting there so creamy and smooth you want to bite them.

She was on the phone, though, distracted as they waited for a *Walk* sign. My hand sank into Boolean's fur. He *was* a mountain, and his fur was the thickest thicket, and his eyes looked at me soulfully. They offered me kindness, because dogs, by some miracle, stay pure of spirit, and can't give a shit about status. We sort of had a moment. I gave him love straight through my eyes, and he gave it right back. Possible values, true or false—Boolean is true.

The binoculars are supergood ones, expensive. I spent a lot of money on them last summer, when I first started watching Hugo Harrison. I had to use a lot of my savings, but they're worth it. I can see the mountain of Boolean inhale and exhale, and I remember the feel of him, because hands have their own memory. I watch his eyes close. His bushy eyebrows fold together in a troubled *V*. I wonder if he's dreaming of home. Of Bern, or of someone's rec room where he was born. I wonder if he's as confused as I am about where he came from and where he truly belongs.

It's cold in the car, and it's getting chilly enough in here that I'd better go home or I'll have to turn on the engine to warm up. We're having an unexpectedly chilly spell for late April. Global warming, it's overwhelming to think about. I even brought my fingerless gloves that Rosalind gave me. She said they're stylish, but they suddenly seem ridiculous, like a lot of objects that aren't whole but you pay good money for anyway—jeans with premade tears, doughnuts, crop tops that say *Amore*. It's getting late, and sitting there in the dark with the motor running, and in a car like this, outside of Hugo Harrison's house—someone might call the police. I've wanted to do it myself, those times I've seen that guy sitting in his truck watching this same house, because what are you up to, dude? In a comic, when the police arrive, it's an exciting moment of old-timey black-and-white cars surrounding the place, exclamation points galore. In real life, it would just be terrifying.

I put the binoculars back in their little pouch and zip them in. I picture the word *Zip!* in an energetic font. I imagine sketching those words, and for a moment I think about the beautiful, individual personalities of fonts—quiet or bold or elegant. Just as quickly, I'm aware that these are the kinds of thoughts my mom and sister tease me about when I say them out loud, so I've pretty much stopped. When I try to explain how a city skyline can look both menacing and reassuring, depending on how it's drawn, or how thrilling it is when good trumps evil on a page since it's such a lie in real life—they look at me like I'm from another planet. Two different planets under one roof are a lot of planets.

I'm about to leave when something unusual happens. A truck arrives. It drives around to the service entrance, where I can't see anything. But, whoa, lights are coming on, too. More lights. Boom, boom, boom—like a Broadway show about to start.

What is going on? There's a sudden flood of commotion. The front door opens, and several young women come out. They line the front walk with votives and light them. Incredible. *Magic.* Inside, it's as if a flower is blooming, or lots of flowers—everything opens, brightens. My eyes blink from the beauty. Actual flowers whoosh in, too. Arrangements on tables, and more outside. Even though the backyard is hidden from here, I know what it looks like. If you rent a kayak at the UW campus, you can see it from the lake. I only did that once, because kayak. Let me tell you, if you put too much weight to one side, you just go round in circles. This is both a life truth and a kayak truth.

The fireplaces turn on, with their long rows of blue-orange flames. Candles are lit. More light! Platters of food, tiers of food, baskets and bowls of food appear. Arlo speeds past stark naked. Boolean is up and about again and tries to snitch a canapé. I say *canapé*, but I'm only guessing. I've never had a canapé in my life, unless you count the crackers and cheese from the annual holiday party Mom gives as branch manager of Heartland Bank. She's worked there since she was nineteen, so long that she's now the boss of her old friend Allison, who operates the drive-through. You may remember Heartland as the bank that got into trouble a few years ago for selling account data. You may also remember that an anonymous person changed the signs of all twenty local branches to read *Fartland,* and they stayed like that for weeks. Still, Mom remains fiercely proud of their *unparalleled customer service.*

Aurora's white Aston Martin arrives and then disappears around the curved drive toward the garage. Sometimes she just (*just,* haha) drives their Land Rover, especially when she heads to places like the Green Lake pool. Another thing about the Harrisons—you always read how much everyone loves him, but, man, people sure do dislike her, maybe Mom and Rosalind most of all. We're required to *hate* her. We used to hate Hugo's first wife, Susan, but now we really hate Aurora. I don't even want to say the words my mom uses for her, in that hard and bitter voice. People online are also downright vicious about Aurora, sometimes even in the comments on her own posts. Is this why they go through so many nannies? Because they hate her, too? It's just another Harrison family mystery that keeps me hooked, same as a good series. I have so many questions, like why Aurora even goes to the Green

Lake pool when they have an indoor and an outdoor pool at the house. I know she goes there because I followed her a few weeks in a row, just to see where she goes on a regular basis.

Whoa. Here she comes now, walking along the glass hallway. She's in a breathtaking green column dress, something the baroness would wear, for sure. In my personal version of Miss Fury, our archenemy, Aurora, is most definitely the evil, gold-digging Baroness von Kampf, who steals the heart of Marla Drake's former boyfriend (close enough) and has his kid, a kid who Marla tries to adopt when the baroness mistreats him. The point is, she's a glamorous-but-evil bitch lady, with luminous, flowing hair that covers a swastika on her forehead. Perfect. I mean, look—Aurora is pure shimmer in those gold heels. Her blond hair even spills down like a waterfall, swooping across her forehead. She's only twelve years older than I am, twenty-eight, but she's living a life that's eons away from mine.

A party. A party!

I'm so glad I didn't leave!

Wow—all of it . . . This is no small hoarded detail, no overheard avocado soap, no Amazon delivery or six champagne bottles in the recycling bin, with one snitched cork hidden in my sock drawer. This is an abundance of detail, as abundant as that food, and just as nourishing. Flowers, orchids! So many orchids! Arlo, now in sleeper pajamas that look charmingly like a suit! (I think charmingly? Him with his sweet, satiny hair—the bow tie carries the strain of forced cheer, even though it's only printed on.) The thump of music begins.

My cell phone buzzes. It's my sister's old one, a Christmas

present from her ex-boyfriend Niles, and the screen is cracked, but whatever. It's her calling, too, probably because I've ignored her three frantic texts. I should have had the car back a good hour ago, and she's supposed to be hanging out with friends. It's Friday night, after all. A time when most people our age (well, Rosalind's finishing her freshman year at Shoreline Community College, and I'm in my last quarter of junior year at Roosevelt High) are out doing something besides sitting in a car and snooping on strangers.

I ignore her. Maybe they'll worry, Rosalind and Mom. I have the sort of ungenerous thought that makes you sure you need to work on being a better person: *Let them.*

Cars are arriving now. Guests! It's silly, but I feel elated. It's electrifying, even if that party is in there and I'm out here. I want it all, I do. I admit it. Just to be in all that light. Part of it. The driveway fills, and then the street. Cars fit into spaces around me, headlights circling, and I pretend to do important things on my phone to look innocent, probably one of the most-often uses of cell phones in general. I sneak glances at the couples, outfitted in stunning dresses and chic suits. The front door opens and shuts and opens.

Oh my God, it's amazing. I've lost track of time entirely. When it's safe (and, uh-oh, my phone is buzzing like mad now), I lift my binoculars again. I see him, Hugo Harrison. He's easy to find. Just look for the center of the hive, the spot where a ray of light seems to almost emanate, the center point, the source of a vibration. His company's name is Psyckē, meaning "the spirit, the breath of life, the essential, invisible animating entity." Imagine what God is giving Adam in that painting on the Sistine Chapel ceiling, where their two fingers almost touch. Hugo's definitely God in this scenario, but he's also the thing, the energy, that God is giving. He's the creator, creating, and it's awe-inspiring. In spite of everything else, it just is. Wild dark hair, thick untrimmed beard, dancing eyes, big nose, eccentric clothes—striped pants, a flowy shirt, a pair of heavy-framed black glasses he might not even need, another mystery, who knows. Boots with red laces, an unkempt appearance that says *I may or may not have showered for you, but you have definitely showered for me.*

I circle my binoculars away from him, even though it's like pulling a magnet away from a magnet. I search around for someone I know (as if I'm actually at that party, right, looking for a familiar face) and am relieved to see Mathew, Hugo's executive assistant. He looks like a Hollywood agent, the way I'd imagine one, anyway. Trim, handsome, harried, wearing those short pants without socks that somehow have become fashionable, no idea.

But wait.

Wait, wait, wait! Wait just a minute here.

Oh *shit.*

Oh my God! My body floods with anxiety. No, *alarm.* Oh no, oh no! What should I do? Should I do something? I need to do something. Talking with Mathew . . . Well, not really talking, but more like hovering around the edges of a group that includes Mathew, is someone else I know. Not *know,* but he's a familiar face, all right? That guy in the truck, the one I've seen watching the house a few times, same as *I* watch the house. No, correction. NOT as I watch the house, because I'm innocent, and we have no idea what he is. He's young. Maybe Rosalind's age or a little older. I've never seen him up close, so who knows. But what I do know—he sits there and watches, lurks. He could be dangerous. I mean, why would he do that, just hang around like that, spying? Besides *my* reason. This guy, I'm sure he's up to no good, and now he's *in the house.*

I need to act, but what do I do? Call the police and say, *Hey, I'm a stalker reporting a stalker?* Even though *stalker* is a very, very wrong word for me. That guy, though. He's *right there.* He's, like, a few feet from Hugo Harrison, and there's no telling what he's planning. My mind is just spinning, my stomach all clenched, because what if something bad happens as I just sit here and watch?

What would Miss Fury do?

I imagine her again—Miss Fury, with her confidence and style. As superheroes go, this is important: She doesn't have any actual powers. No special skills, aside from her fashion sense. No wild backstory involving an emergence of some incredible ability. She's just all the things you want to *be,* that *I* want to be: smart, and observant, and unafraid, yeah. She's things *other people* want me to be, too: stylish, as I've mentioned, so much so that she has her own paper doll in the back of the comic, with a wild wardrobe of cutout clothes. She's decisive, and furious—it's her actual *name.* My best friends, Arden Lee and Clementine—they're always saying I should maybe be angrier.

Miss Fury would scale the Harrison house, sneak through a window, tackle the intruder. She would whip off his mask (he's not wearing one, but whatever) and discover his true identity. She would fix this, is the point. She would make what's wrong right, what's confusing clear, what's dangerous safe. She would be bigger than bad.

I, however, am not bigger than bad. My paper doll would have this T-shirt, these old leggings, and my fury is a seed underground. I'm afraid I'm about to witness something horrible, something I can't do anything about. That's one of the best things about Miss Fury. She has control over stuff that people don't have control over in real life—bad guys, evil. What a joke to believe that anyone has control over those things, but what a comfort, too.

I hate myself for this, but I can't watch. If that guy, what, pulls out a poison dart or something and sticks it into Hugo Harrison, I don't want to see it. I'm just a girl in a car fighting a sense of dread. This is real, not ink on paper.

When I start the car, failure surrounds me, cold and heavy. I drive away from the lights and the celebration, from the drama and even the possible danger, and there's this sense, you know, that I'm more alone than I've ever been in my life.

Maybe this is just how you feel when you could be living in that very house you're driving away from. When you could, at this very moment, be at that party, whispering to Aurora about the odd guy you've seen outside. When, at the end of that hopefully safe and contented night, you could step over that big dog and head down the hall, kissing little Arlo good night before heading to your own room. When they could all be people in your life that you love, and not villains, not archenemies.

When the thing you should maybe be angrier about is that Hugo Harrison is your father, but you only watch him through 2,019 frames of glass.

chapter
Two

THE MEMBERS OF THE SOGGY PAGES BOOK CLUB (ME, Arden Lee, and Clementine) unanimously agree that one of the most annoying critiques a book can get is that the characters are flawed and make bad decisions and are therefore unlikable. Arden Lee once got so worked up on the subject that his paisley-and-satin vest now has the permanent watercolor sweat stains to prove it.

The bad decisions the readers get all pissed about—they're not usually huge and horrible wrongdoings like murder or thievery, drug use, whatever. No, what they get most upset about are failures of love and hope and vulnerability—too much of any of those, usually. Failures of belief. Maybe it makes a person get a little uneasy, you know. You can be sure that you'll never commit a murder, but some tiny piece of you might be nervous about tumbling into too much love or hope or belief. Better shout it from the rooftops, then, or your favorite book-reviewing site: I would never! Who would ever! Well, congratulations on making it unscathed through the gauntlet of being human, I say. So far. And the members of the Soggy Pages agree.

I guess this is a warning that you're about to witness my bad decisions, my failures in hope and love and belief. This might be a wild story with a comic-book plot, a story that sounds like fiction, but it's full of humans, in spite of the robot. And humans are flawed, in case you haven't noticed. Even Miss Fury and June Tarpé Mills are. That's part of the whole point. What do you do with those flaws? *How a character* evolves, *that's the important thing,* Arden Lee said on that sweaty-vest day. *And some people never evolve,* Clementine added, something she knows more than most.

Plus, hope can be a villain that looks a lot like a hero.

———

BEFORE I DRIVE HOME, I MAKE SURE TO HIDE THE evidence of the bad decisions I've made so far. They're not all that bad, compared to what's coming. But I tuck those binoculars far down into my backpack. When I finally arrive on our street, Mom nearly backs right up into me as she reverses out of our driveway with Rosalind in the passenger seat. Our mother, Brandi Diamond (*Brandi with an* i, *Diamond cuz I'm a jewel,* her social media bios read), slams on the brakes when she spots me. She rolls down the window, sticks her head out. She's fixed her hair all fancy, loose blond twirls made with the biggest curling iron, and she's wearing mascara and lipstick. Her eyes are shiny with . . . anger, worry, excitement? Hard to tell. Anything could happen. That's the bio I'd write for her: *You just never know.* She's as multifaceted as that gem in our last name, full of love and rage, loyalty and jealousy, generosity and coldness, flirtatious fun and cruelty. Put that in a blender, push the button, and don't use a lid. It's not the worst plan to be quiet and watchful as you stand nearby with the paper towels, in case there's a mess.

"I was worried sick, missy! Do you *ever* think about other people? You couldn't even call?"

"I'm sorry. I lost track of time," I say.

"Well, you're here now."

Huh. Mom can be a weather system, and I'm a diligent, anxious forecaster, so right that minute I see that she's maybe not all that mad, not really. It's more mad-for-show.

Rosalind, though.

"Do you have any idea how late I am?" Rosalind leans forward so I can see her face. She's so pretty, even when she's angry. Her hair is golden, like Mom's, and her skin is golden, and even her green eyes have flecks of gold. The night is cool, but she's wearing a silky halter-style top in a leopard print. I blink, because two cats. Mom is in her leopard bodycon dress, the one that shows an embarrassing amount of cleavage. *If you have a problem with it, that's* your *problem,* she's said, and she's not wrong. They're either going to a feline-themed party or they accidentally dressed alike again.

"I'm so sorry," I repeat, hoping that leopards care about regret.

"Didn't you notice the windows of the *library* getting dark?" Rosalind snaps. That's where I told them I'd be. Rosalind always says it like that, as if me being at a library is something to distrust, as if the library itself is. She thinks books are an assignment, something a teacher tells you to do, which shows you right away how different we are. Same with Mom, who claims she looooved *Eat, Pray, Love* but maybe just saw the movie.

To them, it's especially suspicious that me and Clementine and Arden Lee have a book club. It's like we're secretly building bombs instead of reading. It's not the worst analogy—private ammunition you're amassing. And it's fine by me if people like Rosalind never discover the power of books and the library itself to be so many things to a person, including a shield and an excuse. Golden Rosalind and her golden friends already have so much power, it's fair that one of the biggest sources of it remains overlooked by them, quietly hidden in the shelter of the library. Let them think books are dull. Let it be our secret.

"I'll be more careful next time, I promise," I lie. When it comes to Hugo Harrison, I have zero control.

"Well, I'll just turn around now that she's back. You can take the car," Mom says as Rosalind presses her lips together, mad.

"No, no. It's fine," Rosalind says in that high-pitched voice that means it's *not* fine. "We're in the car already! Let's just *go.*"

"I'll drop you off, then! I'll turn right back around and come *home,*" Mom says, hurt.

"You don't *have* to!" Rosalind says. Meaning, you have to. It's one of those weird fight-not-fights. A below-the-surface tug-of-war. Golden people—well, I guess if you want to remain golden, you're stuck being passive-aggressive. That's the deal you made. Rosalind looks at Mom, and her expression shifts into something complicated and unreadable. She lets go of her end of the rope. "You can hang out with Karen."

"Karen," Mom says, and rolls her eyes. Karen is Venicenne's mom. Venicenne, one of Rosalind's best friends. Her name is supposedly a creative twist on the romantic Italian city her mom and dad visited before she was born, and has nothing to do with deer meat. Another kid-naming reminder: no creative twists.

"She's *nice,*" Rosalind says.

"Bo-ring," my mom sings. "You never let me have any fun."

Rosalind is either murderous or guilty, I can't tell. "Okay! Hang out with us, then."

"You girls have such great *energy,*" Mom says as her eyes go bright and forgiving. "And I haven't seen Zoe in forever. I miss her so much!" Zoe is another one of Rosalind's friends, along with Sahreen and Eva and Ivan and Marco and, and, and . . . A couple of months ago, Rosalind and Venicenne and Zoe and Sahreen and I took Mom to Pizza Italia in Madison Park for her birthday. They kept telling her, *You're the cool mom!* which she loved, but I think she wished they'd left off the *mom* part.

"Fine," Rosalind says, but her *fine* has lost its edge. She glares at me like this is all my fault.

Luckily, another car comes down the street, forcing a release of our family traffic jam.

"Lock the doors, and don't burn the house down!" Mom calls, because I'm the forgetful one who doesn't think. They roll their windows up, and I watch the car disappear.

Away they go to have experiences I wish I were part of and, at the exact same time, am relieved I'm not part of. There's probably a German word for this. We members of the Soggy Pages Book Club love and honor the unique exactness of such words by giving a round of celebratory toots with the kazoos Arden Lee got us at the dollar store whenever we discover a new one. Then we add it to our ongoing list, which now includes words like *Fernweh,* the melancholic desire to go someplace else. Or *Fremdscham,* feeling embarrassed when someone else is acting embarrassing. Or *Zweisamkeit,* the opposite of loneliness, where you feel completely connected to someone.

I've probably never felt that, *Zweisamkeit.* Some people think being alone is the loneliest thing, and some people feel loneliest in a crowd, but I think the loneliest thing is to be one of three people in a room when the other two like each other best.

OUR HOUSE DOES NOT HAVE 2,019 PANES OF GLASS or three hundred feet of waterfront. We live in a tiny bungalow in Fremont, not far from the Lenin statue and the rocket and the feminist theater. It's the kind of street where Tibetan prayer flags droop from porches, and where there's a random purple house, and empty cat food dishes on steps, and the commingling smells from Thai restaurants and the chocolate factory, which is around the corner. You'd think this would be wonderful, until your cleanest shirt smells of cocoa.

I walk up the path, one shoelace undone, an invitation to trip. Inside, I slip off those boots, Army-Navy surplus, which make me feel capable of things I'm not really capable of, like survival in the outdoors. It's cold in there, too, since we're supposed to keep the temperature down. *Do you know how expensive it is to heat this house?* Mom says, which is both a truth and a reminder of who is absent: Hugo Harrison. *Wouldn't* that *be nice,* she always says, a statement drowning in bitterness that never requires his name. The *that* can be anything—heat, or mansions, or avocado soap. Going on fancy vacations or conceiving two kids and doing nothing to help raise them.

Who can blame her for being pissed? What would that have been like, coming home from the hospital with a baby, with only my grandma, Nana Minnie, there to help? And then bringing a *second* one home? Two little kids and a job and a parade of babysitters, man. So hard, so lonely. Hugo Harrison never chased us as toddlers, or struggled with car seats and high chairs, or wiped our vomit, or practiced math facts, or drove straight over to Alyssa Wilker's house to scream at her for stealing my *Frozen* lunch box in the second grade. Mom's not wrong, you know, when she points out that she's always been here, doing the work of both parents.

Rosalind—she's pissed, too. Yeah, because how *could* he? Who ditches a couple of kids like that? I try to be pissed. But they're like two lions on either side of the door, and it makes me want to run the other way, across the yard and into the woods. What's out there? How do we know it's bad? What if it's great, a whole new beautiful land? What if it's so much easier than *this*? What if that land is ruled by people who are . . . *my* people, in ways that Mom and Ros aren't? Plus, when you're that pissed, how reliable are you with the facts?

God. I feel guilty just thinking that.

I'm starving. After all that glorious party food I saw, I warm up some leftover pasta in Tupperware. I jab my fork in, eat right down to the bottom of the old, orange-tinged plastic. Next, a torn hunk of bagel dunked in peanut butter for dessert. Thus fueled, I head to my room. It's small, but it's my own, and there's always food in that fridge, and I've got lots of books stuffed under my bed from the yearly library sale, so we have enough. We have plenty. Unlike someone very close to me who I love, the shining soul who is Clementine.

If my mother had had an on-again, off-again affair (that is totally the wrong word, but I have no idea what the right one is) with some random, normal, not-wealthy-and-famous guy, maybe we'd never really think about what we didn't have or what we might be owed. It was Hugo Harrison, though, who she met in Il Ladro, the Capitol Hill coffee shop. Hugo Harrison, whose latte-foam mustache the beautiful and sexy Brandi Diamond *(Men have* always *liked me)* boldly wiped off with her thumb. Hugo Harrison, who hadn't yet made Frame but was already making a big splash in the world with Rate Me, while married to his first wife, Susan, the OG wife who now lives in Malibu near their grown son, Phoenix. (Ask me anything about *them,* too.) Hugo

Harrison, who'd waltz in for a night or, at most, a weekend, for about three years, until I was born. One kid, he still came around; two, too many. They had a big fight about it, a messy story involving screaming and a screeching car. The word *trap* was used, and she never took another cent from him after that.

I'm not some kind of a whore. *It wasn't just some . . . We had a* relationship, she always says. But here's my secret wonder and worry: Did they *both* have the relationship? Or did *she* have it, pretty much by herself? Was she all that important to him, I mean. Rosalind is 100 percent sure Hugo would have left Susan for Mom if he hadn't met Aurora in Paris, and *boom,* true love (or so the story goes). Is this a Brandi wish or a truth? The way she tells it, he gave her a ring and a bracelet and once or twice let the *l* word slip, but she also told us that he refused to give her his phone number and that they never went anywhere together in public. Except that art gallery show where she had to pretend not to know him, but where they met up in the bathroom (gross). I was conceived after *an impossibly lavish night at Hotel Sorrento, wink wink* (gross gross).

Does fucking make a father? Try to understand why that particular word is important, please. I mean, stop judging for a second and understand. I just kind of doubt they were making love, or even having sex. At least, I kind of doubt he was.

Two people are never in the same relationship, is what I suspect. And fucking doesn't mean you're leaving your wife or showing up for the kid's first-grade play or even their high school graduation. At least, Hugo sure wasn't at Rosalind's. Mom emailed him an invitation at his private address, even though Ros was furious about it, since she wants nothing to do with him. He probably never even got it—he's so famous now. I don't know if you're ever so famous that you forget two children.

The last time we saw him was when I was little. I don't even remember. Rosalind does, but barely. We were, like, five and three. I try not to be sad about it. It's like missing a hope more than a person, anyway. And hope is something that can stay and stay, unlike people. But after Aurora came on the scene, all offers of money finally stopped, and so, according to Mom, did the occasional email or flirty text he'd still sneak-send in the middle of the night when he was with Susan. *He just couldn't let me go!* she'd say, until he could. Until Aurora, under the Eiffel Tower. Fucking doesn't mean that Brandi Diamond *matters,* or that *we* matter.

I want to matter. What if I secretly matter, like he secretly matters? It sort of seems like having a crush on a movie star, but then again, it's actually possible.

Why don't you make him pay child support?! Rosalind has asked a thousand times, as if money is the most important thing. Allison, Mom's friend at Heartland, asks that, too. Mom always has the same reply. *I have my pride,* she answers, her chin lifted. It makes her sound heroic. Pride can't buy avocado soap or heat or college tuition, but it's clearly more important to Mom than any of those things. On most days I respect her for it, but it's confusing. Why she needs to be a hero more than anything else, you know.

And, sure, I get that she doesn't want a relationship with him, but can't *we* have one? I don't dare just try to reach out to the guy. She'd be *furious.* It never even occurred to me that we *could* reach out until Mom emailed him last year about Rosalind, sending that invite plus a roster of Ros's achievements, like band and volleyball. After that it hit me that he was *right here,* you know? An actual person, living a real life. Not on the cover of a magazine, but close enough to know us and for us to know him. Close enough to . . . who knows. Get to know from afar. *Watch.* Maybe one day be brave enough to break every rule and actually talk to him. I'd have to be *really* brave, and not just because he's Hugo Harrison. He rejected Mom, and when you're on Team Rejection, you don't go trading to the opposing side. You stay loyal, with your pride and your chin up, conquerors against the enemy.

We're never mentioned in any of Hugo Harrison's bios or interviews. Only Phoenix, and now Arlo. *We* don't talk to other people about him, either. Mom used to drop it into conversations when we were little, to the other moms at school and stuff, but it pretty much backfired. I mean, try telling someone that you, regular you, had an affair with someone like Hugo Harrison. It sounds made-up. I once bragged about him being my dad to this girl, Maddie Martinez, in junior high, trying to impress her, and she only laughed and rolled her eyes. *Right,* she said. Clementine and Arden Lee know, but we're a protective vault for each other's secrets. Miss Fury had Francine and Cappy looking out for her, saving her in the nick of time, and I have Clementine and Arden Lee. Secrets—they're all icebergs, just waiting for their *Titanic.*

Mom only has one picture of herself with Hugo. Or at least a photo of her hand and his face and bare chest. Whenever she took any, he'd make her get rid of them right away because of Susan. In that photo you can really see it—Rosalind has his lips (lucky). I have his dark hair and his nose (well). We have her name, though: Diamond. *Diamonds are worth more than gold. More than his money, I'll tell you that much,* she says.

We are required to hate Hugo as much as Mom does now, which is *a lot,* especially after he didn't answer her email about Ros's graduation. Quantity matters. Quantity of hatred is a measurement of loyalty. *That's it! That's the last straw!* she said. I have no idea how many straws there were. This implied that she was moving on forever, that maybe a Kevin or a Terry or a Manuel would finally stay around longer than, say, a year or so. Two people are never in the same relationship, yeah, but also, a person can carry on having a relationship all by herself, in her head, that's what it seems like. When he didn't show up for the ceremony, things were thrown and slammed, and there was yelling. A glimpse of the scenes she'd had with him, I think. It made me wonder if he had his reasons, you know, for staying away. Reasons that didn't have to do with me and Ros, that were bigger than us, even.

That invitation, though . . . It's another thing I wonder. Like, are we also supposed to share Brandi Diamond's truest unspoken hope? The hope way down in there, that she might actually be important to him? In terms of his care or love or attention, is it all of us or none of us? I mean, what if, one day, *we* are important to him, but *she* isn't? It feels dangerous to even contemplate.

I SIT AT MY DESK. I'M THINKING ABOUT THAT GUY AT the party. The stalker guy. If he does anything to hurt Hugo or

Arlo or Aurora, I would never forgive myself. I *don't* hate Hugo Harrison, as much as I try. I was too young to do a very good job of hating Susan, so I try to be good at hating Aurora, just so I don't fail at the whole thing. No one could hate Arlo, that's for sure. God, he's so sweet and adorable. It's hard to explain, but my heart just fills with love when I see his photos. His face makes you feel good about life, the way the green tips of bulbs popping up in spring do, or fluffy clouds in a blue sky, or syrup filling the deep squares of a waffle.

I imagine myself rushing in and saving Hugo, wrestling the bad guy to the ground. It makes me think of an image in *Miss Fury, Summer Issue, No. 2,* so I open it to that page. I study the image to see how June Tarpé Mills drew it, while trying to remember how *I* felt when I saw that guy—stressed and afraid. And then I try to make that feeling come through my hand, if that makes sense. I don't know how this actually works, if all art is God or talent or just this cool and amazing thing called creativity that human beings have inside of themselves, an unextinguishable light, but there they are: two struggling figures. They're versions of each other, male and female, but she's on top. She's winning. She's fighting for the ones she loves. It seems like the most amazing thing a person can do, create something that wasn't here before, bring it into being through your very own imagination and your very own hands. Oh man, I love to draw.

I wouldn't say this out loud, either, but it's pretty good. I mean, it's not as good as June Tarpé Mills's—I have a long way to go. I haven't tried to make my own actual comic yet, because I still have to choose my characters and figure out the story. Mostly, I mess around, learning. I've done so many versions of Miss Fury, but she just keeps looking like the one June made. She's the most important piece, but who should she *be*? No idea. I try to study June's lines, how she made those muscles look so real, but it's important, really important, that this be *mine*.

My original inspiration, *Miss Fury, Summer Issue, No. 2,* is worth a lot of money, so I'm careful with it. I found it last year at the Solstice Parade in Fremont, when I went with Arden Lee and Clementine and Arden Lee's mom, Jackie. We'd just witnessed the extravagant displays and over-the-top floats—the skin painted rainbow tones, breasts in every shape and size and color, a naked gold man riding a gold bike, a woman unfurling giant butterfly wings. And more—a dragon float, a unicorn, an octopus, a giant beach ball. Cars covered in coins and tiny Madonna statues, butt cracks galore! Everyone in some sort of disguise and yet more exposed and free than in real life, shouting and singing and dancing. Then we ate corn on the cob and strolled around the fair stalls.

Jackie and Arden Lee hunted through the vintage clothes, and Clementine looked at the books, hoping to find a *Prince Caspian* to complete her and Apple's set of the Chronicles of Narnia, while I casually flipped through a stuffed box of comics. Archie and Marvel, Richie Rich and Casper, dudes and dudes and dudes, whether they were redheaded high school boys, hypermasculine superheroes, or ectoplasmic do-gooders. But then . . . there she was: a *force* in a black catsuit and a red cape. On the cover she was climbing a rope to the top of a skyscraper while giving a Nazi a swift kick in the face. The city buildings were drawn with edgy light, the moon a large and perfect circle. Even her shadow looked mighty. The title, *Miss Fury,* was written like a take-no-shit statement in a solid red-and-black font. *Summer Issue, No. 2, ten cents.*

Okay, my superhero knowledge was on the slim side, I admit, but who ever heard of *her*? Like, *no one*? Wonder Woman, yeah, but never a Miss Fury. I swear, I could feel the pulpy newsprint power of it right away. Adventure, escape, plus the thrill of a fantastic find. Arden Lee loves a vintage vibe, and I suddenly understood that better—the cool, retro whimsy backed by the weight of history. The art had such *energy.* The artist's name was super intriguing, too: Tarpé Mills. Could be a man or a woman, no idea.

Inside, I saw the year: 1942. A big ad came next, for a book titled *Fun for Boys,* from Knickerbocker Publishing. *Sports! Thrills! Games! How to train your dog, how to be a ventriloquist. Jujitsu secrets—fear no man!* Wow—it was so great, even before we got to Miss Fury leaping into the next page, knocking a gun from a bad guy's hand. So much power, so many exclamation points! My heart actually started beating hard, and I handed over my money, fast, before anyone else could grab it from me. Well, no one was grabbing it from me. It was a version of how Arden Lee always worries that people will steal his library books if he leaves them in the car. I *valued* it already. That comic book belonged to me.

The stall guy, well, he didn't know what he had, and I got it for a buck. When we were walking back home, I lifted it from the bag to show Clementine. Arden Lee and Jackie were walking in front of us so we could fit on the sidewalk. *Cool!* Clementine said, seeing what I had right away. *I'm going to make a comic,* I said. *Like this.* I'd been drawing since I was, like, five, but all at once I was done with animals and flowers or whatever. I knew, just like that, what I wanted to do. *That'd be awesome!* Clementine said, and then I called for Arden Lee to look. *Oh, whoa, wow!* he said, over his shoulder, which made me even more jazzed. *Have you ever heard of her?* I asked, because he knows everything about everything. He shook his head, but Fremont was so crowded that we had to keep walking. I couldn't wait to get home. It's hard to even explain. I wasn't one of those people who always loved comics, all comics; this was something specific about Miss Fury herself.

Maybe it was because I'd just seen all those people, you know, so free and yet in disguise, more themselves than they could ever be in their regular lives, and here was Miss Fury, Marla Drake, same. You had no idea what the gold guy and the rainbow-painted women had to deal with in their normal lives, you know, and here they were, singing and shouting and feeling *everything*, 100 percent, breasts and balls and spirits riding along on a wave of joy and goodwill and strength. Personal strength. You felt their power, not some special superpower, but something inside them all along. This is how she seemed to me, too. This overlooked or forgotten superhero. Full of hidden abilities and her own force. Well, it was just days after Rosalind's graduation, too, when I found it. The big no-show rejection of Hugo Harrison.

When I got home, I was sure I'd discovered my thing, same as Clementine with Pippi Longstocking. I felt the connection that can come when an artist makes something from their down-deep depths and it intertwines with something in your down-deep depths. You recognize it and feel it in this profound way, whether it makes sense to anyone else or not.

I sat on my bed, removed the comic book oh-so-carefully from the paper bag. I couldn't wait to read the whole thing, and then look up everything about this totally ignored character, and the mysterious person who made her.

And then . . . Shit.

Shit, shit! Seriously. I mean, the problems jumped out right away. Miss Fury, she originally got her powers from an African witch doctor's pelt, a concept that was dropped as it went along, but still. There were racist tropes galore. An entire country of people, Brazilians, were used for a plot device, with all the easiest and oldest white-gaze images imaginable. Not to mention a character called Albino Joe, and a gay guy called Whiffy, ugh. People haven't been seeing each other forever, it seems. People not seeing other people, truly seeing them, seems like one of the truest and longest-lasting things about human beings, and I have no idea why.

My heart actually felt heavy. I wanted to cry. I searched *Miss Fury* and *Tarpé Mills* on my old laptop, and what I found made things *more* confusing, because, wow. Tarpé Mills *was* a woman, June Tarpé Mills, a bold, boundary-breaking loner, the first female creator of one of the first female superheroes, who hid her actual first name, June, in order to survive as an artist in a field of men. She dared to draw this strong, powerful, sexy woman and was eventually banned by newspapers after she drew Marla in a bikini. And, yeah, she did it *before* Wonder Woman, still so outrageously famous, probably because a guy created her.

I called Arden Lee. He'd have answers about what to do. Butterflies, ancient civilizations, history, you name it, he knows about it. If I now have Miss Fury and Clementine has Pippi

Longstocking, Arden Lee has All the Books as his mentors and guardians.

Me and Arden Lee, we've been close friends since we met in Mr. Shattuck's class in the sixth grade. We clicked, magnet to metal, bonded by the weird superglue of trauma, thanks to that bully, Shattuck. Two sensitive people, me with my asthma and rashes and general failings, and Arden Lee with his physically immature body, super-mature mind, and stubborn refusal to fit in stylishly or otherwise. And while I was generally overlooked, Arden Lee was a constant target for every cruel kid having a bad day. We met Clementine in the seventh grade. She was new and super quiet, but you know your people. We hauled her into our lifeboat, and a year later the Soggy Pages (no book shall remain pristine, we agreed) Book Club was born. Sure, we have other friends—Arden Lee knows a lot of the drama kids, and there are people we say hi to, and I even had a semi-boyfriend last year, but it's Arden Lee and Clementine and me who are on the raft together. We rely on each other. We love each other. There's no one I trust more.

"If you hear a clacking sound, it's me shaking up a spray can to paint my ass gold." That's how Arden Lee answered the phone that day.

"Hate to tell you. Parade's over."

"It's never too late to be your true self," he said.

How can I ever forget *that*? I went on to explain my sorrow about Miss Fury. The racist tropes, the exotic Brazilians. I told him the good stuff, too. How groundbreaking the work was. I described this scene where Marla Drake/Miss Fury is just coming home after a secret night of fighting Nazis, when Gary Hale grabs her and demands to know where she's been. She totally puts him in his place, giving him a shove and a forceful *Let go of me!* while wearing a stunning blue gown. *I'm sorry! I didn't know I was so distasteful to you,* he pouts, and she ditches the aggressive, jealous asshole just like that, in 1942, besides. How do you *not* fall for her, huh? But there was no looking away from the racism.

"What do I doooo?" I moaned. I fell in love and got disillusioned faster than with Finn Lahruti last year.

"I get it. Imagine how I felt about Roald Dahl."

I remember Arden Lee crying. Crying hard, after finding out about Dahl's anti-Semitism. He was devastated. He loves all those books. He even has a pair of Wonka-like striped pants he got at our favorite store, Second Stories Consignment. What a betrayal.

I still held the comic book on my lap. "Should I burn this thing?"

"You'd have to burn every single comic book before . . . wow, *recently?* Racism was pretty much *built into* the whole superhero thing from the beginning, El. *So many* negative racial stereotypes, Asian characters in particular. But also . . . the complete whiteness, right? There's one hero in those old Golden Age comics, and only one. The white male American dude with his bulgy muscles. The things that got said about Japanese people during the war? You'd be shocked. *Superman, Captain America . . .* Racist. Not to mention *Tarzan.* God. *All* of them."

"So now what? Honestly. What do we do with so much bad shit?"

"I don't know, El. The only thing I *do* know is that we *can't* make it disappear. Erasing it, pretending it didn't happen? It'd be like those families that won't speak about their worst secrets. I mean, awesome! Do something terrible to someone and then bury the body forever! Acting like, la-la-la, *what* racism? You don't get rid of that; you have to *look.* Take it in, and take it in good. If you want to draw your own, learn from what was right, then do a whole lot better than what wasn't."

"I loved her. Love her. No idea. Do I love her still, or not?"

"See why you and Clementine are wrong about insta-love?" A long-standing Soggy Pages debate. "You have to find out the *history.*"

"It still sucks, doesn't it, that the real first female superhero has been mostly forgotten? But Wonder Woman sure hasn't been."

"Wonder Woman had racist stereotypes galore! And William Moulton Marston, the guy who made her . . . Oh my God, El! Look *him* up," Arden Lee said.

That's what I did the minute we said goodbye. Oh, William, William, now world-famous. Still so very famous. Look at all the stuff we don't see and don't know. Before Wonder Woman, he supposedly invented the lie detector test, when it was his wife, Elizabeth Holloway, who actually came up with the idea. Lying about a lie detector test! What feels worse, though, what feels terrible: He was also credited for being the sole creator of Wonder Woman, the most famous female comic book character ever, when she was Elizabeth's idea. *Elizabeth* had that lightning-zap, fingers-touching moment of creation where Wonder Woman came into being, instead of another Wonder Dude. His wives also invented storylines and did the lettering and inking. *Wives,* plural. When

Elizabeth was pregnant, old Willy brought home a mistress, Marjorie Huntley, and then informed Elizabeth that the three of them would live together. Then he met Olive, a young student of his, and she joined them, too. Apparently, he threatened to leave unless the women agreed to this deal. In public, though, he went on and on about female empowerment.

The thing I *really* couldn't shake . . . Marston had kids with all three women, but the kids who didn't belong to William and his OG wife, Elizabeth . . . They were told their real dad had died. They grew up with William but never knew he was their father.

The members of the Soggy Pages Book Club believe that the right book can find you when you need it. A comic, too, maybe. I wasn't sure if *Miss Fury* was right or wrong, but it seemed to be trying to tell me something.

Now I tuck the drawing of the struggling figures into my desk. I give up. It looks like me struggling with me. I'm trying to learn from Tarpé Mills, the good and the bad, as Arden Lee suggested, learn from her and move forward from her work, but it's hard. I wish I were better already. I wish I knew the story I wanted to tell. My chest feels tight, from the cold car and the cold house, probably. Maybe we have a mold problem, who knows. I take a puff from my inhaler. It's something else I have in common with June Tarpé Mills, our asthma, but she was a smoker. It's another edit I will make to improve upon history, because there's no way I'd ever touch a cigarette.

It gets late, past midnight. Mom and Rosalind still aren't home. I don't have to wait up for them, but there's a silly, nonsense part of my brain that feels like I can't rest until they're back, until we're three again, a full triangle. I remember reading once that a triangle is the most stable shape. I wonder if William Moulton Marston's wife, Elizabeth, thought so when he brought home wife number two and wife number three, or if Susan thought so when my mom was on the scene, let alone Aurora.

I go downstairs and eat a few frosty bites of some forgotten ice cream, a former vanilla caramel that's a slimy version of what it once was. I put it back after I'm done, because I have a hard time throwing things out. I turn up the heat.

That's when I open my laptop again, Rosalind's old one, on borrowed time. The kind with a fan that constantly blows, warning of imminent destruction. I head straight over to Aurora's Instagram, where she posts stuff about her and Hugo and Arlo, along with products she endorses—a certain pillow, a white linen blouse, a moisturizer. A cute nursery lamp, her favorite biodegradable diapers, a pair of chic sunglasses. A super-stylish dehumidifier, a . . . You get the idea. It's the likeliest place to see fresh information about the Harrisons, maybe even photos of that party. It's also one of those intimidating accounts that make you feel like shit about yourself. Aurora's so . . . self-assured. You would never in a million years imagine her having self-doubt or wearing the wrong clothes or making mistakes. This is probably the real reason people hate her, even though they love that white blouse and the moisturizer and the pillow.

And, bingo, payoff, because there's a new post. There are new posts practically daily, but I still get an almost-nervous thrill when I see one there, even if it's just a bottle of mint lotion.

It's not a bottle of mint lotion. No, it's not. It's an absolutely precious photo of Arlo, just his face, with his brown eyes, and his tousled dark Hugo Harrison hair, same as me, and his Arlo-only mischief-light. His skin is so soft-looking, so brand-new human in the world. It gives you a stab in the heart, the way parents can just get right in there and fuck up something, someone, so pure. I don't mean to say Arlo is fucked up (although, according to Mom, *he doesn't have a chance, with a father like that*). I just mean that maybe I am. That so many people are. I think of William Moulton Marston's kids, or just anyone who hurts a child, because how *could* you? We start out so new, you know.

I move on to the post itself. And now my heart starts to thump. It starts to thunder, the distant drumbeat of disaster, sure, but of possibility, too. *Local folks! Help! Nanny needed for June–August. Loving, patient, and fun people only, send résumé and relevant deets! Link in bio!* It sounds desperate. And it seems so *dangerous,* just putting a request out there like this for anyone to see.

I mean, what if that stalker applies? Or some other stalker-like person? Or . . .

The thought jabs me, as sudden and fierce as Miss Fury stabs a bad guy with her stiletto.

Me.

I could do it. I could have a secret identity, infiltrate the house of my enemy/non-enemy. Would I be there to save them or defeat them?

I download that application. Just to see, you know. I stare at that first line: *Name.*

But then the room fills with a weird rubber-burning smell. For a second I'm in such a dream world that I imagine the scene in Miss Fury where she grabs the fire hose and flings it at the bad guys, saving Gary Hale. I leap from my chair, but it's not soon enough to save my hair clip now melting into a puddle of plastic on the floor heater.

"Ow, ow, ow," I say, tossing it to the floor before the house catches on fire or something.

I can hear them both, my mother and Rosalind, because how many times have they told me not to do stuff like that?

Oh, Eleanor, Rosalind says.

Are you trying to burn our house down? Mom says.

chapter
Three

THEY'RE HOME, FINALLY. I HEAR MOM'S CAR AND SEE
the swerve of headlights in the driveway. Sure, I've been waiting
for their return, but now I slam that laptop shut, fling myself into
bed, and pull the covers up. I don't want to talk. See? Them together, me alone—I choose it, too, sometimes. Being by myself is
just relaxing, you know. Talking to them or most anyone (anyone
who isn't Clementine or Arden Lee) can feel like a graded per-
formance, where the judges hold up the scorecards. A land mine

of mistakes you're likely to regret and torture yourself over later. When you're by yourself, you can be the gold man on the bike and the rainbow woman, only with no one watching. Full you, no anxiety, just ease. It's exactly how I feel when I read, too.

The door unlocks and in they come, laughing and chatting, any tension between them gone. *I had no idea!* one of them says, and then, *She did it on purpose!* And then, *Did you notice the look he gave her?* And then, *OH MY GOD!* followed by laughter. Shoes clunk to the ground, car keys clank on the counter, the coat closet opens and closes. The voices move to the kitchen. It occurs to me that the words *a part* and *apart* are all the same letters, but opposites. Only the space makes the difference.

I briefly imagine me and Hugo coming in from a night out somewhere. Us laughing at some wild thing that happened. *OH MY GOD!* I say, and we laugh.

They come down the hall, and there are the usual sounds of getting ready for bed: flushing toilets and brushing teeth and quiet good nights. My doorknob turns silently, and a sliver of light briefly appears and then vanishes, Mom making sure I'm not dead or gone, probably. Something about this makes me feel gone.

I'm not sure what it would take to be golden like Rosalind. She just came that way, I guess. Even as a baby, Rosalind was beautiful and healthy, always happy, always smiling at people wherever she went. *Miss Personality! What a flirt! That's just how I was as a child,* Mom loves to say.

And me, ugh, *little crabby pants, always in a mood,* crying if anyone wanted to hold me. The opposite of Mom, meaning: bad. The nebulizer machine for my asthma was always humming and sending out a gloomy, essential steam. I got rashes from sun or lotion or chlorine or some food or plant or air or you name it. I got rashes from life.

One day, you'll come out of your shell, Mom says. But I like my shell. Shells are important, even beautiful, I think, with their swirls and mystery. I'd rather have one than be a *Nacktschnecke,* a naked snail, a slug. I swear, the word *extrovert* is part of the problem, a PR campaign right there. So close to *extra,* shouting that more is better.

The house gets quiet. I remember the nanny application, still right there on my laptop. If Rosalind happens to lift that top, I'm a goner. I sneak out of bed. The cursor still blinks in the same spot: *Name.* I make a folder called *Job Prospects* and move the application. Who am I kidding, though? It would be less terrifying to climb through their high window in disguise than to walk right through the Harrisons' front door.

I stare out my window toward the smokestack of the Theo Chocolates building. Midnight cocoa smoke billows across the roofs of our neighbors, and a slice of the Ship Canal winds like the moonlit tail of a serpent. In the distance there's the neon pink glow of the Psyckē sign on Hugo's building, visible for miles. In the comics there's always a looming metropolis, and a misunderstood hero, unseen until they step out of the darkness in disguise. In truth, I'm not stepping out of anywhere. That tower with its pink light—it's nothing I'm part of. I'm just another tiny human, sitting in its shadow.

"YOU WANT TO DO *WHAT*?" CLEMENTINE SAYS WHEN I tell her and Arden Lee about the Harrisons needing a nanny. Her eyes actually go round with horror. She's a rule follower. Always, but even more so now, out of necessity. It's lunchtime, and we're sitting outside on the big hill in the back of our school. See, you don't have to sit at the clichéd loner table in the cafeteria or hide in the library, even though we love the library. You can find a patch of lawn behind the school. The grass is damp, but no worries. Arden Lee has us and our butts covered, with three garbage bags folded into triangles, like the flags they give to the families of fallen soldiers.

"Innerer Schweinehund?" I say, trying to explain why I keep opening and closing that application. *Innerer Schweinehund* means "inner pig-dog," the weak part of yourself that's responsible for bad decisions.

"That would be so dangerous, El. I mean, *your mom*? Maybe it'd be better to just—"

"Be totally ignored by the guy forever?" Arden Lee interrupts. "Like, *why*? I say go for it!"

This is the two of them right there, so similar and yet so different. Arden Lee, brilliant TikTok book reviewer and daring clothing stylist, sharing his bold intelligence in the outside world while prone to bouts of screechy immaturity at Roosevelt High, and Clementine, who's just got to make it one more year, quiet and undetected. Generally, I'm solidly with Clementine on Team Quiet. When you're noticed, all of your faults leap out, and bad things can happen, too—rage, loss. Better to stay under the radar.

"I wasn't going to suggest being ignored forever," Clementine says. "Just, maybe you could write the guy a letter or something? After you move out and are on your own?"

"A letter, like the Middle Ages!" Arden Lee says. "You could chisel it on a stone tablet." This is them, too—Arden Lee calling Clementine a Luddite (yeah, his vocabulary), Clementine calling Arden Lee tech-reckless (yeah, her own flair with words).

"I doubt I'll really do it. There're a million problems. Like name, for one." *Eleanor Diamond* might spark some memory of a dark-haired baby from sixteen years ago, you know? Does Aurora even know about me and Ros? Did Susan? I'm pretty sure Aurora isn't going to hire Hugo's own daughter by a long-ago mistress. *Mistress* is such a funny word—an accusation that sounds as prim and fancy as a doily, yet there is no male equivalent. Another word hides in it, too. Probably one of the truest things about a situation like that: *stress.*

"Name? Easy! Marla Drake," Arden Lee says.

Clementine groans.

"Address?" I say.

"Galactic Sector ZZ9, Plural Z Alpha," Arden Lee says. It's the address of Planet Earth in *The Hitchhiker's Guide to the Galaxy.* Make something up, is his point.

"References. Experience . . ." Last summer I worked at Armchair Books, closed now. (Insert the weeping of the Soggy Pages Book Club here.) I used to babysit the Farias twins, and I tutored little Malcolm Grigoradias in math. Our neighbor Beth Fernandes (who got married in a bookstore, what a dream) is always traveling to amazing places with her band, and I watch her dog, Otis, when she's gone. That's all I've got.

"Hey, my mom could vouch for you. She loves you," Arden Lee says.

I love her back. Jackie is the biggest Arden Lee fan you can find, and she's a huge supporter of Clementine and me, too. Without her, Clementine might not have made it through this whole year. A lot of other adults would have likely straight-up called the authorities, but Jackie sees the bigger issues and tries to help. So do Clementine's next-door neighbors, who hold her up like a pair of bookends. "Would she pretend to be Mrs. Farias?" I say.

"Is she the lady you babysat for? With the kid who ran away when the front door was unlocked?"

"Oh my God, Eleanor! A kid ran away when you babysat?" Clementine's sister, Apple, is never out of sight on Clementine's watch. And Clementine's watch is always.

I blush. I never told Clementine that. "They were twins!"

Clementine lifts the lid of her plastic container.

"Whoa, that smells amazing," Arden Lee says. Clementine *has* to be capable, but wow. She's made some kind of—

"Tabouleh. Bulgur is cheap. Garlic makes anything amazing."

"But what if you *actually* applied and got the job?" Arden Lee's eyes light up under the brim of his panama hat. He sips a juice box. "You could find out what the big mystery thing is."

"The big mystery thing, like her very own father?" Clementine knows what Arden Lee's actually referring to, of course. Who doesn't? Practically every day you'll hear something about it. A bragging hint from Hugo Harrison or Psyckē Enterprises, reporters dropping leads and guesses. Some new product is coming, and it's big.

"It's a robot. It's got to be." Arden Lee burps loudly.

"Gross," Clementine and I both say at the same time.

"If it's not a robot, it's still related to AI for sure," Arden Lee says. "Or the metaverse."

"I still don't understand AI, to be honest. Or what the metaverse even is," I say.

"Imagine if the internet were an actual place, or an imaginary actual place, a shared 3D virtual world where you interact with other people as an avatar," Arden Lee says.

"Yawn," Clementine says.

"Yeah, just wait until everyone's in it, shopping and going to concerts and buying real estate." Arden Lee sticks a finger into the corners of his chip bag, then licks off the salt.

"If it's just as complicated as this world, I don't see the point," Clementine says. "Plus, everyone's already half gone already, disappeared into their phones. Or *all* gone."

I look at her, and, oh man, do I feel sad. My heart breaks. But she doesn't seem to even be referring to her mom. I guess you just get used to your own situation. It becomes less *bad* and more just *is*.

"Get into his house, Eleanor! Come onnnn! We could investigate. Break into his office or something."

"I think you've been watching too much *Scooby-Doo*," Clementine says.

"I'm a *Bluey* fan, you know that." Arden Lee starts singing the *Bluey* theme song, pretty loudly, too, a shimmy to go with. At school he sometimes does this immature attention-getting stuff. Online, though, he's a subdued-yet-stylish professor.

"I'd totally prefer Miss Fury's suit to Velma's orange turtle-neck," I say. Ros, with her flat, hard abs she frequently features on Instagram—she'd look better in that thing than I would, to be honest. She even has one of those gold belly button rings, which always make me think of a cherry on a sundae. The way they belong but don't.

"I'm sorry," Clementine says. "But it still bugs me. All the emphasis on how fabulous he is, after he—"

"I *know*, okay?" I love Clementine so darn much, but she's told me this a hundred times, and my voice prickles with irritation. This means she's probably right about something that I don't want her to be right about. She thinks I should be angrier at him. It's hard to explain. I don't like to be angry. Anger scares me. Angry people scare me.

"I just worry about your loving heart," Clementine says.

She has a loving heart. I almost want to cry. Clementine and Arden Lee are the best people to be alone in the world with, that's for sure.

"I hate to break this up . . ." Arden Lee does *not* hate to break this up. He loves friendly contention because it's *plot*. But something better than Clementine and me is about to happen, and romance trumps contention any day. He nods his head left, toward the gym building.

"Oh!" Clementine clutches my arm.

Here he comes, Xavier Chen, wearing his signature leggings, black tunic, and starter-beard scruff. Somehow he's a loner who's risen above the loners, the odd kid who's so odd that he's edged into the unexpected, lofty stratosphere of cool, an untouchable cool. In this world, the real one, we are all still animals, and sharks can still smell blood in the water, and in junior high and high school, oddity is still blood. How far back does it go, people making themselves big by making other people small? Way back to when our brains were walnut-sized, maybe, but it's no excuse.

Xavier Chen, though. In a comic, give him penetrating eyes and a hideout with all the sleekest gadgets.

Clementine laughs dramatically, as if we're having the most wonderful time, instead of being frozen in awkwardness at the mere presence of Xavier Chen.

But then . . . a miracle happens.

"Hey," he says to her.

"Hey," she says back, sending a garlic poof into the back lawn of Roosevelt High School.

Arden Lee and I meet eyes in mutual despair. We've probably lost her.

"There's rejection even in the metaverse," Arden Lee says to himself. "You can't hide your vulnerability, even in an avatar."

"Metaverse, avatar, AI . . . None of it is *real*." I shrug.

"Not-real stuff can have a lot of power," he says. "Miss Fury?"

"Okay, okay, you got me."

"There's a difference, though, for sure," he says. "A book doesn't have the power to learn on its own, to change itself, to rise up over the people who interact with it, or made it, even."

I have no idea what he's talking about. It just sounds all doomy and sci-fi, all end-of-the-world, when a lot of this stuff just seems interesting. I've played around with Frame, and it's fun. How seriously can you take a robot?

"Book club after school?" I say to Clementine. We're reading *Middlesex* by Jeffrey Eugenides, and I can't wait to discuss it. But honestly, I mostly say this to bring her back to us. "Right? Right?"

I sound so needy, even to myself.

"He saw me," she says.

A FEW DAYS LATER ROS USES MY LAPTOP TO WATCH some hair-braiding video without asking. I get a total scare. That folder, *Job Prospects,* is right there on my desktop. I delete it. For a while I don't even visit Hugo's house. It was such a close call, but finals are coming up, too, and a monster paper for world history ("The Rise of Feudalism," ugh) is due. There's not a lot of time to sit in Mom's car, hoping for a glimpse of Hugo's dog or whatever. After graduation I'll probably end up going to Shoreline Community College like Rosalind, but if by some miracle I can go to Cornish College of the Arts, I'll need a really good scholarship. So I take only the occasional break, scrolling through Aurora's posts (a day on their yacht, her hair blowing in her face; Arlo's toes in a creek; her favorite brand of socks).

I check Rate Me, too, Hugo's first controversial creation. Rating regular people—it's brutal. That app is gross, infuriating, creepy, sometimes sweet, sometimes heartwarming. But you can't look away.

Whenever I first open it, I do something silly but terrifying: I type my name in the search bar. You can't rate anyone under the age of eighteen, but it's still scary to look. *There are no ratings for this person!* comes the relieving reply, along with that marginally humiliating exclamation point. After that I look up Hugo Harrison. I look up Hugo Harrison *again*. He has close to five million reviews. A four-point-five rating. That many people couldn't have actually met him, the requirement for posting, but there's no way to check these things. New reviews pour in daily. Jerry99classyfifty. Five stars. *Met him tonight. Down-to-earth for a billionaire (ask me about a few others). Funny, too, what a surprise! And he makes a mean Manhattan.* SunnyDeLit4622. Five stars. *What a charmer, that's all I'm gonna say.*

I always search *Aurora Andozza Harrison* next. Her reviews only trickle in. Sometimes the number stays the same for days. Two-point-three average. The last review is one star and only says *Home-wrecker.* The one before that reads *Content removed,* which happens when language gets abusive according to Rate Me's policies.

If I have extra time, I'll type both their names into Google and search the last twenty-four hours. If I'm really procrastinating, I'll look up Susan's Facebook page. (She rarely posts.) I'll check in on Phoenix, enlarge the photos of him with his surfboard to see if we look alike. (We don't.)

The night before my chemistry exam, though, just after I finish that stupid feudalism paper, I just have to get out. There's so much crammed in my brain, I'm sure it'll all vanish the second the test is over. In the living room Mom and Ros are watching some show about matchmaking. I ask to borrow the car to get a Slurpee, though I'm not heading to 7-Eleven.

Ros makes a face. "Ick."

"Are you kidding me? You used to love them!"

"Not anymore. *Chemicals,* Eleanor."

"I doubt it, and who cares," I say.

"I hope you're making good choices, missy," Mom says. This means, *You're not making good choices, missy.* Then she grabs her stomach.

"Oh my God! Seriously?" Lately, I've seen her doing sit-ups, her toes hooked under the bottom edge of the couch. "I'm not even overweight!"

"Did I say that? I did *not* say that," Mom's eyes widen in disbelief. "You don't need to be so *sensitive.*"

"You didn't have to *say* it. You did *this.*" I demonstrate. I feel sad for my little tummy splootch. Like, the poor thing. Clementine and I call them our little hamsters, Hammy and Boo. We like them. I used to. Or else, I tried to. Honestly, it's an effort to like it with all of Rosalind's posts of herself in her bikini, and Mom's fire-emoji comments.

"Seriously, Eleanor. Just go get your Slurpee. You obviously need a break," Ros says.

If Clementine thinks I never get pissed, she's wrong. In my head I see Miss Fury in one of the many scenes where Marla wrestles Era. Era's supposedly her friend, but, man, they fight a lot. Era is on the ground. It's clear who's winning. I hit the accelerator hard when I leave.

I park right across from the Frame House. The street is quiet. It takes a while to calm down, to just settle in to the weird but great alertness of being there. I love all their little outdoor lights that calmly illuminate specific plants or a tree in a way that shows respect for their beauty. Colors flash upstairs, as if someone's watching TV. It's both exciting and disappointing to imagine them doing something that regular.

Suddenly, Aurora is standing in the big windows, looking out toward the street. I swear she sees me. I quickly glance down at my phone, like I'm lost or something. I feel lost. God, she's spotted me, sitting right there, staring in. Fear crawls up my spine. I hunt around in my little backpack, pretending to do important yet innocent things as my heart gallops.

I peek.

She's gone.

Will I look more guilty if I flee now, or should I wait? I wait, because when it comes to Hugo Harrison, my *innerer Schweinehund* rules.

Does every criminal want to get caught? In Miss Fury, they *do* get caught.

Now, now . . . Oh my God. A truck drives very slowly down the street. A blue one, a very familiar one. *That* truck. It's the stalker guy again. Either Hugo's house is spy central tonight, or the dude in the truck is here all the time. He pulls into a space by the curb. I can't see his face, but his body is alert. Now *he's* looking straight at me, I'm certain of that.

His door opens. Wait, what? He's walking. He's walking toward the house. . . . No. No, he's not, he's coming my way. He's heading over to my car. Inside the house I hear Boolean start to bark, loud. The kind of bark that means an emergency, or an intruder.

Shit. Shit!

You're not going to see this in a Miss Fury strip. I bolt out of there. I start the engine, and my tires actually screech. My hands shake with a near miss. I've got to stop this, that's one thing I know. You keep pressing and pressing, something's going to break. Okay, here's a reason those readers hate flawed characters. They're just so self-destructive.

That's it, I tell myself, my heart pounding. I'm done.

chapter
Four

WELL, A WEEK OR SO LATER, I'M FOLLOWING HER. AU-rora. Or, at least, I'm trying to. I know, I know! I have zero will-power. This is the very opposite of being done, because I'm not even sitting in my car, safely hidden. I'm hanging out on a bench in front of the Green Lake pool after school, right out in the open. From previous, uh, *excursions,* I know that she sometimes swims here on Wednesday afternoons. She's going to walk right past me.

Maybe it's not my *innerer Schweinehund.* Maybe it's my

Abgrundanziehung—my "grabbed by precipice." That feeling when you're at the edge of a cliff and are pulled to look over it. The exciting, nerve-racking compulsion to do something dangerous.

She's later than usual, so maybe she's not even coming. I have no idea what I'll do if she appears. Maybe stare *way* over the cliff, or worse, who knows. I'm a wild card. That is, for a generally unwild person. Ros would laugh at that because she thinks I never take risks.

But, hey, I'm not only here to spy on Aurora, okay? Java Jive, the coffee place where Clementine works, is right across the street. Thanks to her, I have an interview in exactly one hour. If I'm going to get myself to Cornish, I need to save some money, big-time. Apparently, I'm going to have to make a complicated drink as part of the hiring process, which is, according to Mom, *much harder than it looks, so you have to listen.* Meaning: *You don't normally listen.*

This summer Rosalind has a job at Heartland as a teller. She and Mom will need both cars, since Rosalind may want to go out for lunch with friends and stuff. *You're going to have to take a bus to work and figure it out like an adult,* Ros said to me. She followed it up with some encouragement. *You can do it, Ellie! I believe in you!* I don't know why her encouragement always feels so bad.

For now, though, I have an hour. I hope Aurora will show, and I'm equally scared she might. I keep watching the main parking lot, but it's a beautiful sunny day, the perfect Seattle day, and this place is packed. Around me there's that child-playing hum of chatter and the occasional scream, and people are zipping around the lake on foot, and bikes, and skateboards. It's like everyone just took the afternoon off. The basketball court even has a pickup game going. I look to see if Arden Lee is there, but I stay where I am. That's the thing about secrets—when you hold someone else's, you have to hold carefully. I won't mention any names, but some people make being there for you all about themselves. When I spot a red flash of satin that I suspect is Arden Lee's tank, I send him silent love and encouragement, because dreams are hard, especially when they have no possibility of coming true.

Parents and kids are carrying their bags into the pool area, floaties under their arms. A duck passes, a flamingo, a goldfish. I still don't see any sign of Aurora. As I said, it's weird that she comes here, because they have two pools right there at their house, one outdoor and one in, but who am I to judge. Maybe she's got a secret self, like Arden Lee, and Clementine. Like me, like Marla Drake.

But I don't see her and don't see her. Maybe I missed her arrival and she's here already. My inner pig-dog is grabbed by a precipice. I go in.

I'm carrying the striped beach bag that I found in our hall closet, which holds a towel and my suit as subterfuge. The key to being in disguise is to actually believe you're doing the thing you're pretending to do, I decide on the spot. I try to walk in there like I'm really heading in to swim instead of searching for Aurora.

Inside, the smell of chlorine hits, mingled with the stuffiness of a thousand exhales. I pass the bulletin board on my left, a messy patchwork of notices. I'm a few steps beyond it when my brain catches up. Wait, wait, wait. I swear, I saw Aurora's logo back there, that intersecting *A* and *H*, surrounded by the clean double circles. She uses it for her profile photo sometimes. I do a semi-moonwalk back.

Wow. Would you look at that. She made a *flyer*. So old-fashioned, so normal-person. It has those little paper tags that you pull off, printed with the URL of the application site. She probably forgot to remove it after they hired someone.

I pull a tag, just because. I'll keep it with the cork in my sock drawer. I'm standing there just holding it like something precious when the doors open. And, oh my God, she's here, she's coming in this very minute, dragging Arlo by the hand. No wonder she's late—she usually comes alone. She looks overloaded. Ragged, even. I know, it's hard to imagine, because you never see her like that, hair escaping from her ponytail, trying to carry Arlo's stuff plus a cup of coffee, and from Java Jive, too, as if our paths are just meant to cross. Well, I made them cross, but you know. She's a living, breathing, harried human being. And Arlo! It's the actual Arlo. He's wearing a little bathing suit and a tank top with a crab on it.

"No, no, no poooool. No pooooool!" he whines. He tries to pull her back toward the doors.

"Arlooooo. Come oooooon." Yeah, there are lots of *o* sounds, the perfect protest vowel.

"Boboooooooo!" Arlo screams.

This is the closest we've ever been to each other.

That's his voice, you know.

My heart is beating so hard, I can't even tell you. I feel like I could throw up from nerves. I'm right there, just holding that slip of paper. And I look like shit. I mean, I'm wearing black leggings and a T-shirt that says *Coffee Is My Jam,* since Clementine said to dress "like a barista" for the interview. The shirt features a piece of toast and a glob of jam, and it makes no sense, but I found it at the consignment store yesterday. Nothing in my closet really screamed *barista.*

Humiliation creeps right up my body. I mean, she's a lifestyle guru, even though she looks frantic and is only wearing a plain blue sundress and the sort of chunky old Birkenstocks Rosalind hates. I imagined her walking past me—*me* seeing *her* up close, not the other way around.

"Um," she says.

"Uh," I say back.

These are our first words to each other, this woman who is technically my stepmother, but who may not know I exist.

"Would you mind . . . ?"

I see the problem.

Bobo, a stuffed monkey, has been dropped a few paces behind them. Aurora is completely out of hands and patience, too.

"Sure," I say.

I trot back and rescue the monkey. I kneel down in front of Arlo and hand him over. Arlo takes Bobo and clutches him like a long-lost relative. He stops crying. In terms of rescuing, it's not kicking Nazis in the face, or even informing the Harrisons about their stalker, but it's something.

I'm looking right at Arlo. I mean, he's close enough to kiss. I kind of wish I could just scoop him up and hold him, but I'm terrified of him, too. I'm not wearing any kind of disguise, right? I mean, it's just me and him and her, and we're all right there in the entryway of the Green Lake pool. His eyes—they're so beautiful that I almost get choked up. His little lips, you know.

My baby brother. It's hard to imagine, but not. At least, my blood and heart and soul can imagine it, because love is just pouring out of me right now, like someone just turned on some faucet taps of tenderness I didn't even know I had. Maybe I'd feel this way for Phoenix if I met him, but I'm not sure. He's older, practically a grown man. The situation with him seems more intimidating and complicated, the whole history of his mom and my own. But with Arlo, the feeling just exists, the way a flower exists, or a mountain, or a pancake. With Arlo, I maybe have a chance. Look, right here: He's so open. *I* am. God.

Now the little guy does something unexpected. He stops crying entirely. His face is so pale, even flushed from upset. But he touches my nose.

"Beep," he says.

I touch his nose back. "Boop," I say.

We could be two robots talking to each other in our own language, but of course we're not. We're two human beings with the same DNA, and maybe it's recognizing itself, or maybe Arlo just recognizes my love.

He pats my head. I'm trying not to burst into tears right there, but I'm smiling so hard at the same time.

Aurora—she seems really, really tired. Tired and strung out in some way that you never admit on social media. Tired, like she's been working really long hours, or maybe defeated by a toddler, but by more than that, too. I don't want to be dramatic here, or read too much into the moment, but I've seen Clementine with that face. With a flash of *haunted* that appears briefly between all of the everyday moments she's trying to handle. It's kind of shocking, an unexpected plotline. Haunted, frazzled, who would guess. But now, with the beep and the boop, Aurora becomes utterly still and focused. She looks at me, hard. For a second I worry that she recognizes me, knows who I am after all.

But wait. No. Maybe she just recognizes my cape, my ability to rescue. She points down to the slip in my hand. I didn't even realize I was still holding it. It sticks from my palm like a fortune in a cookie.

"Are you, um, interested?" she asks.

SO, PICTURE IT: ME AT THE GREEN LAKE POOL IN THAT T-shirt, kneeling down on the hard, cement floor, the screech of kids in the background. My bag is on the ground, half spilled. A tampon and a book that Arden Lee gave me, *AI Universe,* have escaped, telling Aurora too much about me already. The pebbly cement is making painful circles on my knees, but I barely notice because I am looking up at her, the real Aurora Andozza Harrison, home-wrecker and snob, perfect-everything lifestyle influencer, archenemy. *Who wouldn't hate her?* Mom has said a thousand times. *No wonder.*

I don't feel *no wonder.* I feel *wonder.* I mean, she's so real. She's a human-being woman, maybe on the verge of tears. Her whole self looks on the edge of something, even if she's clearly wealthy. It's hard to explain, but her highlights shimmer like coins in a treasure box, and you just know her sundress is more expensive than a Ross sundress, and that her manicured nails aren't going to be squishing up ground beef for a meat loaf.

Interested?

Are you *kidding*?

"That slip of paper? That's me. Mine. I'm the one looking for a nanny," she says, because I haven't answered. I'm just standing there frozen, struck with my own good luck.

"Oh! Sure," I say. "*Yeah.* I'm interested." It sounds so casual, but really, it's the only thing I can force out of my mouth. I want this so bad. This moment seems imagined. I *have* imagined it, a hundred times.

"Live-in? It's just for the summer. We have a permanent person starting in September."

"I've been looking for a summer nannying job," I lie.

"We've been having trouble finding someone who really *connects* with Ar—" Her eyes land on the book. "Hey! Is that *yours*?"

"It's . . . a subject that fascinates me." Not a lie.

"Huh." She shakes her head, as if struck by *her* sudden good luck. "Do you have any experience watching kids?"

All that mental practice with the application pays off. I tell her about babysitting and tutoring. She looks understandably hesitant. Mom considers child-raising to be one of her areas of expertise, so I'm about to pile on all the stuff she believes is important, like monitoring a child's milestones for any potential delay, and being a good role model, and how baby-wearing and co-sleeping are crucial for bonding. At least, these are the reasons we're so well-adjusted, according to her. But then I stop, because I'm not all that well-adjusted. Or, if this is well-adjusted, then I'm really worried for everyone else. "I just really love children," I say instead. And it's true. At least, I think I might really love this particular child already.

Aurora smiles. "Would you want to give it a trial run right now? I had a sitter, and he canceled, and I just *need* to swim. It's the only way I can clear my head to think straight. Maybe you guys could just hang out in the shallow end near me and see how you do? I assume you've got your suit and stuff?"

"Sure!" Sure? Unsure. Very unsure. Panic rises. Just *meeting* them is a lot to handle, a lot to take in—the beep and the boop, the way she says *and stuff* and seems so much younger than I thought. I'd have to put on my suit, too. She'd see my splootch, and I didn't shave my legs. And I rarely swim in pools. I just dunk in super quick and get out, since chlorine apparently messes up my skin. It's one of my rashes. *Oh my God!* Mom says. *You're so sensitive. I had to watch every single thing you came in contact with for years! I never went anywhere without at least one EpiPen.* I don't even know what might happen if I do. An emergency, maybe.

What I'm *not* panicking about is that I have a real, actual interview in about twenty minutes. This doesn't even cross my mind. I'm about to be a no-show, and I've never been a no-show in my life. I am always a yes-show, a 1,000 percent yes-show. Even the *thought* of being irresponsible brings guilt. But I'm caught in a magnetic vortex of hope and possibility.

"Great! I'm Aurora. This is Arlo, and you're . . ."

"Eleanor," I say, and then blush. Like, bad. Like, the red of a thousand blushes all jammed together. My heart clamps down, sick, because I messed this up already. Ugh! If she *does* know about me, she might start wondering about bumping into a girl named Eleanor who's pretty much the same age as Brandi's daughter. God, I'm so stupid sometimes. *You're not stupid, Eleanor,* Mom says whenever I don't get a 100 percent on a test. *You just don't stop and THINK.* My mind searches for a solution, and then I remember what Arden Lee says about books, how believability is in the details. "Drake," I add. "Eleanor Drake. I actually had a nannying job lined up in Eugene, where we used to live, but my dad got transferred right at the end of last year." This exact thing happened to one of Arden Lee's cousins.

"Well, *that* sucks," she says.

"I'll forgive him *some*day," I say, and roll my eyes.

"I can't blame you! So, I swim for maybe forty minutes?"

"Great," I say.

"Stay right in my lane where I can see you?"

"Of course."

"Here's everything." She hands over the bags. The *everything* seems to include a wide variety of stuff—floaties and fish crackers and a water bottle and sun lotion. And Arlo himself, too, after an encouraging nudge forward. Aurora gives a little wave and heads straight for the pool. Now Arlo looks like he's going to cry, and I feel like I might cry. I have no idea what to do. I try to summon Clementine's care and capability with Apple. I suddenly realize that she must have a hundred daily doubts.

"Does Bobo like to swim?" I ask.

Arlo's worried face studies mine and discovers a joke. He shows me his dimples, oh my God. "Bobo is a stuffie," he says.

"Oooh-ooh, ahh-ahh!" I do my best monkey. I give Bobo's feet a paddle. "Kick, kick." Arlo's little teeth are the cutest little white squares when he smiles, like that gum you pop out of the foil packs, but smaller. I just want to bite his face or something. Not literally, but you know. My heart blooms. I am such a goner. "Let's get our suits on."

IT TAKES ME, LIKE, FIFTEEN MINUTES TO DECIPHER *swim diy-pa*. Apparently, there's such a thing as a *swim diaper*. It's about the only useful thing in Aurora's bags, aside from a towel and a pair of water wings. You wouldn't believe all the stuff she has in there. It's like a Target exploded. Probably not Target. There's a baby rain poncho and a single rubber boot, and an expired applesauce pouch. And, man, there's going to be more to this than meets the eye, because it takes me another ten minutes to undo all the Velcro and unbend the little arms from the sleeves and to get the chubby legs out of the shorts and into the swim diypa.

Arlo walks like an overstuffed penguin in those orange water wings I've squeaked up his arms. I hold his hand and clutch a towel around myself as we head to the pool. Last year's bikini with its lively pattern of ironic (I told myself ironic) sea creatures looks only childish here. Aurora waves when she sees us, then dives back under, zipping through the water in her red tank suit, doing one of those amazing flips when she reaches the end. It's strange, though, how she said swimming is her only outlet when she's got all those photos of Pilates and hot yoga and stuff on her Instagram, too.

I hold Arlo as we edge in. He clutches my neck. "It's okay," I tell him. "I would never let anything happen to you." It's the truth, and a vow.

I'm so busy being confident for him that I forget all about the chlorine. I swirl him, and water dots his lashes. He floats around with his chin up, and I pretend he's a dolphin and a whale and, at his request, a *regulah fish.* Bobo watches from the side. What a blast.

"God, I feel much better already," Aurora says when we're out of the pool and Arlo's wrapped in his towel like the most snug, adorable baby burrito. She takes off her swim cap and shakes out her hair. "I just need that, you know?"

Not really. "For sure."

"You're *so* good with him!"

It turns out I am, I think.

"It was getting so *complicated,* hiring someone for just a few months! This big, national search! Ten-page résumés, ugh. I just wanted someone natural, *real.* Like my favorite babysitter when I was a kid, the girl who lived next door."

"That's me," I say. I'm still not sure I have the job.

"As per usual, Leo Gemini was right."

"Leo Gemini?"

"My astrologer. He said my person would soon appear somewhere near the water." She beams. "This is going to be a big year, and every second counts, he told me."

Leo Gemini is about the fakest name for an astrologer I can imagine. Plus, they live by Lake Washington, in a city where water is basically everywhere. I remember General Bruno, Killer Dawson, and all the bad guys lurking in Miss Fury's world. I told Arlo that I would never let anything bad happen to him, and it suddenly seems like a big promise.

Aurora pats her pockets, hunts in her bag. For a lifestyle influencer, she's pretty unorganized. "Oh, never mind. I was going to have you give me your references, but I can't find my phone. Why don't you just come by our house and we can sort out the details. Tomorrow? Four o'clock? At the, uh, Frame House?" She tilts her head, waits.

I know what she wants from me, so I pretend to be politely shocked. I summon Miss Fury, the image where her eyes are wide and accented with shiny white dots of surprise. In the panel, there are no words, only black motion lines of feeling. "Four is great. Thank you so much."

Aurora smiles. "I believe in trusting my instincts. And I can tell you're a really good person." She can? I don't feel like one, standing here in disguise, sharing DNA with her kid.

We say goodbye. As they head to their car, Arlo starts to cry. He even reaches toward me. Aurora retrieves a tiny bag of crackers, opening it with her teeth as they walk, nothing you'd ever imagine her doing in those glamorous photos. Arlo ignores the crackers. She's missing the point. All you have to do is look at him, at us, and you'd see it.

I watch as she lifts him into his car seat and shuts his door. I wish I could explain to him that I'm not going anywhere. We belong to each other now.

The wildest thing? My arms. No rash. I was swimming for almost an hour, and my skin is as clear as the sky on this day that has changed my life.

chapter
Five

I WONDER IF THIS IS HOW MY MOM FELT WHEN SHE
first met Hugo, even though he wouldn't even give her his phone
number. You know, before Mr. I Can Change Your Life turned
into Mr. I Can Ruin It, Too. As I head to the parking lot, I'm
jazzed—an exhilarating promise mixed with pure panic. It's all so
close. *All*—a totally different life, a me that is so much more than
the one I am, the one that is wallpaper, a weed, a shadow. A noise
you're not even sure you hear.

The minute I shut my car door and I'm alone with me, the truth, the likely permanent truth, hits. I'm just regular old Eleanor Diamond, not particularly awesome, definitely not up for the task of being with people like them, and now I've created a mess. The lies already, oh man. The lies I still need. What am I going to tell Mom and Ros? And, sure, I might force Hugo Harrison and his family to look at me, but what are they going to see? In the rearview mirror, there is only a girl with flat, wet hair and red chlorine eyes. I tossed my T-shirt back on over my bathing suit, and now I have two wet boob circles. This is who Aurora Harrison was talking to, this doofy girl. I cringe so hard, my stomach folds like an accordion.

Arden Lee says my inner critic is a real asshole.

I grab my towel to sit on since my bikini bottoms are still damp. I can just imagine Ros getting in and wondering why her seat is wet. And that's when things get so much worse. Oh my God, oh my God. My bottoms are actually *inside out*. Like, actually inside out! Like, so inside out that the ironic sea creatures are pale and nearly invisible, and so inside out that the little white landing strip along the crotch is VERY VISIBLE.

No. Just no, no, no.

I'm horrified. Nearly in shock. I mean, how could this happen? How? Maybe because I was wrangling a toddler brother into his swimsuit and panicking about being a stalker gone wrong and interacting with a famous influencer wife of a famous tech genius who's my stepmother and doesn't know it? Maybe that? Or maybe it didn't happen. It didn't really, did it? I look down. It did. What is wrong with me? I'm so ridiculous. How could I not notice?

Okay, okay, I fairly often put shirts on backward, even ones with hoods, which drop down over my face like an abduction in the movies. I've worn different black flats when we were Mom's dates at the Heartland holiday party, making Rosalind laugh so hard she almost peed. But bikini bottoms? And at a pool, too, where you're already at the pyramid point of vulnerability, in front of Aurora Harrison, who is the sky beyond the pyramid.

I feel around the back of them, just to torment myself further, and yeah, there's the little silky tag, which I know features a sea turtle and reads *Tropical Treat.* Oh my God, oh my God. I can almost feel Ros's disdain shooting straight from one of her Instagram posts. My face is burning a hot red, and my chest is tightening. I find my inhaler and puff. This is way worse than any stupid thing I've done in the past. Worse than PE basketball. Worse than throwing up during the second-grade play when I was wearing a cumulonimbus costume of cardboard and cotton balls. *Puke rain,* said Emerson Fry, who would later anoint Arden Lee with the all-purpose insult *weirdo.* Arden Lee claimed this was a badge of honor, but he was hurt, of course he was. No one's immune to cruelty, no matter how confident your clothing choices seem.

I'm just sitting in Mom's car, in that rare parking spot, so of course other cars are starting to line up behind me, assuming I'm about to leave. I hate that! It makes me nervous, and, you know, I need a minute. Sometimes, you just need a minute, so back off! And now I can't find the keys. Mom's old Taurus is not one of those amazing tech-filled miracles where you just push a button and it starts. You need an actual, real key that turns an actual, real ignition, and I have no idea where this medieval entity called a key is. Hunting, hunting, panic rising. That car is pissing me so off, sitting there insistently with its turn signal on, claiming my spot before I'm out of my spot. I'm not done here, okay? Finally, relief, there it is, the weight of metal. It's in. Only, in nerves and haste and humiliation, I forget to reverse, and lurch forward instead, scraping some underneath thing of the car against the cement curb.

I start giggling madly. I mean, shit. I'm a crotch-out, wet-boobed, maniac driver liar.

Thank goodness, I'm out of here. My heart is beating a little wildly, made more intense by that albuterol.

But then . . . it hits. It hits like a . . . I'm sorry, Arden Lee, all I can think of is *Mack truck,* even though that's a cliché and even though I don't even really know what a Mack truck is. The point is, it hits hard. That interview. The one I've missed by . . . I check the Taurus clock, which permanently reads six-fifteen. A lot. I've missed it by a lot. And I probably only remember the interview now because I'm staring straight at Java Jive. Something worse than horror and humiliation strikes—a gross, deep guilt, the self-hatred that comes with being irresponsible and unkind. Clementine was so excited. All week she's been grabbing my arm and squeezing, her eyes all happy. To the point where Arden Lee was getting a little jealous about us working together, saying stuff like, *Fine, leave me out,* as Clementine said stuff back like, *You should apply, too! It would be so great!*

Oh my God.

Now it's not the hysterical *Oh my God!* of being the maniac driver liar. It's the quietest *Oh my God* of letting someone down.

My mom is so right about me—how I don't think, how I don't

a million things. And my inner critic isn't enough of an asshole to keep me in line, that's for sure.

I pull over. I can't go in there now, like this. My heart jabs with remorse, imagining Clementine and Clementine's boss, Allie, just waiting and waiting for me as the minutes ticked by. I madly search for the email with Allie's number on it. I call, without a plan, not thinking first, because I'm a fuckup, ugh. *You've reached . . .* Her voice is so nice. She *is* so nice. Clementine's always saying so. After the beep I give her a thousand stumbling apologies. I tell her I had car trouble. I tell her I couldn't get to a phone, because I'd locked my purse in the car. Sorry, sorry, sorry, car, car, car, I say. I hang up, feeling slimy and deceptive because I didn't ask to reschedule, so of course she'll know I'm just a thoughtless, uncaring person who maybe got a different job.

Please answer, I beg as Clementine's phone rings and rings.

"Eleanor!" Clementine wails. "What are you *doing*? What *happened*? We were waiting, like, over *an hour* and then just gave up! Are you all right?" I hear the whirl and grind of machines in the background. I also hear her worry.

"I am so sorry. Oh my God, Clementine. My car . . ."

"Your car." Her voice goes distant.

"It wouldn't start?"

"It wouldn't start."

"I had to take it to . . . um."

"Eleanor. I can see your car right this second. You're parked next to the bike store." I look over at Java Jive. I see Clementine in her black Java Jive apron, with her orange braids over each shoulder. She gives me a crisp salute.

"I am so sorry. It's just been quite a morning, and—"

"Don't lie to me."

"It's a long story."

"Well, I don't have time to hear it right now, since I'm at *work*." Let me tell you, people can be super quiet at school, but that doesn't mean they'll take your shit.

"Don't hate me. Something incredible happened."

"I could never hate you, but this better be good."

I RIP OFF THAT BATHING SUIT THE MINUTE I GET HOME. Well, *rip* isn't exactly the right word, because who can rip off a wet bathing suit. I scoot-scoot out of the bottoms and fling off the top, which lands on the back of my chair and hangs there all jaunty, like it's in a party mood. Marla Drake, who, as I have repeatedly mentioned, becomes the super-fantastic and powerful Miss Fury, never has these issues even as her regular self. She's glamorous and elegant even in the worst of times, which, at this moment, sort of pisses me off.

I pace around my room, anxiety thrumming. Out my window I lock onto the neon pink Psyckē sign in the distance, and my mind creates a plot and characters. In this dream scenario it's tomorrow, and I'm at the Harrisons' house, and I'm killing it, and they love me. We're all laughing and having the best time. The fantasy involves champagne and glittery shoes. Maybe one of them has a brief moment (okay, it's Hugo) of gazing at me with a smiling familiarity, a sense that he might know me, and, wow, wouldn't it be something if I were *that* Eleanor, since this one is so . . . *cool*? Hugo and me, boom, we recognize each other, we connect, as if *we* are on the same planet. He's so amazing and easy to be with, and it's like I actually have one of my two parents. He looks at me and sees more than the mess that Mom and Rosalind do. I mean, I know they love me as I am, I'm pretty sure. They say so. They might love me more if I were better, but they love me. But with dream-Hugo, I'm already appreciated, as is. And I appreciate him, too. There's just this simple love-goodness between us. Like the way it should be.

This all comes to a screeching halt, mostly because the fantasy train has hit an avalanche of truth piled on the track. I'm going to their house tomorrow. Eleanor Drake, from Eugene.

I fling open my closet, staring into the abyss of that deep and eternal question: What should I wear? What would Marla wear? A smart suit, a gown. It hits me then that June Tarpé Mills probably spent more time thinking about Marla's wardrobe than the way she portrayed an entire race of human beings. Hey, sure, let's dismiss large groups of people and focus on fashion, gross. Why are people so hard to love? Role models, heroes, parents, your own self, even? I stare dismally at a mess of thrift-shop T-shirts, dresses from a bygone era. My stomach sinks with the pre-despair of certain failure. There's probably a German word for this, too.

"Ellie?" A knock. Rosalind pops her head in. She usually calls me *Ellie* when she wants something, but maybe not this time, because all she does is come in and look around at the piles of clothes strewn everywhere. Her face goes soft with sympathy. She can be kind, too, I should mention that. Like, really kind. When I started junior high and high school, she toured me around, showed me the cafeteria and the band room and the gym so I wouldn't be nervous. She looked out for me. "What happened? Are you okay?"

"I have nothing to wear," I groan. It sounds awful and spoiled, because, look.

"You must have gotten the job."

I almost do a double take of shock. How did she know? But she means Java Jive, of course. We're all so much in our own heads, in our own worlds, that we can forget everyone else isn't in there with us.

"A different one." This is what I should have been doing instead of worrying about shirts and skirts and shoes: I should have been getting my story straight.

"A different job? Like *what*?" She looks suspicious. Well, I'm acting suspicious. We stare at each other. We could be one of those frames in Miss Fury where there's only one big question mark above everyone's head.

"Um." A great start, Eleanor! "Nannying. I've gotten to know this family. Friends of Jackie's. A wealthy family. Really wealthy. They live in Laurelhurst. I'm supposed to go over there tomorrow to figure out the details."

I look at her, my sister. Her eyes are so green, and her hair is so shiny, and I remember that she's my friend, that she's on my side. At our old house we even shared a room, you know. It was always us with our Happy Meals, Mom with the Quarter Pounder, until no one cared about toys anymore. I remember what she always tells me, too, that she's proud of me, that she wants to help, that she wants me to live my best life. The point is, she loves me. And

I love her. And we are the sisters, not Mom and her. I almost spill everything right there.

I don't need to. She zeroes right in like a fighter jet. "You don't mean Hugo Harrison."

"What? Of course not."

"Are you lying to me? You're always so *funny* about him."

"No, I'm not *lying*. What do you mean, funny?" She sure isn't laughing now.

"Like, unclear. Like . . . not on the right side of history."

Rosalind can make Arden Lee tear his hair out, clichés, clichés. "What does that even mean in this context?"

"In the context of *Mom*. In the context of what he did to her and us."

"Whatever, okay? A person can be curious and not be a traitor." But that's not true. I understand what *traitor* means to Mom, even if I can't explain it to other people. Traitor is one of the worst things. Traitor means rage, because *how* dare *you?* Traitor is a barren landscape she might drop you in forever. And *traitor*—well, there are a hundred ways to be one, and sometimes you only find out accidentally. Pretty much, you're required to agree with everything she says or believes, about Hugo Harrison most of all. If she discovers what I'm about to do . . . My stomach hurts just thinking about it.

"I don't even see the point of being curious," Rosalind says, her lips closing with prim certainty.

"Well, it doesn't matter anyway," I tell her. "My job is with the . . ." My eyes dart around the room, land on my artwork. Miss Fury comes to my rescue again. "Von Barons."

Rosalind snorts. "*Von Barons?* That sounds like something out of your comics."

I make a face to indicate how ludicrous she's being. *Your comics,* though—this is how Ros and Mom see my art in general, and Miss Fury in particular, as if it's some combination of Rosalind's brief stint making friendship bracelets plus Saturday-morning *SpongeBob*. When I first started drawing Miss Fury, I showed them some sketches, hoping for encouragement, maybe. But after Ros's *Supercute!* and Mom's *Well, everything takes practice,* I stopped sharing. They don't understand that making this comic means so much more to me than when I tried to draw the neighbor's cat or a bowl of fruit, and how can they? They're not interested in creating stuff, and who can say the exact right thing about something so crucial to a person anyway? I've kept my deep dive into Tarpé Mills and William Moulton Marston and the Golden Age of Comics to myself, too. How serious I am about my art, how I'm trying to learn—it's all secretly mine. I need to be free to suck at it. I need to be free to have it matter without the risk of getting wrecked. Things that matter that much deserve protection.

"The Von Barons are a really great family. They want me to live with them for the summer, and it's going to be awesome. They've got these two kids . . ." My mind flashes on Arlo and Boolean. "Arthur and Bailey."

"Arthur and Bailey? Not *Arlo?*"

It's almost shocking hearing Arlo's name come out of Rosalind's mouth. In a way he's secretly mine, too. The Harrisons are, because *they* matter that much. And after today he matters even more. I have to remind myself that they—Arlo and Hugo and Aurora—also belong to Rosalind, even if she doesn't want them.

"Rosalind! God!" I say, like she's being annoying and beyond. I add a dramatic face.

"Well, I'm happy for you. I hope they pay well."

I hear the edgy competitiveness, even if she will always and forever win. She *doesn't* hope they pay well, not really. Or, at least, not as well as Heartland.

"Yup," I say. "They do." I try to sound smug and mysterious, folding the fabulous amount into myself, when I'm actually realizing right that second that Aurora never even mentioned the pay, and I never asked. I'd do it for free, for the chance to swim around in that pool with Arlo clinging to my neck.

"You're going to leave me with Mom all summer?"

"You *like* being together," I say.

Rosalind sighs. She glances at my laptop, shut tight.

It hits me.

I didn't think, I didn't think! Rosalind's going to go search for the made-up Von Barons, first thing. I would. "And don't bother looking them up and stuff. They're—" My mind hunts frantically for that word that Arden Lee is always calling Clementine. The one that means they are religiously opposed to technology. "Luddites."

"Lud-what?"

"They're not online at all. I mean *at all*, and believe me, I looked. They both made money in tech but don't want to be part of it anymore. They have flip phones, that's it." Lies are pouring right out.

"Whatever," Rosalind says, like she can't imagine it.

"Really," I confirm.

There's an uncomfortable beat of silence, and then Rosalind decides to let it go. She sits on my bed, choosing to save me instead of slay me. I suddenly realize that the saving and the slaying both mean that you're the one with the power. "That's cute," she says. She points. I lift a blue-and-red striped skirt. "No, the yellow one." Plain yellow, with a row of brass buttons down each side. I scoot it on. I grab an orange argyle tee.

She cringes but tries to hide it. "I love it," she says. "Just not with your librarian shoes."

My *librarian shoes* are oxfords decorated with wing-tip holes that I got at Second Stories, the day Arden Lee bought a cheap fur coat that maybe lost a battle on the savanna. Those shoes spoke to me like a worn paperback. Yeah, their vibe is clichéd spinster, supreme shusher, and cardigan-wearing librarian, and I love them. The word *spinster* is so romantic to me, spidery and stubborn, and I adore quiet, and there's nothing better than a cardigan, that cozy clothing friend who only wishes you comfort and peace. It's the very opposite of Ros's turquoise bikini featured in her most recent post, where she stands in the shallow end of Venicenne's pool, caption: *Hot.* When I put on those shoes, I have a different superpower—the silent majesty of knowledge.

Rosalind thinks *librarian shoes* is an insult, haha.

"YOU'D BE AWESOME AT THAT!" MOM BEAMS THAT night at dinner. Okay, this only happens in my imagination. In real life her face scrunches at my news. "You barely have any background for that kind of position!" She rolls the pizza cutter along the take-and-bake veggie, flops a slice onto my plate. The center is still underbaked, something my inner critic might note about me.

"I'll do great." I think this is what *she's* supposed to say.

"I'm not sure how I feel about you living somewhere else for the summer."

"I'll be half a mile away. I'll be home all the time! It'll be a great learning experience."

"You'd have to keep your room *way* cleaner than here," Mom says. Rosalind kicks me under the table, gives me an *ignore her* face. God, I love it when she does stuff like that. I love it when she's on my side. I love it when she's my someone.

"Much cleaner," I say. I wait. I brace for the no that's coming. I can practically hear Mom clicking her Heartland calculator with her manicured nails. I've got an arsenal of comebacks for any roadblocks, like if she insists that she has to speak to the Von Barons. But none of this happens. It's funny—sometimes she's a hawk, watching me and my body for any sign of imminent disaster requiring her rescue, and other times I could leave the country and she'd barely notice.

"Well, at least you got a job. You must have made a good impression," she says.

It's a yes! It's a go! I'm past the prison guard, through security, over the border. My giddiness is like a bunch of tiny dogs dressed in tutus, jumping around on their hind legs, hooray!

"Blakely seems to really like me!" I answer. "I think that's what did it. The few times I, uh, ran into them at, uh, Arden Lee's house."

Rosalind picks the green peppers off her pizza. We both hate them. See how much we have in common? I feel a surge of love for her. All of me is surging, this is so exciting. Ros looks up. *"Bailey?"*

"Bailey?" I echo.

Shit! Shit.

"You said Blakely."

"No, I didn't."

"You did," Mom says.

"I'm tired, okay? Geez, you guys."

I think of her, how can I not? Marla, Miss Fury, in a hundred close calls.

I'm so screwed.

chapter
Six

"HUGO HARRISON USED THE WORD *SENTIENT*, LIKE, three times at that tech conference, according to Mr. Alonzo. It's *got* to be a robot." After his microeconomics class today, Arden Lee's back on the subject of Psycke's mystery product. "They already did the robot dog, so it makes sense. You're going to hear *something*, El. God, I can't believe you'll be in his house!"

Today in our favorite lunch spot, we've got company. The last day of school is tomorrow, and everyone's out here messing around in the sun, signing yearbooks and stuff. Ewan Manning, Lily Shruti, Ana Lee, and the twins, Hannah and Forest Gyles, are sprawled out right nearby. Ewan Manning's brother, Niles, was Rosalind's first boyfriend, and Ewan's even been at our house once or twice, but he pretends not to know me at school. I wish I could be bigger than the awkwardness that I feel around people like them, kids who are popular, good at sports, in student government, and student everything. Instead I feel a strange, embarrassed shame, like I'm wearing a clown nose that can't be removed.

"You could be like . . . What's that book we read about the World War II female spy?" Clementine asks.

"The one with *code* in the title?" Arden Lee says.

We crack up. They *all* have *code* in the title. It's practically a requirement for World War II female spy books. The members of the Soggy Pages Book Club can riff on lots of title trends—the use of *Girl,* or *The So-and-So's Daughter,* or the vanishing or disappeared or lost girl or daughter. Ewan Manning and Lily Shruti and the gang don't know what they're missing.

"*Code-Named Robot,*" I say. Arden Lee snorts.

"The robot dog is creepy." Clementine takes a bite of a rice dish with beans and raisins, probably the ones I snuck from our cupboard. After telling Arden Lee and Clementine everything about Aurora at the pool, Clementine forgave me for missing that interview, because that's the kind of friend she is. Instead of being mad, she grabbed both my arms, her face happy, and said, *That's* wonderful, *El. I know how much this will mean to you, even if I wish you didn't have to do it this way.*

"It's the eyes," I say. Those eerie, unseeing black marbles.

When I think about Boolean, a real dog with real feelings, the robot version doesn't seem anywhere close. When you look at Boolean and he looks back, you see a soul.

"They're empty," Clementine agrees. "No meaning."

It's how I feel when I mess around with Frame, the AI art generator, even though it's really fun and what it makes is cool. Sure, *I* input the words (a polar bear wearing a top hat while riding in a three-masted ship), but the polar bear is never the one I envisioned, and I don't get the deep satisfaction I do when drawing. Sketching is hard, and what I make sometimes sucks, but the desire to do it seems to come from a place that's as old as time. I'm not really religious except in an emergency and when looking at stars. But if God does exist, creativity is maybe a present he gave us to make up for the other shit we have to deal with.

"If he's supposed to be so realistic, maybe he should poop silver balls," I suggest.

Arden Lee is all animated, watch out. He shoves away a whoosh of bangs. "The idea is to make a *better* version, an improved model of what's real. Wag, wag, cutie dog stuff, no poop."

"The *truth*, though . . . We get poop along with good." Troubled lines crease Clementine's forehead.

"They should make the robot dog's lips flap when he's riding in a car with his head out the window," I say. "I love that about dogs."

Arden Lee ignores me. "The errors of being human, the mistakes, the ugliness—that's what they're *eliminating*."

"Who's to say what's ugly? And as much as we hate mistakes, we grow from them," Clementine says. Sometimes I wish we'd just talk about dogs.

"Yeah? People don't *always* grow," Arden Lee says. "Do you want human error when you're getting your appendix out? AI in medical research, robot surgery, it's *miraculous*. Isn't it *good* that we're trying to eliminate those human failures? Robots doing surgery is one of the most revolutionary things ever."

"They don't perform surgery," I say, but I sound unsure even to myself.

"El!" Arden Lee says. "Robot surgery has been going on for *years*."

Ugh. I hate not knowing stuff, even if we can never know all the stuff. "Sorry."

"Stop," Clementine says to Arden Lee. "She gets enough of that already." She means my mom. I stay silent. Traitor land mines are everywhere.

Arden Lee sighs. "You're right. *I'm* sorry, El."

They think Mom and Rosalind always criticize me, which makes them mad. Their support feels good until the guilt hits. I don't know why it feels shameful to be treated badly by my family. Besides, Mom and Ros do love me, even if it's all too complicated to explain to anyone else. Clementine and Arden Lee remind me of that headline I saw long ago and never forgot: *Protective Husky Defends Kitten Against Adult Cat.*

"Thanks for caring," I say. "If I get the job and find out anything, you'll be the first to know." Talking about all this is making me anxious, though. I'm meeting Aurora in a few hours.

"You *already* got the job!" Arden Lee says.

"I could totally screw it up. What if they know who I am already?" I picture Hugo opening the door, standing there like

General Bruno or Gary Hale, or maybe even the newspapermen who covered Marla's bare torso with a blob of red ink when she wore that leaf bikini. Angry and accusing, is the point. "*Why* did I give them my real name? Eleanor isn't exactly common." I have new respect for Marla Drake, what it takes to have a secret identity. Nerves of steel, for one.

"Eleanor Weltzler, Eleanor Reilly . . ." Arden Lee counts our classmates on his fingers.

"Eleanor Delarion, my neighbor, but she's eighty," Clementine says.

"Using your real name is *genius*. Who would do that? It practically *guarantees* you're not her. And, hey—being around them . . . Maybe it'll be great or maybe terrible, but it won't just be happening in your imagination."

Arden Lee glances at Hannah and Forest Gyles. See, he knows what he's talking about. When Arden Lee was twelve, his dad, Leon, moved out of their house and in with his then-girlfriend and now-wife, Cherie, and her twelve-year-old twins. *The perfect daughter, the perfect son,* Arden Lee says about Hannah and Forest. Leon was on the roster for the Sonics the last year that Seattle had a basketball team, and he lives for the sport. Forest Gyles is the biggest big-shot basketball player on the Roosevelt Rough Riders, the kid people say could go pro. For a while Arden Lee visited on weekends, but it was a disaster, including some brutal games of HORSE. Now he only goes on holidays. When Forest's locker gets decorated and stuff during basketball season, we try to be extra nice to Arden Lee.

Clementine is quiet. "Do you think what I'm doing is terrible?" I ask her.

"I think it's *understandable*. I'm just worried. I mean . . . If your *mom* finds out?"

Arden Lee whistles long and low, a soundtrack of bad outcomes. Arden Lee and his mom have their own history with mine, after Jackie accidentally backed into our mailbox once. *What the hell are you DOING?* Mom yelled, racing from the house. Mom already judged Jackie, after she gave us a holiday gift with the tag still on, a food basket from Ross, all these crackers and snacks for, like, seven dollars. *From, what, the* 1990s? *Is she trying to* kill *us?* Mom said. Now whenever Jackie comes up in conversation, I hear it: *I hate to say it, but Jackie is*—I don't even want to repeat it. Let's just say it has the word *trailer* in it, and Jackie is the sweetest person.

"My mother had an astrologer," Clementine says. I've told them every detail about meeting Aurora, even the fake-sounding Leo Gemini. "We went with her once. She disappeared into this blue house with a giant eye painted on it, and we waited in the car forever."

Clementine's situation is so much worse than mine that my anxiety turns to sadness. God. The sorrow doesn't last long, though, because here comes Xavier Chen, sauntering across the lawn.

"Hey," he says to Clementine.

"Hey," she says back.

Can you feel someone else's heart beating? If so, I feel Clementine's. She's smiling a small, shy grin. The most unsure but hopeful smile ever.

"He totally came this way on purpose," I say.

She blushes. "No way."

"A hundred percent," I say.

"You absolutely checked out his butt." Arden Lee is beaming. We're all suddenly giddy.

"I did not!"

"Butt checker!" I call, and me and Arden Lee crack up so hard, and Clementine's shoving us, and Arden Lee gets all nerdy and rolls on the grass. Those other kids are staring at us, because he's holding his stomach from laughter and making a scene, and who cares. Who cares, and I love it, because the day suddenly feels wonderful. It's a blue sky, warm sun, summer's almost here, school's almost out, I'm about to be a spy in my father's house, and Clementine is falling in love kind of joy.

If you want something nice to happen for anyone, it's Clementine.

TWO BLOCKS AWAY I START FEELING ALL SWEATY AND weird, like a big hand is about to reach out and destroy me. Or like a big eye on a blue house is staring down. My heart pounds. Arcs of sweat form under my armpits, great. Miss Fury never has panic attacks. Not even on that high ledge, chasing the murdering imposter.

I pull over.

What was I thinking? I'm in way over my head, even before Mom or Ros finds out. My chest is all tight. I puff my inhaler. As comforting and inspiring as fiction can be, it's not real. I'm not Marla, or even her creator, Tarpé Mills, taking on the big dude artists of the Golden Age, like Jack Kirby and Will Eisner. I'm plain old Eleanor, un-golden, too scared to be bold or angry.

Just breathe, I tell myself. It's what people always say in the movies when someone is in a particularly stressful situation. It's proving to be totally worthless.

My phone buzzes inside my bag. Watch, it'll be Mom. My hands shake—albuterol plus nerves, wow. Wrongdoing can really make you a wreck.

The text is from Arden Lee: *You can do it.*

I almost burst into tears. *AHHH,* I text back.

Are your pants on okay? He adds some laugh emojis along with some hearts.

I smile. When I told them about my inside-out bathing suit, Clementine said, *I bet Aurora didn't even notice,* and Arden Lee said, *Embarrassment sucks, but it won't kill you.* He's an expert about that, since he's always true to himself, something that takes more guts than just about anything else. If you don't like his velvet vest or his hats or the way he skewers people who misuse *theirs* and *there's,* move on, but you're going to miss the way he loves you as hard as he loves books.

I think I'm good, I text.

The circles of typing appear. And then comes the message: *You're GREAT, Eleanor.*

chapter
Seven

I'M NOT SURE HOW MANY PEOPLE KNOW THIS, BUT there are floors that actually have heat underneath them. I find this out when I take my shoes off after the Harrisons' housekeeper lets me in. For a second I'm sure the warmth is in my imagination. The same thing happened when my confused butt met the heated seats in Jackie's Ford Fiesta.

It's my first mistake—those plush white carpets beyond that shiny stone floor . . . I slip off my librarian shoes. The housekeeper, an older woman with short silver hair who I've seen through my binoculars, gives me a disapproving expression. "You can keep those on," she says curtly, but only after I've felt that heat. Apparently, when you're that wealthy, people are supposed to keep their shoes *on* in your house, because if stuff gets wrecked, whatever. It's the exact opposite of what you'd think.

"I'm sorry!" Apologizing already, ugh. Embarrassed already, too.

"Right this way."

It's exactly what you'd expect a housekeeper to say, which makes me get the giggles. I swallow hard and try to think of something serious, like when Mrs. Wei's cat got hit by a car and had a cat cast. But then the words *cat cast* almost do me in. I make a horrible *pffft* sound, and the housekeeper looks over at me like I'm unbearably unsuitable and immature, which, let's face it, I am. Clementine once said that the best thing you can do in any difficult situation is to be kindly honest, and I love that and never forgot it.

"I'm really nervous," I say.

Clementine's magic does not work here. The housekeeper's face remains *Backpfeifengesicht*. I probably don't have the grammar right, but it means a face that gives you the urge to slap it, haha. I follow her into the main living area. And then . . . Well, let me tell you, looking at something from a distance and being inside of it are two completely different things. The whole front of the room is glass, and all of those frames make a giant window to the world. The lake in front of me is vast and shimmery, blue and more blue, with blue sky above. There's a blue swimming pool, too, surrounded by white chaises and bright green grass with a crisp crew cut. I wonder if these are the colors of heaven, or maybe just the colors of money. Money definitely means order. Nothing here looks on the verge of slipping out of control.

I see that long dock as well, and the huge white sailboat with the small zoom-y boat tied to the back. The big boat is named the *Hugo Naut*, something I already knew from my kayak trip and that article in *Sailing Magazine*, but now I squinch to read the name of the dinghy: *Theos.* I make a mental note to look it up later. I'm overwhelmed. Everything is so . . . Well, my mind has gone into shock, because the only adjective I can think of is *beautiful.*

I am in *his house.* This is his. He's, like, *all around.* He could walk in here any second.

If things were different, this could be my house. I could stretch out on one of those chaises, ask the tight-faced housekeeper for a lemonade, or whatever rich people do. I would never do that; I'd get my own. It wouldn't change who I am. The housekeeper would think that about me, too. *Money doesn't change who she is.* She'd like me.

Well, in real life, not so much. She gestures to a sleek leather chair next to a plush white U-shaped couch. I sit. The chair is stiff, even if the leather feels smooth and buttery. "Thanks," I say. I force myself not to apologize again.

The housekeeper studies my face, hard, as if she can see right through me. She's making me nervous. More nervous. "Do you need anything?" she asks.

And, hey! This is something I can get right. I know the answer, from several uncomfortable visits to my grandparents' house in California, before Mom, Nana Minnie, and Papa Joe became estranged. *Estranged* might as well just be called *strange.* I don't even understand *why* they are (*we* are)—something to do with a slight, an insult, and Mom getting pregnant twice without a husband. How Mom wasn't appreciative enough about their help, and how they never let her forget it. Nana Minnie's real name is Meredith, but you can tell she takes great pride in being small. Papa Joe always comments on it between cocktails, *my tiny wife, my little powder keg.* Anyway, the right answer is to *Do you need anything?* is *No, thank you.* They love you more when you're seen and not heard. Or not seen and not heard.

"No, thank you."

The housekeeper gives me a slight smile. Bingo! "I'll let her know you're here."

I snort, because I'm still on the verge of nervous hilarity and that's also exactly what a housekeeper would say next. When she's gone, I lean down and dig my fingers into that white carpet. It's as soft as you'd think.

There's a vase of fresh white flowers on the glass coffee table, and the water is pure and clean and not slimy, the way it was when Niles gave Rosalind roses for Valentine's Day. Ros kept them long after they wilted and lost their petals, and I'd have done the same. Roses, a dozen of them. Finn Lahruti, my boyfriend for all of three months last year, gave me a key chain with an otter on it, a baffling romantic gesture that I spent three more useless months trying to decipher.

Everything is so clean. New and echoey. I can see the huge modern kitchen from where I sit, and there's no *stuff* in it, no loaf of bread on the counter, or pot drying upside down on a towel. No stack of mail or tossed-off shoes or nearly empty tissue box or stray fast-food ketchup packet, nada. In a way it's also the opposite of what you'd imagine, less not more. It reminds me of the poop-less robot dog, the way the mess of a real life has vanished.

I sniff. No smells, either. No odors of last night's dinner or garbage that needs taking out or the thick smell of chocolate from the factory by our house. I wonder where Boolean is, because it doesn't even smell like dog. It just smells crisp and tight and efficient, a credit card swipe through a machine.

My dad's house.

The words seem as ridiculous as *cat cast,* and I almost snort-giggle again. As I sit here in disguise, terror and hysteria have merged. I've existed on Harrison family scraps for the last few years, and this is a feast. Everywhere I look, there's something else to take in. I mean, even those little plugs in the walls are where he might recharge his phone and stuff, so, wow.

I listen for his voice, my missing genius father, my hope of belonging. That tech conference Mr. Alonzo was discussing is over, so he could totally be home right now. But I only hear a boat on the lake and a crow making a point to another crow.

I imagine him walking in. I'd shake his hand, whatever, and our eyes would meet. He'd *feel* who I am, instantly. *I always knew you'd come,* he'd say, smiling.

Oh God, an awful thought: if Mom and Rosalind could see me now.

The pool glimmers. A few white birds scenically glide on the lake. Flowerpots overflow with color. Does anything bad ever happen here? It sure doesn't seem like it. And then . . . Wait a second. Wait just a second! A flash. A person in the yard. A guy, really quick, in the side yard and then gone. He disappears around toward the front of the house. I know him. Oh yes, I do.

The other stalker!

Maybe I have it wrong. Does he belong here? Is he their landscaper or something? This is not what my body is telling me. Alarm bells shriek. Landscapers don't sit in their trucks, spying. That guy—the way he slunk around that corner, I'm 100 percent sure he's up to no good.

Just as I get up to look, I hear the *click click click* of dog toenails, and the stomp-slap of running toddler feet. The stalker will have to wait because, now, a little torpedo zooms through the room and launches onto me. Arlo's wearing a shirt with a rocket on it, appropriately, and tiny khaki shorts. He smells all applesauce-y plus shampoo. I semi-roughhouse, giving him a rib tickle. Mostly, I show Arlo how happy I am to see him. I'm so happy right then that all giggly fear vanishes as my heart blasts off.

"Bool—" I catch myself before I say his name. He's jumping up with excitement, too, and it's like fighting off a bear, but it's a bear I'm not supposed to have met yet. The funny thing is, he recognizes me. Like, that day we met, he *saw* me.

"Eleanor, you have made some serious friends already," Aurora says.

There she is, Aurora Andozza Harrison, hated home-wrecker and two-point-three on Rate Me, looking fresh and beautiful but still so much more . . . *exhausted* than on her social media pages. Her face is all blotchy, and her eyes are puffed as if she hasn't slept in weeks, and she's wearing baggy white shorts and a T-shirt that reads *Gitex, Dubai*. Is *home-wrecker* ever used for men? I'm not sure if William Moulton Marston was a home-wrecker, but he sure did do some major remodeling.

"It's great to see you guys!" I say. Very non-interview-y, but it's what I feel.

Aurora smiles. "It's great to see you, too." She seems to mean it. I'm not sure why it's so surprising, but I said something real, and she said something real back, and it shouldn't be a miracle when this happens, but it is. "And you already met Greta." Another mental note: the unfriendly housekeeper's name. I wish I had a pen.

We take a tour. It's wild, because they all seem to really like me. I'm not even doing anything. I'm just walking around this astonishing place, touring catering kitchens that are bigger than our real one, and on the second floor a theater, and a playroom that's a million times nicer than Chuck E. Cheese. I'm saying stuff like that, too, *It's a million times nicer than Chuck E. Cheese,* and Aurora just laughs and says, *No Whac-A-Mole.* Stuff just spills out of my mouth, like *I can't imagine how much Windex you must use,* and *If you're going to rate beds, bunk beds are number one, and waterbeds are number two, and pullout sofas are, like, fifty-seven.* Instead of rolling her eyes or wincing like Rosalind might, Aurora just volleys an answer. *What about those air-mattress beds when you're camping?* And I say, *Okay, fifty-eight.* I'm carrying Arlo, and he occasionally leans down into my face to get my attention. I do *our* thing: I beep-boop his nose. I'm in this moment, and everything else is forgotten—that stalker on their property, the lies I've told to get here. It's so strange and freeing to just *be*.

They have a library! And, okay, the spines are organized by color, and the Soggy Pages Book Club unanimously disapproves (content before aesthetics!), but still. I spot cool titles galore. We move up to the third-floor bedrooms, the most personal areas of their lives, never photographed. We cruise past the Harrisons' main. The door is shut, darn. Aurora shows me Arlo's room, decorated in an outer space theme, and Arlo flings himself on his toddler bed to be a show-off.

"And this is where you'll be." Aurora opens the door to the adjacent room, a beautiful, airy space overlooking the lake. My room. My room in their house! It's breathtaking—plush rugs and a white comforter, a sleek desk with a modern chair. I want to cry, but panic fills me, too. I would *sleep* here. I've so often dreamed of being part of this family, but now I feel nauseous.

"Wow. Thank you." The person speaking—I don't know her. Out that window I can see the Psyckē sign, same as at home. I imagine Hugo, standing at the end of that dock, watching the light blaze in the darkness. You'd feel like you made the whole world, maybe.

"We were hoping you could start on Monday? Is that too soon?"

We. *We* were hoping. Hugo Harrison knows about me. Or, at least, about the fake Eleanor from Eugene who's going to watch his real kid. Aurora's uncertainty is a surprise. On Instagram, she's decisive. Here, that sweatshirt has a bleach stain on the sleeve, a circle of white, an error. It's strange, you know. She's not what you'd expect at all.

"Monday is great," I say. It's not. It's so not great. It's wrong. A mess.

"We take a two-week trip to our place in Tulum in July. We'd expect you to come?"

My heart pounds with the disaster of it all. How? Plane tickets and passports, my fake name? Getting Mom to agree to a fabulous vacation in a foreign country with the Von Barons?

"That would be amazing." *Schnappsidee*—a really, really bad idea. The kind you might come up with if you were totally drunk. A Schnapps idea. That's what this is. Worse. One that might get me annihilated. One that might hurt people.

At the end of the hall, we reach a shut pair of double doors. "This is Hugo's home office." She rattles a handle to indicate that it's locked. "Off-limits."

"Got it," I say. Arden Lee would be losing it right now. I follow Aurora back down a different staircase. On the second floor, outside of another pair of doors, I hear it: *Clank*. Grunt. *Clank*.

"The gym," she says, as an explanation. "*His* gym."

I nod. My heart thrums. *He's* there, right now, lifting weights. He's probably there a lot. Hugo Harrison, my *dad*, is behind that door. I may have stopped breathing.

"He's just a man," Aurora says. "Okay?"

She sounds almost mad. Maybe she sees the way I'm looking at that door, and remembers that AI book from my bag, thinking I'm another disciple of Hugo's. She's probably sick of them. I have the urge to say I'm sorry again. "I really appreciate you," I say instead. "I'm glad I'm here."

Aurora, our enemy, our Baroness von Kampf, who actually has lovely eyes, looks into mine. It's hard to tell what she's thinking, it really is. For a second I think she's going to hug me. Instead she settles on "I'm glad you are, too."

All at once my throat tightens up with tears. This would seriously be a wrong interview move, but emotion fills me. Because I don't just mean this house, you know. I'm glad I'm in the place he brought me. Here, in this world.

chapter
Eight

REALITY HITS THE SECOND I LEAVE. I'M *NOT* THINK-ing, proving Mom right for the millionth time. She's likely right about everything else, too—that I only care about myself, that my clothing style is "unusual," that one eyebrow is thinner than the other, that you can see dark hairs on my upper lip, that my health is frail with my asthma and rashes, that my splootch is a problem.

I look around for any sign of that guy or his truck, but nope.

I'm the sole stalker who infiltrated the premises. What a mess, what a mess. What a wonder. What a thrill.

They want me to travel with them to Tulum! I text Arden Lee and Clementine.

Wow, El, incredible! You get to be with H.H. the dude, your FATHER, Arden Lee answers.

Father—it's more of an idea than a person. I suppose it's the same with anything you've never had. You're excited for what it could be, but you also can't possibly guess the reality. Like the first time we went on an airplane to see Nana Minnie and Papa Joe. I expected magic. And being in the clouds *was* magic, but I didn't have a clue about the frightening toilet whoosh in that tiny bathroom or the white waxy barf bag in the seat pocket or the nerve-racking thunk and screech of tires as you land, like the plane should have had a *Student Driver* sign on the back of it. *He's just a man,* Aurora said, but I don't have a lot of experience with those. Not in our house. Mom's boyfriends never last long.

But I'll have to get a passport! They'll find out my name when they book the ticket!

PRIVATE PLANE, he texts.

Clementine finally responds. *You'll have to tell your mom maybe for the passport?*

Not if you're sixteen already, Arden Lee shoots back. *I JUST looked it up. But so what? The Von Barons have a house in Mexico!!* He adds a celebration emoji. After we read *Les Misérables,* Arden Lee claimed to be Team Ends-Justify-the-Means, but he's actually one of the most kind and honest people ever. Once, he even ran, like, five blocks to return ten bucks to a lady who dropped it outside of the Tacos Today truck. He just understands why this is important.

So does Clementine. *I can't even imagine it,* she texts. It's hard not to think right then about Pippi Longstocking, staring into the light of the candle, imagining the return of her father.

I wish you could come with me. Both of you, and Apple, too. And, wow, do I ever, for so many reasons.

DRAWING USUALLY SOOTHES ME, BUT I'M TOO ANX-ious to make something that's never existed before, that comes from somewhere true and deep. Instead I play around with Frame, which is just pure fun. I type in a bunch of words that pop into my head: *Camel in beret with pineapple. Rocket ship surprises penguin in winter. Girl spots friendly octopus in fantasy pond.* He's cute. I give him a bow tie. It's mindless. The images still feel empty, sure, but I'm enjoying myself. It makes me wonder why art connects, though. Like, why Miss Fury makes me feel something, and certain books and films, too. Deep enough to cry and get mad and miss the characters. The penguin has no life—he's digital flatness. Frame just makes *content*.

I shut down the app. The deepfake with Mom and Ros begins tonight. If it all blows up and Mom doesn't let me leave on Monday, or take a vacation with the "Von Barons," this little fantasy is done. It'll be a relief in some ways. Fantasies are way more convenient than real human beings, that's for sure.

My mom loves when you do stuff for her and give her lots of

compliments, so I decide to make a nice meal for them. Mom and Rosalind like things that involve the words *lean* or *grilled* or *low-calorie.* I guess denial is virtuous, because when Mom and Rosalind refuse themselves things like food or time to slack off, they can give off the same vibe as super-religious people. Like their diet and rigorous workout/work/study schedule set them on a moral high ground I can't possibly reach. I have to be satisfied with merely looking up to them, you know. I'm okay with that. You can have the moral ground up there if I can have my nachos down here.

I broil some chicken. I do two extra pieces for Clementine and Apple and hide them in the fridge to bring to school tomorrow. Mom would absolutely want to help Clementine and Apple, which is why I can't tell her what's going on. Jackie, Arden Lee's mom, knows the whole situation but does something even harder than helping—not helping, or not helping in the ways that a person might think of first. Clementine's neighbors, same. Sometimes help is loud, but sometimes it's better quiet. The problem is, people like their help to be loud, to be seen and heard. It makes you wonder how often help is really for the other person. Or care-taking in general.

I make kale salad, too, and brown rice, more virtue. I vacuum and do speed-racing dusting, which is what I call it when you swerve around the picture frames and lamps and stuff. I think you're supposed to dust before you vacuum, but whatever. This is more about the appearance of cleaning than actual cleaning. Clementine says that, lately, everything is more about the appearances of everything.

I hear them laughing and chatting outside on the porch before the key rattles in the door. "Oh wow, what smells so good?" Mom drops her purse on the kitchen counter.

I lift the corner of foil so she can see the chicken already prepared and waiting for them. "You work so hard all the time, so I thought I'd just cook for once." Ugh. I hate when I'm aware of my own manipulating.

"You didn't get the job." Rosalind kicks off her shoes and hangs her pack on a kitchen chair. They knew I was meeting with Mrs. Von Baron today. "That's okay, Ellie. It can take a lot of interviews with a lot of people before you actually get hired somewhere."

I don't know why her kindness makes me so infuriated. My teeth grind together. My chest gets all tight. I search around the kitchen for my inhaler. It was right here a second ago, but it must be in my room.

"Did you vacuum?" Mom asks. "I told you, that dust isn't good for you."

This is never going to work. I can't pull this off. Who am I kidding? Is this what Clementine and Arden Lee mean by anger? Is it a gross, disturbed upset, where you also feel like shit about yourself? "I *did* get the job. They want me to move in on Monday." My voice drips with a bitter, victorious *I told you so*.

"What?" Rosalind says. "I thought you said they have two pools and stuff."

"A family with two pools couldn't like me? Well, they do. You should see my room!"

Rosalind makes a face of distrust. "Do we even know these people?"

"Monday? Like, *this* Monday?" Mom's voice climbs.

"They even want me to go on vacation with them."

I'm wrecking it. It's all slipping through my fingers, as fast as sand.

"Vacation? Where?" Now Mom's eyebrows lift in curiosity as Rosalind's fold down.

"Mexico. They have a house there."

"Mexico?" Rosalind says, as if it were a war zone. She'd love to go to Mexico. Niles and his parents went, and she was mad and disappointed she couldn't go, too, even when she offered to pay her own way. "What if you have some sort of . . . crisis? You can't *swim.*"

"I can totally swim! And why would I have a crisis?" My voice is rising. I feel this whirlwind of panic and despair, and, suddenly, I realize how very badly I want this, and how much there is to lose. Not just time with Hugo. Not living in that fancy house and getting to do stuff I've only dreamed of. Just . . . Arlo. My heart and his heart and what happens when we're together.

Rosalind holds her hand out, proof of a hundred possible things that could go wrong. My inhaler sits in her palm.

"Can I just get in the door?" Mom says. "Can I at least take my bra off, for God's sake?" Her face is rapidly turning stressed. Her eyes become small and distant, and the silver streaks in her hair all at once become more noticeable. She walked in happy, and now look. I've always thought of myself as a weather forecaster, watching our family skies for storms. But sometimes it's more like managing a mythological god, where the factors involved are outrageous and impossible.

"I've been away from home before," I say. "What about when Nana Minnie and Papa Joe sent us to camp in middle school?"

"For *three days*. With *me*. You hated every minute of it," Rosalind says. "And it was, like, an hour away, not a foreign country. You don't even have a passport!"

"I can get a passport."

"Aren't you going to need a car to get around all summer? What are you going to do about *that*?" Ros fumes.

"They have one for me." It's true. A Land Rover, similar to Aurora's. She showed me in their garage.

"Mom," Rosalind says, widening her eyes toward Mom as if all this is outrageous beyond belief. Well, it sort of is.

Mom gives the weighty sigh of someone used to handling everything on her own. "Give me their number. I'll call them."

"Mom!" I say now. It's more of a screech, to be honest. A screech of pure need, and opportunity lost, or about to be. No. No, no, *no*. This is bad. I'm Miss Fury in the cockpit of that plane, being shot down by Nazis. I need to think fast. "You're always saying how I need to step out of my comfort zone, and work on my confidence, and try new things, and—" Well, it's hard to remember all of the things I'm supposed to do for my self-improvement. "I have this chance, this great chance! And you *can't* call them. I want to be a *professional*. You're always saying how important that is. . . ." This is manipulation, but also fact. I *do* want to be professional. I don't want my mommy to call my new employer. "She, Mrs. Von Baron, asked if you'd be okay with me doing all of this, and I said, yes, *of course* she is! She's cool. She wants me to be independent and have enriching experiences. She *trusts* me. . . ."

Mom takes this in. "It *does* sound like a once-in-a-lifetime experience."

Oh my God.

It's *working.*

"This is so unfair!" Rosalind says.

"Don't be *jealous,* for God's sake," Mom shoots at her before heading down the hall to her room, one hand already reaching up the back of her blouse to unhook her bra. Rosalind looks like she's been struck. Her cheeks flush. Her eyes get watery. It can happen so fast, the way you're the awesome one and the awesome one and the awesome one, and then, suddenly, not.

Rosalind's face—she's devastated. Betrayed. It makes me think of one of our book club discussions about *The Remains of the Day* by Kazuo Ishiguro, how Arden Lee said that the snooty butler who served the rich dude all those years was *a tragic figure.*

"Maybe you can come over to swim," I say, but don't mean it. I can't mean it. I just want Rosalind to know I love her.

"I don't need your help, Eleanor," she snaps.

When we finally sit down to eat, the chicken has turned rubbery, and the kale is tough and fibrous, with too many bits of hard, inedible stalks. But Mom has gotten all cheerful with me, enough so that she's promised not to reach out to the Von Barons. *Of course I won't!* She expresses only excitement at my promise to come home on my days off. The tension between Mom and Rosalind sits there, though. It's gross and poisonous, and that stuff is usually mine, and maybe I'm more used to handling it. And I *do* wish it were mine again instead of Rosalind's, because I feel so bad for her right then. It's better, honestly, when things are the way they always are, because Rosalind seriously looks like she might fold in half and crumple, or else rage this house to the ground. Me, it just goes in and disappears, like when you water a plant.

Whatever I just got from Mom—I don't want it. Rosalind should have it. She's the one who earned it, even if winning felt good for, like, five seconds. Rosalind's fork tinks against her plate as she eats silently, angry and hurt. Mom asks me what part of Mexico, and what kind of car Mrs. Von Baron drives, and what she looks like, and if we should go shopping and get some new clothes before I leave, and does she need to come with me to the passport office. I know the right answer. They love you more when you don't need anything, so the answer is *That's all right, I'm good.*

Rosalind and me and Mom, sometimes we're like that cheap plastic game you get in party bags, where there are, like, twelve mixed-up numbers and an empty spot and you have to shift the tiles to get them in the right order. Instead of a bunch of numbers, though, there are only three numbers and an empty spot and no right order.

My stomach hurts, but I'm in. I did it. Rosalind, she looks at me like she wishes she could pinch me so hard, same as she used to when we were little.

chapter
Nine

THAT NIGHT I TEXT ARDEN LEE AND CLEMENTINE.
I got Mom to say yes. The thrill of victory is fading fast, though.

I want ALL the details tomorrow! Clementine answers. *Story time.* She means for Apple. They're reading the Chronicles of Narnia in order. If I have Miss Fury, and Clementine has Pippi Longstocking, and Arden Lee has All the Books, Apple has Lucy from the Chronicles. Lucy, the little sister all alone in the world with her siblings, fighting the evil of the White Witch with only Lucy's goodness and a cordial made of fire-flowers, which grow in the mountains of the sun. That cordial can cure any illness and even bring someone back from the dead, but it can't bring Clementine and Apple's mother back from Kansas City, or wherever she is now. Their dad—they have no idea who he is.

You're a force, Arden Lee texts. It's what I say to him, too, when I see him at Green Lake, wearing his silky shorts and tank top, his skinny legs looking so vulnerable. I only say it from afar, and only in my mind.

I take out my pens to face my enemy again, that stalker. I mess around with the sketch I did of him. The Golden Age, the 1930s to the early 1950s, is the right inspiration for my abilities right now, because their work wasn't very refined in terms of the art itself. Like, the more advanced details of the muscles and stuff, that came later, in the Silver Age. In the Golden Age they worked fast, churning out art to make a living, and the comics were printed on the cheapest paper. They were doing this new thing that didn't even seem to have value yet.

And June as Tarpé Mills is in some ways the right inspiration for me, too. Superman, one of the earliest strips of the Golden Age, was created by a misfit duo, the teenage writer Jerry Siegel and the young artist Joe Shuster. But Tarpé did her work alone. Her in-command females maybe originated with her own single mother, who raised June and her brother and sister, by working in a beauty parlor. Tarpé Mills said in interviews that she didn't know where she got *her* inspiration to draw. She was just one of those imaginative loner kids who hung around the house reading books.

But the Golden Age and June herself aren't the right inspiration for me entirely, not with all that racism and homophobia. The Golden Age, and June's career, ended with the Comics Code in 1954, which was great in one way because it prohibited ridicule and attacks on any religious or racial groups. But it was awful in so many other ways, a mess of censorship around queer characters and female ones, contributing to an out-of-control book-banning frenzy like today's. It forbade queer characters and policed the representation of women in comics hard—female nudity, behavior, attire, postures even, because, supposedly, Superman encouraged delinquency, Batman and Robin were lovers who would turn kids gay, and "unconventional" heroines like Marla, who had a job, fought bad guys, and became a single mother after she adopted Baroness von Kampf's toddler, were pornographic and harmful to kids. After the Comics Code and all the banning of comics, female action figures were forced back into being "proper" young ladies who made men the center of their world, and Miss Fury was gone.

Why can't all people be seen and given dignity? That's what I want to know. And if Tarpé Mills hadn't been censored out of a job, would she have evolved? Would she have realized the harm of Albino Joe and Whiffy and her Brazilian characters, while still giving us Marla, who parachutes from a plane in a ball gown? We'll never know, because she was eliminated, as William Moulton Marston and Wonder Woman, whose comics often portrayed women chained and tortured, survived. Looking at my *Miss Fury, Summer Issue, No. 2,* both groundbreaking and problematic . . . I *hope* she would have evolved, but hope is all I have. It's the same question again and again: How much leeway, how many chances, do you give the people you love?

I get a new blank sheet. This is how it is, just paper and practice, individual panels. Since I don't have a story yet, or even the characters, it's all copying. It's how you learn, but not how you go forward. I pick out an image that June Tarpé Mills created, a two-panel scene of Marla Drake. One half is her real self, naked aside from her lace underwear and the red gown she flings off her head. The other is her even more real self, completely masked. June used herself as a model, sketching from a mirror, so I guess *I'm* using June as a model, too. I try to replicate it. It's not nearly as good as June's yet, but why should it be? Her lines guide my lines, until one day my lines will be my own. And this is hard to explain, but I feel it, I feel it deeply, how the making of art is for the viewer and the maker both, because I'm convinced that Tarpé Mills *felt* this drawing when she created it. That somehow she understood, in a deep and personal way, how Miss Fury could be freer in that costume, freer in disguise, freer as Tarpé and not June, than she was even without clothes. And because she felt it, I feel it. When I'm viewing it, I do.

It makes me wonder if Astrid Lindgren felt Pippi, her loneliness and her strength, and if C. S. Lewis felt as small as Lucy sometimes, and as brave, and if the authors of All the Books had to relate to their characters in a real way in order for Arden Lee to relate right back. Maybe this is why I *don't* feel Frame's AI art—the creator, that machine, *can't* feel.

Our house is silent, aside from TV murmurs in Mom's room. I creep out into the hall Miss Fury–style and see Rosalind's light still on. I'd check on her, but this would only make her mad. The thing that's great about those old classic Golden Age comics, but also wrong, too, is how it's mostly the Nazis and mad scientists and evil baronesses that cause harm. It's never the people right inside your house, inside your own family, people who love you, even. Villains are outside, a force in the world to fight and conquer. In a family you might fight, but will you ever conquer? How can you not concede, I mean, when it's all so critical? Maybe there's a normal family where this stuff doesn't happen. Wow, that seems so relaxing. *Normal* sounds more like fiction than fiction.

In my room I put away my pens. I have a sudden memory: the Harrisons' dinghy. *Theos.*

I look it up.

Oh. Uh-oh.

I wonder if it's a bad sign, you know, an ominous one, that Hugo named the large yacht after himself, and the smaller boat after God.

"*BRAVE NEW WORLD* BY ALDOUS HUXLEY," ARDEN says, holding up the scrap of paper victoriously. Clementine and I groan. After discussing *Middlesex,* a unanimous Soggy Pages thumbs-up, we're choosing our next read.

"It's too much!" Clementine says. "With El going to live at her dad's house? The whole rise of tech and the technocrat thing?"

"Is *technocrat* a real word?" I ask. "It sounds like a guy with scissors for hands."

It's the last day of school. It's warm, but not too. I'm wearing my orange shorts, white polo, and orange vest with the white diagonals, which Arden Lee compliments with *Vintage golfer 1930s!* but which I say is vintage Creamsicle, perfect for the start of summer.

"It's the perfect book about creating perfect humans!" Arden Lee says, his eyes bright. "Timely, too. Control of the masses with media and drugs."

"Spoiler alert," I say, and Clementine socks me. The Soggy Pages Book Club hates this expression. We have strong feelings about most book-related issues, from cover art to film adaptations to badly written posts complaining about badly written books.

"Why are we reading it again, if you already did?" Clementine's not a dystopia fan.

"I haven't! I'm just going by the jacket copy."

"I hope this isn't too close to home right now," Clementine says. "Remember what happened with *Orlando*?" *Orlando* by Virginia Woolf is about a sixteen-year-old Elizabethan boy who loves books and becomes a feminist woman at age thirty. She lives for three hundred years, loving men and women both, interacting with the great literary figures of the time. We thought it was amazing, but Arden Lee was emotional for weeks after.

"So it hit a little close, okay," Arden Lee admits. "'He was afflicted with a love of literature.' My God!" Arden Lee clutches his heart.

"It's like she *knew* us," Clementine says. "Still, are you okay with this one, El?"

"Sure, except it's super old," I say. "And two white dude authors in a row. Plus, *Middlesex* was your book, too," I say to Arden Lee.

"Fair is fair, come *on!*" This is how we've always done it, ever since we started our book club in the eighth grade. We each put a title in Arden Lee's fedora, and one gets chosen randomly.

"You better not have cheated again," I say.

"Once! I did that once! And did you love *The Elegance of the Hedgehog* or not?"

"Give me that," I say. I snatch the fedora and look at the other scraps of paper, expecting them to say *Brave New World* and *Brave New World,* but they don't. They say *Lavinia* by Ursula K. Le Guin and *Kaikeyi* by Vaishnavi Patel. I show them to Clementine.

"Okay, okay," she says. I stick the slips back in the hat and hand it to Arden Lee.

"The rise of the machine!" Arden Lee's all excited now that he got his way. He puts on the fedora, and the slips fall down his face. *Lavinia* drifts and lands on his Cheetos bag. It's too hot for a fedora, but Arden Lee believes in suffering for style. That was another reason Arden Lee fell hard for *Orlando.* The passages about how clothes can change the way the world sees you.

"I'm going to the passport office after school," I tell them.

"*Tulum,* wow. You're going to have the best summer," Clementine says, without a trace of Rosalind's envy. How is that possible, when you survive on your paycheck and the few hundred bucks you get in the mail every month from a PO box in Independence, Missouri? Try to imagine how *that* name hurts. The sun right now in this blue sky—that's what Clementine's heart looks like, I'm sure of it.

"Carlos wants to take us to Disneyland," Arden Lee says. Carlos is Jackie's new boyfriend. He's a mechanic at Biggie's Auto, and he's as different from Arden Lee's dad, the towering, handsome Leon, as you can get. "Mostly, this summer, though, I just want to get really good. I've only got one more shot to get on the team, literally." We know he means basketball. It's his biggest secret, this dream. Arden Lee says he *loves* basketball, but it's easy to understand why he needs it so bad, too, even if he's not very tall or even athletic.

All talk of summer plans stops, though, because here comes Xavier Chen. This time he doesn't stop and smile. He doesn't head over to sit with the Gyles twins and their friends, either. My heart cracks a little with disappointment for Clementine, but when I look up at her, she just shrugs.

"Too risky anyway," she says.

"You only have to make it one more year," Arden Lee says. Not even. Clementine's eighteenth birthday is next January. She's already printed out the paperwork to become Apple's legal guardian.

"It's going to be a great summer no matter what," says our sunshine.

ON MONDAY MORNING I'M IN THE PASSENGER SEAT of Jackie's old Ford Fiesta, with Arden Lee behind the wheel. My mom's roller bag is in the back seat, packed with pretty much everything I own. The night before, Mom ordered pizza for my going-away dinner and gave me all of her tips about how to excel at childcare. She even got teary this morning. *What am I going to do without you? I'm going to miss you so much,* she said, and not just in my imagination, either, in real life. Ros reminded her that I'd be back in, like, five days.

Arden Lee pulls up to the Frame House. "Wow. Holy shit."

"I know, right?"

"It's unbelievable. And, man. Suddenly *real*. What you're doing." His expression is almost panicked at the breadth of my lie. "I hope I didn't do the wrong thing, encouraging you."

"You couldn't have stopped me," I say, but his doubt suddenly doubles my anxiety.

For a split second, in Jackie's Fiesta, with the bumper sticker on the back that says *Maximum 15 Clowns,* I imagine every bad thing that could happen. Mostly, I realize that once I leave this car, I'll be alone. No Clementine, no Arden Lee. Just me, wearing the flimsy disguise of Eugene Eleanor in a house full of strangers.

"Hey, it's not all that different from your regular life," Arden Lee says, and then we crack up. "Well, just go see what happens."

"I'm terrified."

"You think I don't know *that* face? Go on," he says.

The ones who see you save you.

chapter
Ten

"LENO, LENO," ARLO SHOUTS, THROWING A PAIR OF
my flip-flops in the air as I try to unpack.

"Arlo, Arlo," I sing back. This place is so clean that my stuff
looks old and shabby—my knit tank top with butterflies on it,
my shorts, a blue-and-white checked dress that Rosalind says
*looks cute, like Dorothy from Oz, but not with those shoes, for God's
sake.* Even my drawings do, and my art supplies, and my original
Miss Fury, Summer Issue, No. 2, brought for courage. It's tucked

away now in that slim desk, in a drawer that's pretty much hidden unless you find it accidentally, like I did. I hang up a few things in the closet. They take up maybe six inches of space. I try to spread out the hangers. If clothes could look nervous, mine do.

The new phone that Aurora gave me sits on the dresser. *You should always have it with you,* she said. She also showed me how to work the baby monitor, the little screen where I can watch Arlo as he sleeps, should he wake up and need anything. She went over some Arlo basics, as well—how they want his naughty behavior handled, his favorite snacks, diaper changes, his sleep routine. His general schedule: breakfast when he wakes, various activities they'll update daily, nap from twelve-thirty to two-thirty, dinner at six. I'm off from then until Arlo goes to bed, so they can spend time *as a family.* It was silly, but those words hurt. Still, Hugo Harrison—the big He, bigger than *Theos*—will be here most evenings. I could finally meet him, tonight, if he even cares about the nanny.

It's a lot for a little kid. It'd be a lot for me. Photo shoots nearly every day, toddler yoga, swimming at the Green Lake pool, a class called Concepts of Coding. It's all outlined in a fat document, which includes maps and phone numbers and explanations and goals.

Concepts of Coding?

No idea, and I can't read all of this stuff right now—the tiny tornado of Arlo is already here, my responsibility. What in the world should I do next? I mean, how am I supposed to fill all these hours with a little kid? No clue.

I shut the closet door, and when I turn around, Arlo's up on the bed, oh my God. Today he's wearing a T. rex shirt and Levi's cutoffs that are so cute I can't even stand it, but now he's jumping, and I realize how big this job is going to be, just keeping him safe, let alone—

"Careful there, bud!"

Shit, shit! He slides off, his elbow bashing into the nightstand. He starts to howl, oh geez. There's no way Aurora *can't* hear this. The neighbors probably can. Boolean noses through the door, worried. Maybe he should be the nanny. He'd probably do a better job.

I clutch Arlo to me, helpless as he cries, trying not to cry myself. Mom was right—I have zero adequate experience for this job. How did she do this by herself, every single day? And with only a fraction of the stuff, namely money, Aurora has. I mentally search through all of the expert advice Mom gave me before I left. Raising us has been her "life's work," and we're her proudest achievements. On her social media accounts it's pretty much what you see—her and Rosalind, the three of us, the Mother's Day posts of all those balloons that Rosalind surprised her with. *Luckiest Mom EVER!* She didn't cover elbow injuries.

"You're okay, you're okay," I tell Arlo, but that's what *I* want. It's not what he is or how he feels. "Let me see," I try instead. It's hard to look him over when he's clinging so hard. *Please be okay,* I pray to, I don't know, Arlo himself or any generous being in the universe. No wonder we want heroes so badly. We need to believe that *someone* is big enough to handle the job of life.

I spot the big red mark on Arlo's elbow. I'm in this beautiful magazine room, in this unbelievable house, and who cares about any of it, because that red mark on his pale skin kills me. "Your elbow got a bonk, and it really hurts," I tell him.

Huh. A strange magic. He stops wailing. Well, not all at once, but it subsides into some gulping sob. He buries his head in my shirt, nods. Boolean collapses to the floor, relieved.

"That sucks," I say.

"Yat sucks."

Oh great. Oh no. Another mistake! "Maybe that's something only Eleanor should say."

"Yat sucks, yat sucks!"

"Stop." I hold up my hand like a crossing guard's sign. This is how I'm supposed to tell him no. Aurora explained that it's not as punitive and gets his attention. Arlo looks betrayed. I mean, I understand that I can't give him everything he wants, but the *stop* thing makes me think of those whistles you blow when a dog barks.

"YAT SUCKS!" Arlo's clearly pissed at the hand, and who wouldn't be.

I change tactics. I ignore all that stuff Mom said, too, about controlling behavior through punishments and rewards. Instead, I use a firm, soft voice. "Those are words for Eleanor, not Arlo. Let's find Arlo words. How about . . ." I make my voice sound like a drumroll. "WHAT A BUMMER!" I whirl him around to make it fun.

"WHA A BUMMA!" he shouts back. It's wild, how even a toddler knows when you're treating him with respect.

But wow. The impossibility of the task looms—keeping him safe, trying not to ruin him. It's a minefield, this job. I've been here all of . . . I look at my phone.

Forty minutes.

Help. Just, someone, anyone! I think of Marla Drake, calling out for her friends Francine or Cappy, or even her bad boyfriend, Gary Hale, when she feels most desperate. She *is* a superhero, you know, and she *still* needs other human beings. She still needs her friends.

A TEXT COMES IN ON MY NEW AURORA PHONE: *Need to see you in my room NOW.*

Oh no. This is bad. Well, I'd want to know what happened, too, if my beloved Arlo sounded like he'd been broken. I'd want to be sure he was okay, that I hadn't wrongly trusted, handing him over to some slacker. Maybe she's going to fire me. I remember the way Rosalind looked at me when I told her I got the job. Like it was a stroke of shocking luck. No, like it was a *mistake*.

I can just imagine showing up back at home for dinner tonight, delivering the news that Mrs. Von Baron let me go already. Rosalind's peach-glossed lips would press into a line, disapproval plus also secret gladness, which is maybe the same thing as being smug. I'd have to tell Clementine and Arden Lee, too. I'd feel worse about that. They actually believed in me.

"Come on, pal," I say to Arlo. I pick him up so we can hurry, but he wails a protest.

"Arlo do!" This actually sounds more like *Arlo dooooooo!!!* with a bunch more *o*'s and a few thousand exclamation points, my God. Already I see that toddlers have maybe earned their reputation.

Except . . . when I view this through his eyes, I get it. How worrying to be hauled up by a panicked girl you barely know. Plus, sure, you want to walk on your own. Who wants to be picked up and carried, unless you're scared, or you've been shopping for hours, or walking around some boring museum or something.

The trickier thing is figuring out whose wishes are more important. Aurora, the adult, demanding I go there right this minute, or Arlo, the little kid, demanding I slow down? Right then I decide who I'm going to pick, as often as I can.

"Eleanor made a mistake," I tell him, setting him down. "Sorry, pal." Ooh boy. I'm going to have to summon a whole new level of patience, if I still have a job. It's great, though—there are no complicated weather systems with Arlo. His feelings are right there if you just look.

We toddle into the hall, Boolean following. I steer Arlo toward Aurora's room, but a few paces away in the other direction, I hear a voice coming from behind those office doors.

It's him! Oh my God. Goose bumps trickle up my arms, because I've heard Hugo so many times before in online interviews and videos, but never this close. Once, he spoke right to me, he must have, that day he held infant me in his arms. I lead Arlo that direction, ignoring Aurora's urgency. I'm not listening in, exactly; I just want his voice to surround me, like it would on any ordinary day as my dad. Arlo and I hold hands outside his door. It sounds like he's on the phone maybe. No. A woman answers. Someone's in there with him.

It's not Aurora, that's for sure, because right then she pops her head out of their bedroom at the other end of the hall.

"Eleanor!"

I'm caught. I'm so caught. I flush red. I stammer, trying to find some excuse for this eavesdropping, but she doesn't seem to notice. Instead she's waving her arm like a frantic airport runway guy. Arlo sees his mom and races toward her. You can tell he's pretty new at running—it's another accident waiting to happen, but he arrives in her arms safely. He's looking smack into her face, like *Please see me, please.* But she has more urgent matters on her mind.

"Come here! I need your help!" I'm not being fired. Maybe she didn't even hear Arlo scream. She shuts the door behind us, leaving Boolean on the other side. It's sad. Dogs should be seen and treated with dignity, too.

We're in her room, *theirs.* It's spacious and cream-colored to the point of loneliness. The color palette is similar to mine, aside from one enormous colorful painting across from the bed. Painting, wait. Is that a *TV*? A TV disguised as a painting? Our TV at home—we have to plug and unplug it to get it to work. The bed. Look! That's where he sleeps. *They* sleep. It's almost embarrassing. But it's a mess in here. Clothes are strewn all over the room—dresses and skirts and tops flung everywhere, layered over the backs of the chairs and tossed on the floor.

"*My* help?" I'm not sure what she wants me to do. Hang stuff up? Sew or something? One time I tried to help Rosalind hem a dress using that sticky tape you iron on, and it was a disaster. Totally uneven, and we wrecked the iron when the tape got baked onto it. Mom was pissed, and we both felt terrible. We chipped in and bought a new iron, but it wasn't as good as the old one.

"Hugo's having dinner at home tonight," she says. "I just want to . . . look great, you know?"

She has zero makeup on, and her hair is pulled up into a messy ponytail, and she seems . . . young. Or maybe she just seems her age. Aurora doesn't even *resemble* that woman on her social media pages, confident and chic. She could be her insecure younger sister at best. Maybe it's her pleading voice, too. I remember her and Hugo's age difference, like, fifteen years, and wow, I suddenly feel bad for her, being with a powerful older guy that she desperately wants to look great for. I get it. I mean, I've let someone else be the judge of my worth only about a million times, and not just guys, for sure. I was obsessed with everything from my hair to my clothes to my breath during those three months with Finn Lahruti, otter-giver, who didn't always wash *his* hair, who wore the same gray hoodie all the time, and whose breath smelled like whatever he last ate. It's just . . . I would have never expected the gorgeous and supremely polished Aurora Andozza Harrison to hand over her value.

"You always look great," I say. It's so true.

"Nooo!" She groans. "I'm a nerd. I know nothing about clothes. I seriously need to get better at that stuff, and fast."

"You're kidding!" She must be. I mean, she's the least nerdy person I can imagine. Her entire Instagram is clothes and shoes and style. Her home, her *whole life* is style. I say this. "Your whole life is style. People go to your page to see what *you're* wearing." To see what she's wearing, to hate what she's wearing. To love-hate her and everything about her.

"Not what *I'm* wearing."

"Yeah. That robe, even." I point to one hanging in her closet, a silky navy gown with gold peacocks on it. I blush. I just confessed that I stalked her page enough to remember it.

"What robe?"

"Peacocks?" It's stunning. I even remember the photo, her at a window, the robe splayed.

"This?" She lifts its sleeve. "I'd never wear it! Too slippery. Have you ever tried to wear satin? You lie in bed and it's like . . ." She mimes a sporting event I try to remember the name of.

"The luge?"

"The luge, exactly! *I* don't find these things."

"You don't?"

"I could never find these things. I don't even care about them, honestly. They're not even interesting to me."

"Wow." I'm too shocked to ask something I should: What *does* interest her? If I'd asked her right then, well, the full disaster of the future might have been avoided.

"Our family manager, Laura, *she* does it all. She does everything for us. Her and *her* assistants. I barely have anything to do with it."

"Oh," I say. Laura. I wonder if that's who I heard in Hugo Harrison's office.

"When we got together, Hugo and me . . ." Everyone knows the story. Two people visiting Paris, sitting on the same bench under the Eiffel Tower, instant fireworks. "He worked with me on creating an image, a brand, a *story*. He said, *What kind of character do you want to be?*"

"Character? I mean, you're a person. You're you."

For a second the stress dissolves from her face, and Aurora laughs. "Wouldn't *that* be nice? But it wouldn't exactly sell stuff."

"Sure, it would." I can't believe it. That *I'm* trying to encourage *her,* the influencer.

"The real *anybody* wouldn't sell stuff, let alone the real me," she says. "I've been around a lot of rich and famous people since I met Hugo, and you know what? A lot of them are truly awful, and you wouldn't want to buy anything from them, and a lot are really awesome, but just regular people, when you come right down to it, so, same. There's a science to it. Making people feel inferior enough to buy into what you're selling, ugh."

I make a face. I want to say how horrible this is. How the more I get to know her, the more real she is, and the more real she is, the more I like her, and wouldn't that be the better way? But I didn't compliment her sweatshirt with the bleach stain, did I? I was in awe of the peacock robe.

"*There's another AI,* Hugo told me when we met. *Add Impact. Impression, influence, power.* I don't remember all the words he used. But *add impact* is supposed to be my role. Or, what Laura does for me. She's the one with the style. All of these . . ." She gestures at the mounds of clothes. "Seriously, I'd be in my sweats all the time."

My head, wow—it's spinning. It's a lot, a real lot, to find out so soon. I'm not even sure who I'm looking at. I mean, so she didn't choose the stylish white blouse, or the expensive sunglasses in the shape of suns, or the vanilla candle, or the hand cream? I thought I had a good idea of who she was, and now this person is a total stranger. Her Rate Me score, too—people are hating a fictional character, same as in online book reviews. And, man, they do love hating those fictional characters.

"Do you want me to help you hang this stuff back up?" I ask. I'm guessing that's why she texted me. It's a disaster in here.

"Oh no. No, Yvette can do that."

"Yvette?"

"Our housekeeper. You haven't met?"

"Greta?"

"She's *not* the housekeeper." Aurora rolls her eyes, as if that subject is too big for the moment. It's all big. It's so big that I almost want to go back to being sure I knew stuff that I didn't have a clue about. Ignorance about your own ignorance is pretty cozy. It's *so easy* to think you know things, and comforting, too. "But *please.* I need your help."

I'm still confused. "With . . . ?"

"With what to wear! Laura isn't answering my texts. You have such a great sense of style."

"*I* do?" I actually think she's making fun of me, but then I realize she's serious.

"And you manage to make it look so easy."

Oh my God, she *means* it.

I'm having this weird . . . I don't know how to explain it, but almost this out-of-body experience. I mean, being in this house, for one. Arlo, who is my brother, for two, is right here, sitting in Aurora's giant closet, trying to put her shoes on his feet. Three, my actual father, if you can call him that, this man who had sex with my mother enough times to make me and my sister, whose face is on magazine covers, is right down the hall. And now Aurora is saying something about me that I would have never even made up in my wildest dreams. If I told Rosalind . . . Well, I can't tell Rosalind. Aurora gave me the nicest and most startling present, and I just stand there staring at her, wearing my thrift-store red capris and paisley tank that Mom says looks like a hippie acid trip, trying not to cry.

"Uh," I say.

"Just, what of this stuff would look good together?"

chapter
Eleven

I EAT DINNER ALONE IN THE CATERING KITCHEN, BE-
cause this is "family time." After I down my food, I sit on the
stairwell just a few feet from them, out of sight, doing something
familiar: spying. Whoever Greta is, she eats with them, so I wonder if this means she's my family, too. Greta, not-a-housekeeper,
sits on one side of Hugo, with Aurora on the other. Arlo's strapped
into a booster seat next to her. He's making faces so someone will

look at him. No one is, aside from Boolean, who's hoping he'll drop a bit of food.

Instead we're all looking at Hugo, me included. Especially me. Because there he is. I don't know why some people have charisma and why most people don't, but wow. That's my actual father, the enemy who created us and then ditched us, the man we're supposed to hate but the whole world loves. I'm on the love side right now; I've secretly been on the love side for a while because just look. He's a creative genius, and the need to create is something we have in common, something no one else in my family understands. And, God, it would be so cool if he could be *my* parent, you know, like Ros has Mom. I've never been this close to him before, unless you count the times he visited when I was a baby and held me for those few minutes. That's when I would have been closest.

He sticks his fork into a slim slab of fish. There's a side of vegetables, artfully displayed, brought out by Jak, the chef. I just downed the same food in the catering kitchen, scooped straight from the pans, though I barely tasted it, honestly, since this show was about to start. Hugo's been telling a story about how his executive assistant, Mathew, almost destroyed their entire presentation at the summit meeting by bringing the wrong laptop or something. I missed the specifics because I was staring at his arm hair (dark, like mine, whereas Mom and Ros have arm hair that is pale and shimmery), and his teeth (straight but not too), and his eyes (full-on twinkle). He makes the story dramatic and hilarious, and Aurora laughs. She might as well be a television audience of millions, because he's just giving his all, and it's magic. I'm smiling so hard right on the steps.

"*Of course* you saved the day," Aurora says. "Did you even *need* that laptop?"

He beams at her. Note to self: *Compliment gets beam.* Watching them, I feel sad for my mom. There's Aurora, his wife, and she gets to live this amazing life, and my mom was just someone he fucked. I wonder, you know, what makes you the woman he fucks and what makes you the woman he marries. The screaming and yelling and screeching car tires maybe automatically put you in the former category. What it makes me want more than anything is to be neither. I want to be June Tarpé Mills, who exists on her own terms. Or Marla, who does the choosing.

"I told you about Mathew and the car, didn't I?" Greta says. Arlo drops bread on the floor, and Boolean snatches it in that way that makes you wonder if dogs even taste. "He practically backed up over the lawn. I couldn't believe it! What is *wrong* with him? He seems shifty to me." It's weird, but she sounds exactly like Mom, talking about Jackie. Her voice has that same edge, implying that Mathew's bad driving was malicious, not an accident.

Aurora rolls her eyes. If I were there, family, she could do it to me, and I'd do it back.

Hugo waves his hand, like *whatever.* "Mathew's harmless."

Now something shocking happens. Greta makes a sour, disapproving face, and she directs it straight at Hugo. Like, who does that? "Huc. Do I need to remind you what happens when you're *careless*?" Her voice bites. It's the last word, the know-it-all voice of a . . .

Oh man. I know who she is. I do, I do.

"Mom, will you ever let it go? For God's sake, I was *eight*."

"And sixteen, and eighteen, and twenty-four . . ."

I never thought it was possible, but the twinkle in his eyes . . . poof. It's snuffed out, just like that. Greta—is that a nickname for Margaret? It must be. I remember Hugo's origin story—how can I not? It belongs to me, too. Margaret, his mother, raised him after his father, Albert, died young. This woman is my grandmother. It's so strange how Hugo's mom sounds like *mine*.

"*You* were the one who left him alone for hours with a computer and a credit card," Aurora says. "An eight-year-old is *going* to buy ten pounds of candy and a bike in every color."

I snort. It's not a story I've ever heard in any interview. Why haven't I? It's so funny and great, except none of this feels very good right now. It's all hard to follow, too, this storyline, because shouldn't he be glad Aurora is sticking up for him? He isn't. Not one bit.

Hugo's face turns hard. I've never seen that, either, in any video or interview, even when he doesn't like a question. He looks *pissed*. And not at Greta. His voice is ice. "Aurora, *stop*." He holds up his hand like a crossing guard, the way we're supposed to with Arlo.

Right there on the stairs, my face heats with shame for Aurora. This is a family, all right. It could be me and Rosalind and our very own Brandi Diamond. That same complicated *yuck* descends.

Aurora pushes her chair back, devastated. She looks so cute, too, in that blue floral skirt and the yellow striped T-shirt I paired it with. She was so excited to see him, but her face has gone pale, and, oh my God, here she comes.

I fly out of there.

I make it to my room, whew. A few minutes later Greta arrives. No knock, just there she is, with a wriggling Arlo under her arm.

I search her face for a resemblance. I wonder if she knows about me and Ros, what she thinks about us if she does. But there's no time for pondering our shared DNA. "You're on," she says, dropping Arlo on my bed as if he's the day's junk mail and then leaving abruptly. God, that's my *grandmother.* It's not the Margaret I pictured, the smart, fun one who would have raised a magnetic genius like Hugo.

It's not even Arlo's bedtime yet. He looks . . . struck.

"Hi, starlight," I say to him.

"Leno," he says. He's getting tired. His skin has gone translucent, and his eyes glaze. I lift him up. He sets his head against my chest, and my heart breaks and fills, both.

I carry him to his room, change his diaper, and get him into his jammies. I read to him. He loves books, how awesome. And he has a favorite, I can already tell. *Again, again,* he says, pressing *All the World* into my hands. I read it again, again because it's been a rough night, and we really need lullaby rhymes about peace and families. It seems like maybe Arlo is like Arden Lee in that he has All the Books, but he especially has *All the World.*

I tuck him in. "How 'bout a kiss?" he says, like some old-timey romantic.

"Absolutely," I say.

"Mama?" he asks. She's supposed to come in and say good night.

"Any minute." I hope I'm right. If she forgets, if she's too wrapped up in her own problems, I'll be as devastated as Arlo.

I pretend to count the glowing stars on his ceiling. I'm on twenty-two when Aurora appears, thank the ceiling heavens and the real ones. "Great job today, Eleanor," she says, but I can tell she's here for Arlo, not me. This is how it will be, figuring out when to be available and when not, like an appliance they use or ignore.

"Thanks. Good night," I say.

"The monitor," she reminds, and hands it to me.

In my room again I watch the screen as Aurora kisses Arlo good night and murmurs love-things. She ruffles his hair and turns out his light. I wonder where Hugo is. It's strange to have the very same wonder I've had all my life, but right here under his roof.

I keep my eyes on the small lump of Arlo as he settles in to sleep. He seems like a little bear or a bunny from one of his books, too alone. I'm here, I got what I wanted. There's a father and a baby brother and even a grandmother, but I'm suddenly very sad. I pick up my phone, Rosalind's, with the cracked screen. There are lots of messages from Mom and Arden Lee and Clementine, but my own real world feels far away. Mom's expecting a phone call, but I can't. I feel translucent, too, just like Arlo, too translucent to be a good liar. And I don't want to tell Mom what just happened. Not because it makes Hugo look bad, but because it makes Aurora look small and defeated. *More later, I promise,* I text to her and my friends.

It's so true. There will be more, much more.

IT'S TOO EARLY TO SLEEP. I DECIDE TO START *BRAVE New World.* It opens in this super-creepy factory, where babies are being manufactured on an assembly line. They're divided into five castes from the most smart and strong to the least, all brainwashed into fulfilling their social destinies. It's hard to concentrate because every time Arlo rolls over or rustles on the monitor, I'm on alert. I'm super glad there's all this amazing technology to watch him, but while reading that book . . . it's eerie and unnerving.

In this quiet house I hear whining, really loud. Boolean is sitting right outside my door.

"Hi," I say.

"Hi," he says, or he would if he could talk. His eyes plead like crazy.

"Are you hungry?" I ask. His ear twitches like he definitely knows that word. Still, he sits and stares. I feel so bad that dogs have to play this endless game of charades.

"Do you need to pee?"

He barks and jumps up on me. It's like being wrestled by a bear. "Okay, okay." I shove him down with all my might. Here there's a person for everything, but not a person for a dog. I look down that long hall, lit with small, tasteful lights. Empty. They're probably in there together, Hugo and Aurora, in that main bedroom way at the end.

Boolean and I go the other direction, heading for the back staircase. Yeah, I remember the monitor. Outside Hugo Harrison's office I hear him talking again. He's not with Aurora in their bedroom after all. I hear her, too, the maybe-Laura woman, in there with him.

This all seems bad. Very bad. I don't know. Just, you'd think he'd want to be with Aurora tonight. She was excited to see him, for sure, but then that stuff at dinner . . . No idea. This feels uncomfortable and wrong.

Downstairs, the dishes have been cleared, and the house is spotless, and those beautiful, tasteful low lights are everywhere, like, if you have this much money, it never even has to get dark. I follow Boolean to a back door leading to the lake, the dock. I hope I don't set off some alarm.

It looks urgent, poor guy. Everyone's forgotten about him. I risk it. I slide the door, bracing for the shriek, but nothing happens. I leave it slightly open so we don't get locked out.

The yard is lit beautifully, too—the trees, the shrubs. The pool glows, an aqua rectangle, still inviting even if the water is ripply from the wind picking up. The lake is choppy, and the rings of the boat mast clang. The rubber bumpers of *Theos* squeak against the dock. Boolean lifts his leg on a bush and pees forever, what a relief. The grass is prickly under my bare feet as I head toward the dock. What a night, and look where I am, I think, as I stand at the end. The moon is nearly full, and I could almost reach out and snatch it from the sky, that's how close it seems. From here, nearly the southern tip of Laurelhurst, I can see the zigzag of Husky Stadium, and the Ship Canal bridge, and . . . oh wow. There it is. The huge pink Psyckē sign, the neon glow of the hero-or-villain headquarters in the rising metropolis. I wonder if you can see it from every corner of the city.

I glance around, on alert for that stalker. I'd grab a rope from the boat, tie him up, my catsuit shimmering blue-black in the moonlight. But no, there's not a soul out here. Boolean races toward me, happy again, but he's running fast and wild on the dock, as a catastrophic scene plays out in my mind, him falling in or knocking me into the water. How could I save *that* big beast? Miss Fury has a cat.

"Boolean!" I clap my hands for him to settle down. "Come here." Under the golden light of the moon, the house is like a stage play with all those windows, lit in shades of tech blue from the TV lights from Aurora's room and the computer screens in Hugo's office. The monitor in my hand hums in the same shade. I spot another blue glow in a room right under Aurora's, Greta on her phone. She looks out toward the yard, her arms crossed. I wave, but she doesn't wave back.

Inside again, I slide the door closed behind Boolean and me. Boolean's not exactly quiet—he gallops like a horse version of a dog, up the stairs and down the hall, ruining any chance to listen in outside Hugo's office. But *that* door very suddenly opens.

"Hey," Hugo says.

I swear, my heart stops. I can barely believe it's him, right here in front of me. *He's just a man,* Aurora said that day, and it's true—he's a human being, and whoa, not a whole lot taller than I am, I see now. He's wearing a black T-shirt and worn jeans, and his feet are bare, and kind of funny-looking, same as all feet. But he's also THE Hugo Harrison, and the guy who left us, the invisible main character made real. I'm a total wreck. It's hard to breathe. I want to sock him, or throw my arms around him, or cry. I want to confront him, have him spill all the reasons that he left us that I'm sure are there—the way that Brandi's anger was just too much, maybe, the way it is for me sometimes. I want to tell him about us, me and him, how we're similar and connected. I want to show him all he missed out on, but still could have.

Instead I only manage to stand there, wishing I were wearing something fabulous, like the yellow fish-tail gown that Marla Drake wears when General Bruno surprises her, instead of my capri pj's with the tiki print that Arden Lee and I found at Second Stories Consignment.

"Hey," I say back. We just spoke to each other, all normal.

"The new nanny, right?" He does this little finger pistol shot, bam, right at me. It's supposed to be playful, but it's pretty accurate. Bam, bam, bam, make it three shots. My sister and my mom, too.

"Right." I look straight in his—whoa, are his eyes *green*? I always thought brown from the pictures, like mine, but they're greenish, like Rosalind's. I stare into those eyes like a dare, like *Here I am.* Like *See me and recognize me, what we share, who we are.* He blinks, but it may just be a regular blink. And why would he blink in recognition? It's not like I'm on his mind. It's not like any of us are. *Go! We need nothing from you,* my mom yelled at him that day, which is the kind of thing you say when you're rejected. The kind of thing that makes someone do as they're told. He's on my mind every five seconds, but he's just living his life.

"Awesome," he says.

The door is cracked open, and I can see into his office. There are several huge curved screens on his desk, like the command center in some space show. It's cluttered in there, a mess of office and tech stuff, not sparse and clean like the rest of the house. He sees me seeing. Instead of slamming the door shut like you'd expect, he angles his body ever so slightly so I can get a better view. Maybe he liked the way I looked straight at him, full of curiosity, no idea. But he lets me peek inside.

That's when I see something I shouldn't. Some*one*. The back of a woman's head. For, like, two seconds, I see her sitting in a chair. Her long blond hair.

I feel a weird wrongness, like, gross. Because who is she, and what's going on here? Is that Laura? Why is he in there with her, and not with Aurora? Hugo grins, like . . . *Ugh.* Like he's got this great secret he just kind of revealed.

"Thanks," I say, and smile. I actually smile! Oh my God. Do you see why I need someone like Miss Fury? Do you? She would never smile in this situation. She would understand what was going on and what was expected of her. She would handle things, clearly and directly, same as she handled Gary Hale and General Bruno. She'd leave a bad situation via a three-story bedroom window if necessary.

"We really appreciate you. You're awesome," Hugo says. He smiles. We've had five seconds of interaction; he doesn't know me. It's the kind of encouraging thing you'd say to any new employee, but those words and that smile . . . Maybe my baby DNA remembers a moment exactly like that, because my heart clicks, like a key in a lock. Who am I kidding, it's way more than a click, and way more than him holding me so long ago. I've been looking at his face in one way or another for years now. It's my face. It's just looking back at me, finally.

And, wow, the weirdness vanishes. My body starts to fill with flowers or something. Rainbows. Music. The most glorious happy everythings. Two seconds of his approval and I'm a goner. I'm suddenly sure that there's some reasonable explanation for that woman in his office, same as I'm sure there's a reasonable explanation for him leaving us. Sure, it's late, but he's changing the world, so, okay, he might not keep regular hours. Who cares, who cares—I'm appreciated. The flowers in me bloom, and the rainbows rainbow, and the music soars.

He ducks back in there with maybe-Laura.

Boolean ducks back in with me. He collapses onto the floor of my room, shaking the tectonic plates of our earth. That dog has glommed on to me like he's been held captive and I'm here to rescue him.

I pace with energy that has nowhere to go. It's stress and nerves and excitement, but there's not a drop of fury. I couldn't put anyone in their place if I wanted to. And I sure as heck couldn't escape from this third-floor window using my extraordinary athletic abilities.

A worry knocks at my mental door. Like, what if hope is an affliction? What if the biggest symptom is a belief in reasonable explanations?

That moment at the dinner table, when Hugo held up his stop-sign hand to put Aurora in her place . . . It's still with me. It gnaws in the background, causing a restless distress. It's hard to forget Aurora's utter humiliation.

It's not exactly anger, but I go on Rate Me. I make a fake account, using an—*another*—alias. I don't write anything in the review part, but I give Aurora five stars.

chapter
Twelve

THE NEXT MORNING MY SCHEDULE ARRIVES WITH ITS
own ping sound on the new phone. I'm supposed to meet Laura
and the team at nine a.m. in the driveway, with Arlo fed, bathed,
and dressed. After breakfast a pair of little denim overalls and a
white shirt appear in his room, a pair of tiny white sneakers next
to them.

Arlo has a blast in the tub, so I have to do some high-level negotiating to get him out. He looks adorable, but how I'm going to keep white clothes white on a toddler is beyond me.

Already, day two, I'm getting slightly more comfortable at the house, so I go to the catering kitchen to hunt for the cleanest possible snack to pack. Jak, the chef, resembles one of those guys you see on Capitol Hill in Seattle, with the big beards and the porkpie hats and the tattoos involving swords. He's super easygoing and friendly. When I saw him this morning for breakfast, he even made me an omelet, and now after he sets me up with a banana and crackers, we're practically friends. He just finished making Aurora strawberry waffles, and there's actually a can of Reddi-wip on the counter. He shrugs and tells me it's her favorite and mimes squirting it into his mouth like Niles did that time he and Rosalind made Mom a Mother's Day brunch.

When I get to the driveway with Arlo, there's a big SUV sitting there, and a bunch of people. My new sense of comfort pretty much flees. Arlo must feel the same, because his little fingers reach toward me and wiggle like he's in a Broadway musical dance number, wanting up. I'm glad about that, because he'll dirty those white shoes in two seconds if he does something reckless, like actually walk in them. Poor Boolean—I have to keep shoving him away because big dog, big hair. He'll make a sweater on me in two minutes. A photo shoot involving all these people—you'd assume this was for some special occasion, like a holiday card, maybe, but no. This is all for Aurora's Instagram, and photo shoots are a regular thing in the little guy's life.

A woman approaches. It's Laura, I'm sure. I recognize her

hair. I think I do, that shiny blond I saw in Hugo's office. It's eerie, how much she looks like Aurora. And even stranger, I realize, they *both* look like the OG wife, Susan, when she was younger. Aurora herself isn't here yet.

"Eleanor, the new nanny?" She reaches out her hand, and I shift Arlo around so I can take it. Her fingers are long and thin, and even her seconds-long grasp is efficient. I spot her wedding ring and, whoa, a giant engagement ring. They're unusual. Braided silver-gold bands, the diamond surrounded by green stones.

"Yep," I say.

"Perfect. I'm Laura. Mostly we'll be needing you to just step aside and be on hand for any meltdowns."

I kiss Arlo's head in answer. We pile into the SUV after I buckle Arlo in his seat. I'm getting a serious case of *Fremdscham,* secondhand embarrassment, the kind you feel on behalf of someone else, because Aurora is seriously late. There are two photographers, a hairstylist, a makeup person carrying a tote, and another woman hauling a few black clothing bags, but no toddler mom. The SUV starts up, and we pull out of the driveway.

"Will Aurora be meeting us there?" Wherever *there* is. The Frame House disappears in the distance.

"No," Laura says. She might look like Aurora, but they're not at all alike. Laura is total, crisp certainty. "Can you please turn on the air? It's boiling back here," she commands the driver from the bench seat in front of Arlo and me. She has her elbows slightly out, the way you do when you want to keep your armpits dry, haha. I notice that Laura's wearing the exact shade of denim pants as Arlo's overalls, and a matching crisp white shirt. I get a creeping unease. It's a pretty common outfit combo, though, right?

I whisper things to Arlo to try to make him laugh, because he looks miserable. "Boo ba loo," I say. Nothing. I peek at him between my fingers, nope. I take the new plastic bottle of water from the cup holder, crack the top, take a swig, and burp in his ear. He cracks a smile. Bodily sounds for the win.

"Let's not spill that," Laura says. Arlo and I look at each other, and I know he's only two, but I swear we understand each other. Like, we have that whole conversation siblings have when you've gotten in trouble and feel the imminent hysteria of *uh-oh*. I make my eyes really big, like there's a monster in the room, and I see the glitter return to his eyes.

During the drive the team discusses something called a shot list. I have no idea where we're heading. The windows are darkened, so it's possible that these are my last hours, and I'm the mafia hit heading to the river.

It's not a river. It's a neighborhood P-Patch. I've actually been here before. I helped Clementine grow some beans and some carrots and a couple of tomato plants that Jackie got for her at Fred Meyer when Clementine wanted to show Apple how things grow. It got to be too much, trying to raise Apple and vegetables both, so we stopped. But now we all pile out and walk through the gate, which is decorated with frail, faded wind socks and a hand-painted sign.

Laura walks through the patchwork of gardeny mess, spots where it's more garden gnomes and decorative stuff than actual vegetation. She aims straight for the back, where there's a large, orderly section that looks recently planted. The dirt is dark, straight from the bag, and there are charming rows of tomatoes and strawberries and who-knows-what, with tiny fruits already emerging. It's like *Brave New World,* all perfect and perfectly engineered.

The team sets up their cameras. I try to put Arlo down, but he basically climbs back up my body, so no way. But now . . . What? Laura is getting her hair fixed and her makeup touched up.

Suddenly, I get it. I feel sick. This is so . . . I don't know, but I also feel tricked. Aurora isn't coming. Aurora was never coming. Laura is the one getting her photo taken. Laura is the one in all those photos.

The makeup woman heads our way, and I'm terrified she's going to put makeup on Arlo, but she just tells us it's time. I'm pretty sure they're about to get the meltdown they anticipated. I try to think fast. "Hey, bud. I know you don't want to do this, and I can't blame you," I whisper to him. "But let's get this over with, and then we are going to play so hard and have an awesome time, and we are going to get an ice cream sandwich." I can't think of a situation that isn't made better by the promise of one of those.

"I-cream sawish?"

Has he ever even had one? Well, he's going to have one today if it kills me. "Just you wait."

I have to basically pull him off me, but I hand him to Laura. I can't watch, honestly. It's just too painful, and weird, and disturbing. I'm worried if he sees me, it'll make things worse, so I wander away where I can still see him. The photographer clicks: shots of Laura and Arlo from the back, in matching clothes, walking down a row; the two of them bending over to examine a strawberry, Laura's hair falling across her face. It looks like Arlo and his mama spending a summer day together. I'm Marla Drake for sure, minus her glorious pink hat, when she discovers the baroness's toddler but has no idea who his real parents are.

"Checked shirts!" Laura calls, and the wardrobe woman unzips the second outfit from the bag. She's unfastening Arlo's overalls, inching on a pair of jeans, draping the shirt over the white tee. The makeup woman washes a smudge from his cheek as Laura tosses on her matching checks. "Yellow socks! I told you I wanted yellow socks!" Laura's eyes blaze.

"I've got them!" the wardrobe woman snaps. Once the socks are on, she returns with a jar. She empties something into Laura's palm that she and Arlo examine as the photographer aims and shoots.

I'm spending the day with Aurora, the Aurora in the Instagram photos, for the first time.

I get it—Laura has a job to do. She's "adding impact" on behalf of the real Aurora, now at home eating waffles with Reddi-wip. But I would give this fake Aurora one star. I'd give this whole morning one star. I'll tell you one thing: I don't get why people are always urging you to be yourself, when that sure doesn't seem like anything anyone wants. And I'll tell you another thing: Arlo is not here on earth to be social media content, okay? No kid is.

"I think we got what we need," the photographer finally says.

BACK AT THE HOUSE WHAT *WE* NEED IS A NEW DIA-
per, pronto, and then it's lunchtime. I also have a promise to fulfill.
I ask Jak about ice cream sandwiches, not expecting any miracles.
I might have to take a quick trip in the Land Rover, my first, but
Arlo's hungry now and nap time is approaching, and I want to
practice driving that car before I take Arlo anywhere.

"We've got the cheap kind. Where you get twenty-four in a
box for a couple bucks," Jak says. "H.H. loves them."

"They're the best." I smile. It's something else we have in
common.

"I don't think Arlo gets them. They're just H.H.'s secret thing."

"Is Arlo allergic? If not, he really deserves one today."

"Nope, and right on," Jak says.

We take our food out to the back lawn, and I lay out a blanket
in the shade. Arlo eats his ice cream sandwich first, and I even let
him lick the white paper wrapper. We do some hard playing after.
We run and chase, and Arlo laughs so hard, he gets the hiccups.

After I put him down for his nap, I go on Aurora's Instagram.
The photos are already up. There's a beautifully written post about
spending the day in the garden, and what it means to watch things
sprout. Sunlight shines down on little Arlo and fake Aurora. Seeing it, you'd feel love and wholesomeness. You'd feel envy. It's a
perfect scene. Ideal. The likes pour in. This is the one place where
people mostly say nice stuff to Aurora, even if they don't mean it.
The comments are full of hearts and tears emojis. The viewers love

the photo of the two of them holding hands, walking down that row. I'm witnessing it: the viewers being influenced.

The photo that really gets me, the one that's especially upsetting, is the image of fake Aurora holding her cupped palms toward Arlo. She's showing him a ladybug. That ladybug, well, now I know what was in the jar. I imagine that ladybug, minding his own business out in nature somewhere, captured to be of use. And I'm pissed, you know. He's not here to be social media content, either.

AURORA POPS HER HEAD INTO MY ROOM. "EVERY-thing okay?"

"Sleeping Beauty." I show her the monitor.

She smiles. "How'd it go at the farm or whatever?"

"P-Patch," I say. "They got some nice photos."

I feel a little mad at her. I wonder what she did all day as Arlo worked as a prop. Maybe it's more than a little mad, because I flash on an image of Marla Drake having it out with the baroness. Okay, Marla's got her on the ground, an arm behind her back. I want to tell Aurora that the photos would have been way better if she'd been in them. No. Better yet would be no photos at all. Just her and Arlo actually at that P-Patch. She could've shown Arlo a ladybug that just naturally happened to be nearby. She's wearing a white T-shirt right now, and a pair of denim shorts, faded and ripped, matching Arlo, and they didn't even plan it. Okay, her shirt has a splotch of strawberry juice on it from those waffles, but so what. Honestly, life has splotches, a lot of them. What's going to happen to poor Arlo if he grows up thinking he should never have them, splotches and mistakes and mess and imperfections? God, poor kid.

"Hey, I'll be back for dinner," she says. "I'm heading out to meet with my astrologer."

"Leo Gemini. Such a great name."

She looks surprised. "Whoa! You remembered. You were actually *listening*," she says.

That's what people do, right, when other people talk? Or what they're supposed to do. "Hey, I wanted to ask . . . You said it was okay to use the pool? It doesn't seem like anyone uses it. I'll bring the monitor with me, of course."

"Oh sure! The pool stuff's in the cabana. I just prefer Green Lake since it's more private."

"Thanks," I say. More private than a private pool makes absolutely no sense, but there's no time for follow-up questions.

"I'm out of here! I'm going to be late." She heads down the hall, her woven handbag hitting against her hip.

I see them on her hand, then, as she holds the strap of her bag. Her wedding and engagement rings, the braided silver-gold bands, the big diamond surrounded by green stones, same as Laura wore. It makes me think of William Moulton Marston, supposed creator of the lie detector test, and his wives, deceiving the public about their life, lying to their own children, too. How can you tell what's real? That's what I want to know. That whole morning we disappeared into an image of flawlessness. I mean, why do we even need to create a metaverse, an immersive virtual world, an augmented reality powered by tech? It's already right here. It's already a simulation.

chapter
Thirteen

I FIND A STACK OF CLEAN TOWELS AND HALF-deflated floatie toys in the cabana. I recognize some of them from Aurora's Instagram posts: a huge swan, an island with a palm tree. They were probably used once, for fake playing. I choose a lounge chair and prop the monitor on the patio table, along with a bottle of water and an orange I found in the catering kitchen fridge. I stretch out on the white canvas cushions. Boolean finds a spot of shade on the lawn.

"God, I'm sorry you have to wear fur on a day like this," I tell him.

It's truly a bitch, he says, or would if he could talk. His tongue lolls out. Heavy panting ensues.

I call Clementine and Arden Lee before I talk to Mom. I need courage for all the lies I'm about to tell her. In terms of those fake photos—well, I'm pretending to be someone else, too, aren't I?

I catch Clementine on her break. She tells me how she got really scared last night because Apple cut herself bad. A situation like that—an ER visit and no parent—it could sink her. But Mrs. Kumar from next door came over, and Apple was okay, thank goodness. I tell her about dinner last night, and the fake Aurora, and she says, *How sad,* but she has to go. We say *I love you.* It's been a rough few days, so I try to really hear it and really say it this time.

Arden Lee's just finishing practice, and he's still out of breath. He chugs water as we speak. *Basket, swish, two points!* he says victoriously. I'm so happy for him. I tell him about the woman in Hugo's office late last night, and he says, *Are you sure she was* human? and I laugh. When I share what happened at the photo shoot, he says, *The* human *wasn't even real!* We also talk about something I just remembered—how Olive Byrne, William Moulton Marston's second wife, used to write all of these super-traditional homemaker-y articles for *Family Circle* magazine, total lies of her true life. She interviewed William as an expert for some of them, too. *She added impact, huh,* Arden Lee says, because he also listens.

Finally, I dial Mom. She's at work, but I'm pretty sure she'll pick up. Calling her from here—a snake of betrayal slithers up, tries to circle my neck. The strange thing is, I *want* to tell her about all of the amazing stuff here. It makes me proud of myself, like I've accomplished something by being with them, even though I'm me and not Eleanor Drake.

"Eleanor! You just love to make me worry, don't you?" Mom answers.

"I'm so sorry. I've just been really busy."

"Well, how's it going? How are you doing? It's not easy raising kids, is it? You can't just have your nose in a book all of the time."

"It's a lot, yeah. He's so sweet. Um . . ." The Von Barons have two kids, ugh. "They *both* are. It's a pretty incredible house. My room is amazing. I'm out here at the pool."

"That sounds wonderful! I'm so happy for you. You're doing great!" she says. Haha, not really. What she actually says is, "Just living the good life, huh? Are you being careful about chlorine? Well, I guess you can pay for the doctor yourself since you're making the big bucks."

"I'm being careful. How are you and Rosalind?"

"Our day has been *hell*," she says. She tells me how her car battery was dead, but how Rosalind knew just what to do and called a guy who was just incredible and so nice and brought a new battery, and how they could have missed the morning meeting with Allison, but they didn't because Rosalind has this innate knowledge of how to handle difficulty. The situation with Allison is just getting worse and worse, though, she says. What a bitch! No one respects her, and when she called out Mom during the meeting for being abrupt with a customer, everyone looked at Mom like, *You've got to be kidding.*

I cut in. I tell her that Arthur is crying and I have to go. Arlo's not and I don't, but I just feel like shit and I don't know why. Bad in the kind of way that can get ugly, like, self-hatred ugly.

"Oh?" she bites. "Well, maybe you can call when you're not in such *a rush*," she says.

I'm a shit daughter, and a shit person in general, I think after we hang up, because look where I am, and look what she doesn't have. A boat putters past, then a kayaker, who waves. I wave back. I realize I forgot my book, and I suddenly need it, bad. I just need to read, because when you open a book, you get to step into another world, and, boom, you're out of here.

It's warm. The water looks so inviting. That chlorine, though—maybe that time at the Green Lake pool was just luck, because I've been told this fact about myself from forever, that I get rashes from chemicals, lake water, too much sun. Rosalind is like Mom, who turns brown with two seconds of sun exposure, but I'm a wreck, a *hothouse flower*.

It's true that you can feel eyes on you, because right then I look up toward the 2,019 frames of glass, and there she is, Greta, Hugo Harrison's mother, my grandmother, watching me. She's wearing a caftan, and her short silver hair looks severe. Even from this distance I can tell I'm something she disapproves of. I wonder if she'd disapprove of me more or less or the same if she knew who I was. Arden Lee always says we have to remember that a person brings themselves to every situation. Meaning, stuff we take personally isn't necessarily personal. She probably disapproves of everyone, and I'm just part of everyone.

I'm not sure who I'm angry at, or if I'm even angry at all, but

I say *fuck it* about the pool. Just fuck it. I fling off my T-shirt, toss it on the other lounge chair, and stand there in my ironic sea-creature bikini. *Fine, go ahead and look,* I say silently to Greta. Glare all you want. I bring the monitor to the pool edge, and then I get right in. I make sure not to cringe when the cold hits my stomach, so there. I duck my head, and, wow, it's so awesome below the surface. Bubbly and *away,* kind of like a book, but quieter and more watery.

I pop my head up and I see him.

The stalker.

He's right here! Right by the house! Oh my God! He's looking up at the windows, as if searching for a way in. My Arlo is there, sleeping.

I leap out of the pool. I'm not in a catsuit. No, I'm not. I'm in my bikini with the ironic sea creatures. I run. I'm not thinking, okay? Pure action. I'm just going to tackle that guy, I swear. I've never tackled anyone in my life. I spent the whole unit of flag football terrified, and all we had to do was rip a strand of red nylon from its Velcro. So maybe you don't always think so clearly when it comes to love. And maybe I already love Arlo more than I've loved anyone in my life.

I race across the hot patio, jump over a short hedge, shoot across the lawn, and . . .

The guy turns. He looks at me, totally perplexed. I'm sort of hunched down, ready to barrel into him using my head, because I'm not at all using my head.

He's wearing a blue polo with khaki shorts. My mind is so full of its own story that I don't see the emblem on that polo, or the words underneath. And I don't see the equipment he's holding, either, until I'm right in front of him. A long, long pole with a brush on the end. I'm running too fast to stop myself, and, boom, I bash right into him. It's not my head ramming his stomach like in my original plan. It's more a confused bumbling collision. He stumbles backward. Luckily, we don't crash right through the glass, the glass he's there to clean.

Northwest Windows, his shirt reads.

"What the hell?" he says from the ground.

It is understandably baffling to have a girl hop out of a pool, race toward you, and then semi-but-not-tackle you.

"Oh geez," I say. Unfortunately, I have to speak while untangling my limbs from his. Up close he's much younger than I'd thought. Much more innocent-looking, too. Way less of a dangerous stalker. He could be my age, though he definitely doesn't go to my school. He's got a bit of peanut butter by his mouth. He's not cute in any predictable way, maybe not even cute at all, just . . . Oh man, his eyes . . . Those eyes don't seem the slightest bit menacing. They're just stunned, and stunning, deep pools of brown. His hair is dark and curly, like it's living its own life and doing its own interesting thing and, ugh, I'm struck. I just am. Arden Lee would be so pissed because he hates, *hates* anything remotely insta-love. This is in no way Finn Lahruti with the otter key chain, shit, shit, shit, who I was never really even attracted to, not in the way you read about. This is the way you read about, and I've never been more embarrassed in my life. He has a compelling oddness that calls out to my own oddness. I don't know how to explain it. He looks intriguing, probably in a way that'll work great in college or whatever, but maybe not so great in high school. It would work for me, okay? It *is* working, as I move my ankle from under his shin so he can get up. My bathing suit has played a major role in humiliating me again, because his shirt has two wet boob marks from my ironic sea-creatures bikini top.

He doesn't respond. He just stands there holding that hose with the brush on the end of it.

"I'm so sorry," I say. "I thought you were maybe, I don't know, an intruder or something."

He does something unexpected then. At least, I doubt I would have done it if the situation were reversed. He laughs. I mean, so hard that his eyes water.

"I'm so sorry," I say again. I don't explain how I've seen him in his car, multiple times, because clearly I need to rethink all of it.

He regains composure, swaps the pole-hose thing to his left hand and holds out his right. "I'm John William Gemini," he says. I mean, what guy our age does that? Shakes your hand? Arden Lee, maybe.

"Gemini?" The astrologer. The astrologer's kid! No wonder he's around so much.

"Yeah, I know it's a mouthful. People call me Nino."

"Nino?" Yep, broken robot again. But it's hard to see how we got from John William to Nino.

But Nino's been through this a hundred times. "My mom's an artist? My name was inspired by this painter, John William Waterhouse? They called *him* Nino." Oh, my heart. He talks in insecure question marks, too, and his mom is an *artist*. Of all things!

"Oh," I say eloquently.

He takes a pinch of his shirt. "I'm from Northwest Windows? Window cleaning?"

My mind spins, imagining his fascinating house, with an artist and an astrologer for parents. I want to know more. I'm not the sort of person who has crushes, whoever that person is. I mean, I thought I might be like Arden Lee, who says he just can't summon up the energy or interest to care about sex. But all at once (I know, I know! Arden Lee is going to *kill* me) I feel bad about all the romantic songs and stuff I always make fun of. I'm totally Marla-meets-Gary-Hale, giving him the same big eyes. It's so strange, how there are parts of the current you tucked away for the future you and you don't even know it.

"You have a really long pole," I say. OH MY GOD! There are also parts of the current you that have always been there, and that will always be there. I blush. I mean, my whole body is hot. My cheeks blaze, and I don't dare look at the rest of me, because I feel the red heat traveling down my chest. Soon I'll be as vivid as that dancing lobster on my suit.

Now he's explaining about the pole, how they can't use a cherry picker out here because of all the landscaping, and so they use this, along with special ionized water that dries in droplets, not in streaks, and I have no idea what he's even saying, to be honest. It's hard to concentrate. I don't even know what a cherry picker is.

"With this many windows, it's important they're clear, right?" He looks at me with those deep brown eyes. It's a beat too long, as if he's trying to say two things, maybe something important about the Harrisons. It sounds profound. Really profound, and I almost feel a little choked up, though I have no clue why.

Arlo, well, he saves me. He starts crying. I hear him on the monitor.

"Got to go!" I hurry back to the table, grab the monitor, my towel and shirt, my phone, and my water bottle, and dash inside the house. I am such a fool. I don't even say goodbye. I don't even tell him my name. It's pure *scham* minus the *Fremd*. Embarrassment for my own self, ugh.

I go to Arlo. I change his diaper and make blubbery sounds on his tummy, and then we head to the kitchen for his snack. Arlo's eating yogurt in his booster seat when Greta appears. She runs her thumb across his cheek to clean it.

"You better tidy up out there," she says to me.

When I look toward the pool, I see that my lounge chair is slightly out of alignment with the others, and that the orange I brought out is on the grass. Boolean's staring down at it, like he wishes someone would play ball with him.

"I'm so sorry," I say. "I will." So this is why Aurora prefers the pool at Green Lake. I look down, guilty. That's when I see it: no rash again. Just regular arms, slightly tan from the sun.

It makes me wonder how true that rash thing is, or ever was. It also makes me wonder how many fictional stories people tell you about yourself. And how many you might believe for a long, long time. Yeah, Arden Lee would totally kick my butt for saying *fictional stories,* but you know what I mean.

chapter
Fourteen

THAT NIGHT AURORA'S MEETING HUGO AT PSYCKĒ
Enterprises before heading out to dinner. She tells me they're
going to a restaurant he loves, with the same owners as this celeb-
rity hot spot in New York, a place that's gotten three stars. I may
not have the number of stars right, because this seems low. Also,
sidenote, so many things have stars lately that we'll probably be
giving stars to actual stars any day now. Like, Sirius would get

five, but for sure there'd be some person who'd say, *Three-point-five, rounded up to a four.*

Anyway, apparently the whole restaurant is like a movie set, and every waiter is like an actor, where they play out this whole narrative involving the patron, though the patron isn't necessarily aware of it. *Like, you're in a play,* Aurora said, *and you don't know you're in a play, and the waiter says the witty line he always says, and then you're hooked. Hugo loves it.* She shrugged. It makes me want a number three beef soft taco meal at Tacos Today.

Aurora needs the right outfit. I guess if you're in a play, you have to have a costume. She wants my advice again. This is still completely astonishing. It makes me feel downright glorious, my insides shining like a five-star Sirius. I bring Arlo and this noisy toy school bus he likes to Aurora's room. It keeps saying, *It's GOOD to make friends!* in a voice so annoying you want to smash it, but he's happy. I try to explain to Aurora that I don't know anything about clothes, that I just pick stuff I like. That's the only clothing advice I have, which, if you ask Rosalind and Mom, is the worst advice ever, because they are constantly looking at me like I stepped out of a Ross Dress for Less after a tornado. "Clothes-wise, I have no idea what I like," Aurora says, and so I suggest this shimmery silver sleeveless dress with a velvety orange-red scarf and a pair of these cool orange shoes with Lucite heels. They remind me of the chunks of amber where scientists have discovered ancient mosquitoes.

I'm bummed that I won't get to spy on Hugo at dinner. Another whole day is almost over, and I haven't even seen him. Before Aurora gets showered and dressed to go, she sits with Arlo as he eats and invites me to hang out if I want. I do want. I want to hear about her time with Leo Gemini, and about all things Gemini. Plus, the dinner that Jak made smells fantastic. In the dining area I notice the windows. You could walk right through them, they're so clear.

Aurora doesn't tell me anything about Leo Gemini, only more stuff about the restaurant, and how she's trying to remember what Hugo ordered last time because she wants to get the same thing. *It must have looked really good,* I say. But she tells me that it's more about making him happy. She *didn't* order what he suggested last time, and he got all hurt. I make a face, like *What?* I mean, it seems like a pretty petty thing to get hurt about, but she explains that lots and lots of things can feel like rejection to some people. And that rejection can feel like criticism, and criticism can be like pouring water on his sandcastle, or blowing up his whole beach with a bomb. Those are her actual words. *Blowing up his whole beach with a bomb.* She says another thing that might haunt me forever: *When men feel rejected, women pay.*

The point is, she's really distracted. It's giving me William Moulton Marston vibes again. His wives pretty much tippy-toed around him, since he was known to fly into rages. There's no real way to edge Aurora into talking about the Gemini family. She's sneaking pieces of Arlo's and my flank steak, and who can blame her. It's delicious, and she's going to a place with three stars. But she sneaks it, right? In that upsetting, mostly female way where you're not supposed to eat, or you're apologetic for eating, or embarrassed about eating, or you eat in secret, or eat way less than you want to, et cetera et cetera. I'm not judging—I do it sometimes, too. Mom and Rosalind are constantly on diets, so I pretend to be on board with a wedge of romaine or whatever, then go fix myself a sandwich because I'm so hungry. It makes me wonder when in history women learned they weren't supposed to feed their bodies, but it was probably when we learned we were supposed to disappear. So, maybe always.

After dinner Aurora goes upstairs to get ready while Arlo and I play stuffed dino and tiny cars. Dino stomps around while cars drive away superfast. We have fun roaring and pretending we are much bigger than we are, and I gain important insight into why kids love dinos so much. Aurora emerges. She smells *so* good, like fresh oranges plus ginger. She looks fabulous in the outfit we picked.

"Orange scent with orange clothes, so fun! You look amazing!" I tell her. The Aurora of her Instagram page would have never needed to hear this, but the real Aurora does. Arlo runs to her and wraps his arms around her legs.

"Well, I'm off," she says. You'd think this would be exciting, going to some fancy restaurant with Hugo, but she's dawdling and acting all anxious. This seems surprising, since he's her *husband*. I don't know. I never lived with two parents, so I don't have a whole lot of an idea what married couples are like. Mom has had boyfriends—there was Kevin, who was always doing something embarrassing she hated, like wearing a dirty shirt in public or getting his hair cut too short. They broke up after he met Nana Minnie and Papa Joe, and he said something about Africa being a country, which was *the last straw*. And then there was Terry, who might have been the reason for some of those diets. He was always pointing out women who he thought weighed too much—on

TV, in restaurants, everywhere—even though he had a belly like a bowling ball. He also gave Mom gifts that were actually for himself, like the Bullet blender he wanted over at our house. They broke up right before he was going to move in, just before I started junior high. We still have the Bullet.

The point is, I never really saw marriage. I assumed it would be cozier. More relaxed. More, um, soft slippers, and less too-high high heels. I didn't think it would be so much like a job. Because, wow, Aurora is working like she's an incompetent employee with a difficult boss who she's trying really hard to manage. I used to think marriage was something I wanted, but now it looks pretty stressful, to be honest.

"Have a great time!" I say. I realize that I'm trying to pump her up so she can pump him up, whoa. It makes you wonder just how many people it takes to support a large ego. My mind flashes on wobbly gymnastics pyramids and old churches with flying buttresses. What's that statement about it taking a village? That's for raising kids, I'm pretty sure, but same difference.

"Wish me luck," she says.

I'm beginning to think she needs a lot more than that. It's another thing I didn't know about marriage. That it needs luck, plus a whole lot more.

I PUT ARLO TO BED. IT'S ONLY BEEN A COUPLE OF DAYS, and I have *All the World* memorized. I totally get why he wants to hear it five thousand times. It's the sweetest book, and the images are soft and kind. The gentle words whisper. Being at the Harrison house, I also understand why kids are given quiet, sweet things like that story, and stuffed animals, and Mr. Rogers, because the world, the real one, is a lot to take in. Even at my age it's a lot, let alone at two, almost two and a half. Here we are, Arlo with *All the World,* and me with Miss Fury, and Clementine with Pippi Longstocking, and Apple with the Chronicles of Narnia, and Arden Lee with All the Books, and it just makes me wish that Aurora had a book, too. Some people think books are just for reading, haha.

I'm in *my father's house.* I swam in his pool, and ate his food, and I'm sitting on the edge of this bed, my feet resting on his big dog. I've been spending nearly every waking minute with his kid, my little brother. But I'm no closer to feeling related to him, connected to him. The weird thing is, I almost felt more connected to him when I was imagining him, and not here in this house.

It's quiet, aside from the buzz-hum of the monitor. Jak's probably gone home, the housekeeper, Yvette, too. I wonder where Greta is. I feel her here, the way you feel the presence of all disapproving people, as if they're in the room even when they're not. It makes me want to obey her and never make a wrong move, but it also makes me want to defy her and destroy everything in sight.

Picture Rosalind rolling her eyes on that one.

I get up and peek my head around the door. Empty hallway, silent house.

"Stay here," I tell Boolean. He gives me a weary look, then puts his head down on his paws and sighs, as if he's already seen his fair share of disastrous mistakes and their tragic outcomes.

I creep down the hall, then take the stairs to the second floor.

The members of the Soggy Pages Book Club know that if you really want to find out about a person, you look at their bookshelves.

The library. God, it smells great in here! The best smell, like a bookstore, crisp and delicious. What beautiful, sleek shelves! One whole wall is books about programming and tech. Hey! I spot *Brave New World* over there, the exact opposite of *All the World*. It means Hugo mixes fiction and non, a Soggy Pages thumbs-down.

I scan the spines, sorted by hue. In red there's *The Elements of Style* and *Maus I* and *Maus II,* and Zadie Smith's *The Book of Other People,* and Amy Hempel's *The Collected Stories.* What a fascinating mix! In blue, Neil Gaiman's *Anansi Boys,* and Don DeLillo's *Falling Man,* and Annie Proulx's *Bad Dirt,* and David Foster Wallace's *Infinite Jest,* and so on. Modern classics in green and orange and purple, wow. My heart fills with love, because *so many books*! I mean, he's one of us, *they* are, and maybe Aurora *does* have her own cherished novel. The Soggy Pages would give an honorary toot of our kazoos. In yellow I hook the spine of *Electric Light* by Seamus Heaney with my fingertip. The cover is smooth and clean. I hold it in my hands carefully, like the precious thing it is—someone's own thoughts and feelings and very soul. Art, but with words. Twenty-six letters instead of cyan and magenta.

When I open it, I realize something disappointing. It's *so* new that the pages are still tightly bound together, and the spine is straight and entirely unbroken. This Soggy Pages member can tell you with zero doubt that this is a book that's never been opened.

I choose another. *The Great Gatsby,* same. *The Picture of Dorian Gray,* same. *The Talented Mr. Ripley,* same. *The Secret History,* same, same, same.

My heart crashes. These books are only here for looks. All these voices, you know. People, saying interesting things, saying, *See me, hear me,* and no one cares.

I try the tech wall. I open *The Mythical Man-Month.* The spine relaxes. There's a highlight, even: "Adjusting to the requirement for perfection is, I think, the most difficult part of learning to program. . . ." It's proof that someone was actually listening. *The Pragmatic Programmer,* read. *Clean Code,* definitely read.

Is this a relief? No idea. Lots of people have books for show, though, right? Arden Lee's stepmom, Cherie, has a shelf of books she's never read, just sitting in their rec room to look impressive. No wonder it smells so new in here. You probably just buy the whole set as a decoration. This house—it's a set, same as that restaurant.

I head back upstairs. I walk past his office, the most forbidden place, the heart of his heart and brain, but I don't dare try the door. Instead I go to their bedroom.

Guilt descends as I step inside. If Greta catches me, I'm dead, but tell that to the part of me that longs to know more about Hugo, all the stuff that isn't shown in the interviews. Private stuff, beyond the disturbing, oversharing details we've heard from Mom, like the scar on the inside of his thigh, and other things about his body. The way he moans in his sleep. She told us a few things about them having sex, too, which I've tried to block out. No one, no kid, wants to hear that stuff, okay?

Their room's been tidied up, and it's easier to see everything without Aurora's clothes strewn around. Their nightstands feature matching glass lamps and wood clocks, and Aurora's holds her laptop. Otherwise the surfaces are bare—no drooping phone cords or hair bands. Mom's bedside table is jammed with lotion bottles and cups of half-drunk coffee, pens and pain relievers, the framed card from Rosalind with the poem about mothers. Could she have even lived in a house like this? Could she have kept her emotions and her stuff in check to fit this image of flawlessness? I mean, how long until her truth would have spilled out on the white rug?

I move one of the lamps ever so slightly, just to see if the nightstand was speed-race dusted, but no. It's been dusted all the way around, and underneath, too. I didn't notice that electronic frame before, on Aurora's dresser. Photos of Arlo and her and Hugo appear and then fade, each one replaced by the next. *Real* photos—Aurora in the hospital after Arlo was born, her hair all sweaty and cheeks flushed, holding the tiny swaddled infant in her arms; the three of them at their beach estate in Mexico, the ocean behind them. I feel a painful crack down my heart, like that time a rock hit the windshield of Mom's car when Ros and I were going to get Slurpees.

Now I carefully slide open a drawer from Hugo's dresser, the one that sat ignored earlier. Disappointing: boxers in shades of gray; socks, but in wild colors. There's nothing else in there. No telling trinkets or silver cuff-things that Arden Lee and I found in Carlos's drawer after he moved in with Jackie. Carlos also had a pair of dice, and this big, gaudy high school ring, and a photo of his daughter when she was a baby, which made us feel guilty for looking. Here there are no photos of me and Rosalind when we were babies, that's for sure. There's no photo of Phoenix, either. It makes me wonder, you know, if Phoenix and Hugo even talk to each other, or what their relationship is like. He seems absent in this house, as absent as we are.

I search underneath the rolled-up stuff to see if there's anything else hidden under there. Way in the corner my hand hits the tight plastic edge of a Ziploc bag. It's full of . . . Impossible for my fingers to tell. Marbles? Round objects, with weird indents. I slide it out. I almost scream.

Oh shit! *Shit.* What *are* these? A bag of fake eyes? Glass eyes—brown, green, and blue. They look at me but don't. I get my courage up and pluck one out. The glass is cold and hard. The eye is greenish, like Hugo's, like Rosalind's. I mean, it's too weird. I seal the bag and put it back. As I do, my fingers hit another one. Nothing can scare me after that. I yank it out and see a small chip-thingy inside. A tiny green rectangle, with metal squares; viewed from above, a miniature city.

The photo in Aurora's frame changes to one of Hugo and Aurora on Halloween, and it's shocking and surreal, because he's Superman and she's Wonder Woman. Wonder Woman! Should he be William Moulton Marston instead? I'm not sure why, but I'm suddenly overwhelmed with the desire to take this chip. So I do. I put the whole bag in the pocket of my tiki pajama bottoms and close the drawer.

It fills me with a thrilled terror. What if it's the most important thing in the world to him, this one chip, hidden here? What if he discovers it gone tomorrow morning, and it becomes a household emergency? What if he doesn't even notice? At first I think I stole it for Mom. On her behalf, I mean. She'd rather have some piece of expensive jewelry, haha, but that's not the point. *What* I took from him isn't the important thing—it's *that* I took from him. When Mom says her sarcastic *It must be nice* whenever she sees him going on an amazing trip or whatever, she says it like it's something she deserves. He's robbed her of that, you know. And I've always just gone along with that as truth. It's been happening for so many years, I never even questioned it.

But as I'm standing in their room, the lake water all shimmery out there, that chip in my pocket, I think, *Wait.* Why *would* she deserve it? I mean, all of this is his, and it's here because of *his* success. She's not owed it just because she was with the guy. Even if she had us kids, she's not owed the payoff of his hard work. Me and Ros, though . . . *We* might be. A person can change their mind about a partner, but a kid is permanent. I want that chip for me, is what I'm saying. I want to take something important to him.

Wait. I think I hear footsteps.

I listen.

Yep, those are footsteps, all right. Of course, because this is asking for trouble, and I've been in here way too long. I'm *going* to get caught. First this whole Eleanor Drake thing, and now . . . I am *definitely* Miss Fury, discovered in Baroness von Kampf's bedroom. I stand there, my whole body frozen in position, my fate decided by the artist.

The door pushes slowly open. I brace myself. It'll be Hugo or Aurora or Greta. Whoever it is, it's going to be *over.*

chapter
Fifteen

BOOLEAN'S NOSE APPEARS.

"Out, out!" I mouth, and wave my hands. He's making for the bed. Oh man—his front paws are up there already, now his big hindquarters. I'm sure he's not supposed to be on the bed. I grab his collar and drag, yanking and pleading. Greta's going to hear this, for sure.

I manage to haul him out. I shove Boolean's big butt into my room and close the door. I make *sure*-sure it's truly shut this time. We're safe, we made it.

The monitor, however, is back in that bedroom.

These are the things that make you wonder if you're *determined* to destroy your life.

I race down the hall, retrieve the monitor, race back. But look. That office is just a few steps away.

Oh, Eleanor, I hear my mother say. *You just don't* think.

I listen at the door of the billionaire scientist's laboratory. All I can hear is the blue-light buzz-hum of technology, his computers left on. I imagine that buzz-hum getting louder and louder, not just in this house, but everywhere, like a warning of imminent catastrophe. Not just my world coming to an end, but all the world as we know it.

This is so unwise. Who knows what kind of security gadgets are operating here. Ones I can't even imagine. He could be watching me right this minute.

I push the handle. I expect to hit a lock, but that's not what happens. It goes down all the way, easy, no problem. It's open. I could go right in.

When it comes to defiance, and even spying, I hit my limit. I hurry back to my room, my heart beating harder than it maybe ever has in my life. If I were Miss Fury . . . Well, clearly, I'm not. I set my hand to my chest to calm down. I force myself to breathe.

I hold my net gain in my hand. One silly chip-thingy. It looks cheap and meaningless in that bag. For a moment, though, I fantasize that it's like the vial that Miss Fury steals, the one that holds the most dangerous and closely guarded secret substance, Acrothorium. That stuff is so powerful, it can disintegrate what looks indestructible. It's capable of destroying lives and empires, just like that.

WHEN I'M FINALLY CALM, I SIT DOWN AT THE DESK and pull out the drawings I brought, and my art supplies, too. My bad guy, my villain—he isn't one anymore. He's Nino Gemini. Not a stalker, but a window washer. A really odd yet attractive window washer. Remembering him, I'm filled with the ohmygod of my humiliating semi-tackle. I crumple up every drawing I've done of him so far, because they're all wrong. I was wrong.

I take *Miss Fury, Summer Issue, No. 2* out of the drawer. I thumb through, pausing on the pages where Bruno and the baroness and Gary Hale are in Rio. That Nazi, Bruno, insults a South American waiter with the racial slur *half-breed*. Tarpé also spells out their speech in an exaggerated caricature of an accent, and the Brazilian men are portrayed as hypermasculine and aggressive. There are more tropes coming in the next issues, brave gauchos on horseback in the countryside, seductive spicy women dressed in frilly samba attire. I wonder for the hundredth time if I should crumple this, the whole book. Tarpé—she was wrong, too.

As I sit here with my pen, something else gnaws at me—the thing Aurora said about Hugo Harrison, and how he gets super pissed when he's criticized. He's got so much power that you're not allowed to disagree with him or think badly of him. Aurora, with her clothes and the food, ordering what he does, sneaking my steak, she's trying to get everything *right.* I get it. I remember Mom, patting her stomach to indicate my splootch. Miss Fury is amazing, the way she can kick those dudes to the curb, the way she's sexy and brave. The way she's the true first female superhero, created not by the famous William Moulton Marston but by the overlooked Tarpé Mills. Yet there's another problem: Miss Fury's body is still that supposed ideal, one that even William Moulton Marston would approve of. It's oh-so-similar to his Wonder Woman, his perfect female fantasy, with her pointy boobs and slim waist, curvy and slender both.

Tarpé Mills said that she never used a model, that she stood in front of a mirror and looked at herself to draw her figures. But Marla and Miss Fury—no real woman has or ever has had that shape, not even Tarpé Mills. It's another trope.

What do we do with so much bad shit? I asked Arden Lee.

Learn from what was right, then do a whole lot better than what wasn't, he said.

I text him right now. *Is every woman in the Golden Age comics a male fantasy, batting her eyelashes at the dude?*

He loves this kind of discussion. He answers right back. *Miss Fury doesn't bat her eyelashes. Otherwise, yep.*

I type, *Should we just ditch every single old issue from that time?* I wait, watching the text circles of thought.

You can't ditch history. Sometimes you want to, but you can't. Before I answer, he sends another text, the pile of shit emoji. I send the same shit back.

Now I do what Tarpé herself did—I stand in front of the

mirror by the door. I lift up my shirt, study my actual body. I sketch her again, Miss Fury, Marla Drake in her disguise. I make her breasts look more like my own—flatter, rounder. I make her waist a little wider. I give her a soft stomach. I try to capture the way I really am. I try to see . . . me. The character doesn't look as . . . well, *good,* I think. That's my honest first thought, because parts of my brain still operate like William Moulton Marston's, I guess. It's probably hard for a brain to think for itself when it's been trained by other people for years and years. Since its very first days, and even before.

I start to color her in, the soon-to-be superhero on the page. She's not just a bunch of vague lines. She's got a long way to go, and I don't even know she's mine yet. But I try to like her, the way she really is. I try really hard to see a young woman, not just a collection of faults. Not just a series of parts I can improve.

BOOLEAN HEARS THE CARS ARRIVE. HE BARKS AND flies down the stairs, as much as a huge dog can. I try to listen to the story play out.

They chatter. Hugo sounds happy, maybe the super happy of being intoxicated. Aurora laughs, and I smile, so glad to hear that things are going well. I hear her heels clicking as she heads into Arlo's room. I watch her on the monitor as she leans over and kisses him good night. She tiptoes out. I hear the door of their room close.

He's still in the kitchen. I want to see him so badly. I look like shit, but who cares. This is how I look, me, his daughter, in my same old pajamas. I grab . . . What? My empty water glass. I hurry down the hall so I can bump into him accidentally on purpose.

I make it as far as the office, that mysterious and confounding place, that big question mark of a laboratory, when he arrives at the top of the stairs.

"Oh, hi," he says.

It's definitely alcohol happiness. His eyes shine. The smell of wine forms a cloud around us.

"Hi! I was just . . ." I lift my glass in the air. I realize how stupid this is—my room has a bathroom, and I can get water any-time I need it. "Getting a snack."

"Snack attack," he says. It's something a dad might say. He'd pick you up when you were a kid, say it into your neck, and tickle you. It's friendly enough that I suddenly feel super guilty, not only for lying to him about who I am, but also for stealing a chip from his underwear drawer.

"Snack attack!" I make a doofy gesture, sticking up my finger as if he's got a great point.

I'm sure he's about to walk past me to meet up with Aurora in their room, but no. He's holding the office door handle, just as I did earlier tonight.

We stand there looking at each other until I realize he's wait-ing for me to leave. "Right!" I say, which makes zero sense.

He smirks.

"Well, good night." Okay, that's that. Five seconds with him. People would die to have even that, I know, but this is my dad. I want to know if he misses us or thinks about us ever. I want to know why he was okay just letting us fade out of his life. I want to know if he ever felt odd or unseen or alone, even with his own family, like I do sometimes. I want to know if we're the ones who are the same, as Mom and Ros are, because I want that so bad. I want to know if we might like each other, as people. If he would like me. See? If I were my real self and not Eleanor Drake, the nanny, I'd probably overwhelm him with emotion, same as Mom did.

I step away, giving up, when he says it. "Hey. Aurora says you want to study computer science. Machine learning. AI."

She did? I do? Here it is, the first chance to tell my father the truth of who I am. Instead I give him who he wants me to be. I know how to do that, just as Aurora does.

"That's right! Yeah, I love that stuff," I lie. "I can't even believe I'm standing here with *you*. . . . I mean, it's incredible." The truth, 100 percent.

"Cool," he says. And now he does that thing again. He opens the door so I can look inside. When I *do* see, he lifts one eyebrow. He grins. The eyebrow says, *Get it?*

I think I do. I should be marveling, struck with awe, but instead I have the uneasy sense I'm Marla Drake, when General Bruno reveals the disturbing scientific invention that will allow a man to be rebuilt, piece by piece. Hugo's watching my face, though. So instead of Marla's shock and outrage, I grin back.

Now he squinches his eyes, as if actually taking me in for the first time. "You look really familiar," he says.

My breath stops. Yeah, and I know why. We look the same. He might have Rosalind's eye color, but his teeth, his smile . . .

The way he's standing there right this minute, nose wrinkled . . . I look like that, a lot. People so often don't see what—or who—is right in front of them.

"No idea," I say.

He shrugs.

I shrug.

Same shrug.

I blush. I turn so red that it's a confession.

He heads into that office.

I never do go get that snack.

What I see: that woman, the one I thought was Laura, the long hair . . . She is in the exact same spot, in the exact same position.

It isn't Laura.

It isn't even human.

Arden Lee, who's always right, is right again.

"Good evening, Hugo," I hear her say.

chapter
Sixteen

NO ALARM BELLS RING OVER THAT MISSING CHIP. NO one notices its absence. On Friday morning I stuff a few belongings into my backpack for my weekend off. Arlo's still asleep. I tried to explain last night that I'd see him on Monday, but time must be a strange concept for kids and animals. *Here* and *not here,* too.

It's mostly been just Arlo and me together over the last few days, aside from one trip with Aurora to the Green Lake pool, when Arlo and I swam around in the shallow end. I still have no idea what she does all day, but she seems to be perpetually stressed. I haven't seen Nino again, or much of Hugo, either. He's been coming home late, and then he and Aurora have a glass of wine together. They talk about everyday things, like Aurora's headaches, or what Leo Gemini said, or Mathew's new girlfriend. And they talk about not-so-everyday things, like *the release*, which I think means that robot. I hear him in the morning, those weights clanging in the gym, his loud voice over the blender as Jak makes him a smoothie. But there've been no more encounters. I'm the nanny, Eleanor from Eugene. With my Boeing worker dad and teacher mom, the details are so boring, I've barely had to add any new ones. I also got paid, money sent right into my Venmo account with its playful, anonymous username. In one week, I've made three times what I make at Armchair Books in a month.

I'm zipping my pack when there's a sound on the monitor. It's Hugo, in Arlo's room. Weird. I've never seen him in there before. *"Whoa, oh, oh, sweet child o' mine,"* he sings. He's play-ing air guitar, too, and dancing toward Arlo's bed. The lyrics are about innocence and pain, no idea what song. I just wish he'd be quiet and that he had picked a different time to show up. Arlo woke up crying last night from a bad dream, and it took me, like, an hour to get him to go back to sleep. He's going to be so cranky if he wakes up this early.

It's silly, but for a minute my throat gets all tight, and I think I might cry. There are those lyrics, *sweet child o' mine*, and, ugh, I just wish . . . Too many wishes. So many that you can't take them all apart and name them. They're just one big ball of wishes, which, I guess, is pretty much the same thing as longing. Hugo leans down and picks up Arlo. Arlo's all sleepy and disoriented and looks around the dark room, confused. The nanny part of me wants to tell him to stop, but there's a daughter part that maybe just wants to be lifted up that way. Ugh, it's hard to admit that.

But, yeah, what *is* happening? Because Mathew, Hugo's executive assistant, appears in Arlo's room, too. He's talking to Hugo in his brisk way, referencing a problem that's now fixed. Mathew reminds me of a buzzing fly, annoying people, sure, but getting his own thing accomplished.

Hugo gives Arlo to Mathew. This is all really bothering me. Arlo likes things in a certain order. First, as he wakes up, there are lovey-hugs and quiet chatter. You open the blinds and check the day. You talk quietly about sun or clouds or birds. He doesn't get handed off to some assistant while he's still in his frog pajamas.

I haul my bag up to my shoulder. I feel inside my pocket to make sure the chip I stole is still there. Now the monitor only shows the gray-blue emptiness of Arlo's bed, that eerie hue of twilight and dystopia. I shut it off. But I need to understand what's going on. I just have a bad feeling about this.

I hear them in Hugo's office—Mathew, Hugo, and Arlo. "Arlo no want!" he cries. I can't tell what's happening. It's upsetting.

"Good morning, Arlo," the robot says.

I feel a horrible swirl inside. Maybe this is the missing anger that Arden Lee and Clementine are always talking about. It feels more like helplessness, though.

I should bust in there, Miss Fury–style, and stop what's going on. I'm not Arlo's parent, though. Hugo is. Well, Hugo's mine, too, and look at the mess he made of that.

I force myself to leave. I have no power here, that's for sure. And there must be some reasonable explanation. Downstairs I bump right into Greta. She seems to be waiting for me.

"Good morning." Her tone cuts. "You're off, hmm?" She seems to be implying that I'm up to something bad. I am, but I'm beginning to wonder if *she* is, if *they* are, because what is going on here? I just don't get it, why you and your assistant would wake up a toddler and bring him into your office with your creepy robot. Maybe that's a normal morning around here, who knows.

"Good morning," I answer. "Yeah, I was just heading out."

"Did we get your NDA?"

"NDA?" Okay, I have no idea what that is. For a split second I think she means NDE, near-death experience. I might be having one right now, as she stares at me with eyes that make me think she knows that Eleanor Drake from Eugene is a fraud.

"Nondisclosure agreement?"

Wait. I've heard of them. You sign something to say you won't reveal secrets about a company, right? "I never got one."

"Aurora didn't give it to you?" Greta is unpleasantly surprised. I'm sure she has many fine qualities. I mean, there's a lovely blanket in Arlo's room that she crocheted for him, and the Soggy Pages Book Club will confirm that no character is all bad, but she seems bitter and displeased a good portion of the time. If, or when, she discovers my identity, I doubt I'll be making cookies with Granny. I'm also worried I got Aurora in trouble.

"Oh, she probably did," I say, throwing my own self under the bus for Aurora's sake. I mean, she's got a lot of tire tracks on her back already. "I'll be sure to turn it in!"

"Good," Greta says as she leaves. I suddenly feel so nervous and uncomfortable that I don't even stop to grab one of Jak's amazing breakfast sandwiches he's carrying to the kitchen table. I just give him a wave, and he gives me a thumbs-up, and I head out.

Outside I breathe in summer, and the delicious murky-water smell of being by the lake. I startle when I see Aurora sitting on the front lawn, though, with Boolean next to her. No one's ever out front. Aurora's painting her toenails. It's all hard to understand—why she's here, up so early, and painting her nails when she gets manicures.

"Tangerine Fling," she says, and holds up the bottle.

"Nice," I say.

She tilts her head, examining the job she's done so far. "Kind of a mess." She doesn't sound unhappy about it. Maybe the opposite. Not exactly happy, but defiantly pleased.

"Arlo's with Hugo in his office?" I watch her face, but it's hard to read.

"Right." She waves her hand near her toes to dry them.

"They woke him up. He was crying," I press.

"He's part of this research," she says.

"Research?" It's another Miss Fury frame. The one where the baroness discovers that the evil scientist has involved her child, little Darron, in a series of mysterious and deadly experiments, but she barely seems to care.

"Machine learning," she says. "Believe me. I've got my eye on it."

It's pretty unconvincing. But I *have* to believe her. If I don't, I swear, I'll *definitely* be in a Miss Fury storyline, when Marla kidnaps the baroness's child to save him.

"Well, thanks for the week," I tell her. "I'm going to miss the little guy."

"You've been amazing. He *loves* you." She spits on a finger, tries to remove a smudge of orange. You never see a smudge like that on Instagram.

"I love *him*." It's true. So true. What does *machine learning* even mean? What are they doing with my baby brother? I don't get *this*, either, Aurora out here, acting strange. "Are you okay?"

"Is trying not to lose your shit *okay*?" She raises her foot and admires it. "Not bad! I like."

She's acting slightly . . . unhinged. "It's none of my business," I say.

"Sometimes I just hate looking at that thing," she says.

I wonder if she's referring to the robot. But then I understand. "That pink sign?"

"This is the only place you can't see it."

"Oh," I say. You'd think it would be amazing, that neon declaration that says you own this whole world. It's brighter than the stars and the moon.

I spot a familiar truck, blue, driven by a very attractive nonstalker. He doesn't park across the street this time. Nino Gemini looks straight at me as he pulls into the driveway. He waves and I wave back.

Aurora lifts one eyebrow. "You two know each other?"

"We met the other day." *Met*, meaning tackled. I blush.

"Huh," she says, intrigued.

"Does he come here a lot?" I ask. I still don't understand why a window washer would sit in his truck and watch the house at all hours.

"He's my best friend's son, so you'll see him around. Lucky, right?" Now she grins like mad. "Hmm. Maybe I'll ask them to come to Mexico with us in a few weeks. I just *love* love."

I put my face in my hands.

"I am *definitely* asking them to come to Mexico."

"Aurora!" I shriek. We sound like we're in junior high. The tension and weirdness evaporate. Aurora and me, we're suddenly two friends having a blast. I keep forgetting how young she is.

"What?" She fakes innocence. "They've come with us lots of places. He's homeschooled." She shrugs, as if this explains things.

"His mom, too?"

"Homeschooled?" She laughs, and I do something I would with Clementine or Arden Lee. I shove her playfully. I shouldn't do this. She's my boss, even if she's also my twenty-eight-year-old stepmother. "Nah, they're divorced. She's kind of . . . an introverted artist type. Stays to herself. She's a painter. Gwen Geary?" Aurora says, as if I might know the name. I tuck it away for future reference.

"That's so cool." I remembered that, of course. I remember *every* word Nino said. I want to tell Aurora that *I'm* that same type, an artist, or that I want to be. After Ros and Mom, though, I don't dare. *Well, everything takes practice,* Mom said, meaning, *You're not there yet.* As if creativity has an end point of perfection.

I *know* I haven't arrived. I need room to suck and be imperfect and figure it out. I hope there's never an end point.

As I watch the back of Nino getting his equipment out of the truck, it hits me, about the bad pedicure. Maybe with all the pressure to be perfect, Aurora just wants the joy and freedom of sucking at something, too. It makes me feel close to her, sitting on the grass in her cutoffs and sloppy tank top.

"Too bad artists are a dying breed, because, hey, AI."

It's a beautiful summer morning, and I'm sitting on the greenest grass near the bluest lake, colors that might look unreal but *are* real, the most original art there is. Behind me there's the most incredible glass house you've ever seen, with a genius inside, a man who's my father, who I hope I'll get to know. A boy shuts the doors of a truck and strides toward us with a big smile. Everything is possibility, everything is future, but when Aurora says that, I feel a sense of dread. In *Brave New World,* to create perfect humans in a perfect society, the first things that had to go were the messy truths of love and raising kids and creativity, the freedom to be a unique individual. I'm not sure what's going on with that robot, but I just feel doom. I hope we don't lose the best things while trying to construct something flawless.

"I'm out of here," I say.

"You're not going to stay and talk to him? He's heading right over."

Nerves win. My own flaws feel like neon signs. There's a chance to be perfect if you hide.

"Chicken," she says, and I flap.

I wave to Nino again, and he waves back. It's easy to get a ten out of ten on a wave. Talking, having a real relationship, not so much. Ros, pure gold, would have no problem.

I get all the way to the Land Rover when I remember that NDA. I should've told Aurora. Oh well. I make sure that chip is still in my pocket before I start the engine. Heading home, I say a prayer to the God of Motor Vehicles that I don't wreck their jillion-dollar car.

I'm down the street before I realize that I forgot to say goodbye to Boolean, which makes me so mad at myself.

chapter
Seventeen

FOR TWO WHOLE MINUTES I'M PURE SOARING EN-
ergy. It's this exciting escape from my own lies, in an expensive
car. Wow, the sound system in here! I could drive south and keep
going.

But I go home. We've lived in our house for about five years,
after our last rental was sold. *A fresh start!* Mom had said, though
she'd looked tired. It's a place Hugo has never been. Mom's so
proud of *doing this all on my own,* and *holding this family together,*

but when I imagine him beside me, arriving here, I visualize her pride slipping, tumbling, crashing.

Whoa, it's such a weird mess of feelings. I mean, our house is small, *so* small, and I never realized it before. My room at the Frame House is practically the size of our living room. And it's a mess. There's so much stuff. Our couch is a purple velvet that Mom thought was *sexy and romantic* when she bought it. Now it's worn and faded, and so is the matching modern throw rug. *Modern*—we got it at Home Depot on supersale, so what do style words like that even mean? There's a cup of half-drunk coffee on the end table, white swirls of milk gathering in constellations, and Rosalind's laundry sits in a heap on a chair. A pair of Mom's old tennis shoes have been tossed off by the door, and one has something tarry on the bottom. The venetian blinds have a few bent spots from the time Ros and I hate-love wrestled. Mom had yelled, *Someone's going to get hurt,* but only the venetian blinds did.

In the kitchen there's a scattered stack of mail on the counter, and a colander filled with browning bananas. Gnats circle, miniature vultures. A lasagna pan soaks in the sink, and there's another cup of coffee in the microwave, warmed but forgotten. In the fridge a bowl of mac and cheese covered with plastic wrap is still here from when I left, along with take-and-bake pizza leftovers and the tiniest wedge of butter flecked with crumbs and jam. I make a peanut butter sandwich on a paper towel plate and carry it to my room.

My room: It's a mess in here, too, but it's my mess. I hate it and I love it and I never want to leave and I want to get out of here and never return. It's such a relief to be home, and it's so sad here. I belong at my father's house, I belong at my mother's house, I don't belong anywhere.

I feel so strange. The smallness, the mess, the evidence of being alive—it's truth, a lot of it. There's nothing hidden. You can almost see the struggle of our lives, the struggle of living in general, how it takes a lot of effort and energy and will sometimes just to be a human on our complicated Earth. No wonder we don't want to see that, the truth and the struggle. The thing is, the too-bad-est thing is, that we can work our butts off to hide it, to make it all pretty and pristine, but the struggle is there anyway. Try to hide it all you want, try to force it into some endlessly positive shiny thing, but it's a lie.

Instead of apps that rate people and show photos of settings and characters, there should be an app for this, for mixed feelings.

I TAKE A SHOWER IN THAT TUB WITH MOLD GROWING between the tiles, which features an array of shampoo bottles with a quarter inch left. Then I head over to Clementine's. In the Land Rover I sniff my shirt. It smells kind of moldy, too. It probably always has, I just never realized. I roll the windows down and wave my arms around, trying to dislodge the odor, ugh. Be free, mold!

Clementine's house is our favorite place to hang out. There are no adults, aside from Clementine, who could out-adult most real ones. When we're over there, we never do the clichéd things teens are supposed to do when they're unsupervised, like have parties and drink or whatever. Instead we're the grown version of ourselves. Clementine cooks for us, and the Soggy Pages meets, and we say what we really think. Of course, Clementine's *always* unsupervised since her mom took off last year, leaving her the house and a scrawny bank balance.

Our house is small, but Clementine's could fit into it, same as those nesting dolls. But hers is super tidy and organized, as if Clementine's afraid things will landslide out of control if she leaves a spoon in the sink. The paint is fading and the linoleum is cracked and the floor tilts, but there is no horse and no Pippi, just Clementine, doing her best to take care of Apple without anyone knowing they're alone. Talk about wearing a disguise.

When I drive up, Arden Lee's shooting hoops in Clementine's driveway, using that rusty old basket with the shabby fringe of net that came nailed to the garage. This is Arden Lee in the full-on glory of sucking, just enjoying what he does badly. We do not sigh and tell him, *Well, everything takes practice.* He's vulnerable in his love, so we quietly encourage, with only the occasional *Nice shot.* Arden Lee is about five foot three, as skinny as a pencil with eraser knees, and there's no way this dream of his will ever come true. I mean, he will never achieve his goal, there will never be enough classes, or trying, or practice, or whatever to get there—to some level of being a pro ballplayer like his dad, or even a member of our high school team.

But, God, *why* do we always think about some end point of achievement, like the dream is shit unless it happens? So what if the dream is fiction? Arden Lee and Clementine and me, we know that fiction *saves.* Sometimes it brings you somewhere you couldn't see before. Arden Lee's dream is safe with us. Maybe even sacred with us. It takes a lot of courage to suck.

I get out of the Land Rover to the sound of *bamp bamp bamp clatter* as the ball hits the pebbly cement driveway and smashes into the rim. Clementine looks up from the dandelion she just plucked from a sidewalk crack, its roots dirty and suddenly exposed.

"Hey!" I say. Arden Lee whistles in admiration of my sexy ride. I haven't even been gone a week, and I've missed them so bad. It's just so good to see my friends that I want to cry. I seriously want to just bawl my eyes out.

Instead I run, my arms flung out, like a dramatic scene in a movie featuring reunited lovers. In the movies you never see friends do this, but cue the music. There's none of the withering humiliation of the Nino Gemini run-tackle. Clementine catches the hug, and Arden Lee joins from the back. He takes it up a notch, jumping up and down and screeching, "ELEANOR!" He can be like a little dog, the easily excitable kind that loses its shit when a doorbell rings on TV. Whenever Miss Fury races toward someone, she's taking down a bad guy, but my racing always has something to do with love.

"Group hug," Clementine says, as you do.

CLEMENTINE MAKES US A BEAUTIFUL GREEK SALAD, minus the expensive olives. I feel bad that we're using resources that she needs for her and Apple. We bring her stuff, though, and

I see the bags of groceries Arden Lee bought with Jackie's help. When Clementine's not looking, I jam some money from my paycheck into the container of tea bags, where she'll definitely find it. Clementine loves her tea, even in the summer. The members of the Soggy Pages Book Club are generally against the tiring, forced pairing of reading and sex, the *Reading Is Sexy* T-shirts and book bags, but we do love our traditional reading accoutrement, tea in a good mug.

We carry the food to Clementine's backyard, a square of sandpaper grass, always dry. There are lots of holes back there, and you have to watch your step so you don't twist an ankle. The previous renter must have had a dog and kids, because we've found old chew toys and Barbies. Once, I even spotted a Super Ball poking up from the ground, an undiscovered planet in the universe of dirt, like the hopeful last scene in a movie about the world ending.

Arden Lee chooses the folding lawn chair that Clementine repaired with duct tape. I sit in one of the molded white plastic chairs with the wobbly leg, and Clementine sits in the other. I can hear Apple's voice rising over Clementine's fence as she plays next door at the Kumars'.

"Well?" Arden Lee shakes his copy of *Brave New World,* salad balanced on his knees.

"I skipped around. I didn't really finish," I say.

"I did more than skip. I quit," Clementine admits. "I hated it."

"You're *supposed* to hate it!" Arden Lee leans so forward in his woven chair that he threatens to tip as he defends his literary territory. I should mention his stylish shorts: green plaid, with a vintage Hawaiian shirt, and his favorite fedora. We *all* dislike it when readers say they hate characters and situations that the author meant for them to hate. "The *whole point* is to be grossed out by the creepy stuff they did to achieve the 'perfect' society!" Arden Lee makes air quotes around *perfect*.

"I get it. I'm just so tired of hating things," Clementine says.

"When they were manipulating little kids, I just couldn't do it," I say.

"Totally agree." Clementine sips her lemonade. Or rather, her water with the tiniest sliver of lemon and lots of sugar. "If that's the future, let me off here."

"You guysssss. You can't just shut your eyes! We need to talk about technology!"

"Let's talk about it without reading *that* book," I say.

Clementine gets up from her chair and says, "Hang on a sec."

She disappears into the house. "You always do this with my picks," Arden Lee whines.

"That's a total lie."

"We didn't even discusssss," he cries.

"Individual liberty is valuable. Human beings are. Love is. Creativity is, relationships are. That should go without saying."

He shakes his head, chews his salad. Arden Lee doesn't like when we look away. When you have All the Books, you're not someone who averts your eyes.

Clementine appears, carrying a paperback. Okay, this is weird, because she only goes to the library. Anything she reads is covered in crisp plastic, a barcode on the front. This is an old, well-loved book, with a crinkled cover and yellowed pages.

I narrow my eyes. "Where'd you get that?"

"*The Agony and the Ecstasy,*" Arden Lee reads. "Sounds vaguely pornographic."

Clementine blushes. Not about the *vaguely pornographic,* either, but about my question.

Arden Lee and me—we get it at the same time. "Xavier Chen?" he says. We both realize something else, too, I can tell. There aren't exactly words for this, so it's more something that just happens. The way that Arden Lee has shared his vulnerability about sucking at basketball, and I've shared my vulnerability about sucking at art and being a daughter . . . Clementine is sharing her vulnerability at sucking at love. Or, at least, being new at it.

"He stopped by. He thought I'd like this. He, uh, heard me complain about the other book."

Because Arden Lee's a best friend and an all-around great person, he stops looking hurt about his Soggy Pages pick. And neither of us mentions that we *always* put the slips in Arden Lee's hat to choose our next read. There's a bigger thing we have to do here. "Cool," Arden Lee says.

"What's it about?" I ask.

"You might like it, El. I've only read a few pages, but it's about Michelangelo. How he had this pure, innate *fire* for being an artist, like, in his soul, and what that meant to him and his society. Like, the opposite of *Brave New World,* where they deprive their citizens of art because they think that art and literature can't be contained, and are therefore dangerous—"

"Exactly!" Arden Lee can't help himself. "That was so important! They were brainwashed to *not feel* all the mess and pain of life, but literature and art awakened that in them, awakened them to their own oppression, too! Like when John was talking about how you read words and you're *pierced*. How transforming pain into meaning is *the point* of art and life . . ."

Clementine and I ignore him. "Michelangelo's talent was something so ancient," Clementine says. "So true and deep. So *essential*. I think that's why he gave me this."

She hands it over, and I see it's, like, seven thousand jillion pages with teeny-tiny writing. Written in, like, the 1970s or something, by another old white dude. I only say, "We might need to add on some time for this one."

Clementine smiles.

Arden Lee takes his hat off. He puts the book inside and pretends to pluck it out, as if it's been chosen.

WE TUCK AWAY OUR BOOKS, AND ARDEN LEE HANDS around the foil package of the brownies he baked. "Okay, tell us every detail," he says to me. I've already told them a lot this week— Aurora and her fake Instagram, bashing into Nino, meeting both Hugo and a grandmother. But I haven't confessed everything. I haven't said a word about the unread library, or that robot, or the chip right here in my pocket.

"What's it like to actually live with him?" Clementine's never had a dad, either, so I'm the first of us to travel into the fatherland, a spy in a foreign country.

For a split second I feel conflicted about spilling the bad parts.

I just want him to be great, someone I could straight-up love. But then I look at my friends' familiar faces. We dislike all the clichéd phrases in books, like *dizzying sense,* and *companionable silence,* ones you see in reviews, too, like *took me apart and put me together again,* and descriptors such as *meet-cute* and *enemies to lovers.* But we have a mixed relationship with *found family.* We get it, the feeling, and yet sometimes Clementine says, *Bring back best friends!* The word *family* is just so complicated, with its particular disappointments and hurts, the way your shared DNA makes pain more painful. *Best friends* is mostly just beautiful. They are.

I tell them *almost* everything.

"All those unread books." Clementine shakes her head.

"You've got to find out about that robot," Arden Lee insists. "Really, Eleanor. Research? What the hell. You might, like, save the world. Miss Fury, for real."

"What is machine learning anyway?" I ask.

"Didn't you read those books I gave you?"

I snore and mime sleeping.

Now he mimes screaming. "We're all taking part in this stuff whether we know it or not. Well, same as all history, honestly. Okay . . . Machine learning . . . It's a subset of AI. It allows a machine to learn without being programmed. From the data it gets, it detects patterns, learns how to be an even better, smarter machine. Kind of how we do. Only, at a certain point, even the scientists have no idea how it works. It becomes so smart that it's smarter than our own ability to understand."

"What's he doing with Arlo?" Clementine looks as worried as I feel. "He's a *child.*"

"Arlo's probably helping to teach the robot, but what the robot is *for* . . . That's the thing you need to find out, El."

That chip is burning a hole in my pocket, like the all-powerful Acrothorium, capable of disintegrating metal. What if it contains a shocking truth that could harm Psyckē and Hugo? Those chips are *always* the downfall of the villain in any story, and I'm trying to love the guy here. But what if it has some important information about what's happening with Arlo?

I reach into my pocket, hold up the baggie with the chip inside.

"What's that?" Arden Lee's eyes widen.

"No idea, to be honest."

"Is it his? Where'd you get it?" Clementine asks.

"Hugo's drawer. Bedroom drawer. Just . . . Something came over me, and I took it."

"Oh wow," Clementine says. "Eleanor."

"I'm a horrible person," I say.

"You're the least horrible person I know," she says.

"You could never be horrible, El," Arden Lee says. "Plus, I do love it. You sly devil. You girl detective."

I feel kind of sick. "I want to know what's on it, but I don't want to know. It's probably nothing. And I have zero idea how to read it, anyway. It looks old. You stick it in something, but what, and then what?"

"I know someone who could tell you."

Arden Lee and I look at Clementine. We're kind of surprised, because Clementine knows the two of us and Xavier Chen and that's about it.

"Wait," Arden Lee says. Well, sure. Xavier Chen is quiet enough to contain worlds. "He's this awesome guy and he's tech savvy, too?"

The corner of Clementine's mouth tips up again in that smile that looks so very, very pleased.

She holds out her palm, and I drop it in. She closes her fingers around it. "Let's just see," she says, because seeing can change everything.

chapter
Eighteen

BEFORE MOM AND ROS COME HOME FROM WORK, I put a pot of spaghetti on and warm some jar sauce in a pan. What would Jak think of this gourmet meal? Who cares, because add some Parmesan dust from the big green plastic container, and you have magic, if you ask me. I'm glad to see my mom and sister. They're my people, right? My family, the only one I've ever known. We've laughed our heads off together, and had the flu at the same time. We've done Christmases and power outages and school-clothes shopping, you know? Here there are three stockings and three place settings. Only one person held this small family together.

They drop their purses and then change their clothes. Mom pours a glass of wine, and Rosalind cracks open a Fresca. "It's so good to have you home," Mom says. "We miss you!"

"We haven't even been making dinner," Rosalind says. "We just stand around at the counter eating takeout and talking."

The warm feelings I had about the three of us—boom, they're gone. But maybe my mind has also been collecting their wrongdoings like kindling, stick by stick, placing them in a mound and waiting for a match. "How adorable," I say. "We, we, we, all the way home, haha." It's sarcastic. Jealous, too, and it just pops out. What's wrong with me? I'm the one who's been off having the experience of a lifetime at that house. I pour the hot noodles into the colander as the kitchen window steams. Outside I count three crows on the wire. One flies off, perfect.

"Wow." It's clear from her tone that Ros is shocked at the crime I just committed.

"What?"

"Don't sound hostile or anything," Rosalind says.

I glare at her, and honestly, I'm not sure if I've lit the match or Rosalind has, but Mom definitely splatters it with gasoline. This is something else that's hard to explain, it all is, but I wonder if Mom's the one who actually gathers the kindling and readies the fire. Maybe she doesn't even mean to, exactly. "What a *brat,*" she says.

It likely won't sound very bad to people in other families, but what I say next is horrible in mine. That I say it at all is. I don't even know why I do it, except that Clementine's right. I *am* angry. I turn away from the heap of squiggly noodles and stare back at Mom. "Thanks a *lot*."

She and Rosalind look at each other in shock. I mean, you just don't do this, talk back. "What did you say?" Mom's voice is pure venom.

"I said, thanks a lot for calling me a brat. That's real nice."

"How *dare* you." It's so weird, but I feel like I've stepped off a cliff of not caring. Like, whatever, bring it on. I have no idea how we got here so fast. From noodles and dinner to rage. Hugo and Aurora have made me brave, maybe.

"We had a whole day planned for you tomorrow, too," Rosalind says. "And you drive up in *that car* and then act like *this*?" It's vicious, and her eyes flash. It feels like hatred. Now there are two of them, facing me like wild animals. Rosalind's beautiful face has gone ugly. Mine has, too, probably, though it's never been beautiful. It's never been her face, the one that looks like mom's, the face that *could be a model,* according to Brandi Diamond. Of course, I look like Hugo Harrison, I can tell you that much now. "Talk about ungrateful."

Immediately, guilt and regret pour in. I'm silent. A whole day planned for me, ugh. I *am* ungrateful. "Oh yeah?" I manage to choke out. It's half-hearted. I hate to even admit this, but it's also hopeful. Like, I want to know what they had planned. I want to know that they thought about me when I was gone.

"I got a membership at Gym Dandy, and it comes with a guest pass," Rosalind says. "We thought we could all go, and maybe have lunch at that vegan place, but I don't even know now." She picks up a fork at the table I set, presses the tines into the place mat. Gym Dandy is where Mom and Ros go. Rosalind has always gotten the guest pass before.

I'm supposed to be remorseful, but I get pissed all over again. I've never, not once in my life, wanted to go there. The red sauce *blop*s on the stove. I turn it off. "How is that for *me*?"

Mom's face turns to That Other Face, the one that waits just below the surface for any sign of criticism or betrayal or rebellion, which are maybe all the same thing. "Get out! Just get out! You spend the week at a fancy mansion and act like this? *You* left *us,* missy, and we're supposed to sit around and wait for you? Why'd they even hire such a self-centered brat?"

"Is that your favorite word?" Oh my God, what is wrong with me? I'm throwing all my cherished belongings into the blaze. She comes toward me, and I shove past her. I run to my room, slam the door. I put my back against it so she can't come in. I'm breathing heavy. I have no idea what just happened, how this all went so rapidly wrong. Okay, it probably wasn't rapid. They've likely been pissed all week about what I got and they didn't, and I've probably been pissed for years. And she doesn't even know whose fancy mansion it is yet, either. I'll be annihilated when they find out.

I can hear them both, talking in heated voices about the enemy in the house. *Who does she think she is?* Rosalind says. She's never talked back. She's more appreciative and more loyal. I'm the only brat.

I'm Miss Fury behind that shut door, with the knife flying toward her head. I feel like I'm made of pure poison. Think of every gross thing, all rolled into one, that's me. It's what I deserve, this grossness.

Eventually it's quiet.

I imagine that food growing cold, red sauce and noodles, blood and guts. After a while, I hear dishes clattering. I wish I could leave, like maybe forever, but this is the place that made me and still has me, maybe forever, too. *You can't escape history,* Arden Lee says. *History is who we've been and who we'll keep being until we do something different.*

I hunt for my inhaler and take a puff. I haven't used it all week. Maybe it's the mold. This isn't like the rash I haven't gotten, either, is it? I mean, I do need this inhaler, right? My chest is tight. I've been on albuterol since I was little. Every tiny bit of dust or allergen spins my system off the rails, and it's been that way since I was born. *You always had one problem or another,* Mom has said again and again. *I was at the pediatrician's every week! Up with you all night long. The nurses were always telling me, "We don't know how you do it. You are so devoted!"* I wonder if I'm like that robot, unreal, constructed by a human.

I take out the drawings I brought home. My new Miss Fury looks so inadequate with her splootch and her regular, not-golden body. She looks so *alone.* She *is* alone. I try to draw a new super-hero, an equal, who can stand beside her. It's Clementine, sort of. I give her orange braids, and a shiny turquoise one-piece suit that deflects harm. Is kindness a superpower? It should be, but it never is in the comics. Behind her and all around is a threatening zigzag of blue light, but she stands there holding a candle. It's like the one Pippi looks into, trying to see her father.

As much as my friends are there for me, and I am hopefully there for them, I can't tell them about tonight. I've never told anyone about these things. I don't know how I'd even explain them. People wouldn't understand how bad *Thanks a lot* can be. Arden Lee and Clementine might think I'm horrible, or my family is horrible. Rosalind and Mom might be all buddy-buddy, but they do love me. Niles used to always say how much Ros did for me and how I never appreciated her enough. What Mom has to do for us all by herself—I can't even imagine. I think of her, you know, alone in the middle of the night, responsible for two little kids. Sitting in a Goodwill rocking chair trying to get a baby to sleep, and helping us with homework after a brutal day at work. Do other families have this confusing ugliness? I don't even know. Compared to Clementine I have it good. Mom might be cruel sometimes, but she'd do anything for us.

Rosalind doesn't even knock. For a minute I think we're going to make up. Like, maybe it'll be us on the same side. Her face is all soft. She looks at me with the stern kindness of a parent.

"What is going on here?" she asks.

"What are you talking about?" So much for softness.

"Are you hiding something?"

"What would I be hiding?" My heart starts to thunder.

"Who are these people? Did you vet them thoroughly? Who gives a car like that to a . . . ?"

"To a *what*?" The thundering stops. Or else becomes another weather mass.

"I just mean, you're a kid with no experience, and now you're driving that? Like, where'd these people get their money? Is it, like, *drugs* or whatever?"

"*Drugs?* What in the world?"

"You met them through Jackie?"

"Jackie doesn't do drugs!"

She rolls her eyes and exhales, as if anything is possible, and I should know that. I've never even seen Jackie have a beer, but that's not the point. Like, why we're here, with Ros implying I could never just get a good job, *that's* the point. "Something's up," Ros says. "It's better for you to tell me now than for me to find out on my own."

Wow. She's really aiming for an Academy Award in the role of Mom, but the thundering resumes. That's the last thing I need, her hunting around for some truth. The real truth—it's way worse for the three of us than what she's imagining. "You *never* give me any credit," I fume. It's true, but I'm also fighting for my own Oscar. "This is a *great* opportunity for me. With a *wonderful* family. They believe I can do this job, and do it well, and you are just *ripping* me down! Can't I *ever* have anything for once? Something good that's *mine?*"

She folds her arms, stares out the window, where she can see the Land Rover. She sighs. "Okay!" she says quietly. "I'm sure it's all fine. But you need to say you're sorry to Mom."

"*Me? I* do?" Probably I do. I'm relieved Ros is backing off, but honestly? "She's so *mean.* And you guys gang up!"

"You have no idea what her life is like! How hard it is. The sacrifices she makes for us, El, really? I feel so bad for her! And then you act like a little shit on top of it. You made her cry. All she said was that she missed you."

We will never be on the same side. Not truly, not ever.

THE NEXT DAY THE THREE OF US DRIVE TO GYM DANDY. I sit in the back seat and wish I could vanish. Mom's voice is curt every time she speaks to me. I mumble and want to cry. Rosalind and Mom chat all friendly about this cute guy, Roscoe, who they sometimes see there. When we arrive, Ros hands over her card. She has a new gym bag. The woman behind the counter asks me if my mom is going to get me my own membership, too.

I shake my head. It seems awful to feel sorry for myself. With my new job, I can pay for three gym memberships, so what's the big deal.

I lift weights, but my arms woggle in protest. When Ros lifts, her midriff ripples like water, the gold belly button ring moving up and down. Her weights sound like Hugo's when they land, capable, driven. Probably, she's more like him, too. I try to ride a bike, but I'm suddenly really tired. I wish I could go home and read. Mom and Rosalind talk about the reps they did last week, and the goals for next, and Mom takes Ros's picture for Instagram. Roscoe arrives, and Mom and Ros poke each other like girlfriends. Mom laughs, all cheery, making the point that she's unbothered by my misery.

I miss Arlo. I don't necessarily miss the tensions that are also there at Hugo's house. But I do miss my brother's pudgy little hands and his eyes that seem like stars, both ancient and bright.

The vegan restaurant is a new one they're trying. They get the eggplant moussaka. Nothing sounds good to me, so I only order carrot cake, like the brat I am.

chapter
Nineteen

IT'S AN OLD BOOK, SO I HAVE TO HUNT FOR A COPY.
Luckily, there's one available at the Green Lake Library. After
today with Mom and Ros, I need the library. I need it to wrap its
big, comforting book arms around me.

There it is: *The Agony and the Ecstasy.* Well, yeah, that about
sums up life. Whoa, it's thick, and it's been here so long that it
smells like deep water plus an old closet. I briefly imagine all the
people who've read it before me, which can give you the creeps

but is also wondrous. I've always believed that everyone who reads a book leaves part of themselves in it, adding their experiences to the whole. The story plus the readers—it's humanity between covers. The good parts of humanity, the ones that want to respect and understand other people.

I walk up and down every aisle because I'm in no hurry to get home. I let myself be reassured by solar systems and royal families and forests and all of the biographies of people who lived through the wildest things you can imagine. Truth stranger than fiction for sure, and fiction trying to tell the truth. It's all so consoling. Here there are no lies about what's real or not; you know right up front: nonfiction, fiction.

I check out *The Agony and the Ecstasy* plus a few others, because it's still so amazing that you can just walk out of a place with a bunch of books and no one chases after you. Free! Wow, I'll never get over it. Then I head down the street to Java Jive. Clementine's working today, so we can't really talk, but I want to show her that I got the book. I spot her at the register. I wave, but she doesn't see me. I wave harder, really hard, book in hand, arms overhead. Clementine, God! She still doesn't look up, but several people inside do. One guy even starts to wave back, arms overhead, too, and—

Oh shit. Shit! What is Nino Gemini doing at Java Jive? Well, for one, he's sitting there thinking I'm waving at him, when I absolutely am not.

He gets up. He's coming outside. He's—

"Hey!" he says.

"Oh hey!" I say casually (haha). "What are you doing here?"

He looks puzzled. "I always come here. What are *you* doing here?"

"Just saying hi to my friend Clementine."

Now she spots me. Us. She waves, calm and reasonable.

Nino turns scarlet. It's a common descriptor in books, one that Arden Lee questions. He once showed us the color on his phone to prove that it's a reddish orange, and yet an argument could be made that this is the exact shade I'm seeing on Nino Gemini's face. "She's your friend?"

"Indeed." Okay, I'm a dweeb who uses the word *indeed* in times of stress.

"So, um, you were waving at *her.*"

"Mm-hmm."

"And I was just that person who thinks someone is waving at them when they're actually waving at the individual behind them."

"Yes. Yes, you were." My confidence is rising. Me tackling him is now becoming fractionally more equalized. I mean, we've got a long way to go, but an embarrassing and unfortunate wave interception is a nice first step.

He puts his head in his hands.

When he looks up, he performs a miracle. "Want to get a coffee?" he says.

FIRST I HAVE TO ENDURE ALL OF THESE BIG-EYED *What is going on here?!* stares from Clementine as she makes our drinks. I don't even bother introducing them, as they clearly know each other. Clementine starts right in on his order without even asking: a hot chocolate with a shot of espresso. And then she does mine, an iced tea, because it's cheapest, and I totally forget that I can afford the big caramel one with the whipped cream. I show her the book, and then we say goodbye. Clementine makes all of these elaborate thumbs-up *You can do it!* hand gestures behind Nino's back, like the coach sending me in from the bench during the big game.

"Want to walk?" he asks.

"Sure."

On the way to the path that circles the lake, we cross in front of the pool and then the basketball courts. I spot Arden Lee. He's there with the Over Thirty team, trying to one-on-one a guy or whatever. Arden Lee's knobby little elbow is trying to block this dude with thick, muscular calves who likely has a job and a mortgage. My heart fills with pride and also worry, the way it does when someone you love a lot is doing something they love and need a lot. Love is just so risky, whether it's a person or a basketball, and I care about his heart.

"So, you're not going to believe this, but I've read that book?" Nino Gemini says. Lest you think I forgot about him right next to me, let me assure you that I haven't. My throat is totally dry from nerves, but I'm sweating like that super-old guy on Arden Lee's team, with his shiny face and swampy underarms, ugh.

"Really? I was guessing no one's read it since . . ." I thumb through, and a whiff of old book cologne wafts out. "1961?"

"Michelangelo," he says. "My mom's an artist, I told you? I'm

211

homeschooled, and she's maybe too heavy on the arts and too lax on the math."

"So lucky." If Nino were in a regular high school, he'd probably be in a world of his own, like Xavier Chen. Tarpé Mills was like that, too, and they say the same thing about Hugo, how he didn't fit in. That's hard to imagine when people are drawn to him like he's a banquet and they're starving. Nino Gemini is less a banquet and more one of those strange dragon fruits you see in the grocery store, pink and prickly and who knows what's inside.

"I thought you'd love math. Aren't you into programming and AI and all that?" Whoa—Aurora's been talking about me, and here's my lie, causing a new problem. It's beginning to seem like lies are a nightmare of magic-trick scarves, where you keep pulling and pulling with no end.

"I'm more interested in the overall concepts? Like, its impact on humanity and stuff." *I'm more interested in Hugo Harrison* is what I should say. Hugo, and who we are to each other. I should tell Nino the truth of who I am right now, but I can't. Who tells the truth of who they are when they first meet someone anyway? Name one person who's that brave besides Arden Lee.

It's a late Saturday afternoon, crowded to the point that we're getting nudged by dog noses and strollers. By mutual agreement, we aim toward a free bench and sit. The remaining blossoms on the cherry tree next to us swirl down like snow.

"Its impact on humanity?" He looks hopeful.

I rapidly change the subject. "Hot chocolate with an espresso shot, huh? In the summer, no less. Revolutionary."

"Want to try?"

He hands it over. I take a sip, and our saliva mingles, maybe magically. "Wow," I say.

"Right?" He runs his finger over his lip to politely tell me that I have a foam mustache. He's a thoughtful person. I wipe it away. He asks me where I go to school, and then we're off, chatting about everything, discovering a mutual love of Sharpies and onion rings and unscheduled days. He cracks me up a few times, and I make him laugh, too, and his hand edges so close to mine at one point that I think he might hold it.

Man, I like him. It's going along so easy, you know. Our drinks are finished. "How's it been, working for the Harrisons so far?" he asks.

"Yeah. It's, um, interesting." Since he works for them, and his dad is Aurora's best friend, I'm doing what Aurora does with Hugo, searching around for an answer I think he'll approve of. One that will make him like me, and where we'll agree. I wish so bad I was one of those people who only says what's true for them, and not just about onion rings. Did I mention how intriguing he looks? Very intriguing. And how his eyes just make you want to fall into them? Very fall-in-able. But now he looks at me kind of funny. His nose scrunches, and he studies, really studies, my face. I'm afraid he's noticing how similar I look to Hugo. Maybe I've just tilted my head in the same way he does. "What about you?" I ask him. "Do *you* like it?" Classic deflect.

"Well, my dad and Aurora spend a lot of time together, so, you know, I, uh, hear a lot."

I wonder what this means. Now *I* squinch *my* nose. We're sitting on this bench squinching at each other, and I swear, he's going to ask me if I'm Hugo's kid. "They're best friends, huh?"

"Um . . ." He rubs his chin like he has a beard, which he certainly does not. It's adorable. "I don't want to say anything negative about your new employer when you just started."

I get a sudden bad feeling in my chest, as if darkness is taking a seat in there. "You can say something negative. It's okay." But it's not. I mean, yeah, I'm searching for information about my father, but the truth is, I'm searching for *good* information about my father. I want to like him, and maybe even love him. I want to understand the reasons why he left us, because there *must* be reasons. I mean, I live with my mom—even *I* see reasons. I want to admire the man who made me, too, even if, especially if, Mom and Ros despise him.

"Well, you asked about them being best friends, but my dad's an employee? He likes her. They have fun together, sure. Just, anytime she needs him, which is a lot, especially lately."

I suddenly feel very sorry, though for who, it's hard to tell. For Aurora, who thinks that she and Leo Gemini are real friends, or for Leo Gemini, who doesn't have any real choice about it. The word *real*—it sure comes up a lot in the Harrison universe.

"Oh. That's too bad."

"I think it's an issue for their employees? In a general way? I've heard that at Psyckē, they play it up hard, how it's a great privilege to work there, for him, how they're changing the world. But there's all this unpaid overtime and people working to the point of exhaustion to please him, only he doesn't really even notice them.

But it *is* a privilege to work for them. I'm grateful. My dad is, too. He's an astrologer. Before this, he just did people's charts."

"There's probably not a lot of astrologer positions on LinkedIn," I say.

"Exactly. My mom worries that they take advantage of him? My parents are still close, even though they're divorced. My dad's gay, but they're each other's person. She's protective of him. She's already pretty pissed about Frame."

"For the bad art it makes?" I think of my camel in a beret. The way the images feel soulless.

"For the theft."

If I were actually a huge AI fan like I told the Harrisons, I'd probably know what he was talking about. Ugh, the biggest problem with pretending is the need to keep pretending. "Right," I say. "The theft part is so wrong."

This seems safe. Theft is generally not awesome. I'll look it up later. I've made a mess, though, a bigger mess, because Nino thinks we're on the same side. Employee and employee, theft hater and theft hater. "It's like if she'd had lung cancer or something, and he worked for a tobacco company, right?" he says. "I don't know why I'm telling you all this. You have a very understanding face."

"I do?"

"Like a flower or something."

I turn scarlet. He turns scarlet. Fuck it, Arden Lee, it's scarlet, all right.

Something marvelous is maybe happening. Absolutely destined for catastrophe given that we are *not* two employees, not at all.

There's so much potential marvelousness, and he's being all confiding, so I risk it. "You've got to tell me something. . . . I've seen you around their place before. Watching it? In your car sometimes. Like, *why*?"

He freezes, caught. He stares at me, like I've just snared him in my FBI sting operation. Finally, he speaks. "That's so weird. I thought I saw *you* there before. I almost went to talk to you one night."

Oh man—Mom and Ros are so right, the way I don't *think*. Questions go both ways, and now he's just snared me in *his* FBI sting operation. "Um," I say. "Before I started working for them, I wanted to see what they were about. What I was getting into." Truth.

He nods, as if he understands this. "Are you a daffodil or a Venus flytrap?"

He's asking if he can trust me. Well, look, I'm Hugo Harrison's daughter—of course he can't.

"Daffodil."

"Okay. So, I watch the house because . . . something weird is going on there."

"Like what?" Like, a million things.

"My dad said he saw this woman being carried in and out of that house. I saw her, too. I thought she was real. They bring her, *it*, back and forth in an SUV."

I think of the NDA. I don't know where my loyalties are supposed to lie. It hits me, how DNA has the same letters. "The robot. The big surprise product he's releasing soon. You'd think he'd keep it a better secret."

"So you saw her, too. The thing is, why is he bringing her *home*? What is she going to *do*? Something seems . . . off. Wrong. And Aurora . . . Dad says she barely comes out of her room lately. What's going on with *that*?"

I nod but say nothing about my sleepy brother being carried off. I watch a family having a picnic on the grass. So normal, how rare.

"Maybe we should find out," he says.

My stomach starts to hurt. If Hugo is a villain, my heart will break. And if I don't have him, I won't have anyone. Arlo, though. With his pure sweetness, with his little spirit just trying to be two years old in a big world . . . All he has is trust.

"We should."

Nino and I meet eyes, in a pact, in a shared mission, and maybe something more. We are so brave, because neither of us blinks. We see each other. It's calamitous, because he's got that warm glow, not a shiny gold glare, not a blue tech hum, but the sincere and deep light of a good person.

Tell my heart, tell my whole body, that *insta* doesn't exist.

chapter
Twenty

CLEMENTINE IS A CONSCIENTIOUS EMPLOYEE AND never uses her phone during work, so I don't start getting texts from her until that evening.

How do you know J.W., the hot hot chocolate guy?!

It takes me a minute. J.W. John William, his real name. *That's Nino Gemini! The window washer! Nino is what his friends and family call him!*

NO WAY. He's a regular!

So, you think he's hot?

ARE YOU KIDDING?

Clementine and I both like dragon fruit. I send a smiley-face emoji, then another one with hearts. It's so summer-fling-fun, the shelf of pink-covered romance books, when it's really another shelf entirely. Dystopian fiction maybe. Or not a shelf at all, just some old box stuffed full of Golden Age of Comics back issues from the *Bell Syndicate*. Good and evil, glamour and intrigue. Stuff cooked up in laboratories in order to destroy the world.

Something seems . . . off. Wrong.

Rosalind cooks dinner, since she says Mom needs a break. She makes veggie burgers, and we clink our forks and sip our water in uncomfortable silence. Rosalind acts like the peacemaker and asks me if I've had the chance to use the Von Barons' pool yet, and if the chlorine has bothered my skin. I don't know why, but I tell her I haven't gone in. Maybe I want to sound like I'm working as hard as they are, or maybe I don't want to risk sharing the new, rash-free me, or maybe lies are just a regular part of my disguise now, even meaningless ones about swimming. I wonder what the price would be to take it off.

Ros also asks me what it's like to drive that Land Rover. *I'm jealous! Must be NICE.* The only other expensive car that's ever been in our driveway was Niles's BMW, which used to be his dad's. I tell her it looks better from the outside than it is in, that the stereo system is broken, and that it smells superstrong from Mrs. Von Baron's perfume. None of this is true. I'm trying to even out some scorecard that's been wrongly shifted in my favor, I guess. I'm up and they're down, and that is not the way it's supposed to be.

I do the dishes and go to my room. Clementine doesn't like to leave Apple alone after being gone all day, and Arden Lee is having a *NeverEnding Story* movie night with Jackie and Carlos, so it's me with me tonight. Carlos seems to really be trying. Sometimes his ideas would be perfect if Arden Lee were eight or nine, but that's okay. Arden Lee will take all the ages of ideas that Carlos has.

My door is closed, but I can still hear them—Mom and Ros watching *their* favorite movie, the one about a couple who falls in love on a cruise ship. Ice clinks into glasses, and then I smell popcorn. It's hard to relax, but I stretch out on my bed and read a few pages of *The Agony and the Ecstasy*. It's wild, you wouldn't believe it, but it opens with a thirteen-year-old Michelangelo sitting before a mirror, trying to draw himself, making his face more perfect for a sculpture he's planning. I cheer when he convinces this older mentor to take him on as a student. Michelangelo is just this young guy, and he's got a passion, an actual soul-burning passion, for his art. How can I not think about Tarpé Mills and me, and all of the artists going back eons, sitting in front of mirrors, learning from those who came before? He's trying to make art that originates in his own body and spirit, his authentic self.

I set aside the book. On my old laptop I look up Nino's mom, Gwen Geary. She has her own Wikipedia page, even. *Gwen Geary is a contemporary feminist painter known for her depictions of women from Greek mythology and the Arthurian legend. Her work comments on the objectification of "other" in Pre-Raphaelites like John William Waterhouse and explores themes of the portrayal of women's power in historical art, particularly the trope of the enchantress.* John William Waterhouse—the inspiration for Nino's real name. Tons of photos pop up, too. Her work reminds me of those fantasy images you see everywhere, straight out of some tale about King Arthur. Hers, though, feature women who look contemporary and real. There's a painting of an older woman with short, spiky blue hair instead of the more typical long braid of the Renaissance, standing by a fantasy waterfall, her arms sagging with age, her neck lined. Another shows a woman with a gray ponytail and a nose piercing, who's still somehow straight from mythology as she rides a boat down a river, her gaze far off.

Wow. Nino's *mom*.

Now I look up *Frame app* and *art* and *theft*. What Nino meant . . . Apparently, Frame works by gathering up millions of images from artists everywhere. It learns to recognize the patterns in the works, and then re-creates them in essentially the same style. So when anyone uses Frame to make art, or display art, or sell art, they're basically starting with plagiarized images, the heart and soul and talent of other people. In terms of a job and being paid—an artist's own work plays a part in eliminating need for any future work. And once their stuff is in there, once a piece of art gets used as a dataset, there's no undoing it. What the machine learns, it can't unlearn.

Theft, all right. Add an exclamation point in a dramatic font. It's artistic plagiarism, the worst word of all, if you ask the members of the Soggy Pages Book Club.

What would it be like to see my drawings, or a version of them, appear on Frame? The ones I did of my body, even? Just taken from me to be used and reused and changed, as if I, the person who created them, never existed?

I'm sad. It's disappointing. I mean, I like Frame. It's fun. I really admired Hugo for making something so cool. For a moment I'm overwhelmed, just truly blown away, by all the taking and using, by all the ways people don't see each other—stereotyping, judging, diminishing. Overlooking each other entirely. The Brazilians in Miss Fury, and Whiffy, and all those characters of the Golden Age and beyond—they're real human beings made into caricatures for profit. Those blank glass eyes in Hugo Harrison's drawer . . . I hate this, but they just make sense, you know.

Do I have enough evidence already that Hugo is a villain? Honestly, what could ever be a reasonable enough explanation for pretending that two kids don't exist?

As if he heard these very questions, my phone buzzes with a text from Arden Lee.

Can you meet up? The three of us.

Now????? It's eight-thirty. Not late, but not a time we usually get together.

The chip.

Dread thrums in my body again. *He found something SO FAST? Just tell me.*

We have to show you. The rocket, in twenty?

I send a thumbs-up. The rocket is a few blocks away, a huge old statue from an Army-Navy surplus store, now decorated with lights and the Fremont motto: *De Libertas Quirkas,* which means *freedom to be peculiar.* There's probably a German word for that.

I lie, of course. I tell Mom that Arden Lee needs my extra charger, so I'm meeting him quick. After I shut our front door, my hands start to shake. The word *evidence* circles my brain like a shark. Only, it's me it's going to destroy.

Am I going to be okay? I text Arden Lee. But he doesn't answer.

I SPOT THEM, STANDING LIKE TWO BEAUTIFUL, ODD space explorers under the sparkly lights of the rocket. Arden Lee holds Jackie's iPad. I seriously consider fleeing, but they spot me, and Clementine waves. I get a lump in my throat. I'm so grateful for them, I can barely stand it.

"El," she says. She hugs me. She hands me the chip back in its baggie. This is bad, bad.

Arden Lee nudges his toe to Clementine. The nudge says, *We can't stall this forever.*

"He's not my father, right?" It's my best guess. Or the thing I most fear. I'd have no one then.

"What?" Clementine looks confused. "No. No, he *is*. But the chip . . . It doesn't have some great big takedown of him on it or anything. It's not going to save the world. It's mostly just private stuff, old emails and documents from like, a bunch of years ago, and . . ."

"Just tell me."

"Some baby photos."

"Baby photos?"

"You and your sister. I mean, we've seen the ones your mom has in the hall."

I let out a sound. A gasp, a half sob of hope and disbelief. "Show me," I say.

Arden Lee opens the cover of the iPad and then a file he's saved to the desktop. He clicks. One at a time Arden Lee enlarges an image, then moves to the next. It's us, all right. There's Rosalind as a baby, being held in arms that must be Hugo's. I recognize her, with her little baby chick fluff of golden hair. And there's me, in a romper, lying on a blanket on the grass. Rosalind sits next to me, legs crossed, her hand on my head protectively. And there's one of me alone, so very newly born, eyes squinched, the world too bright as it always would be, but you just have to look anyway.

My throat cinches. I blink away tears. I wipe my eyes, but, damn, I can't stop them. I start to cry. My friends put their arms around me, and we're a huddle of astronauts as the ship prepares for blastoff. I was wrong. Hugo *did* have photos of his babies in that drawer, same as Carlos. Why would he have them? Why would he keep these? One reason, right? Only one? I hold that baggie like it's life itself. Worries about robots and artists and unseeing eyes vanish. My heart fills with love and grief. All these years we could have had together, you know.

"Does this mean he loves me?" I ask.

"Oh, El," Clementine says.

I don't know it yet, but in that moment I'm Miss Fury for sure, parachuting out of that shot-down plane. Trying to save her life, but falling, falling, right into the hands of the enemy.

chapter
Twenty-One

ON SUNDAY MORNING I GET A FRANTIC TEXT FROM
Aurora, asking me to come back a day early. Like, basically *now*.
I'm scared that they discovered that missing chip. *Everything okay?*
I ask. The family is heading out on a boat trip, she says, and she's
desperate for another pair of hands. Relief. *Be right there,* I answer.

I tell Mom that something came up with Mrs. Von Baron,
and her eyebrows go down in a concerned *V. I hope she doesn't*

make a habit of this, she says. According to Nino, she will definitely make a habit of this.

I pack up in a hurry, making sure to remember my inhaler and
my drawings and that chip. After seeing what was on it, I *want* to
return as fast as I can. When I got home from the rocket, I went
immediately back to my stalking habits, hoping for more, more,
more of him, the man who kept those photos. He had seventy-five
glowing new Rate Me reviews! Okay, okay, they couldn't be based
on real encounters, since they occurred in Nevada, and Southern
California, and Missouri, when Hugo was home, but still, they
were all so good! I read a new interview, too, in *Esquire,* with
a reporter named Shaun Shrupti, titled "Beauty and the Best."
It featured an image of Hugo holding the high-heeled foot of
what had to be his robot. The suspense is building and building.
He's incredible, he really is. And there's part of that incredible
man, even a secret part, that loved and maybe still loves two little
babies, grown now.

I just wish Arden Lee and Clementine didn't seem more worried about me when I left last night than when I arrived.

⬛⬛⬛⬛⬛⬛⬛⬛

THINGS ARE STILL BAD WITH ROS AND MOM, SO I GET
in the Land Rover with both the relief and the guilt of fleeing.
The Frame House beckons with its shine and newness. I greet
Boolean, then drop off my stuff and head to the boat. "Thank
God," Aurora says when I arrive. She holds out her hand to help

me aboard. Wow, that boat—it's a chic house on water, with teak furniture and bright decorative pillows. Aurora doesn't bother to chat but instead heads over to Hugo, who stands by the wheel. He ignores her, and both of their faces are tense. I follow Arlo's voice. He's down below with Jak, who's unloading a ton of picnic food.

"Boo boo!" I say, and Arlo drops a bag of snacks and runs to me. I lift him up, and we have a cheek-kissing reunion.

"Little dude was being a big helper!" Jak says for Arlo's benefit.

"Is that right? Way to go!" I ruffle Arlo's hair. "What exactly is going on?" I ask.

"The guests are late. Hugo and Aurora are arguing about who will be captain." Jak makes big *uh-oh* eyes. He slaps the fridge closed and hauls up a cooler. "I'm out of here. Have . . . a time."

I snoop around down there, discovering bunk rooms, one that's clearly Arlo's. I spot his bag and make sure he's slathered in sun lotion, and then we hop around and play on the triangle bed before Arlo climbs up the ladder again. On deck I watch Jak hurrying away as Greta heads toward the dock. She's wearing one of those floral skirt-type bathing suits, a gauzy cover-up, and a big hat, which is bound to blow off in two seconds. She frowns, as if going out on this big, beautiful yacht is quite the chore. I imagine this grandmother meeting my other grandmother, and then I have the shocking realization that they'd maybe get along great. Arden Lee hates when characters have shocking realizations.

Aurora keeps looking at her watch dramatically, making a point that the guests are still not here. I hope they hurry, because Arlo only has two good hours before he'll need a nap. We sit at the outdoor table, playing with a sticker book I found in his bunk. It's marine-themed, and Arlo puts an anchor on my head. It's an excellent choice, metaphorically speaking.

"T knows *nothing* about driving this thing," Aurora confides to me. She's definitely pissed. "Ugh. I just don't have time for this!"

For not doing much, she sure seems frazzled all the time. But I make the same face she does, just as a mirror would. I don't bother to ask who T is. "Did you have a great Saturday?" I ask. According to her social media pages, she and Arlo were at Shilshole Beach, eating crab legs and corn and potatoes cooked over a bonfire.

"I was home. Doing a bunch of, uh, paperwork." So those were Laura's toes in the cute strappy sandals, then. I wish Arlo had a stand-in, so he didn't have to work so hard.

Finally, a couple strides down the dock. "Ahoy!" the guy shouts. They've got a little girl with them, and an older woman, who seems to be the nanny. I doubt we'll be hanging out.

T has the scruffy start of a beard and expensive deck shoes, and his wife, or whatever, has blond hair swept up in a Dairy Queen swirl, two strands framing her face. Greta greets him in the longest hug ever. She actually holds him at arm's length and studies his face, beaming. Before long we're underway, and it's the strangest role reversal ever. T shouts commands at Hugo, and he just follows orders, hauling up the buoys and stuff as T points and yells. The woman, Jennifer, sits by Aurora. They can't find a groove of conversation and just keep staring at Arlo, the way people do with kids and dogs when they don't have anything to say.

The little girl, Hailey, goes below with her nanny. She and

Arlo seem like two people who've met before but decided they have nothing in common, and I see the girl and her nanny playing a board game. By the look of it, it should be called a *bored game*.

I try to appear enthralled with sticking a plastic jellyfish on a laminated beach, when I'm really listening in. There's all this BS-y social catch-up stuff, asking each other about work and the kids and all, but what I notice is how Greta keeps complimenting everything that T says. He's talking about how a long crack appeared in his driveway and he had to fix it, and she's going, "You're always so incredible at home maintenance, Trev."

Trev. Trevor! I should have guessed. Hugo's biography rolls through my memory: his birth here in Seattle to his mom, Margaret, and dad, Albert, long dead. His brother, Trevor, two years older, who he used to play video games with, igniting his love of programming. My *uncle.*

It's a glorious day, suddenly made a million times more interesting. It's hard to concentrate on how glorious, because, oh man, the stickers are finished, and Arlo is totally done sitting still. Keeping a little guy safe is tough enough on land, let alone on a boat that's zipping through the waters of Lake Washington, heeling over as it picks up speed. Luckily, it's lunchtime and Arlo gets buckled into his booster seat, and I get a break from chasing. The food looks amazing. The other nanny and the girl are still below, so I have no idea what to do. But Aurora hands me a plate, like I'm part of her family. I *am* part of her family, even if I'm the only one who knows it.

"How's the bot business?" Trevor asks Hugo.

"The robotics are beautiful. We're working on her *relational potential* now." Hugo wiggles his eyebrows in intrigue. His family's in on the robot secret, I guess, but even they don't know what her purpose will be.

"She's going to be the perfect wife?" Jennifer guesses.

"Hugo would love that," Aurora says.

"A friend for sad, lonely people!" Trevor makes a pouty face. It's total *Backpfeifengesicht.* At least, *I* want to slap it. Bummer. He's been my uncle for such a brief time, too.

"Hey, that would save lives." Hugo's voice is defensive, but it seems like an act. I don't think the robot is going to be a friend.

"I seriously don't understand why you didn't just start with someone else's machine and add your own AI," Trevor says. He's got a black olive in his teeth from the tapenade, haha. Go, olives, you little condiment revenge pros.

"We're out to change the world, T! Fix the most essential issue that *exists.* Every detail must be flawless. The eyes especially. I examined *hundreds* of them."

"Hers look like mine," Aurora says quietly.

"They look like *Susan's,*" Greta says cruelly. "And her face musculature was off for more than *a year.* Her eyebrows . . ." She makes her own look all wonky. Trevor laughs.

"Uncanny valley!" Jennifer shrieks.

They all seem to know what this means, though I have no clue. Aurora flushes in anger. "Do you have any *idea* of all that's involved?" She takes off her sunglasses and stares straight at Jennifer and then Trevor.

"Whoa, Aurora! Down, boy! She always thinks she has to

protect me," Hugo says, as if it's unimaginable. It *is* unimaginable, that someone so powerful would need defending from the group around that table. "But she's right, because—" Hugo reaches for a hunk of papaya. He pretty much smashes it into his mouth as juice drips down his wrist. I hate to admit it, but even *this* is compelling. "There are *hundreds* of reasons you might cross into the uncanny valley. Think of all the data in any interaction—visual, dynamic, shit down deep in the unconscious, flashing through your cranium so fast, you're not even aware! What do you expect of a person, if you come close, speak, touch, say this word or that word? If you smile? What happens to another person's pupils, the crease around the mouth? The vertebrae, the muscles? We need our subjects to *believe,* the way you believe in a story, without pause, without the snap that breaks the belief. We need to replicate the *essence of being human.*"

Hugo's voice has amped up, and his gestures have gotten large, but his audience is unimpressed. Greta looks bored, and Aurora watches a party boat pass with her lips clamped tight, and Trevor and Jennifer eat shrimp, Trevor sucking the juice from a tail like they've heard this a hundred times. Even Arlo only gnaws his pita. But I can't take my eyes off Hugo.

"Uncanny valley is innate," he continues. "It's animal instinct, our most basic protection. We're on alert. And yet! And yet . . . This is an immensely possible endeavor, because human beings *want* to believe in magic, too. Badly enough to shush the unease, to be successfully *tricked* by light and mirrors. And high tech." He laughs. Aurora rubs her arms as if she's cold.

"How's it going in the appliance business, Trev?" Greta asks.

"There's been a huge run on Insta-Hots," Trevor says. "Unbelievable sales numbers."

"So great!" Greta covers his hand with hers.

Right then and there I watch Hugo deflate like a balloon. He might be a giant in the world, but here he's a puddle of wrinkled rubber and escaping helium. I'm not a giant in the world, but I've experienced that same thing. Hugo Harrison, genius billionaire, all at once feels more like my father than he ever has. I understand him in some deep and inexplicable way. It hits me, hard— his biography, our shared story, our plotline. Single mom, no dad. One older sibling.

You have to find out the history, Arden Lee said, and here it is.

Uncle Trev may not be one of the most famous men in the world, but he's golden, all right.

HAILEY'S NANNY COMPLETELY IGNORES ME AS THEY play Jenga. This whole trip feels like Jenga, anticipating who might pull the final piece that will cause the whole structure to topple.

I read Arlo *All the World* and lay him down for his nap. Family drama must take it out of him, because he falls asleep immediately. I feel exhausted, too. I can't believe it, but I actually feel sorry for Hugo, who maybe wants the one thing in all the world that money can't buy. I find a chair in a quiet corner near Arlo's room and take out my phone.

Uncanny valley: It sounds like the setting in a glorious novel about the Amazon, or a land that time forgot, or a place way in the future where the last people on Earth discover untouched beauty. That valley would have a waterfall, and astonishing tropical plants, for sure.

But no. Uncanny valley isn't a place at all. It's a moment, that very moment when a realistic robot goes from cool and interesting to creepy and disturbing. When our curiosity switches to unease, alarm, and even horror. When our instinct gives the warning that a "human" is a fake and might be dangerous. I wonder if this instinct was hardwired into us for the future we're facing, same as the urge to run was hardwired for our prehistoric past.

The goal for robots is to override our instincts. The fake should be so perfect that our warning system never kicks in. The success of the thing is how well it pretends to be something else—

Someone as harmless as we see ourselves.

"Whatcha looking up?" Hugo Harrison says.

He startles me. I look at his nose/my nose. I want to get to the part where I see him as my dad who kept those photos all these years, but mostly he's still just the guy that used to have sex with my mom. That's what we've always heard about the most. Now I try to picture them even having a conversation. It's like what Arden Lee says, though, how he can't understand kids who want their divorced parents to get back together, because his are like salt and pepper. Mine aren't like salt and pepper, even. Mine are pepper and a banana.

The thing that he wants, the one thing money can't buy—it's what I want, too. "Uncanny valley," I say.

"You know what? I really like your inquisitiveness, and your interest," he says. He jabs the air between us with one finger. "A-plus."

I blush. His praise is helium into my balloon. "It's all totally fascinating," I say. It is. *He* is.

The thing is, I don't realize that I just changed everything between us. It was the perfect moment to be there, giving helium, receiving helium.

Just like that, he's big, buoyant Hugo again. Honestly, it's hard to tell which one is the real him.

chapter
Twenty-Two

THAT WEEK THERE'S A PHOTO SHOOT WITH LAURA and Arlo at a state park, the two of them on a forested trail in matching khaki shorts and white tees. We go with Aurora to toddler yoga, a private lesson taught at the Bellevue Botanical Garden, where we Downward-Dog in the Japanese teahouse. There's also Concepts of Coding, that this guy, Chester, teaches by the pool. It basically involves me putting stickers in various spots on a train track so the train goes different directions, because Arlo refuses. I've barely seen Hugo, and if that robot is still in the house, it's leaving Arlo alone.

"Swimming saves me. No one can hear you cry underwater," Aurora remarks as she towel-dries her hair in the Green Lake pool locker room before we go home. Well, maybe not *home,* but at the Frame House I don't wake up wondering where I am anymore.

"Are you okay?" I ask. I ask her this a lot. I've never seen anyone *less* okay. It's hard to understand why she's always in a rush, stressed, slamming her laptop closed when you walk in, like she's got weighty secrets. Now Arlo's out of his damp bathing suit, but his hair is still flat and wet, and it makes his worried eyes look even larger. On Aurora's Instagram today she's wearing a new bikini aboard the *Hugo Naut.* Laura must work out a lot. Her body and Aurora's look similar, but Aurora has stretch marks from having a baby, and her muscles aren't as firm. It seems sad to erase those truths of Aurora or any woman. I mean, look at Arlo. Here's a brand-new human being who never existed before, a real, beloved tiny person, who will have his own story, and feelings, and dreams, and his eyelashes are so beautiful. You'd think we'd want women to show off any bodily evidence of what it took to make that happen, but no.

"All you can hear is *blub, blub, blub,*" Aurora says. I really like being with her, you know. Once, when we were both kneeling on our mats in the teahouse, she glanced at me and I glanced back, and the whole absurdity of what we were doing hit—on our knees, our butts in the air. And she cracked up. Just busted up laughing, and so did I. Arlo rolled on his back like a puppy and laughed with us. Desiree, the instructor, told us to focus, as if we were naughty elementary-school kids. It was just a great moment.

Before I met you, I thought you did hot yoga and stuff, I said, back at the car.

Toddler is my speed, she said. *Actually, I kinda hate yoga,* which made us bust up all over again.

Aurora's been revealing other things about herself, like how she's deathly afraid of heights, and wishes she had more friends, and how she went through a whole year as a kid eating only frozen corn and fish sticks. I've been helping her with her outfits pretty much every evening. I see why people like Nino's dad just do whatever she asks, because . . . Well, this is hard to admit because it's the biggest betrayal of all, but I kind of love her. In Miss Fury we get a few nice glimpses of the baroness. Her humanity. She's not all bad. Sometimes we see where she and Marla both have the same struggles as females in the world.

"I'm worried about you," I say.

Her eyes get watery. We're there in that uncomfortably steamy locker room, and I can't wait to get outside, but I don't dare move.

"It all got so far off track," she says, mostly to herself.

I don't know what she means exactly, but it reminds me of Concepts of Coding, where one decision changes the direction of the train. I assume she means her life, and the way it altered the day she met Hugo in Paris. She's been telling me stuff about him, too. Them. The way there are three people in their marriage—her, him, and his idea of himself, which also has to be fed and loved and cared for. She tells me how she tries to build him up, but the more she does, the more she herself disappears. It reminds me of the baroness again, her and General Bruno. But it also reminds me of Mom, telling us stuff we don't want to know. So much stuff that you start wondering if it's the whole truth.

She has this perfect existence, so it's hard to feel sorry for her. But she's also just a human being who doesn't see how incredible she is, and I want to make her feel better. I know nothing about her life, though. I'm just me, an almost-senior in high school, pretending to be the nanny. I'm still literally a kid, even if the adults in my life keep forgetting that. I mean, the sex thing that happened with my mom and Hugo Harrison—I had to look it up. She told me when I was, like, nine, and I hadn't even kissed Finn Lahruti yet.

"You're amazing," I say. Aurora shrugs.

We gather our bags, and Arlo wants to be carried. He waves his hands toward Aurora, *up, up, up,* but she misses it, so I lift him instead. I kiss his hair, still smelling of chlorine, in consolation. My kiss will never be her kiss. My *up, up, up* will never be hers.

When we pull into the driveway a few moments later, Aurora stops to stare at that incredible house, its 2,019 panes of glass.

"Frame would never exist if it weren't for me," she says.

"He doesn't deserve you," I say. It's the kind of thing I say to Mom when she talks about how she's done everything for us while Hugo Harrison lives his grand life.

I have no idea that Aurora is actually confessing something.

━━━━━━━━━━━

THAT SAME AFTERNOON, DURING ARLO'S NAP, I'M reading *The Agony and the Ecstasy* by the pool when Nino appears with his equipment. He spots me and waves. Michelangelo's friend has just asked him, after a hundred days at work, if he gets tired of drawing leg after leg and arm after arm and torso after torso, and he's just answered that they're *never* the same, that every leg and arm and neck and hip are different, with a true character of their own.

I set down the book and head over. "You got new glasses," I say. They're round and adorable, like two little cookies on his face, so cute I could bite them.

"I can see even better now," he says. "Hmm. Daffodils have brown eyes with flecks of green."

Neither of us blushes this time. We stare right at each other, all fake confidence. He taps the toe of his sandal to the toe of mine.

"We should exchange numbers. I forgot last time."

"We should definitely exchange numbers."

He hands me his phone, and I hand him mine.

"Anything interesting happen this week?" he asks.

I don't tell him all I've learned about Aurora and the Harrisons' marriage, or anything I've discovered about my father: How he leaves the garbanzo beans on the side of his plate, how he lifts weights in the home gym to Cat Power's "Ruin." How he gallops Arlo around on his neck as Arlo holds his hair like reins. How he'll do something unexpectedly sweet—leave a heart of flowers on the table for Aurora—and then something unexpectedly mean—zone out when she talks. How he mostly doesn't notice my existence but will sometimes ask me a question from the practical to the whimsical, like how long my dad's been an engineer (*fifteen years,*

I answer) or what my favorite summer memory is (*being here now,* I say).

I also don't tell Nino how these small pieces make me realize there are hundreds more, and how being here makes me too aware of all the days I haven't been. Hugo—he has so much to learn about those babies in the photos, too, on that chip still hidden in my bag.

"Not really," I say.

"Hey." Nino picks up my hand. "Once upon a time there was green polish."

" 'What we know of others is our personal secret,' " I say.

"*The Agony and the Ecstasy?*"

"I wrote it down for our book club," I say.

"You're in a book club," he says. He's doing that adorable thing again, where he's rubbing nonexistent chin whiskers.

"With my two best friends. I forgot you don't already know everything about me," I say. "It seems like you could."

"It seems like I will? Tell me a thing right now."

I'm Hugo Harrison's daughter, I want to say but don't. That's what I should tell him.

"When I'm at the eye doctor, and they say, *Better here or here?* I want to say, *Better somewhere else entirely.*"

"If I weren't at work, I'd kiss you?" His glasses steam.

Can you feel insta-everything? I kind of want to grab his butt and squeeze. Just, gimme him. "If I weren't at work, I'd let you?"

"I'd better get going. The Harrisons hate a smudge."

chapter
Twenty-Three

"AND DID I TELL YOU WE HAVE A NEW IT GUY, DAVID?" Mom says. It's night, and I'm on the dock. Mom's voice is coming through my ear right next to Hugo Harrison's yacht. The pink neon light shouts for attention in the sky.

"The one with the great smile," I say.

"He has a great smile. And he's there in a second if you have any issues. Rosalind sure has a problem with him, though. She gets downright bitchy when he's only trying to help. I told her she needs to see Dr. Paula about her PMS, because *honestly*."

"Right," I say.

For days after our argument, I got the chill—the cold, abrupt voice Mom uses when you're being punished. It's like being sent to Siberia without the airplane ride. Little by little there was a thaw, winter turning to spring. I served my time, and she's back to being friendly. It's funny, I worried about getting away with this whole thing, but it's actually pretty easy. Now that we mostly talk on the phone, I realize I'm primarily the listener, which works out perfectly. If I just keep asking her stuff, I can go a whole conversation without revealing anything.

"Acupuncture can be helpful for mood disorders," she says. "Maybe Ros isn't happy. Does she seem unhappy to you? She's been biting my head off right and left."

"No idea," I say. "How's that annoying Denise at work?"

"Oh my *God*," she says.

Out of nowhere Boolean blasts outside. A demon has overtaken him, and he zooms around, hunched low, totally off the rails. Totally ignoring Hugo, too, who's calling his name and clapping his hands for him to come back.

"Mom, I've got to go."

"How are things over there, anyway?"

"I've got to go *now*."

"Okay, honey, we'll talk when you can!" Actually, she does not say this, not at all, are you kidding? In real life, the chill returns to her voice. "Well. Since you're so *busy*."

Boolean races down the dock. He's aiming right for me, and

he'll knock me into the lake, I'm sure, but he takes the corner with supreme canine skill and bolts back.

"Boolean!" Hugo shouts.

"Who's that?" Mom asks.

Shit. Shit!

"Uh, the neighbor. The dog got loose."

"I thought you said they had a cat."

"The neighbor's dog! I've got to *go*!"

"Seriously, you—"

I hang up. I'll apologize later, because Hugo's on the lawn, heading my way. God, I hope she couldn't make out his voice. Boolean zooms past on lap three. "Boolean," I say, low and commanding. "Cookie."

You can almost hear the click in his dog brain. It's like Concepts of Coding, when I make the train choose a different track, only this train screeches to a halt. He sits, the perfect gentleman. Wow, the things he'll do for a treat that's gone in two seconds. And, sure, there's a robot dog, but does he make you feel this mix of frustration and joy? This one, this real dog, he's 100 percent himself—comedian, skilled zoomer, giant love boy. His mess is his charm. I grab his collar and haul him off the dock.

"How'd you do that?" For a moment Hugo's not too busy or involved to notice me. He's right there, real human with a real human, and because he sounds proud, I want to say it: *Remember me? I'm your daughter. I'm here. I know you've never really forgotten, not with those photos right there, tucked in your drawer.*

"It's what I do with Arlo sometimes. Distract him with something he likes even better than the bad thing he's doing."

"Hey, cool. Good with kids *and* dogs. Impressive." *It's me, Eleanor Diamond,* I shout inside. *Impressive me—I'm yours, yours, yours!*

"I'd better give him a cookie now, though," I say, taking one from my pocket. "A deal's a deal."

"I'm taking notes," Hugo says.

"It's a short note: *bribe.*"

He laughs. God, it makes me happy. Like I just climbed a mountain. "He's been wild since we lost the dog walker, Sierra. We've got to find another one."

Boolean crunches his dog biscuit, and then Hugo turns to me under the light of the moon and the neon.

"Wanna have the coolest experience you'll ever have in your life?"

I'M IN HIS OFFICE. LET ME REPEAT, I'M *IN HIS OFFICE,* the secret laboratory, the lair, the inside of his brain, the place few people are ever allowed. I'm taking mental photos so I can tell Arden Lee and Clementine everything. My heart is beating hard.

He's going to show me the robot, I'm sure, but I don't see her anywhere. Just a long desk, and four different screens and boxes full of stuff, their flaps open. The swivel chair where the robot sat is empty.

He gestures to it. I sit. I remember the scene in Miss Fury, when General Bruno takes Marla captive after he discovers that she has the metal-disintegrating powder, Acrothorium. She uses it to destroy Nazi tanks, but he wants it for his own terrible aim—to build a man with human parts.

He reaches for a headset. "Okay?" he says, asking for my consent.

"Sure," I say. I try not to look as scared as I am.

He puts it on my head. Niles had something like it, and you could pretend to play sports without playing sports. It covers my eyes, sends me into darkness.

"Your favorite spot on Earth . . . ," he says.

I realize it's a question. I haven't been very many places. I think of the time Arden Lee and Clementine and Apple and I went to Bainbridge on the ferry last summer. We just hopped on and got off and walked around, but it seemed like a dream. It doesn't sound like enough.

"Hawaii," I say. Of course I've never been.

The light fills the screen. The beauty does. I'm suddenly in a world, and that world isn't even Hawaii, it's so much more, I can tell you that. The colors are extraordinarily vivid and beautiful, the light is, and there's even warmth, a breeze, some beautiful scent. I'm walking without moving. A trail opens to a beach, and the sky is magnificent. The ocean is. There's a turtle, and flowers, and, and, and . . . My whole body fills with a sense of peace and love and a feeling I've never ever had—just of being in exactly the right place, a place where I belong.

"What do you think?" Hugo says.

His voice is an interruption. I don't answer. I walk. The flower is the most beautiful flower. The shell is the most beautiful shell. The ray of sun is like holiness shining down.

Hugo lifts the goggles from my face. It's abrupt. I'm almost angry. I'm standing in the middle of the room, though I didn't realize I'd actually gotten up from the chair. "Why did you do that?"

"You'd never want to leave."

He's right. It's so wild, but I could stay there forever. God, what happens when you create a perfect world that's more desirable than the real one even though it's not real at all?

"What is it?"

"It's a virtual reality simulator, coming next summer from Psyckē." Next summer, after the robot.

"But what *is* it?"

"It's called *Heaven*."

I don't say anything. I just want that headset back. Maybe this is how people feel when they take drugs. Whatever that headset is, it's incredible and dangerous and amazing and way too powerful.

"You thought you were going to see the robot, didn't you?" Hugo says. And then he winks.

BACK IN MY ROOM I'M SHAKEN. I WATCH ARLO SLEEP-ing on the monitor. Worry fills me. I hunt around for my inhaler, until I feel its reassuring weight in my palm. The tightness in my chest isn't my lungs, though.

I text Nino. *Something strange is definitely going on.*

He calls me in two seconds. I open my bedroom door and peek out, making sure Greta isn't right there listening in.

"Hey," I say.

"Hey," he says.

It's the first time I've heard his voice on the phone. It makes me feel immediately better—less alone, and taken in by his newness. *Hey* can be the sexiest word in the universe.

"FaceTime?" he asks.

"Sure," I answer.

In a second he's back, looking more familiar than he has a right to in his plain blue T-shirt. He gives me a spin around his room, a quick view of band posters and a bookshelf. I tell him what happened—how I thought I was going to see the robot but got a sneak look at *Heaven*. He tells me he read something about that, virtual experiences that simulate your own death. Fake-outs of the most crucial life events.

It's all fine, right? Older, more important people are making sure of that, aren't they? It's hard to explain how large the experience was. It sounds like I'm describing a game, pretending to swing a golf club when you're not actually swinging a golf club, but it was so much more. I remember this kid at school, Turner, who had to go away to some rehab place for tech addiction. I couldn't fathom it, but now I can. Those people who fall in love with bots, too. The manipulation, the trick, is just so, so good.

But then all of that stuff just exits my brain because Nino says, "Can you believe we're going to Mexico in two weeks?"

"What?"

"They didn't tell you yet? Aurora asked my dad if we could come."

We. My heart thumps with thrill and nerves. Man, I hope my passport comes in time. "Really?"

"Really."

We both giggle madly. And then we start talking. I find out he hates sushi (like me), loves music from the 1990s (unlike me), and collects old detective pulp fiction, his favorite titles being *Lady, That's My Skull* and *The Case of the Dancing Sandwiches* (sort of like me). He passed out when his mom tried to do the frog dissection unit during his homeschooling (could have been me) and has been feeling really, weirdly happy lately (because of me?!).

My heart is a glowing sun. His glasses flash, two discs of reflection. He shares a few stories about his best friends, Ralph and Phoebe, and I share a few about Clementine and Arden Lee. I decide to take a risk and tell him how much I love to draw comics, how much I *want* to but probably suck. *Isn't sucking part of, like, the creative process?* he says. *It's probably the magic piece no machine will ever have—the failing and the trying again.* Then I take an even bigger risk and tell him I never knew my dad. It's not the whole truth, but it's the center of it. *Oh man,* he says. *That's got to be tough. You'd probably do anything just to see the guy for five minutes.*

I would, I say. *I definitely would.*

It's the second time I've been to heaven in one night, but this one doesn't involve a headset.

It's really late when we finally get off the phone. But I get out my drawings and my pens. I have my real-ish Miss Fury, my me, still in process, and I have my Clementine, with her candle, and now I sketch Nino. I can't even believe that I first drew him as the enemy, the bad guy. I made assumptions that fit my own story, and I was so wrong. Lately, it seems like the real magic of human existence comes when we actually see each other. When we look with clarity and love and generosity and compassion.

Nino sees. I felt him do it.

I draw him. I dress him in a sexy window-washer work suit. Plain old blue. His clarity is his power. I make his glasses flash, two discs of pure light.

chapter
Twenty-Four

WHEN AURORA TELLS ME ABOUT MEXICO, I PRETEND to be surprised. We spend the next couple of weeks doing our usual classes and outings, but also packing, finding her fun outfits, and getting Arlo's stuff ready. Hugo's always working. He goes on a trip to Palo Alto, and Aurora and I watch movies together in the evening and eat popcorn, just like Mom and Ros do. One night Nino and his dad come by, and Aurora calls it Practice

Tulum, and Jak makes carne asada. I feel shy with Leo Gemini at first, but he's this super funny and warm guy, not the romance novel cover model you'd imagine from his name.

At home on my days off, we put our Soggy Pages meetings on hold because Arden Lee goes to Disneyland with Jackie and Carlos for a week, and then Apple gets sick. I tell them about *Heaven* and about Nino, but it's hard to talk when Arden Lee's about to board the pirate ride and Apple has a worrying fever. I get ready for my trip. I buy a new swimsuit, emerald green with zero ironic sea creatures, and text my friends a photo. Clementine says the suit looks sexy in an old movie-star way, and Arden Lee says it's gorgeous, and Rosalind says it would look better if I didn't stand around so awkwardly. Mom says, *Mexico just seems like Hawaii without the Hawaii,* and thinks this is hilarious. She's allowing me to *handle this trip as an adult,* which means I don't even have to talk her out of calling Mrs. Von Baron. She never mentions that voice she heard on the phone.

My passport arrives just in time. It's a different sort of enchanting book, small and blue, with promising, empty pages. I look like a convict in my photo, but so what. Rosalind laughs when she sees it, but I don't care. I almost cry saying goodbye to Clementine and Arden Lee. This feels enormous. Hugo's not even joining us until later, but I'm in it, you know. His life. I'm part of it. I almost forget I'm Eleanor Drake, especially when Aurora and I are hanging out on her bed, Arlo snuggling between us, Boolean on the floor. It's them I've fallen for. Us together.

AT THE AIRPORT THERE'S A SEPARATE CHECKPOINT for security. It's the part I'm dreading, imagining the bells going off or whatever, being found out as I hand over my passport. Nothing happens, though. The officer checks my face and my photo and wishes me a good trip. Relief floods in, excitement, too.

We actually walk outside to where their plane is parked. We climb the stairs that have been rolled to the doorway, same as presidents do. It feels like a simulation, proving that real life can seem fake, just like fake can seem real. Our luggage magically disappears. I sit in a cushy seat that still smells like new leather, Arlo beside me. He's standing and wriggling and getting up and down and walking around. Then we buckle in and take off. Arlo peers out the little cave-opening window at the miracle of clouds. When he does this, with his hair all baby-shiny, but his little jeans so earnest and grown up, my heart fills.

I've only been on an airplane twice before, going to California to see my grandparents, and it was nothing like this. We sat in the back, where people lined up to use the bathroom, so there was a nearly constant eye-level view of belts and zippers and belly over-hangs, hands pressing on your seat back for leverage, butts prac-tically in your face. Still, the clouds were cotton candy and the farms were a patchwork quilt, and we stared straight down into the semi-flattened volcano of Mount Saint Helens. We got a thrill-ing bag of pretzels and a ginger ale that Mom said was good for our stomachs. She handed us gum and made us open our mouths dramatically when we descended so our ears wouldn't pop.

On the Harrisons' plane, there's a flight attendant just for us. She's wearing a navy-blue uniform with thin red piping, like those crisp, efficient airmail envelopes, capable of things regular envelopes aren't. She hands out champagne because Aurora says that every flight is worthy of being celebrated. She's right, and it's a great thing to say, and it makes me mad at all those people on Rate Me and even on her social media, influenced by a her that isn't her. This is the one who influences me.

We drink the champagne, even though I'm underage and technically working. It makes me feel all buzzy and slightly dizzy, part of this group in a way I wouldn't be if I'd ordered Mom's ginger ale. Nino's across the aisle, and he and Aurora and his dad work on one of those word puzzle games Arden Lee likes. But Nino keeps peering up at me from behind those adorable glasses. Every now and then Aurora squeezes my arm or makes wiggling eyebrow innuendos, because she's definitely feeling the—okay, apologies to Arden Lee for the cliché—electricity between us. It feels like electricity. Or at least an energy, a magnetic connection that says without a doubt that things are going to happen here, probably involving mouths and mouths and skin and skin and fate and fate and memories and memories.

If you can make that with machine parts, then I am very sorry and very sad to hear it.

That energy—it feels like the essence of being alive.

A LARGE BLACK SUV PICKS US UP AT THE AIRPORT. WE drive through small towns with tiny stores and houses, past long stretches of what I realize is jungle—lush patches of trees you can barely see through. There are cenotes here somewhere, and Mayan ruins, and yet the house at the end of their long drive is as futuristic as the one in Seattle, made of cream stone and tropical hardwood, long rectangles with glass fronts facing out to the turquoise waters of the Caribbean. Everything is earth-toned and echoey, serene to the point of chilly, even with that warm sun and tropical foliage everywhere. There are two pools, and a bar area with slouchy white canvas furniture and round wood tables. A huge outdoor dining spot spills toward the beach.

Inside, the living room features a singular L-shaped couch and an enormous teak table, and our athletic shoes squeak as we walk around. The staff brings in our bags and offers us cool drinks and slices of melon sprinkled with salt and paprika. The entire staff wears white—the men in khaki pants with white shirts, the women in white skirts and white tops with colorful scarves as belts. When Miss Fury travels to Brazil during the Nazi invasion, the clothes all fit the expected clichés. Suddenly, here, this makes me sad, the frilly colorful dresses and jungle loincloths of the comic, and these white uniforms chosen by the Harrisons.

"Wow, huh?" Nino's never been here before, either, though his dad has.

I nod, but it all feels like a lot. It's exciting but stressful, the anxiety of being out of your element, and Arlo's also getting cranky. He had a too-short nap on the plane and whines to be picked up and then down and then up. My mind is going toddler, too—high, low, up, down, emotional, overwhelmed.

Aurora is ahead of us in the sleek hallway, her heels clicking.

"I have a surprise!" she sings. She seems happier than I've ever seen her. She's relaxed and having fun with Leo. Maybe it's the tequila in her and Leo's drinks. Or maybe it's because Greta has been left at home, and Hugo won't join us for days, and neither will Laura.

Nino and his dad meet eyes, worried. They know Aurora way better than I do. Nino shrugs.

"Ta-da!" she calls.

We step into a bedroom that features three queen-sized beds with crisp white covers, each with a ceiling-height teak headboard and orange and blue pillows. Huge windows face the beach. Attached I see a spacious bathroom with hardwood vanities and silver sinks, white bathrobes on hooks.

It takes me a minute to realize what's happening. It's not until the staff drops my bags in front of one bed, Nino's in front of another, and Arlo's in front of the third that I understand that we'll all be in this room together.

A tidal wave of panic rises. A bed—three beds—does not equal sex, okay, but I've only messed around a little with one guy (I will not mention the otter key chain again, as I trust no further reminder is necessary), and I'm a regular human girl who drools and maybe farts, plus Mexican food and a shared bathroom. Nino and I barely know each other, and what would my mother say, and God, Aurora, what are you thinking? I swear, people of her generation and Mom's and even my grandma's were all about sex, even at my age. Have you heard the lyrics to their songs? *We* need to worry about climate change and getting into college.

Nino blushes.

"I thought you'd be *happy*," she says. "Plus, I know this place seems immense, but Leo's got one guest room, plus Laura and Mathew, and this is where Arlo always stays with his nanny—"

"It's amazing," I say. "Incredible. I can't believe I'm even here." The men who brought our bags have already disappeared before I could even say thank you. I guess the idea is to serve us without being noticed.

"You'll have more chaperones than I hope you'll want." Aurora indicates Arlo, and then points to a security camera near the ceiling.

"Oh," I say.

"And your dad will be right down the hall." She waggles a finger toward Leo, who takes another swallow of his drink and looks tense. "I mean, I remember what it feels like to be young and in l—"

"You're still young, are you kidding? You're not even thirty!" Leo interrupts her, saving us from humiliation. "Look at you! Young and brilliant and beautiful!"

He's laying it on pretty thick. "Aww." She pinches his elbow playfully. "You're such a good friend. I'm going to get changed."

As she and Leo head out, Leo looks over his shoulder and mouths, "Sorry?"

"It's great!" Nino mouths back. "Hey, roomie." He nudges my foot.

"Hey, roomie." I nudge back.

"CHEESY CRACKERS!" Arlo wails, killing any romance.

Nino finds a snack cup in Arlo's backpack. Arlo snatches it and glares at him.

Aurora's right—there's probably no better chaperone than a toddler, as every couple with a kid likely knows.

Later I realize that every room has those cameras. It's different from the Frame House, where there's only a central security system. Because we're in this country, and not in Seattle, *otherness* is what's cool and what's suspect both, same as in Miss Fury. It makes me feel bad again, the way there are eyes everywhere, people watched but not seen.

ARLO GETS A WONDERFUL DINNER OF BEANS AND rice and grilled chicken as Nino and his dad swim in the ocean before it's time for us to eat. Arlo settles into his bed with the guardrails and drifts right off, and I carry the monitor to the outdoor dining area. The sky turns all rainbow sherbet, and then the sun sets. The peaceful garden lights snap on, and the torches stuck in the sand are lit, the flames waving. The smell of the ocean and the warm night air just fill my body with the satisfied joy of *elsewhere*.

I've never been somewhere this elsewhere before. Only California, which managed to seem different and yet not very different, like another room in a house, but not a different house altogether. Somehow, I'm not the staff of this house, either. Aurora has set a place for me at the table, and it's her and me and Leo and Nino. Here, we are family, the closest to it I've been so far, not listening in from upstairs.

On the outdoor table candles flicker romantically as we eat. Aurora's wearing her gauzy white sundress we packed together, and

I'm wearing one I just got. It's maybe Hawaiian, with palm trees and a big sun in an inconvenient location smack on my stomach, I realize now, but so what. I feel breezy and free and full of possibility in ways I never knew I could. Then again, who wouldn't feel breezy and free and full of possibility with this much money? At this house, with torches poked into the sand, with staff bringing you platters of pork in some luscious sauce and big round mounds of guacamole with warm chips—yeah, you feel pretty good.

Aurora tells a story about her college days, when she first met Hugo. They're in this bar, and he's trying to impress her playing pool, and she's just mocking him because he's awful at it. She's such a geek and into her studies that she has no idea who he even is. Who he *already* is, because even though he hasn't made Frame yet, he's done Rate Me, and he's been in every magazine and on every talk show, and how in the world can she not know him, especially when she's studying computer science.

We're just listening and laughing along, probably because our glasses keep being filled. Margaritas now, and my mom would just die. Either that, or she'd start revealing all kinds of shocking stories about her early party days. I've never drunk this much in my life. I mean, one time me and Arden Lee and Clementine tried to share a bottle of wine that Clementine's mom left behind in the house, but my cheeks got all red, and Clementine drank hers too fast and started slurring her words, and Arden Lee pretended to love it, but I could tell he didn't. Now I can kind of see why people drink, because I feel all warm and confident and sexy, and the lights are dreamy, and the air smells like flowers, and Nino keeps brushing his arm against mine. I swear, if he keeps doing that, I might just climb all over him in that gorgeously glowing pool tonight, cameras or not. Maybe this is why we're not as sex-obsessed as past generations. Romance, you know. Like, they had more of it. It's hard to have romance when you've got pandemics and racism and a warming planet.

The point is, I'm not even really paying attention to what she's saying. The point is, it's not until Nino and I are taking an after-dinner walk on the beach, both of us barefoot, holding hands, holding electric hands and electric fingers, that I realize it. She was a *student* when they met? She studied *computer science*? This isn't at all what we've heard in the interviews—their passionate meeting under the Eiffel Tower. Him being instantly charmed by her style and beauty and personality, swept away by her sophistication and elegance. Did she say *geek*?

Whatever, anyway, for the moment, because Nino stops walking. We face each other, and he has stars in his eyes, and now he's kissing me. He tastes like margaritas, which is now my favorite taste in the whole world, because kissing is way more delicious, way, way more than I ever could have known. Finn Lahruti, well, never mind. I don't even know what that was. I want to just pull Nino down on the sand and run my hands all over him. I don't, though, because he breaks away.

"Whoa," he says.

"There's got to be somewhere in that big house we can be alone." I kind of shock myself. Sure, it's supposedly okay for girls to be sexual and want sex and stuff, but that just doesn't match up to still being punished for it left and right. I mean, we're not blind, we know the world we live in. But here I am, being all Miss Fury, pre-censor.

Nino doesn't seem shocked. He just laughs. "I like you, Eleanor," he says. "A lot."

When we get back to the house, the table's been cleared, and every stray glass or crumb or item of clothing that was strewn around has now been picked up. Everything gleams and shines as if no one has ever been here.

A staff member interrupts Nino and me when we come inside. "Excuse me, Eleanor?" she says.

"Yes?"

"Mrs. Harrison wanted me to give you this."

It's the baby monitor. Aurora offered to watch it while we were away, but now it's back.

I'm not truly family, not to Aurora. Leo is staff, too, and so is Nino. So is everyone here, aside from Arlo and Aurora herself.

I don't know why I only realize it now, but Marla Drake's "friends" were always the people who worked for her. Francine was her maid. Cappy was her doorman.

It seems so lonely.

chapter
Twenty-Five

MAYBE WE'RE AURORA'S FAKE FRIENDS, ON THE PAY-roll, whatever, but over the next few days, we have a blast. There are no robots, no AI or missing dads. I don't draw, and I barely even read *The Agony and the Ecstasy*. We all swim in the pool. Leo takes forever to get in, going inch by inch, his elbows raised like chicken wings as the cold water inches up. *Just jump!* Nino says for the millionth time. Leo never jumps, and I kind of love him for it. Aurora swims with Arlo, swirling him in circles in his floaties. He looks at her and clings, as if he's made of gravity and she's Earth. It makes me so happy for him. I don't ask her about her college days, or being a geek, or anything about Hugo. She's so relaxed and at ease, I don't want to break the spell.

That pool—I still don't get a rash. I don't even use my inhaler. It's like I can breathe here.

We walk the beach, too. Sometimes it's an *Erkenntnisspazier-gang,* a thinking walk, or it's a talking or playing one. We pair up, Nino and Arlo, or Nino and his dad, or Aurora and me and Arlo. Nino lives mostly with his mom, but he and his dad are similar in lots of ways. They're both funny, and slightly offbeat, and Leo doesn't talk in question marks, but he deals with the world in one, like the way he gets into a pool, or won't walk barefoot on the beach, or stays up late talking with Aurora even after he says he's tired. I can see why Nino's mom feels protective of him.

It's probably the way Arden Lee and Clementine feel about me sometimes. *Miss you,* I text them, sending photos of my toes in the sand.

Love you, Clementine texts back, sending hearts.

Check this out, Arden Lee texts back. It's a photo of him in a thrift-store sequin jumpsuit, playing with a whole new style direction ever since Carlos has been sharing all his old favorite music. *Twenty bucks! Très glam rock, 1970s!* Me and Clementine send back flame emojis.

We have huge breakfasts with anything we want. I try not to want, and only ask for the same thing Aurora does, because I don't want to be a brat. It's weird to be served like this. It's uncomfortable. I don't know how a person actually gets used to it. This feeling of freedom and relaxation, though—I love it so much. For hours at a time, I totally forget that this isn't my real life. I totally forget I'm wearing a disguise, a non-me, a new me, in another loose sundress that makes me feel all summery and sexy. At night, listening to the ocean roar in and trickle out, I wonder if this fake, secret, hidden me is the real one.

I can't entirely forget the old Eleanor Diamond, though. I check in with Mom every day, by text or a call, as I promised.

"Well, you certainly seem happy," Mom says. Guilt crashes down. Happy can be an accusation when someone else isn't.

"It's fun, even if I'm babysitting twenty-four seven." It's not really true. Even Leo takes turns with Arlo in the pool, riding him around on his neck. I see how lucky Nino was, and is. It makes me understand how a dad can be, what a dad is. It's so wonderful to watch, but it also pulls my heart with a longing and not-having. I haven't really seen what I've missed right in front of my face. Sure, there were maybe a few birthday parties when I was little, where you saw the dad scooping ice cream or helping with the trampoline. Or those fathers in the auditorium after the school play or during graduation, holding the bouquets to give to their daughters. (The sons never seemed to get bouquets.) But I never just spent days living with nice-dad stuff. Like, Leo Gemini always offers Nino the sun lotion before he uses it, and he remembers the things Nino told him from the day before, and shares the details about a handcrafted leather goods store he thinks Nino would like. With Arlo, Leo Gemini kneels down to talk to him at eye level.

"What's with all the selfies you're sending?" Mom asks. "I know what *you* look like."

"I thought you'd like to see where I'm at and what I'm doing." I want to say that Rosalind's whole Instagram feed is selfies, but that would be bratty, for sure.

"Well, yeah, but not *just* you. Where's the house? Where's Mrs. Von Baron? You've only taken little corners that show nothing."

"They don't like me to share photos of them and their kids. There's this thing called an NDA? You're not supposed to—"

"I know what it is! You're not the only one who does. It wouldn't apply to *me*. I'm your *mother*."

The way she says it, those words mean *you're mine*. Your most private corners are. As stressful as it's been to be Eleanor Drake, it's also felt kind of great. Secrets, private thoughts, creativity, reading books, even—they're the best, because, sorry not sorry, you can't come in. I hear Mom getting all fight-y, though, and the last thing I want is her contacting my employer. "I'm sure they didn't mean you, Mom. I'm just being super cautious. I'll try to send more."

"I *miss* you," she says. She says it like her heart is being pulled with longing, but I don't want that need on me. I don't want to be missed like that.

"I miss you, too," I say, but it feels bad in my mouth. I'm glad Rosalind is there.

"God, Eleanor, come hoooome."

"Soon!"

"I *love* you."

I say it back, but what I love right then is being here. Who knew that a place could make you feel like a totally different person. The freedom, the openness, and the sexiness, yeah. But, also, the glorious sense of just belonging to yourself.

"GOD, I SHOULDN'T BE SLACKING OFF LIKE THIS, BUT I could stay here forever." Aurora sometimes talks like she's the burdened CEO of a major corporation. Her straw hat is tipped down over her eyes, her legs stretched out on the lounge chair. On social media the fake Aurora is home, canning strawberries for jam. On Rate Me someone claims to have bumped into her at the Anthropologie store in University Village, where she was a total bitch to the saleswoman. Rating, one star. Maybe it was Laura. It sure wasn't Aurora. Wow, it's so easy to attack what—who—isn't real to you.

"I'm going in," I say. The pool, I mean. These are the kinds of things we're saying to each other—easy, relaxed ones. Trusting ones, even though my passport reveals my real name right under my picture. I should be asking her about that robot, and about the Eiffel Tower, and my father, and a hundred other things, and I should be telling her the truth. The monitor hums, and Nino and Leo are down the beach somewhere, cruising the shop stalls. Aurora rattles the ice in her glass, and in a moment a staff member in white appears, ready to refill it.

The days are a lazy dream, but they fly by. Six days, seven, with only a week left. In the mornings we hit the button on the wall that lifts the window screen. It's a treat and a surprise every time, watching it rise to reveal the ocean. It's a treat and a surprise to see Nino every morning, too. He looks more and more familiar. He cleans his glasses on his T-shirt and puts them on. *Beautiful,* he says each morning—meaning me, this place, this temporary life.

He *is* more and more familiar. I know that he crinkles his nose when he gets asked an uncomfortable question, and that he always brings his plate to the kitchen even though Aurora tells him to stop, and that he's saving his money to travel for a year before college. Also, that he worries he missed important social skills being homeschooled, and that he's tried to write detective noir, and can't watch movies where there's a devil, a slasher, or a dog that dies. His best friend, Ralph, is an activist who is passionate about corporate injustice, and his other best friend, Phoebe, will go anywhere for bubble tea, and they sound a lot like Arden Lee and Clementine in the way they love him. He twirls my hair in his finger. When we race in the pool, he denies letting me win, but it's hard to tell. He laughs when I do my victory strut, a butt-out, arm-waving, head-bobbing dance in my emerald suit.

I've told him that I've never traveled anywhere but here, that *I'm* saving money to go to Cornish, and that I worry about *my* social skills, even though I went to regular school. I can't watch movies where there's a zombie, a serial killer, or a missing parent.

I bet, with your dad and all, he answered. He remembered. He listened. Same as his own dad does.

I tell him, *I really like your social skills.*

He tells me, *I really like yours.*

We sleep in our own beds, but I'm aware of him over there, on the other side of Arlo, emitting the energy of a solar flare. I think of my drawing of him, the light rays flashing from his glasses, but even with his glasses off, he shines.

Lying there oh-so-close to him, I keep thinking of Miss Fury's deft roof crossings, or those art heist movies, where they evade the cameras through some fancy technology that is never explained. People in catsuits leaping at great heights, navigating under and around thin red laser beams, getting to the prize. I tell Nino this.

We could do it, he says, and does a sneaky slink with his arms. It's so goofy I want to climb over there right this second, forget about the cameras. But we're not sleek or sly, and I'm in my Candy Land T-shirt and neon pink boxers, and Nino's in Nirvana and penguins.

Instead, we kiss when Arlo's napping, or after he's gone to bed, as one of the staff watches the monitor. Nino pushes me up against the wall of a hotel down the beach, and in the ocean I wrap my legs around his waist, big waves knocking water up our noses. I wish I could see him tomorrow and the next day and every day after that. Aurora is so happy that Nino and I are together that she beams and takes all the credit.

I try to push out the fact that I am deceiving her and Nino both, but the truth pushes back. That chip is here with me, too, in the zippered pouch of my suitcase. I don't think things through and I'm a brat and worse. But I'm also a person who cares about people, these people. Aurora's been really good to me, and so has Nino, and they deserve more. Every now and then when we're all hanging out and having fun and Hugo is somewhere back home, it's easy to forget that he's my father. He's never been one and still isn't. But I can't forget that Arlo is my brother. I keep the sand out of his mouth and make sure his sun lotion is reapplied after swimming, and I wrap him in towels and give him snacks and naps and all the love in all the world, and I do it as his sister, in disguise. Not being truly seen hurts, even when the choice about it is yours.

Once, my passport slipped out of my bag onto the floor, and Nino asked to see my picture. The picture with *Eleanor Diamond* right underneath. *It's bad,* I said, my head filling with *Erklärungsnot,* explanation alarm, the panic of being caught without a good one. He let it drop, but I had a hard time sleeping that night.

Another time, Nino and I were in the ocean when a wave actually knocked us right over and dragged us to shore on our butts, filling our suits with sand. When the bubbles swirled over my head, when my feet were above me and the surface was too, too far away and I couldn't catch my breath—I thought I might die.

"Oh my God," Nino coughed. He looked terrified, his eyes big and round with the horror of what could have been.

It felt like a warning.

THE MORNING HUGO IS SUPPOSED TO ARRIVE, THERE are red flags tied to the poles on the beach, indicating riptides. No swimming allowed. It feels ominous. We've never seen those before. We thought the ocean was one thing.

The staff is extra busy and seems stressed, and Aurora snaps at me over some missing diaper wipes and never apologizes. Even Arlo is crankier and more out of sorts than he's been in days. Last night was almost a farewell party for the four of us, Aurora talking wistfully and sharing funny memories of the past week, like when Leo screamed because he thought some liquid soap was a jellyfish in the outdoor shower, and when Arlo got brave and dunked his head underwater, and the time she startled Nino and me kissing by the tropical plants and a palm jabbed Nino up the nose. After we went to bed, she and Leo stayed up really late. I read books to Arlo, but he cried and wanted me to be with him until he went to sleep, so Nino just went for a walk on the beach by himself. I took a puff from my inhaler for the first time during the whole trip.

In the late afternoon the house fills with noise—Hugo's booming voice, his laugh, his presence, the sound of thunder, if thunder were brilliance and creativity and the need for attention. Leo gets quiet and goes into town to go shopping alone. Nino tells Hugo that he's off to go take a surf lesson, but I see him leave with his book. Arlo raises his arms to be picked up, but Hugo doesn't notice. He's busy lavishing praise on the staff in their white uniforms as they smile with smiles that never reach their eyes.

By dinnertime a photographer is snapping pictures of Laura and Arlo on the beach. Hugo and Mathew smoke cigars and sip tequila by the pool. Hugo's shirt is off. Oh man. Oh wow. I spot the ribbon of black just above his shorts. I don't know why I never connected it, one of the facts that I have about his body to the book me and Clementine and Arden Lee are reading. But then again, when Hugo got that tattoo, I doubt he thought much about Michelangelo, either, the artist who spent four years painting the Sistine Chapel ceiling, where that image appears.

I see that tattoo, is the point. The one just under his waistband that we've heard about since we were kids. All of a sudden

I think about Brandi Diamond and him together, years ago, in some room, having sex. She couldn't tell what the tattoo was at first, Mom told us. She made two wrong guesses that embarrassed him. *A flock of birds? Oh wait. Hands! Doing sign language.* A tattoo should speak for itself, I guess, so he felt humiliated, and she was proud about that.

But I see it as Hugo reaches for his drink on the side table—the line of black. They're hands, all right. Two fingers touching. It's *the* moment, the most well-known one in the entire painting on the entire Sistine Chapel ceiling, where God's finger touches Adam's at the moment he's created.

"Do you know it takes eight to twelve years to harvest an agave?" Hugo tips back his drink. "After that they only use the heart. And then the plant is done, kaput. You have to grow the next one from scratch."

"Whoa," Mathew says.

Right then I'm not sure who I feel worse for in Mom's story of Hugo's supposed humiliation. People can be so proud in their anger and superiority when it just seems sad. It seems way less powerful than the power they imagine. Because it's clear to me even from that distance what that tattoo is. It seems clear, very clear, who has the power.

chapter
Twenty-Six

THAT NIGHT AT DINNER NINO AND I AREN'T INVITED
to eat with them. We're actually told this by one of the house staff
members in white. She tells us that the family and their adult
guests will be eating privately outdoors. *Family.* She offers to pro-
vide takeout menus or a meal on the side patio. It's silly, but I feel
hurt. Nino's not surprised. *Totally expected,* he says. *No big deal.*

I feed Arlo in the kitchen and give him a bath. I put him in
his cutest pajamas in case his dad, our dad, comes to see him.

Like, maybe extra cuteness will help get him attention. But no one comes to say good night, not even Aurora. I put him to bed, and then I carry the monitor around, searching for Nino. In that spacious living room, I see the adults around the table, the torches flickering behind them, twilight sprinkling the waves with glitter. My phone buzzes with a text.

Takeout at Flammarion? Nino asks.

Flammarion is the farthest edge that the monitor will go, the very-most end point we can travel on the beach and still keep a watch on Arlo. It's not all that far, honestly, and there's a houseful of staff members to help him should he need someone, but Flammarion sounds like a distant land that's ours. Nino named it after this wood engraving from the 1800s that's on the cover of his dad's favorite book, *The Compleat Astrologer*. It shows a guy in a long robe sticking his arm through an imagined filament where the very edge of the Earth meets the heavens.

When I arrive, there's a blanket spread out on the sand, and even in the glow of the setting sun, I notice how tan Nino's getting, and how bright his eyes look. Back at the house there are torches, and candles, and landscape lights, but Nino's eyes are the real shine.

"Hey," he says. "Burritos. Ta-da!" He makes a wide-armed gesture at our feast, mysterious bundles wrapped in foil, cardboard cups full of sloshy ice. Funny, but I missed regular old takeout, the kind me and Mom and Ros get for a treat. My heart lifts, like I'm reuniting with an old friend I haven't seen in a while. Sloshy ice in a cup is just great, that's all.

"Thank you! Man, this looks *amazing*."

"Right?" It's seriously two burritos in foil and two cups with straws sticking out, and he's as thrilled as I am. "My dad is sad he's missing this."

"Really?" In spite of our takeout joy, it seems hard to imagine that Leo is having *Futterneid,* food envy. He's included; we're not. Is it even fair to be hurt? What would Hugo do if he knew I was his kid, not just the nanny? Would I be at that table tonight? This experience has been like lifting a curtain and discovering a hole of want that goes on and on.

Nino makes a face, like *of course.* "The Hugo Show is exhausting."

I heard Hugo's voice when I headed to the beach, loud and rollicking, telling a story where everyone laughed. I wonder if it's exhausting for him, too, to perform all the time, or if it's more exhausting to be the audience. I mean, the audience can always escape the performer, but the performer can never escape himself. I try to tell this to Nino, but it comes out in such a jumble, I don't even know if I'm making sense.

"That show back there . . . ," Nino says. "It's *nothing.* Have you ever been to his *office*?"

Psyckē Enterprises, the sprawling complex on the hill with the neon pink sign on top. "Not inside." Because, yeah, I've been in the parking lot, sitting in my car, watching the guys in their hoodies and jeans going in and out; the women, too, always more dressed up than the men, in smart, cute outfits. They're busy ants in a colony, ID badges strung around their necks.

"When you're there, you realize how many people he affects. That building alone is a whole city, and he's Oz. All the offices in there are glass. You see straight into them. Not his, though. His, you can't tell where it is. It's all mirrors. You have to know."

"It sounds cool, actually."

"So many people. CFOs and CEOs, project managers and whatever managers. Design teams, and HR, and social media, and marketing, and publicity, and who knows what. They've got their own language. It's all about a utopian vision, creating a better world. They really believe it, too. He's basically their guru. If you doubt him, or ask questions, or *don't* believe . . . Boom. That's what I've heard. You're out."

"But he *is* a visionary," I say. "And so is the person who made this burrito." It's delicious.

"That whole 'excuse the guy because he's a visionary' thing, though . . ."

I stay quiet.

"Shouldn't we require our *visionaries* to *see*? Clearly, I mean? Other people, not just themselves? And shouldn't we be super careful who we're allowing to make decisions about this stuff like AI? I'm worried about all this unchecked power, aren't you? Frame, Rate Me, this *Heaven* thing you told me about . . . Whatever that robot is going to do . . . I don't know, Eleanor." Nino swirls the ice in his cup, takes a noisy slurp. "What's going to end up happening here? In these types of movies, humanity is never the winner. Like, I read detective novels from the fifties, where there's always a bad guy and a good guy, and the bad guy always gets what's coming to him, and I've got to say, that's pretty great."

"That time period, though. Talk about unchecked power.

Even in those detective novels, I bet, if they're anything like the comics from that time."

"For sure, for sure. I just mean all this shit is disturbing. What happens when we value what's *not* real more than what *is* real?" He takes the top off his cup and drinks the last of his soda. "And I feel bad for the kid, you know. Hugo just looks right through the little guy."

A thread of unease pokes through a needle and makes a stitch and then another inside of me. Irritation cinches, too, because Arlo and me, we're not less just because our family situation isn't as perfect as other people's. It's not fair to be annoyed when Nino doesn't realize he's feeling sorry for me, too. I peel the foil of my burrito, take another bite. There at Flammarion my own story of being unseen merges with the bigger one he's talking about, and I wish I could do more than sit here feeling helpless. I want to believe I'm Miss Fury, capable of standing up against bad stuff, but I'm only a girl on a beach eating a burrito.

I watch the lump of Arlo on the monitor. "I'm the kid, too," I tell Nino. "I'm Hugo's daughter."

I don't plan it. The moment has arrived, is all. Which is a funny expression, because it's actually you arriving to the moment, not the other way around.

"Wait a sec, *what*?"

"I'm going to tell you something very weird and uncomfortable and I feel horrible that I didn't tell you right at the start so I'm going to beg your forgiveness right now and hope so bad you won't hate me." A rush of words that really mean one thing: *please.*

He sets his cup on the blanket, and it promptly falls over, the ice spilling as swiftly as my secrets. I stick my arm through the filament where Earth and heaven meet, and two fingertips touch, and I tell him a story of creation—mine, and Rosalind's, too.

"Oh, Eleanor," Nino says.

"Do you hate me?"

"I don't hate you, of course not. But *wow*."

He exhales. It's a lot. It's strange and disturbing, and I see it on his face. Too late, I realize I've also made him part of my secret, a coconspirator. It's awful. I am. What will a robot do with complications like *this*? If we want a machine to be as humanlike as possible, it had better be messed up, I'll tell you that. Messed up and unpredictable in ways no algorithm can ever decipher. Sure, a robot can replicate our best parts—our creativity, our talents, the ability to solve the world's most difficult problems, and on and on, but maybe what makes us most human is the way we can entirely fuck things up.

"I'm so sorry," I say. I'm trying not to do what Mom might have done with Hugo, at least at first: cry and beg. The strange thing is, Nino looks way more sad than mad.

"Hugo's kid . . . Man. I wish you would have told me. Like, from the beginning."

"I wish I did, too." I also wish I'd never said a word tonight. I wish I could be Eleanor Drake forever. "I'm so sorry I lied to you."

We crumple our trash, head back to the house. The filament between us feels impermeable. I wonder if I'm going to be sent to Siberia without the plane trip. Instead, just before we reach the house, he does the kindest thing—he takes my hand.

"I'm so sorry again," I say. My voice wobbles. "I just wanted to know him so bad. What I did, what I'm doing, is wrong."

"God. I'm sorry you went through all this," he says. "I mean, it's not a kid's fault, what a parent does."

It sounds so simple. When he says it, it even sounds true.

———

IF I FELT A NEEDLE AND A THREAD STITCHING UNEASE, what happens next is an unraveling. Is this how a machine breaks down, one piece destroying another, causing the whole thing to crash? Do you need a crash to build something new? That night Aurora and Hugo have a fight. It's loud. Loud enough that the whole house can hear, I'm sure—Laura and Mathew and Leo and every white-uniformed staff member who stays on the premises. In the morning a lot of people will have to pretend they never heard a thing.

I lie awake, frightened by the anger. Arlo doesn't stir, thank goodness. He's a still, small mound in the bed next to mine, surrounded by a stuffed dino and a monkey and a dog, because you need all the friends you can get when you're little in a world so big. Across the room Nino sits up in the dark. I sit up, too. He reaches for his glasses and puts them on as if they'll help him hear better. "What's going on?"

"No idea," I whisper.

Before we each climbed into our own beds just hours ago, he kissed me, brief and gentle. His kiss said, *We'll figure it out from here.* I'm not sure, though, really. For once in my life, not being my true self is what maybe wrecked things. Now the circles of his glasses point my way, catching the only light in the room.

Their voices get closer. Their footsteps, too. Someone is pacing, someone following.

Now we can hear them clearly. "How could you do this?" Aurora cries.

"It didn't mean anything!"

"A *she* is not an *it*!" Aurora yells.

"Oh shit," Nino whispers.

A *she*. I feel sick. Poor Aurora.

"*You're* the one who matters, the only—"

"That's a lot of phone calls and texts for not mattering! I saw! You can't tell me, when I saw with my own eyes. Have you been with her when we've been gone?"

"No! It was months ago. We met for lunch, that's all. *One time!*"

"Lunch? You expect me to believe that? Hugo, I'm not stupid."

"That's all it was, I swear. I don't know why she keeps calling and texting! She's clearly not okay! It was zero, Aurora. Zero, zero, zero! It couldn't matter less. She's *nothing*." His voice retreats, harder to hear again. This fight is like a tornado, moving across a plain.

My throat tightens. I'm not stupid, either. Of course he and the woman had sex. *Zero, zero, zero! She's nothing!* The tornado blows a house down, my house. No matter what Mom has told us, his words reveal our rotten foundation, the one I've always feared was there.

Nino sits on the edge of my bed. "Eleanor?" He puts his arms around me. I want to cry. I want to sob and weep for all I never had and for what I do have, this situation that stamps some giant black mark of insignificance onto me, a permanent bruise. Zero, nothing. Can a bruise cover your whole body?

Aurora's voice is back. She's talking about a dog. It makes no sense.

"Dog?" Nino whispers. We hear the word again, again. *Dog, dog, dog.*

They're back. The storm is. The footsteps are practically right outside our door. Their loud voices jab and then retreat. "You could have *anyone,* you know that? Anyone! But Sierra . . . honestly? Our *employee?*"

After the fight dies down, and after Nino returns to his bed, I lie in devastated silence until the sun rises. That shark is back again, circling, circling with a thought.

The shark bites.

At least Sierra got his phone number.

chapter
Twenty-Seven

THE NEXT DAY AURORA GOES MISSING. WELL, THAT'S how the other people in the household see it, but probably not how Aurora does. It sounds so passive, *goes missing,* as if it's something that happened to her instead of something she made happen. As if she needs rescuing, when she's maybe actually saving herself.

That morning Hugo is a force, magnetic in his need. He strides around the house barking directions, his hair all wild and his flip-flops smacking the stone floors. The staff in white scurries, offering him plates of food and drinks, while Laura and Mathew are on their phones, trying to locate Aurora. *My dad can't take it,* Nino said, and so the two of them have driven off somewhere. Hugo rails, pacing while eating a piece of pineapple, scaring Arlo, who keeps saying *I want Mama* until I take him outside.

Hugo finds me swirling Arlo in the pool, the ripples making soothing sounds that are lies. He stands above us. Arlo doesn't reach his hands up to be held like he usually does. Maybe he reads the mood or has just given up. Maybe I could have had Hugo in my life, if Mom had been . . . I don't know. If Mom had been who he wanted her to be. If Mom had been . . . more, or less, or whatever the right math was. But what if it was for the best that he wasn't there? What if his absence was the biggest gift I could have gotten, a prize, the Fates looking after me, not the reverse, as I'd thought all along? What if this is true for Clementine, too, and Arden Lee with his dad? You think, what a tragedy that they aren't there, but maybe it's pure, good luck. The thing that saves you, even if you feel destroyed.

"Do *you* know where she is?" he asks.

"Me?" God, he's standing right over me. I can practically see up his shorts, gross. I avert my eyes. What if I saw that scar on his thigh Mom told us about? Ugh.

"She trusts you. You're special to her." His voice has gotten all soft and charming. His words cast a spell. *Special.* Oh God, it happens, a hand madly erasing in my mind, making a new sketch, filling it in with explanations, reasonable or not. I mean, I already knew he was a cheater, didn't I? This is hardly news. It's not even news to Aurora. He's probably done it before, even with her. Isn't that just what happens with brilliant, dazzling men? The whole philandering thing? And wait. Wait! There's still one crucial piece I shouldn't forget. What about those photos, huh? Keeping us in that drawer, in that special place, it's not *zero, zero, zero*.

"Me?"

"It would help if *you* helped." He gives a pained smile. As I stare up at him, he looks so large. I still want to figure him out, as if I could build a knowable human if I had all the parts. As if I could build *me* and understand *me* if I had his whole.

"I'll try."

He nods and turns to walk away. I almost do it right there—I almost tell him who I am. It would be like the dramatic scene in Miss Fury when the baroness reveals her child's true father. Instead I lift Arlo from the pool and then towel him off. I slip my sundress over my head. I text Aurora, no answer. I text Nino.

Where are you???

Some cenote? Dad's in the water, floating on his back wearing his goggles. He won't get out.

Ughh, I type. I send a crying emoji and a scream emoji.

Is Aurora back?

Not yet. Does your dad know where she is?

He thinks El Sol, probably. They have the best pool. You can rent their cabanas.

I'll check there, I answer.

You might want to stay out of it? They do this. He's done this before. He gives her some innocent explanation, and she decides to believe him. She'll be back.

I set Arlo down. Staying out of it is not what Hugo wants. *Thanks,* I text.

It's past Arlo's nap time, but I'm not leaving him here. I bring his bag, and we take off down the beach. He makes it about ten steps before he wants up. Up it is, then. I prop him up on my hip. Arlo seems to weigh twenty pounds, then fifty, then a hundred as I trek down the hot sand.

I head straight for El Sol. The other day Nino and I sat under one of their grass-roofed beach huts and kissed. They do have the best pool, beautiful and winding, private and serene. It's exclusive and quiet. I spot the orange of her suit in one of the cabanas. Her eyes are closed, and one arm is flung over her head. Her hair, the drama—it's pure baroness. Two empty margarita glasses sit on the table beside her.

She sits up when we approach, all sweaty-faced, her eyes red. She holds out her arms to Arlo, but he doesn't want to go. I can't blame him. It makes my stomach ache, because Arlo shouldn't have to be around this stuff. He should get a few good years just being awed by dragonflies and the way sun plus rain equals rainbows.

We plop onto a chaise, and a waiter heads over. Aurora orders another drink. I love Aurora, I do. But, oh man, she is disappointing me so deeply right now. I want her to be bigger than the man who hurt her. I want her to be MOTHER, where protecting Arlo and loving Arlo is bigger than her own feelings. It's not fair, because I didn't think that same thing about Hugo a few minutes ago. I sure didn't.

"So, you found me," she says. My heart is breaking. I wonder about the robot again, all robots. What would it take for them to truly be humanlike? What data would be crucial? Experiences the robot has with the people they love, and the people they hate, and the people who created them and betrayed them and stayed by them. Experiences they were never even part of generations ago. A perfect, solo, self-contained robot—it's nothing that could ever exist in real life, never. We are all connected, each of us impacts the other, how obvious, okay, but how monumental. That intense, ongoing web of connection, going back eons and only moments, impacting what hasn't happened yet, too—*that's* humanity. Irreplaceable humanity. All that's most sacred intertwined with all that's most messy.

"Can you please come back?" I ask. Maybe I should be asking instead if Arlo can stay, or if I can help us all pack up and go right this minute. Or maybe I should be running off with Arlo myself, just like Marla Drake does with the baroness's child, kidnapping him in order to save him.

"I'll go back, but I'm done. I'm finally done. That's it. Time to go nuclear." I have no idea what she means by this, but she looks determined in a way I've never seen. She shakes her head. "Hugo wouldn't even be who he is without me." She's said stuff like this before, so I think what I always do. Like, I doubt it, you know. I think he *would* be who he is. He's the one with the brilliance, right, and she's his wife? He could have picked a different one, and he'd still have that mind.

I shrug.

"Without me, Frame wouldn't have happened," she insists. "It wouldn't do what it does."

"Wouldn't have happened?" I'm sure I look skeptical, and wow, wow, we can be so wrong about so much.

"Wouldn't have happened! At least not right then, in that way. Eventually, maybe. But my work on it was pivotal. When we met, he was a visiting professor at Stanford, and I was his student. He asked me to be part of this team that was . . . Well, at the time text-to-image synthesis suffered from severe artifacts. Distorted and illogically placed objects, a wrong blending of foreground and background . . ."

"Wait, what? I have no idea what you're even saying. Was this after you two were in Paris?"

"Paris?"

"Meeting on the bench under the Eiffel Tower."

She snorts. "We didn't even go to Paris until after we got married."

"But that's the story."

She ignores this. "We'd figured out a way to train a transformer to autoregressively model text and image as a single stream of data without using pixels directly as image tokens, using a two-stage training process that first compressed images so that an inordinate amount of memory wasn't used, two fifty-six–by–two fifty-six RGB image down to a thirty-two–by–thirty-two grid, each element able to assume over eight thousand possible values, and then—"

"Aurora." I put my head in my hands. "None of this makes sense to me."

"Okay! The point is, without *my* work, Frame *wouldn't* work. The images it creates would look like shit. Told ya I was a geek."

"Seriously, Aurora? Seriously?" Oh my God. When Leo Gemini told her she was beautiful and brilliant, he wasn't laying it on thick at all. He was telling the truth. She *is* brilliant. How did I not know? How did any of us not know? Is this fury? Is it? Then why does it feel so intensely sad? So crushingly disappointing? Because this isn't like the dramatic scene in Miss Fury when the baroness reveals her child's true father. No, no. This is pure William Moulton Marston. And I knew it, didn't I? That *Miss Fury* came to me for a reason? It was trying to tell me something, all right. And not just about Miss Fury and her creator, Tarpé Mills, but about the one who stole her light, the one who is still seen as she remains unseen.

Arlo finally crawls from my lap and sits in Aurora's. She puts her arms around him. This is the truest story: Hugo off on his own and Aurora and Arlo together. Back at home Mom and Ros. It's not me and Hugo, the same, like Mom and Ros are the same, the creative ones, with him the genius innovator. I'm on this chair by myself; I just am.

"Why don't you tell people, Aurora? Everyone should know what *you* made!"

"It wasn't *just* me. Yeah, the ideas and the direction were mine, but there was a team. And our work was built on the talent and labor of other people, going all the way back to Harold Cohen's AARON back in 1973, and Alan Turing in the fifties. You know, *Imitation Game*? And *that* all goes back to Ada Lovelace, way back in 1842. The mother of computer programming, not that anyone's made a big movie about *her*. She was the first one to write about poetical science—the idea that machines might one day do more than calculate, that computers might be able to make art."

"I've heard of *Imitation Game*, but I've never heard of Ada Lovelace."

"Exactly."

"But he gets all the credit? For what you made?"

"It's a long story."

I want to challenge that, because *why* wouldn't you take what you deserve? Why would you let him claim your talent, your creation? Why would you let people think you're just an Instagram influencer, someone who only cares about looking good, who people hate-follow? And why would you go back to him, honestly? To someone who took that from you?

But then I remember William Moulton Marston again, his lies about the lie detector test. Elizabeth, allowing him to take credit for that and for Wonder Woman, too. The way he came home and informed her that Marjorie would be his second wife, like it or not, and Olive his third. And Olive herself, allowing her children to be kept in the dark about their real dad.

I wanted to be like Miss Fury, fearless and feminist, or like Tarpé Mills, creative and fierce. But instead I'm one of William Moulton Marston's poor kids of his poor wives, because, yeah, it's an old story, all right. A story about people in power wielding power, deciding who is seen and who isn't.

"Aurora, we could tell the truth! I'm sure you have *proof*."

Aurora only looks at me like I'm the kid that I am, a kid who needs heroes and villains, who needs the good guys to win badly, so badly, when that's not the way the world works.

"It's going to take a lot more than that. People *do* know. The information is out there already. We wrote a paper. We wrote more than one paper. It doesn't matter. People want to believe in the brilliance of Hugo Harrison. And the magic of tech. I did. For too long."

Arlo starts to cry.

"Can you take him?" Aurora says, and hands him back, as if he's a problem too large for her to handle at the moment. The way he looks at her, it's killing me. And so is the way she's not looking at him. Oh, it's the pain of *Weltschmerz*. World sadness.

Hugo isn't a hero, and neither is William Moulton Marston, that's for sure. And Aurora herself is only human, and so is my mom, and Susan, too. Elizabeth wasn't a hero, and neither was Marjorie, or Olive, or even Tarpé Mills. Heroes and villains—they're so comforting, so thrilling, even, but they're just not real. They're pen and ink, or pixels. They're distorted and illogically placed objects, a wrong blending of foreground and background that no brilliant solution can fix. Heroes are lies. But, man, I'll tell you. There are a lot of children who are very, very real who sure could use one.

chapter
Twenty-Eight

WE PLANNED TO STAY THROUGH THE END OF THE
week, but Aurora wants to go home. There's a rush of packing. Suitcases are hauled into the SUV as Hugo sulks and is left behind. It's
a long, somber flight. In the air, up in the clouds, Nino sleeps, and
so does Arlo, and I watch the white haze, trying to find the words
to tell Aurora that I can't do this anymore. I want to go home, too.
My home. I hurt Nino, and I'm still lying to Aurora, who right now
heads my way and plunks down in the seat next to me.

"I may need you to work more hours," she says. "I'll figure something out for your weekends off, but if we can do longer days, that'd be great."

It's the last thing I'm expecting when I'm about to tell her I quit. "Aurora?" I want to tell her everything, but she's already handling so much. "I don't think I can—"

She knows what I'm going to say. "You can. You have to. Please. It's important. I need you. It's *urgent*."

What's so urgent? Watching Arlo so Aurora can hide in her room and go to the pool? Her eyes plead. Beside me Arlo's cheeks are flushed with sleep, his hair damp. Why did William Moulton Marston's wives never tell their kids the truth? Why didn't his children ever suspect it? Power, sure, but hope, too. Longing and need. Messy love. I don't want to leave my brother.

"Okay." I rub my forehead. "Okay."

Finally, out the tiny plane window, I see our city, looking like the hills and valleys of Arlo's favorite book, *All the World*. Somewhere down there, a red truck *does* have apples in the back, and a flock of birds *do* fly around a church tower. That book seems so innocent and sweet, but it's good to remember that things like that are true, too.

IT'S STRANGE TO BE HOME, IN THIS NOT-MEXICO place, with evergreens and skyscrapers and jammed freeways instead of palm trees and beaches and lazy breezes. At the Frame

House, Boolean trots out, and Yvette, the housekeeper, brings in the bags. Aurora and Leo talk quietly by his car. Nino and I stand in the driveway, saying goodbye. I wish we were just a girl and a guy with new vacation tans, sand still in our suitcases, thinking only about fun and kissing and being together.

Instead I tell him what Aurora revealed, about her and Frame. It spills out, not in orderly code but in muddled emotion, because I'm going on and on about William Moulton Marston, and the women and the kids, too.

"Eleanor? Let's get that fucker," Nino says about Hugo Harrison, my father.

I flinch. I wish he were just a fucker. The night before, when we were still in Tulum, Hugo stopped me in the outdoor breezeway and said, *Hey. Thank you. You're really great, you know?* Even William Moulton Marston wasn't just one thing, was he? My mind plays a slideshow of those photos, Hugo holding tiny me and tiny Ros. Hugo keeping those images in a special, hidden place. I can't forget that we're his, and he's ours. I wish I could.

"Seriously, we need Ralph," Nino says. "He's this secret vigilante *activist.* . . . His dad was abusive, right? And I think it made him . . . I don't know. Really passionate and pissed about those in power harming the little guy. He does all *kinds* of things. To speak out against this stuff . . ."

I stare down at my sandals. Shake my head.

"I'm sorry," he says. "I forgot for a sec. I mean, he's still your . . ." He sighs. "Are you going home?"

"I was. But Aurora asked me to stay. Begged me to."

"Ahhh." He mimes putting a knife in his heart and pulling it out, but he looks unconvinced. I remember what he said about his dad, showing up for her at all hours.

His keys are in his hand. I wonder where we stand. If we stand. "Are we . . . ?" I trail off.

Nino looks into my eyes, like *really* looks. Hard enough to see the actual me, my worry and my care. "Yeah, we're okay. Hey, I'm going to really miss seeing you every day," he says in answer, glasses flashing, as his dad heads our way.

"I'm going to miss *you*."

"I'll see you at Flammarion," he says.

THAT NIGHT I HEAR THEM IN ARLO'S ROOM—AURORA reading *All the World,* and Arlo's high little chipmunk voice. They're on the page with the birds. *Where they go?* he asks.

Up high, she answers. *Up and away.*

She always comes back, Nino had said, and I guess it's true. She's here, doing the usual thing.

Out on the dock I call Mom to tell her I'm back. Mrs. Von Baron had to return early, but they didn't tell me why, I say. I wish I didn't know. I tell her I'll still be home on Friday, and that I can't wait to see her and Rosalind then. Out here under the darkening sky with that neon Psyckē light in the distance, I mean it. When I say it, my whole body misses my normal life, our cluttered kitchen and Mom's blond ponytail with the butterfly clip and the way Ros snorts when she laughs hard. But then Mom tells me that they're headed out to get dinner and she can't talk. She tells me that I'm lucky I got to go to Mexico at all, instead of just staying home and working hard all the time.

The *Hugo Naut* bumps against the dock, *Theos* bobbing behind. I have a brief fantasy of getting in it and zooming away forever. Instead I FaceTime Clementine and Arden Lee. They both pick up, thank goodness. Seeing their faces—my heart rises and fills with the happiest, longest word on our list, *Flughafenbegrussungsfreude,* airport greeting joy. Clementine's sitting on her old couch with Apple, *Prince Caspian* open on her lap, and Arden Lee is sparkling in a chain-mail tank top and hoop earrings. He turns down some music when he answers. Albums are spread all over his bed.

"You look fabulous, Arden Lee," I tell him.

"Wow!" Clementine agrees.

He belts out a lyric about not needing heroes, of all things, or home. He shimmies like a diva. "Tina Turner! Look at all these albums Carlos gave me! It's a whole new world. Wait. Eleanor? You're in Seattle."

"Back early. Family crisis," I tell them.

"Are you all right?" Clementine asks. "What happened? Tell us everything."

"There's a lot of everything. I'll give you all the gory details on Saturday? I'm pretty exhausted, but I just wanted to tell you I was here."

"As long as you're okay," she says. "Otherwise we're coming to get you."

"I'm okay."

It's getting late, so we send around a bunch of nostril shots and kissy-faces and say goodbye. I call out to Boolean, who's scratching his back like a goof on the lawn, and we head inside. In that spacious bedroom with all the glass, my suitcase sits on the floor, still packed up. I could put my shoes on right now and leave, tell Aurora that staying is impossible. I've seen enough, haven't I?

What's enough, though, to let go of every last piece of hope? It's those baby photos, yeah, but I also keep seeing Hugo on that boat, his face struck with rejection, that other way we're alike. But I shouldn't forget, either, how the origin stories of comic book villains and heroes are always essentially the same, with their tragedy and abuse, wrecked children who grow up to be loners with deep longings. The hero transforms those longings into helping others, while the villain transforms those longings into destroying others.

I couldn't bear to destroy anyone. And my hope is way larger than just Hugo Harrison loving me or not. I have an *All the World* hope.

I sit at the desk and take out my drawings. It seems like forever since I even held a pen. I set aside my Clementine superhero with her candle, and my Nino with his beaming lenses, and my me, my plain Miss Fury. She's still missing something. I have no idea what, but I set her aside, too. Now I sketch an Arden Lee. He's wearing his sequin jumpsuit. Darts of light shoot out from each tiny, shiny disc. He's so bright, he's as bright as Arden Lee's face was tonight as he sang.

Aurora interrupts with a tap on my door. My instinct is to shove my art in a drawer, but I don't. If you want people to see you, you also have to be willing to be seen. She's here with the monitor but heads right to the desk. She stands over me, looking at my work.

"Eleanor, you're *good*."

"Really?"

"*Really*. I didn't know you're an artist."

You're an artist. Are. Already am. My chest blooms with emotion. With gratitude. My cheeks get hot.

"Want me to take this tonight so you can work?" She waves the monitor. *Work.* A thing taken seriously. Something she understands, because she had this, too—the desire to use her talent to create.

"Give me that," I say, and laugh. I reach out my arm for the monitor. "I *am* at work."

Aurora makes a face, like *No way.* I swear, her expression says, *You're here, in a house, with us, like a family.* She doesn't realize all that she's giving me with that, or maybe she does. She ruffles my hair with affection.

The idea of me pulling a Miss Fury and kidnapping a child from the baroness is absurd. It would never happen in a million years. The thing is, she's his, and he's hers. Well, he's *his* most of all, but for better or worse, she's his lifelong struggle, his imperfect beginning, his origin story.

She says good night. At two a.m. Arlo wakes with a bad dream. When I go to his room to comfort him, I see a strange thing. A thin line of blue light glowing under Aurora's bedroom door. It's from her laptop. I listen. I hear the *tip tip tip* of typing, the rustle of papers. There's no doubt about it. It sounds urgent, all right.

BY MORNING HUGO'S HOME AGAIN. ARLO'S THRILLED to see him. He rides his dad around like a horse, as he does, Boolean barking excitedly, as Greta says stuff like *You're going to hurt yourself* and *You're not as young as you used to be.* It's such a dad thing that I feel that deep hole of lost chances again. It makes me think of Nino's father floating alone in the old water of that cenote.

It's hard to know what's happening. Aurora took a long bath before dinner and wears one of our outfits, a lime-green shift dress and blue high-heel sandals. She and Hugo are extending small kindnesses. They're General Bruno and the baroness. *She'll be back,* Nino said, and maybe this is *back.* He brings her a tall glass of sparkling water, with a lime he sliced himself. She laughs at something he shows her on his phone. Greta goes to her room, looking mad, as per usual. I'm not sure who she's disgusted with, maybe both of them. If so, it's the first time I'm on her side.

Jak makes an incredible dinner of barbecued salmon and risotto, and the pool glitters and the yacht bobs, and on the hill in the distance, the pink Psyckē sign reigns. Maybe everything will just go back to normal, whatever that is. If anything should be ditched from the past and present, it's that word.

AROUND MIDNIGHT, ACCORDING TO MY PHONE, someone goes into Arlo's room. I stir at the sound of his door opening. I bolt out of bed when I see the shadow. My heart pounds in panic. But it's only Hugo. *Only* is a word we give too often to family members, probably. Hugo murmurs to Arlo as he lifts him from his bed. Arlo whimpers, but Hugo jiggles him and starts to sing. I don't know what he's doing, but it's wrong. I feel that wrongness in my whole body. Hugo's not seeing the most basic thing here, that Arlo was sleeping and shouldn't be disturbed for a need that's not his.

I get up. In my old shorts and the *Gym Dandy* tank top that Rosalind gave me for Christmas, I'm nothing like Miss Fury. I'm me, mad. I wish Clementine could see it, this anger, here without a doubt.

Hugo sees me in the hall. "It's fine. Go back to bed," he says. I keep trying and trying to locate some father feeling for him, but it doesn't happen, unless this anger *is* a father feeling. Arlo lifts his head from Hugo's shoulder in confusion. He starts to cry. He holds his arms out to me, but Hugo pushes past. He shuts his office door firmly, sending the message that this is none of my business. Well, he's wrong about that. My little brother is very much my business.

It's weird, and I don't get it, but I can hear it through the door: That robot is talking to Arlo. No. That robot is *soothing* Arlo, using words a parent would. I'm seriously getting the creeps, because she asks him if he'd like a story to feel better, and Arlo agrees. And then the robot begins to read. I hear the lilt and rhythm of a story. A stolen story, like that stolen art, and so many stolen ideas. *All the world is old and new.* The words after that aren't the right ones that Liz Garton Scanlon wrote. They're words from some other children's book, or maybe many of them, data just cobbled together to get an expected response.

And Arlo, no! It's working. He quiets. His crying has stopped. Is this the point? Is this the test? To make him cry, to make him stop? To see what he'll do, how thoroughly he'll be deceived? That's how the success of the robot is measured, right? How well it pretends to be something it's not? And this one is pretty successfully pretending to be . . . Oh my God. A mother? A loving parent? At least, Arlo's responding to it as if it's truly speaking to him, truly reading, truly having his best interests at heart, when it doesn't even have one.

I'm frozen in place. And horrified, because Hugo Harrison is monumentally powerful, sure, but this robot and everything else Hugo and Psyckē create involves *hundreds* of people. His CEO and CFO and his board of directors, his stockholders and employers, are all on board with what is happening in that room right now—using the pure light of Arlo for profit.

I hover by the door. I want to burst in there, but what can I do? It would take a superhero to fight that much power. Not a girl.

Back in my room I keep my sight fixed on that monitor, my stomach churning with upset and anxiety. I watch that empty bed until Hugo lays Arlo back where he belongs.

chapter
Twenty-Nine

IN THE MORNING ARLO HAS LITTLE CIRCLES UNDER his eyes from fatigue. I dress him for a photo shoot on the *Hugo Naut*. The photography team will make it look like he and Laura are on some great voyage rather than right here on Lake Washington, where I can still see them a few feet away.

I'm seething. Here it is, my fury, building and building. I know it's reckless, but I go into their bedroom again. Aurora is gone, a mysterious "meeting" that will take all day. I wonder if the meeting is really her and Leo going to that place they love for lunch. Greta is home, but fuck it. Fuck her, with her pinched mouth and disapproving eyes that contributed to Hugo being Hugo, her criticism inputted like data.

Boolean follows me, an oversized and hairy conscience. From Hugo's dresser I grab the baggie with the fake, unseeing eyes, models for the eyes of that robot. I want them *gone*. I'm too angry to be scared. I stride from the room, down the stairs, and out to the end of the dock. I can see the *Hugo Naut* and the film crew right there—Laura-fake-Aurora with my baby brother, and the little boat that bobs behind, *Theos,* meaning *God*. I grab an eye and hurl it. I hear the plink, and it floats on a wave and then sinks.

Sure, I get it, the goal. Robots as the perfect parents who never make mistakes, creating the perfect children, just like in that awful book, *Brave New World*. An impossible and never ever reachable goal, because children need to be seen more than anything else, seen by real eyes from a place of real love. It's the largest failing of human parents, the not-seeing, isn't it? Of humans in general? The stupid robot can only fake-see just like a bad parent only fake-sees.

Now I throw handfuls. Oh, it's creepy. It's eerie, but what isn't creepy and eerie about people and machines pretending to have hearts and souls and love and troubles? Pretending to have compassion and creativity? Those eyes bob and stare. They float off from each other, gazing oddly, wrongly. Down they go, hooray.

I don't see them anymore. But I still feel them there, under the water. And, yeah, okay, I know. When I was in the Harrisons' room, it would have been the perfect moment to put that chip back. The perfect moment to say, *Enough is enough,* to leave that hope where I found it. But nope. The chip is still zipped up in my bag, protected, the way you protect, *should* protect, the things that matter.

Ugh! Try replicating *that* illogic in a robot.

AFTER THEIR SHOOT I TAKE ARLO TO THE POOL. IT'S Wednesday, but Aurora doesn't show. Whatever she's doing must be important to her, to miss her swim. As we approach the building, I look for Arden Lee out there on the court, but I don't see him. I wonder if he's home listening to Carlos's albums, wearing some glam-rock outfit his dad would hate. I wonder if new acceptance and new understanding and new experiences can change the program.

Arlo's irritable, and every little thing is a frustration. He's upset that the water wing blowhole is up and not down, and that he wanted to pull up his swimsuit even though he can't do it himself. He cries when we get in because the water's too cold, even though it's the same temperature as always. It's hard to stay patient, but then I remember that I like things to be the way I expect them to be, too, and that my own suit is hard to get on, and that the water is definitely colder than the pool we just spent a week playing in in Mexico. He was also woken up last night. Kept awake for a good hour, at least, when he needed his rest.

I swirl him in the pool where I first fell in love with the little guy.

"You're not just a dataset," I tell him.

"Dada set," he says.

JAK MAKES ANOTHER BEAUTIFUL MEAL THAT NIGHT—grilled shrimp on greens with polenta cakes. Aurora is acting like nothing is wrong, like nothing has happened, like nothing is still happening. This is how you manage to overlook something bad, I guess—you pile enough normal-looking stuff on top until you're convinced it's not there anymore.

I watch from the stairway, mad. At her, you know, because come on. Arlo needs someone. He needs at least one person. One parent on his side, so he's not all alone.

"Let's make it old-fashioned," Aurora says. "Pony rides, games. Here at the house? With the neighborhood children, and kids from . . ."

I wait, because Arlo doesn't really play with other children. They're talking about a birthday party, happening in two weeks. It's outlandish, because it's for his *half* birthday. Apparently, people love celebrations. The public does. Birthdays and vacations and weddings and dogs.

"Way too faux-humble," Hugo answers. "This should be *huge*. The team will have ideas for locations. Don't dream small. Dream viral. It could be anywhere."

"He'll be more comfortable here," Aurora says. On Rate Me today, someone saw her in Hawaii and said she was a total bitch while buying a sarong.

"I understand my own kid. And he's not my first, remember? I know what kids like. Do you?"

Kids like a dad who doesn't abandon them, for starters. Aurora's face goes blank. He always makes her doubt herself. I'm expecting her to give in. Instead she says, "We're having it here."

Greta sits there all sour-faced. Honestly, I want her to just say a nice thing, just once. Yeah, like that would ever happen.

"That's a great idea, Aurora," Greta says.

Grr, unpredictable humans! It's not always a big mystery why some people want to replace them with a better model.

"Here, on the agreed-upon date and time," Aurora says firmly.

It's almost like she's already sent the invitations.

chapter
Thirty

ON THURSDAY IT'S ME AND ARLO AND JAK. ALL DAY and all night. I don't even see Aurora when I head out on Friday morning. Instead Yvette has the monitor, and I see Chester, the Concepts of Coding teacher, pulling up the drive as I leave. I roll down my window.

"Class today?" This is strange.

"Doing a little extra babysitting," Chester says cheerfully, and waves.

Whoa—Aurora must be *super* busy. He's a great guy, so I brush it off. Plus, I'm meeting Nino today before I go home to see Mom and Ros. We've talked on the phone every night since we've been back, and, between us, the tension of my lie is fading. But I'm still Eleanor Diamond being Eleanor Drake, with its avalanche of mess. How can he meet my mom and sister, for example, this boy who works for Hugo? My deception has made us something shoved in the back of a drawer, a secret, even if it's maybe about love.

I'm nervous. His house is only, like, a ten-minute drive from us, but the tucked-away street off the grand and curving road of Ravenna Avenue feels like another world from our hippie-shabby corner of Fremont, with its statues of Lenin, a troll, and a rocket. Here the homes have charmingly cluttered gardens and adorable porches. I pull up to the little Victorian with its gables and elaborate trim. His mom will be gone, he said, but it still feels intimidating to be at the home of a real artist like Gwen Geary. Some things feel familiar, though—chipping paint, weeds popping up between the stones, the sense of a person trying to manage a lot.

He opens the door before I even knock, so he's been watching for me. There he is, looking all shy, and I suddenly feel shy, too. He's the same Nino of that extravagant house in Mexico, the one I saw waking up and brushing his teeth and with his hair all saltwater messy, but he's also new. This is where he actually lives, him and his mom, who I've never even met. I realize there's so much more to know about him, the actual him, the one whose real life is here.

"Hi, you," he says, and kisses me quick.

"I'm here," I say back.

"So . . . we don't have a chef. Or a pool, aside from the blow-up one my mom got when it was a hundred and three one summer."

Inside, their place has old oak floors and surprisingly high ceilings, and it smells like a mix of pine and baking and that damp-soil smell that probably means there's a leak somewhere. A few of Gwen Geary's paintings hang on the walls. I recognize one I saw online—the woman with punk blue hair standing by the waterfall. And another: an older woman with saggy breasts and wrinkled arms, riding in a boat down a river. I move toward a third painting that seems really familiar: a woman in a flowing robe kneeling by a lake, seeing not her own reflection but one of a man. It's so realistic—her pale skin, and the way the light falls on her shoulders. She's so *compelling*. The expression on her face shows confusion and a deep disappointment. Her eyes—they look kind. Like they've seen a lot of life. I don't think I've seen it online, but it looks so familiar. I get the shivers when I see her signature at the bottom. *Gwen Geary*—it's so powerful. "Wow," I say. "These are *amazing*."

"Just her favorites. Her studio is full of them. After a long career there are *a lot* of canvases."

"This is the coolest house ever." It's not just the paintings—there's other art around, too. I spot little statues and quirky objects, a tiny tiger next to a lamp made from a green glass float. It's like meeting Nino's mom without meeting her, seeing the inside of her brain, her artist mind.

"That's nice of you. Dad thinks it's just messy. You should see his place. Total opposite. Small and modern. Sparse."

"Opposites attract?"

At the word *attract,* Nino yanks my T-shirt and pulls me toward him. "You're in my house." It *is* hard to believe. I love it here, too. "I baked you cookies," he says. "Your favorite, snicker-doodles."

I don't even remember telling him that, but *he* did. "You bake, too?" It's another thing I didn't know. We kiss. The kiss is delicious, but there's been so much kissing and messing around in Mexico. Here we are, alone, the chance for more. I want more. The hallway is lined with bookshelves. We bash into them as we bumble to his room, all mouths and hands.

Whoa—a bed. His room—I remember it from FaceTime calls, but I didn't see these photos. Him and two friends, Phoebe and Ralph, probably, and three . . . Little League statues? Nino, *baseball*? But, hey, I can ask later.

I'm nervous, but not enough to stop this wave. We crash onto the blue bedspread, and it goes instantly messy, the pillows a lumpy, lopsided pair. My teeth bump his lips and maybe it really hurts, because his hand goes to his mouth and he winces. I hear a car door slam and worry his mom is home.

"Is that—"

"Our neighbor."

But the idea of his mom bursting in has wedged its way into the want. I'm thinking that *this* might be the biggest benefit of becoming an adult and having your own place, the not-getting-caught part. I try to concentrate on zippers and buttons, but it's taking a lot of concentration, like, I expected sex to be a little smoother than this. Instead it's similar to that book of Arlo's, where he tries to zip the zip and lace the laces and snap the snaps, but he just doesn't have the skills yet.

There. Nino's skin and my skin, wow. I mean, not all the way, but shirts are off, and so is my bra, and his pants are semidown, and my flip-flops have been lost somewhere, and his skin is like water and mine is like water, one river.

My hands are under the waistband of his shorts, and I'm tugging them, ready to arrange his hips over me, and the whole idea of getting caught has been totally lost, like, who even cares. Walk in, whatever. I'm gone, just disappeared into the moment, when Nino catches my wrist.

"Wait, wait," he says.

Wait, wait? Wait, why?

He sits up. I swear, I'm in this wild fog, and I have to wait a second for the fog to clear to even hear him or see him entirely in focus. God! How frustrating! I try to urge him back down, but he says my name.

"Eleanor, wait."

Ugh! Okay, okay. He's sitting up, and I see him mostly naked, and I could almost laugh, because his erection makes it look like he's sitting on a . . . broomstick? Like the cutest guy witch, warlock, whatever, sitting on a broomstick, I don't know. My mind is a frustrated mess. *"What?"* I ask.

"Let's just . . ."

"Nino." A swoop of disappointment crashes in to where the wave was. Embarrassment, too. I mean, he doesn't want me, and I want him, and it feels awful.

"Obviously I want you *badly*," he says, as if I'd spoken aloud.

"I mean, if you can't tell." He gestures to his own body, and I feel bad for guys, for one split second, for having such an obvious display with nowhere to hide.

I say nothing. I hunt around for my clothes, but they're on the floor, so I just grab a corner of that blue bedspread and cover myself. The sheets are a yellow floral. Super faded, like he's had them a million years. So different from the crisp, smooth white ones at the Harrisons'.

"The thing is . . . I think I like you. A lot. So much that I want this to, uh . . ." He clears his throat. "*Mean* something, you know? And we haven't talked about this, and how it might change things, or contraception, all of that—"

"I just assumed you'd have a—" I sound defensive. I mean, I'm worried he's thinking I'm reckless, when I'm not reckless. He told me he'd had sex before, and that they'd used a condom, so I'm not assuming it out of nowhere. This is all a whole lot more complicated than I thought it would be. Like, *why*, though, but it is. There are all these feelings that go with it, more than just the feeling-feelings. I thought we would just . . . I don't know. Have sex and like each other even more after.

"I do, of course I do! I . . . How to explain? It seems like we should more than just fall into this. I did that before, I told you. Today I baked you those cookies, but I *really* wanted to make you a great, special dessert, right? Something memorable, something you love, in case this was going to be a day we'd remember for a long time, a day in our story together, right? Our long story?" He's talking fast, the words tumbling out, his face flushed. "And I realized that I don't even have a clue what your favorite dessert is. No idea. Like, so much of our time has been about the Harrisons and all that stuff, about him being your dad and them not knowing, about whatever is going on over there, and my mom and Frame, so much stuff that's not *us* yet."

I want to grab my clothes and disappear, because this just feels so humiliating. I mean, I appreciate what he's saying in some ways. But the awful truth is that I want him right now more than he wants me. At least, I don't think we need to know every detail of each other in order to have sex. I don't think we even need to love each other yet in order to have sex. And it's embarrassing, because isn't the guy supposed to feel this way, and aren't I supposed to be talking about love and our future and needing more time, blah blah blah?

Seriously, for a minute, I just want to get out of there. Maybe not even be with a person, ever. Just me, by myself, forget the whole thing. Like, I'm imagining him calling and me just making up a bunch of excuses to never see him again. But then I remember a moment when we were in Mexico. We were putting on sun lotion. There's that spot you have on your back where you can't reach, right? Nino said, *Let me help,* and I said, *Thanks.* And he tapped that unreachable spot and said, *It's like we were built with a reminder that we need each other.*

I almost choke up. The fog of wild want, that desire, it dissipates, and I see Nino, this guy I care about, looking at me with such clarity, like he *sees* me. And he's telling me that he wants to *really* see me, like maybe for a long while, and I realize it's not blah blah blah, not at all.

"Strawberry shortcake," I say.

"Yeah?"

"Nothing too fancy, but it's what's actually my favorite."

"Come here," he says.

He holds me awhile. We get dressed. The rumpled bed looks like a failure and a success, what could have been, and what will be.

WE EAT COOKIES AND DRINK LEMONADE, TWINING our bare feet together as we sit on a couple of towels on the dry yellow grass of Nino's backyard. Part of the fence is broken, and the neighbor's dog stares at us through the slats, the real stalker of this story. Nino tells me about their old dog, Brutus, and I tell him how protective Boolean's become of me.

"Do you think dogs are what people are supposed to be?" he asks. "Like, they're a goal and a road map to happiness right in front of us that we ignore?"

"They do eat their poop," I remind him.

"True," he says, and sighs. I can see that Nino is the type of person who wants to believe in something bigger, too. A hero, a villain. Goodness. "Your text last night . . . You said you figured out what the robot is for," he reminds me. "You were going to tell me today."

I completely forgot. How is that possible? Nino is how. God, look at him, sitting there with his glasses askew from our tumbling. His adorable butt on that towel that once read *Hawaii.*

"It's going to be a caregiver for kids. Maybe even a substitute parent."

"A *parent*?" He's horrified, and he's right to be.

"He makes Arlo interact with it. To teach it. I don't understand it all, but the more data the robot or any AI gets, the more it learns, and can learn on its own, I guess. The child learns from the robot, and the robot learns from the child. And then there's a point where even the creators don't understand how and why it happens, because it learns beyond what we can."

"He *uses* Arlo?" *Uses*—it's the perfect word. "Does Aurora know?"

I nod. It's terrible to admit.

"This is awful. And this is going to be for other little kids? We've got to stop this."

"Like, *how*?"

"Destroy that evil robot."

It sounds so great. It does. Two kids on old Hawaii towels, taking down a powerful giant with billions of dollars and a whole company and the world behind him. I make a face. He sighs again.

"What is *wrong* with us? We're okay handing over the most important parts of being alive?"

It feels hopeless, like all the biggest issues do—climate change, gun violence, racism. We badly want to do something, but what? How? Aren't the adults around us supposed to protect us from this shit? Parents, companies, our government? Come on, come on!

He pulls my T-shirt until I'm sitting on top of him. We kiss, only that, like it's the end of the world, and the end of the world tastes like snickerdoodles.

chapter
Thirty-One

I'VE GOT AN HOUR OR SO BEFORE MOM AND ROS GET home for dinner, so I look up Nino's mom again. I stare at Gwen Geary's photo as she stands next to the very same painting in their living room—the woman seeing the reflection of a man instead of herself in the pond. Gwen seems so confident in her jeans and T-shirt, her long braid over her shoulder. Nino resembles her, way more than he does his dad. I feel proud to know them.

It hits me then.

It can't be, can it? That painting that looked so familiar . . . I'm not sure I saved it, so I have to go back into Frame and hunt through my drafts. It's the image that popped up after I typed in *Girl spots friendly octopus in fantasy pond.*

Oh my God, I'm right. There it is. It's Gwen Geary's art, but not. It's her world, her kneeling figure, the one from Gwen Geary's mind and heart and hands. But the woman is a girl, and there's an octopus in the water instead of the man. It's wearing a hat. I was having fun, but her whole meaning, her whole message, her *voice*—it's gone.

I feel sick.

I mess around on Frame. I type *Pre-Raphaelite,* like, three times before I get the spelling right. Then I type *boat* and *woman* and *river* and *Gwen Geary* and *dolphin in a bow tie.*

It's terrible, because up pops that other painting in their house, transformed into something silly and empty. There's the boat with the woman in it, but a cartoon dolphin in a bow tie leaps from the water. The woman is young and beautiful, her saggy breasts and wrinkles gone. She's been given a tight body and an unlined face.

Gwen, standing there in her jeans, she's fighting forces so much bigger than she is. She's trying to *do* something, using her art. And she's saying, *Here I am, me, no matter what, no matter who you see or don't see.* At first I thought Frame was fun and harmless, and then, after learning about the theft, I thought that was sad. But it's more than just *sad*—it's wrong. And I feel it deeply, the wrongness. Taking someone's creation is taking their voice, their vision, the strength they're summoning to speak against all that's broken in the world. Their light, you know.

I delete the images I made, and then I delete the app itself. But it won't make this go away. Once a machine learns something, it can't be unlearned. And the machine has learned Gwen Geary.

"YOU BARELY POSTED ANYTHING ABOUT THE TRIP," Mom says. She and Ros are home from Heartland. We've brought the groceries in from the car, and now the bags are strewn around the counter. Mom reaches into one and waves a bok choy. "We're going to try a new diet."

"I never post a lot," I say. "And you guys don't need a diet."

"But people post when they go on trips," she says. "That's what you *do*. We were over here just starved for information."

"Starved for information, diet, haha," I say. They give me that *You're an alien and we're from Earth* look again.

"It's called *flexitarian*," Rosalind says. She uses her teacher voice. "It's semi-vegetarian without giving up things like burgers."

"I don't think you can be semi-vegetarian," I say. "Like, you are or you aren't, right? If you're semi, you're not? Semi-vegetarian just means you eat a lot of vegetables."

"Seriously, do you have to make fun of everything?" Rosalind asks. I can tell she really missed me.

"Seriously, fun? It's like opposite day in every sentence."

Rosalind makes a face that says she has no idea what I'm talking about. Maybe I'm trying to distract them from my trip, or maybe I'm just back, you know. Back to me and them, and feeling left out already even though we've been home for all of five minutes. In my mind this was going to look different. Then again, it always looks different when I imagine it.

"Well, you can show us your photos now that you're home," Mom says.

"Sure," I say while panicking. I knew this moment would come, and I have no real plan for it. I open my photos. They're still unpacking stuff, so they're not paying 100 percent attention. I show them a few of me goofing off on the beach that Nino took with my phone.

"Looks pretty," Mom says.

"You're sure working hard," Rosalind says.

"Where's Mrs. Von Baron? It's like you don't want me to see her," Mom says. "Are you worried that I'll chat with her in the grocery store if I know what she looks like?"

"She just hates getting her picture taken. Like, *hates*."

"Well, where are the kids?" Ros asks.

It's clear they've been discussing this, my secretiveness. I can tell it's been a thing. How fun for them, to chat and wonder and suspect things about me. I scroll. Rosalind's looking right over my shoulder, so I have to go fast. I find one with me and Arlo in the pool where you can only see the back of his head. "Arthur and me," I say.

"Cute," Rosalind says.

"Must have been nice to play around that pool for a week and half," Mom says.

"Who's that guy?" Rosalind says. "I saw a guy."

Shit! "There's no guy."

"Where?" Mom says. "I want to see. Who is it?"

"Lots of people work at the house!"

"Sitting by the pool, his legs dangling in?" Rosalind's eyes narrow.

"They let everyone use the pool, same as me. Staff." Would it be so bad to tell them? About Nino, anyway? Why is every part of my body screaming no, no, no? It's probably like basketball, and drawing—I need to be free to have it matter without the risk of it getting wrecked. Things that matter that much deserve protection, they do, they do.

"Summer romance," Mom says, and elbows Rosalind, and they laugh. She hated Niles at first, downright hated him, and was kind of mean to Ros about it until he mowed our lawn and fixed our Wi-Fi and brought her this special coffee from Maui that his parents like. Nino—I just can't see him doing that kind of thing.

I put my phone away. I reach into a bag and take out the hamburger buns. I pretend to be mad, or else I *am* mad; it's hard to tell. I think I am, but I don't know why. I'm just tense and overwhelmed. I can't stand carrying this secret anymore.

"Well, you sure look all tan and relaxed," Mom says. In my imagination I make the words sound glad for me, instead of tinged with jealousy and resentment. Imaginations are handy in situations like this.

"Those are for tonight," Rosalind tells me when I head the buns toward the freezer.

"I almost went to Mexico once. With *him*."

Oh God. We all know who *him* is. Him is only and ever one person. Both Rosalind and I stay silent. Maybe she doesn't want to hear this, either.

"I didn't tell you?" Mom's face brightens. "Yeah. He wanted to take me on this trip. He loves that place, for some reason. Why? No idea, it seems like Hawaii without the Hawaii to me." She laughs again at that joke.

Rosalind works hard at fitting a bag of peas into the freezer when there's plenty of room. I take what feels like five minutes sliding a carton of milk into the fridge.

"It was right before we broke up, broke up the *first* time, or I would have gone. You and I *both* would have gone, Ros. You were just my squiggly little tadpole right inside my own belly." She pats hers. I hate when she talks about us being born. I think this is something you're supposed to like or maybe even cherish, but I hate it.

"There's still time. You can still go," Rosalind says, as if Mom is ninety-five and on her deathbed, but she's in her corner, you know.

"They have a house there. Must be nice. Did you know that, Eleanor? Right in the same town you went to. You could have gone to visit. Did you see it?"

"There are lots of houses there," I mumble.

"Their pool looks a lot like the one you were at," Mom says. I freeze. Rosalind catches my eye, and we stare at each other, and our eyes have a conversation, but two different ones, I think. I hope. Hers is about Mom doing this thing again, about the Harrisons and their stuff. Mine is about whether she knows, or they do.

"*She's* not camera-shy, that's for sure," Mom says. If we know who *he* is, we most definitely know who *she* is. Aurora, the hated Aurora, the villainess. The true Mrs. Von Baron, the evil baroness, if Mom knew anything about the Miss Fury storyline. "I swear, that woman posts every five minutes. What is she *doing* to her kid? The poor thing! He's practically in every other picture. I don't get it, I really don't. My God, the sunglasses and the clothes, *endlessly*. What a bitch. I cannot understand for the life of me what he sees in her."

A door shuts inside me, that's what it feels like. "I'm sure she's more than what you see in some post," I say. Aurora's not perfect, far from it, and she's not a perfect parent, for sure, okay? But I care about her. And she *does* hate getting her picture taken, so there.

"What?" Mom says. The level of my betrayal right now . . . It's immense.

"I'm just saying, you don't know anything about her."

"I know plenty, Eleanor. *Plenty.*"

I do something incredibly dangerous. No, I don't yell or throw things. But I roll my eyes. I don't even intend to. It's like they just curved up and swirled around on their own.

"Don't you *dare* roll your eyes at me, Eleanor Diamond."

"I'm done here," I say. I swipe a box of granola bars off the counter and stalk away. I can feel the thrum of possible danger in the air, but there are no thumps of footsteps, no grab of my shirt. That's the most unsettling thing about anger and fury, not being sure when it might erupt into violence or when it won't. You always have to be prepared, in case.

I shut my door. Man, I want slam it, but my body is also filling with regret. I was so flip and so careless. My heart is pounding and I'm sweating. I feel sick. I only want everyone to love each other. It's hard to understand why that's so difficult.

I can hear them.

"Can you believe her? My *God*! Who does she think she is?"

"I wanted one of those granola bars," Rosalind says.

"Well, go get it! They're not *hers*!"

"Yeah, she'll bite my head off."

"She's so *emotional*. Jesus Christ! *You* never rebelled like this."

I wonder, you know, how many rebellious brats are really just kids speaking the truth, truth that no one has dared to say before.

chapter
Thirty-Two

THE NEXT MORNING I'M SO HUNGRY FROM ONLY eating granola bars and some crackers that were still in my travel bag that I swear I could eat that smell of bacon coming from Clementine's house. Bacon—a luxury for her. Arden Lee's mom, Jackie, must have sent over more food. I didn't bring any groceries, but I'm going to tuck more cash into that tea jar.

I knock. They don't hear me, though. Even from out on the porch I can hear them talking loudly and laughing inside, having fun. I open the door and go right in. There they are in the kitchen, Arden Lee and Clementine, these two people I love so much. The sight of them . . . How to explain? It gives me the same feeling as when I open a book—that comfort, that ease, but the sense that I might have a great time, too, and maybe discover something crucial, like acceptance. I get choked up seeing them, Arden Lee leaning against the sink, holding a glass of orange juice, wearing his rainbow tank and satin shorts; Clementine in a sunflower sundress, double suns, standing by the stove, turning bacon over with a fork, kissing Apple's head before she races past me to play next door. There's been so much, too much going on. I practically fall over this doorstep, into their company. When Arden Lee and Clementine see me, their faces light up. Seriously, they fill with light. Clementine smiles so big and says, "Oh yay!" and Arden Lee claps. Can a heart burst yet feel as full and whole as it was meant to be?

"Hey, honeys, I'm home," I say.

———

THEY SEE ME, AND I SEE THEM, TOO: HOW HAPPY THEY are, and how they're having a blast, and so I don't pile on all my troubles right then. We just hug, and I sneak a piece of fruit from the bowl and help by getting the pancakes out of the oven where they're warming. But I see something else, too. Some*one.* Xavier Chen in the backyard. He's moving this little lawn sprinkler on a dry patch of grass, yanking the garden hose so the thing is centered. It's husband-y. Not the yard-stuff part, just the way he's trying to help Clementine with this house. He's showing his . . .

How else to say it? *Love.* He's showing his love, just scooting that thing around.

I lift my eyebrows in a question.

Only one side of her mouth goes up in a grin, pleased. A new expression. "Do you mind?"

"Do I *mind*? Are you kidding? I'm so happy! That *you* are."

"Freudenfreude?" she asks.

"Super *Freudenfreude!*" It's the happiness you feel when your friend is happy.

"Where's my kazoo, damn it!" Arden Lee shouts. He's grinning like a big goof. He feels it, too.

"In your wazoo, as per usual," I say. We crack up so hard. Way more than that joke deserves, for sure.

"He's reading the book," Clementine confesses.

"He's reading *way* more than the book!" Arden Lee says, trying for innuendo that doesn't quite work, but who cares. It's wide and generous and delighted.

"CLEMENTINE!" I swear, my heart has wings and is flying around the room.

When I step outside with my plate and hand Xavier Chen his, piled generously with pancakes smeared with peanut butter, the way Clementine knows he likes them, I have a moment where I want to say those things you always see dads say in the movies. Like *If you hurt her, I'll . . .* The slightly misogynistic things, come to think of it, that don't give the person in question the slightest bit of credit. Clementine, she can take care of herself.

Instead I just say, "Hey."

And Xavier Chen says, "Hey."

Then Arden Lee races from the house, a wild satiny rainbow, whooping and hollering, "PANCAKE CITY!"

"Welcome to the Soggy Pages Book Club," I say as Clementine pulls up another lawn chair, and Xavier Chen balances his plate on his knees, and Arden Lee makes a bacon mustache to get attention, and as that sprinkler, that small fountain of hope on dry grass, attempts the impossible in the name of love.

WE DISCUSS *THE AGONY AND THE ECSTASY,* CLEMENtine's new favorite, Xavier Chen's old favorite, my and Arden Lee's middle favorite. I'm behind in my reading. I'm just at the part where Michelangelo sneaks back at night to carve his name right across a Madonna statue no one knows he created, and they're already at the part where Michelangelo has won a competition to carve a giant statue of David facing Goliath. Mostly we talk about how astonishing it is, the way this guy, this one dude, with all of his brilliance and talent and creativity, just burns and fights to express it. Not for profit or acclaim or world domination, just because his soul's got to do it. It's, like, the human spirit, you know? Creativity and love, the best parts. The most enduring pieces of it, hopefully.

Xavier Chen leaves before we do. He's super quiet, but not shy, if that makes sense. And he's thoughtful. He understands that we need some time now, just us three.

"Well?" Clementine dares ask.

"He's THE BEST," I say.

"Cutest couple evah!" Arden Lee says. "God, he *adores* you."

"You think?" Oh man. Clementine's in love! This is what it looks like. You can see it right on her face.

"Are you *kidding*?" Arden Lee and I say at the same time.

I imagine it for a second, how it might be if Nino ever joined us. It's hard to picture quite yet. I wonder about meeting his best friends, too, Ralph and Phoebe, what that would be like. No idea. This proves Nino's point, I think, that we still have a lot to learn about each other.

"You should bring Nino!" Clementine says, sort of reading my mind.

"Soon," I say. For a split second I feel bad for Arden Lee. I don't want him to feel left out of the whole relationship thing. Now *he* totally reads my mind.

"If you two feel sorry for me, I'm going to be pissed," he says. "Look at us, I'm drowning in love! If I ever want more, I have time. Come on, do we finally get to hear about Mexico?"

I TELL THEM EVERYTHING, ABOUT NINO, AND HUGO and Aurora's fight, about Aurora and Frame. I tell them about Arlo and the robot. A caregiver, a parent.

"That's so awful, El. Apple would be taken right in by that. She thinks clowns are real. And those big stuffed characters at parades, where you see the person's eyes right through the mesh mouths."

"Wait. They're *not* real?" Arden Lee says. "I thought they

lived in circus-tent houses and drove Volkswagens and ate, uh . . . probably sherbet."

"Cotton candy, but the blue kind," I say. This is not the time for a riff on clowns, but oh well.

"This AI stuff," Arden Lee says. "Some of it—what it's going to do, how it's going to really help people . . . I've been reading a ton more about it." Of course he has. That's what he does. "It can determine who might get pancreatic cancer, one of the deadliest and least treatable kinds. *Early,* you know. Life-savingly early. So much stuff to really help humanity. But this soul-stealing shit . . . They've got to protect us."

"The mysterious 'they.' *Who's* going to protect us?" I ask.

"Who ever has?" Clementine says. The three of us stare out at the hopeful fountain of love, which looks so very small in the face of such troubles.

"*I've* got to do something," I say. I'm imagining . . . Well, yeah. I'm still imagining her, Miss Fury. Saving Arlo in some dramatic rescue as the world burns. But Arden Lee and Clementine look at me like I'm a kid in a cardboard spaceship.

"Like *what*?" Arden Lee asks.

"Kill the robot?" I say. They crack up.

"Does this mean you're giving up on your dad?" Clementine asks.

"I should, because he's not a great guy, even if he might love us? He kept those photos. . . . How do you know when enough is enough?"

I'm looking into the faces of two people who struggle with these same questions. I remember my drawings, my regular superheroes. Clementine with her candle, Arden Lee with his circles of light. Me with my . . . no idea.

"Ughhhh," Arden Lee moans.

"Yeah," Clementine says, and that's all. She keeps trying to call her mom at the phone number that hasn't worked for, like, two years.

"Kids deserve better," Arden Lee says.

chapter
Thirty-Three

"I HOPE YOU HAVE A GREAT WEEK," MOM SAYS AS I
shove my stuff in my pack on Monday morning. "And I do hope
we can get on a better path."

She *does* say this, in real life, and I want to believe she means
it, but I hear the forced cheer that means she's taking the righ-
teous high road with impossible me. I *feel* impossible when she
hugs me goodbye. I'm convinced I'm a shit person she has to manage. I wish this weren't so hard. Me, her, people in general. I wish

people could just respect each other and be kind. It doesn't seem like that big of a wish.

"Bye," I say.

Rosalind pops her head into my room before they leave for work. "You're being very hurtful," she says before snapping the door shut behind her.

God, I *am* horrible. I wait until they're heading down the street before I lock the house and get in the Land Rover. My phone—the Aurora phone—beeps with a text.

Arlo is with us. Come to Psyckē at noon to pick him up.

It's strange because Aurora rarely goes to Hugo's headquarters. I send a thumbs-up, and she drops a pin of Psyckē's location, like anyone wouldn't know where it is. That pink sign blares over our whole city, like the globe on the *Daily Planet* building in DC Comics.

It's only eight. I head over to the Frame House to drop off my stuff. In some ways it's like I'm home. Boolean and I have a sweet reunion, and my room feels familiar, and I pop my head into Arlo's room just to see his stuffed animals arranged on the bed because I've missed him. In other ways the clock is ticking. This is going to be over soon. I feel *Torschlusspanik,* gate-shutting panic.

I decide to go for a morning swim and put on my ironic sea-creatures bathing suit. The green one, it just wasn't me. Man, it's a gorgeous day, and this house—how can anyone be unhappy here? You have all anyone could want in the world, so why do you need more, why do you need the world itself, and the admiration of everyone in it?

I face the sparkling lake, the dock, and the *Hugo Naut.*

Boolean finds the spot of shade nearest to me, making me feel hot just looking at his big hairy self. Nino will be arriving soon to clean those windows.

I sit by the pool for a few minutes first, reading brittle, yellowed pages about Renaissance Italy.

We've agreed to finish our book by our next meeting. A shadow crosses my vision, startling me.

"That NDA," Greta says. She's not that tall but seems to tower. "Laura says she still hasn't gotten it. It's been weeks, my friend." *My friend* means *my enemy.*

Good morning, Grandma, I want to say. The words sit right there, ready to spitefully leap.

"I gave it to Aurora," I lie. "She said she gave it to Mathew." More lies. I have to force myself to stop.

"It's a condition of your *employment.*"

I'm sad that we share DNA. "Got it," I say, instead of *Go ahead, fire me.* There's a gross burn where my ribs meet, like I've swallowed a vial of Acrothorium and it's stuck there. It feels dangerous, capable of destroying me or other people.

She goes back inside. Her little heels click on the patio. I read the same page again and again, but the words don't penetrate. There's a filament between us, me and the book, and I can't poke my hand through it.

Forget it. I step toward the pool and dive into the deep end, where I basically already am. The water feels incredible, refreshing and crisp, and I swim a few laps. When I pop up, there he is, Nino. Grinning at me, holding something behind his back.

He hands me my towel when I get out. We kiss, and yeah, he's working, and Greta probably sees, and this is risking a job he needs.

"Look." He reveals the book he brought me. One of his pulp detective novels.

"The Corpse in My Bed," I read, and laugh. The cover features a woman in a scandalous, shimmery two-piece outfit, with a guy smoking a cigarette behind her.

"I was, um, hoping you weren't thinking this after the other day at my house." He's grinning and joking, but maybe not, too.

"Oh my God, no," I say.

"I thought of another way to explain what I meant, about waiting."

I don't really want to talk about it anymore. I have to respect his feelings about it, is all. "Yeah?"

"It's like Flammarion."

I smile. "I was just thinking about it."

"The very edge of the Earth meets the heavens, and my arm is stuck out through the filament, but I want us both to walk through together. Like, really together."

God, he's the sweetest. And, man, way more romantic than I am, that's for sure. "I like that," I say. "A lot."

"The cover looks a little like your Miss Fury, too. The dark hair? From 1954, like, ten years later."

"You looked her up!"

"I'm interested. And I'd really love to see your own art."

"I love that you'd love to see it," I say. I do. I'm so pleased, I swear, I'm wearing that same smile as Clementine.

I KISS NINO GOODBYE.

"Don't get abducted at Psyckē," he says. "If you find yourself in the UFO being carried up into space, send a sign."

I give him a two-fingered salute that I think is from *Star Trek* but might actually be a Hawaiian expression of gratitude. He waves his hose, haha.

I'm nervous to go to Psyckē. Really nervous. I remember all the stuff Nino told me about it, how it's like a city, and I'm afraid of getting lost. Well, that lasts for all of two minutes, because I'm barely in the Land Rover when my Aurora phone starts buzzing. *Get Nino to drive you over. H and I will leave in one car. Tell reception you're there to see us.* Then a heart emoji.

Instantly my nervousness turns to an unsettled dread. That heart—it's for her and Hugo, I'm sure. She's back, all right. So much for being done, finished. So much for protecting Arlo and herself. Why is it so hard to do that? Protect children, yeah, but also ourselves? We all need a personal superhero, one who won't allow bad people to get near us.

"Hey!" I call to Nino. I show him the phone.

Water drips from the windows, soap, too. If he leaves without finishing, it'll be a mess. Streaks are forming already. He shrugs. "If they say so."

It's the first time I've been in Nino's truck, so I take inventory. Mom's car smells like pine air refreshener, with back notes of cigarettes smoked long ago. But Nino's old truck smells like cracked, heated vinyl seats, with back notes of sun-sand-beach and songs of the 1970s.

"Eleanor, meet Bowie."

"Bowie?"

"Dad's had this truck forever. Since he first heard David Bowie and felt seen."

"Nice," I say, and make a mental note to look him up when we get back. I don't think this thing has airbags, so I hope Nino's a good driver.

He is.

It's another thing I didn't know but do now.

THE PINK SIGN ON THE TOP OF THE BUILDING SEEMS enormous from down here on the ground.

"Ready?" Nino says.

"I guess." Cool air hits as we enter. All we can see from the stylish lobby is the long curve of the reception desk, the command center of a sci-fi ship. I approach the receptionist.

"Eleanor Diamond to see Aurora and Hugo?"

"One minute, please," he says. And then, "She'll be right with you."

Hurdle number one accomplished, I think. But when I turn back to Nino, he looks like he's been punched. He's pale, and he's running his hand through his curls, and even his glasses are knocked sideways.

"Are you okay?"

"Eleanor," he breathes. I have no idea what the problem is, none. Zero. I'm so busy living in the world inside my head, you know, like we all are.

"What?"

"*Diamond.* You gave that guy your real name."

I SWEAR, MY HEART HAS STOPPED. I FEEL PARALYZED, and I'm expecting . . . I'm not sure, maybe a SWAT team, or a swarm of security guards or something. But no. When the elevator door opens, it's just Aurora, wearing one of the cute outfits I helped her create—a teal-blue skirt and a lime-green tank with yellow checked flats. She's smiling but looks tense. Maybe she didn't hear. Or was too distracted to pay attention.

"Hi, you two," she says. "Come up to the lab. Arlo's there."

Nino and I meet eyes. *The lab?*

"You look nice," I say, as I always do.

Aw, thanks is her usual reply, but not this time. "*Tricked* by light and mirrors. And high fashion." She swipes her badge to start the elevator. When the door opens, I see the glass cubicles that Nino told me about, along with an enormous central area featuring the statue of a man's head with a visible brain, the neural pathways lit in neon. The whole area buzzes as people tap on keyboards, looking up to smile at Aurora as she passes. We cruise by an enormous pop-art painting of Hugo himself on the huge back wall. As we follow Aurora, I'm a bomb about to go off. My name, my name! *Eleanor Diamond, you are such an idiot. You never think!*

Aurora's phone vibrates. "They're in the boardroom now." She takes a crisp turn. She didn't hear the *Diamond*. It doesn't seem like it. I exhale, and the bomb stays intact. "Arlo's just about finished."

"With what?" I ask.

She clears her throat, as if she's having a hard time swallowing. "The preview for the shareholder meeting this morning. Before the product reveal."

"The product?"

"The robot," she answers. "They're trying to transform the most problematic aspect of human existence: parenting. Imagine a perfect machine doing that job, a machine that lacks the complications of human emotion, and the effects of traumatic history, and the failings of patience and energy and time. A constant companion, always at their best, intuiting a child's needs by learning from children themselves."

"It learned from Arlo?"

"Not just Arlo. Lots of children."

"Aurora . . . ," I plead.

"You know, I should have just worn my Stanford University sweatshirt today. Did I ever tell you that I won a prestigious prize for my PhD thesis?"

She doesn't wait for an answer. We reach the boardroom, an enormous tinted-glass room that we can't see into. The outside wall is painted with another image, *that* image, that very same one—those two fingers touching, the ones Michelangelo painted on the Sistine Chapel ceiling. It's the tattoo just below Hugo's waistline. Michelangelo's genius, etched into his own skin.

Aurora opens the door. I see the long table with a laptop on it, a screen at the front of the room. A bunch of men and women mill around, holding champagne glasses and tiny plates of pastries. Arlo rides on Hugo's shoulders. There are identical folders on the table, too, blue and white. All these people. It's not one man doing bad things, you know?

Aurora's 100 percent Erica von Kampf, the baroness, shining her admiration at Bruno and his men. She murmurs something to Hugo that makes him laugh, and then she takes Arlo from him. She has way more important things on her mind besides my inconsequential last name. She heads us toward the door, but Mathew stops her.

"Aurora. We mentioned the need for the greatest discretion?" He points to one of the blue folders, barely visible in her bag.

"Oh! I'm so sorry." She sets it on the table, beams. "What a thrilling day, huh? Are we proud of this boy or what?" Aurora squeezes Arlo's chubby leg.

"He was great," Mathew says. "Perfect."

Now she hands Arlo to me. "Let's get you guys out of here. Someone needs a nap!"

She corrals us into the hall. "Oh wait, wait," she says. "My keys. And his diaper bag. Just a sec!"

"Oh my God," Nino says when we're alone.

But Aurora pops right out again and hands me the stuff. "Meet you back at the house? Not sure what time. The car's in my usual spot." Her usual spot. I have no idea where that is—it's my problem now. She gives a little wave and ducks inside again. We have to find someone to swipe their badge so we can even start the elevator to get out of there.

OUTSIDE, THAT PINK SIGN SHINES DOWN ON US, taking over the sky.

"I hungry," Arlo says.

"I'm going to swing by the house, get my things, and go home." Nino looks so mad. Furious.

"You're not going to finish the windows?"

"I can't do this anymore. I mean, there's a point where if you're not against it, you're for it, right? I mean, little kids . . . It's beyond stealing art. Or that *Heaven* thing." He stares up at that sign. "Did I ever tell you what my friend Ralph did?"

"Which thing? The caramel corn?" He once gave Nino, like, three giant tins of it, unsuccessfully trying to convert him into a fan. "Wait. He's an activist, you said. You mentioned a protest about a homophobic teacher?"

"Better. *Bigger.* I told you, he's kind of a secret moral crime fighter? Did you ever hear about that elder care facility that was abusing its residents, Le Ville?"

"I think so."

"You can't tell anyone this, but he changed the sign on the building. No idea how he did it, and he won't say. He doesn't want us to be implicated if anyone ever finds out it was him. But he somehow stole the first *L* and the two letters at the end, so now it reads *evil*. It's been, like, a year, and it still says that."

"That's so great."

"It was seriously high, too. Like, four stories."

We both keep staring up.

"Wait," I realize. "Wait just a second. Heartland Bank, after they sold customer account information . . . He wasn't the one who changed all the signs to *Fartland,* was he?"

"I'm sworn to secrecy," he says.

"My mom has worked there forever. And my sister just started."

"Oh God, Eleanor, you can't tell anyone!"

"Are you kidding? What Heartland did was *terrible*. Of course I won't tell anyone." I won't tell, and my whole body is filling, honestly. With hope or light or something. With the idea of *someone* doing *something*. A hidden Ralph, in disguise, going up against villains so much larger than he is.

"I so hungreeee!" Arlo wails. God, Arlo. Me too, me too, but lunch isn't going to fix my hunger.

It isn't until later, way later, after Nino's gone home, and Arlo's napping, that I see it. That blue folder, in Arlo's diaper bag.

chapter
Thirty-Four

ALL AROUND US THOSE WINDOWS LOOK LIKE CRAP.
Streaky and hard to see out of, but Aurora doesn't even notice.

"Mama!" Arlo says. "Up!" He holds out his arms, and she
scoops him out of his seat.

"What a big day you had yesterday," she says.

He looks pleased, but I doubt he's even remembering it. He
just hears her love words, her approval, and wants more. Man,
that approval stuff can be a power for good or evil, that's for sure.

"Can you take Arlo away for the afternoon?" Aurora hands him back to me. "How about the pool? The party planner is coming to finish up some last details, and I don't want him underfoot. This is going to be *big*." His half-birthday party on Saturday, in just a few days. After I saw that blue folder, I imagined . . . the baroness, rescuing her own child from the mad scientist. But no. She's back in it, this whole life with Hugo. *This is what they do*, Nino had said. And look at her. All excited about this ridiculous party.

"Big, how?" Arlo gets shy with a lot of people, especially if they're unfamiliar.

"Full-court press, literally." Her face is completely unreadable. Aurora still doesn't mention my name. *Diamond* got lost in all that glitter and gold of yesterday, and in whatever is coming. Stock prices shooting skyward, probably. "This is going to be a party no one forgets," she promises.

———

I TAKE ARLO TO THE GREEN LAKE POOL. THE PARK IS super crowded, and I have to wait a jillion years for this giant old RV to back out of a spot. It has a license plate that reads *Captain Ed* and a peeling bumper sticker, *Home of the Redwoods,* and it bumps up over the curb and crashes down again before the driver gives me a friendly wave for my patience. We walk past Java Jive, and Clementine spots me and blows me a kiss, and I blow one back. I want to run in and tell her about Psyckē, but Arlo's pumped to go to the pool, and I don't want him to see me upset.

Some of the guys on the over-thirty team are shooting hoops, and I spot Arden Lee. He's going one-on-one with this big, gray-bearded bald guy who adeptly jets around, blocking him. And then . . . Well, it's like a miracle. Arden Lee reaches for the ball and makes a clean steal from the old guy. He sprints down the court and loops that thing right into the basket. It's beautiful. It's so beautiful, I wish he could see himself, just shining in the world. I wish I could cheer, but this is his thing, so I only cheer inwardly. Still, I cheer so hard.

I'm about to head in when I see something odd. The game stops. Arden Lee is talking to the guys, and everyone's patting him on the back. He trots over to his gym bag. I don't understand, because there should be a good hour or more before his practice is over, but he slings the bag over his shoulder and heads the other direction. No idea. None at all.

The pool is quiet. Everyone is swimming outdoors today. Arlo and I pass the bulletin board where I first spotted Aurora's flyer. It feels like a million years ago. It feels like something is ending, or a lot of things. Once we're in the water, I try to soak up every minute with Arlo, his wet eyelashes when he dunks, his slippery seal body. I worry, I worry so hard, that he's going to be gone from me, and soon, and I won't see him again for a long, long time. What will happen when I meet him again when he's, say, fifteen, after thirteen more years of him being used? Of being *perfectly* unseen, falsely seen, by both his parents and some robot? What an experiment. The whole thing is, anyway, raising a kid, I guess. Two imperfect people, or one, or none, in charge of a small being with universe eyes.

I know it, I do. I've got to tell Aurora the truth about me, and soon. It's my only chance for a real relationship with Arlo.

We change and then go outside. It's hard to notice the spectacular sun and the blue sky and the green grass, or any of the already perfectly imperfect parts of being alive—drippy Popsicles, overtired kids, a child's lost water shoe on the lawn. But it's not hard to see Arden Lee. He's sitting right outside, in a tree-shaped spot of shade, his arms circling his knobby knees. He's not in his shorts and tank. He's wearing a cute silver romper and a bright, tropical-patterned visor.

He pops up when he sees us. "Hey!" he says. He's been waiting for me. I can't remember when this has ever happened. He seems serious. I start to worry. I feel like I'm on one of those intervention shows or something, but with only one person intervening.

"Hey," I say. "What are you doing here? I'm so happy to see you."

"Up," Arlo says to me.

I lift him. "This is my friend Arden Lee," I tell Arlo. "Can you say hi?" He cannot say hi, not that I blame him.

"Little dude!" Arden Lee says. "Give me five!" Arlo does not want to give five; see above. But then Arden Lee does a peekaboo move behind my shoulder, and Arlo smiles.

"Why aren't you at practice?"

"I think I'm done with basketball."

I'm shocked but try not to show it. "Really?"

"I wanted to tell you first. That's why I'm here. It kept running through my head, the thing you said the other day. *How do you know when enough is enough?* Tina—she became her full self, her full powerhouse self, when she finally ditched Ike, that abusive punk."

I have no idea what he's talking about. It's probably from a book he's read. "Tina?"

"Tina *Turner*? Musical *goddess*?"

I squinch my face in apology.

"It hit me, El. It hit me hard. There are lots of things to love, you know? I might want to try one that loves me back."

chapter
Thirty-Five

THE NEXT MORNING HUGO FLIES OFF ON ANOTHER
PR trip. Aurora is deep in party preparations for Saturday, three
days away. It reminds me of that night I watched the house before I knew them—the florists, the food, the golden sparkle. The
excitement. Yesterday a red-and-white tent got set up on the lawn,
along with a riding ring. This morning a miniature carousel arrived with a small matching Ferris wheel. No way I'd get on that
rickety thing.

"It's too big," she says about the wheel. "It's all you see." The flurry of activity is making Arlo nervous and clingy. He looked at one of the men setting stuff up yesterday and rudely said, *Go home.* Right now he's sitting in his seat at the table, his back to the whole thing, alternatingly eating blueberries and watching them fall, a tiny Newton discovering the laws of gravity. He's pretending that none of the stuff out there is happening—a useful life skill, if you ask me.

"It looks great, Aurora."

She folds her arms. "I'm really pissed at Nino. He left us in the lurch, and at a time like this! Look at that!" She points to a window the new cleaner hasn't gotten to yet. Nothing is truly a lurch for them, though. A new window washer arrived within minutes of Yvette making a call. "What was he thinking?"

"No idea."

"Don't you two *talk*? And Leo won't pick up my calls. I don't know what's going on."

She's not pissed, really—she's hurt. I see that, and I get it. I wish I could explain that friends don't quit, but employees do. I can't bear to break her heart, though. She's had four new one-star reviews after she's been spotted at a taco truck in Mercer Island, a Seattle coffee shop, a beach in Capri, and a restaurant on Coronado Island. The taco truck might be her. I mean, she loves tacos, and she gets impatient when her order gets messed up, but she's mostly been home, doing this party stuff. Her Instagram shows her and Arlo by a sandy shore, sharing peach slices at a picnic table, bathed in yellow light.

"I have a surprise," she says. "For *you.*"

"Really?"

Even the taco truck people would forgive her if they saw how sweet she could be. God! Why oh why can't people be one consistent thing—kind or cruel, selfish or caring. There would be so much less struggle if good were good and evil were evil. If bitter grandmothers didn't crochet beautiful blankets, and if sisters were only on your side, and mothers and fathers were as perfect and reliable as machines could be. If talented cartoonists weren't racist, and homophobic, and misogynistic. If visionary fathers weren't men who used their kids and their brilliant wives.

I take Arlo from his chair and follow Aurora. The baroness—she's never one thing, either, all right. She's smart, and funny, and charming, and her voice is full of music notes sometimes, as Aurora's is now. When we get to my room, she gestures to a dress laid out on the bed. It has a lacy yellow top, which connects to a white skirt with a pattern of squiggles that resemble question marks. She chose it *for me,* and my heart cinches and blooms, both.

"Aurora," I say. "That's so nice of you!"

"For the party." She smiles.

I hold the dress up in front of me so she can see. This is maybe how bridesmaids feel, contemplating the scratchy, well-meant choices of other people. Asking, *Is this me or not?*

"I love it," I say. "Thank you so much!" I suddenly wonder if Nino will be there. We talked a bit last night, but he was at his dad's house, and he told me things had gotten complicated since he quit. We couldn't talk long.

"We won't need you on Saturday morning. We'll be doing family photos, so if you can show up an hour before the actual party, that'd be great."

"Sure." I try not to let *family photos* stab me in the heart.

"Come on," she says. "Wait till you see." She grabs my arm, and we're girlfriends again, sisters, and we head to Arlo's room. On his bed there's a pair of yellow shorts and suspenders with the same squiggly design, along with a tiny white polo shirt. We'll be matching. *Like siblings* is my first thought. My initial instinct is joy and a sense of belonging. Arlo races over and, like a mini diva, tosses the clothes straight to the floor. "No party!" he declares.

Aurora ignores him. "My dress is similar to yours." She gives my arm a squeeze. I see her non-baroness eyes, her true self, and the moment is here. It's time she knows who I am.

"Aurora?"

"Laura and the team thought we should all match," she continues. "That way any post related to #PsyckedUp will have a high probability of looking amazing. *Nothing* can mess this up."

The moment passes. I'll tell her after the event. I can't wreck this for her. She's trying so hard. I suddenly remember Hugo and that restaurant he loves. The way everyone in it is a character playing a part. The whole experience is a show. The yellow clothes are costumes.

Like a bridesmaid, sure. But maybe more like a paper doll.

AND THEN ON FRIDAY NIGHT, EVERYTHING'S READY. In the morning food, flowers, balloons, servers, workers, clowns, and, get this, *a pony* will arrive. And guests, of course. Aurora's buzzing around, all happy. Hugo is back from his trip and appears for dinner. He's in a supergood mood, too, walking around in his bare feet, patting Aurora on the butt whenever he passes her. I sit on the stairs and listen in, still a part but apart.

"My dude, the star!" He tickles Arlo under the chin.

"What happened with the *Vanity Fair* guy?" Greta asks.

"It's fine." Aurora rolls her eyes.

"You don't need to fret about this stuff, Ma," he says. "He's landing in, like . . ." He checks his watch. "An hour."

"The *Times*?"

"Yes."

"*PCMag*?"

"What do we care about *them*?" He pops a carrot into his mouth with his fingers, crunches. "Bringing in a whole new era, little comet." Hugo tickles Arlo's ribs.

"A comet is what killed life on the planet," Aurora says.

"Asteroid," Greta says. "There's a *difference.*"

This, tomorrow, the whole event—I have no idea what's going to happen, but it's not a two-year-old's half-birthday party, that's for sure.

chapter
Thirty-Six

I GET ARLO READY FOR BED. BOOLEAN FLOPS ON THE floor beside us. We read *All the World*. The pastel families, the peace and the goodness—it's a place to rest. "You're two and a half tomorrow," I tell him.

"I two."

"Champion man," I say, and kiss him.

"Peon man."

I smile, but maybe that's where the trouble lies, when people feel only too small or too big. Flawed or grand. In the shadows or golden.

"I love you," I tell him. "Always."

"Love you," he says.

Hugo doesn't wait until it's dark, or until Arlo's asleep, even. Not this time. There he is in the doorway. "Wait, wait, wait!" he says to me. "Party boy can't go to sleep yet! We have one last rehearsal."

Arlo's in bed, sleepy-eyed, with one arm around the neck of a dino. An asteroid, not a comet, did those guys in, but what does it matter. Stuff happened that made them gone.

"Wakey, wakey!" Hugo, with his big nose and those bare feet, his T-shirt reeking slightly of the onions and garlic from dinner, picks up my brother. I've tried to love Hugo. I've needed to love him so bad. But little Arlo is so tired that he slumps against him, and this grown man, his father, doesn't notice or doesn't care. My anger alights, flushing my cheeks and making my eyes blaze. It's criticism. That's something Hugo *does* notice. He's got a radar for it, all right. He tilts his head. "Don't tell me that you *object*?" He says it like I'm a peon. Like I belong in the shadows.

"Object, object," I say. First the word that means *protest,* and then the word that means *a thing, an unseen thing.*

"Are you making some kind of point, Eleanor Diamond?" he asks.

It's a blow, and it steals my breath.

His face gives nothing away. He's all calm smugness, the guy who moves the queen, checkmate, on the board. And I look back at him with . . . God! Need. Terror. This could go either way—

everything I ever wanted, or else ruin. Will I live my whole life with this particular hope? That the people who were here when I came into the world, the people assigned to love me and accept me and care for me, might do those things without me having to perform and measure up and give and disappear? It's the most basic hope, probably, as deep as your own DNA.

"You know who I am." I'm shocked, but why should I be? I gave them my name. Does Aurora know, too? It sure didn't seem like it, but I can't think about that now.

"You told my receptionist! During one of the biggest meetings of my life!"

I want to say, *I was right here in front of you this whole time, but you didn't want to see,* though the same was true for me. "I'm sorry," I say instead. These are the first real words I say to him as myself. Sorry that I lied, sorry that I'm here, sorry that I'm a burden, a new problem. Sorry for every possible thing he might already dislike or disapprove of.

I wait. He could hold out his arms to me right this second. He could reveal his hidden love. Or he could shut down, close the door on us. Arlo squirms. He reaches for me, but Hugo holds him firm. Even Boolean can't take it. He just can't deal with that stress, and he leaves. I need him, but he goes.

"I don't like being lied to," Hugo says.

His arms do not open; no love is revealed. My hope gets stabbed. It falls. I wish it would fall forever, but I'm beginning to understand it may never do that. It might just keep popping up and up, every time I'm sure it's extinguished, like those mean trick birthday candles that light again every time you make a wish and blow. Well, robots won't have these true-life things, either, will they? Unmet hopes and unfulfilled longings, the ache that's rapidly filling my chest. Still, I want more than a wish; I want a father. I want a father and a mother and the grandparents and the flock of birds and the big tree.

I want more than this hole, so deep and wide and permanent. See, Hugo? I'm disappointed, too. *I* disapprove.

"I'm sorry," I say again. "I wanted to meet you. *Know* you."

"You could have just called me. I'm right here."

Just. "I wasn't sure if you . . . would be open to it. My mom said no, but it seemed like maybe . . ." How to explain? All the stuff Ros and I heard for years, but those baby photos, too.

He ignores this. None of it's important to him, not really. Do I see him? That's the thing. Do I recognize his genius? "What I want to know, what I really want to know, is *why* you're all prissy-faced, doomy about the robot, huh? You don't *get* it?" he asks. "You don't *appreciate* what I'm trying to accomplish? Everyone else understands how huge this is. What's *your* problem?"

"It's huge, all right." I can't even believe he cares about my opinion. I'm nobody. It's probably like when Mom gets honked at by some driver and stays mad for days.

"Jesus! You say that like we're not changing the world. We're going back to where it all *begins,* where it all gets fucked up, and we're making that right! Wouldn't you have wanted that from me? Perfect guy? Perfect dad?" I can see Arlo's distress level rising—his whole body shouts it. If Hugo handed him over, Arlo would be fine, but Hugo doesn't. He doesn't even hear Arlo.

"I just wanted you. You know, *around*."

"Bullshit. This *is* me. You don't seem all that pleased. Listen. I've done some astonishing things in my life. But what could I have accomplished without all the crap from my mother? If she gave me one ounce of credit, huh? A kid, they want to be loved. They want someone to think they're awesome. The robot gives a kid what they really *need*."

It's a dark night in the metropolis. We're two comic-book figures fighting on a high-up ledge. "What they need is to be seen. By a person. Even if that person isn't perfect. Your robot could never do that. It can never be human," I say.

"I'm not trying to make a *human*. Human is the *problem*. She's *better* than a human. She knows exactly what to say, and when, and how. You should see these kids when that robot praises them and showers them with approval. They shine!"

"Leno," Arlo whines.

"That's a terrible kind of shine. Too much praise is as bad as not enough." Am I wrong? Ros might think so.

"Are you *kidding* me? You want to meet me and know me, and I get *this*? You're supposed to be my *kid*? No one treats me like this."

"Your robots are only going to make more robots," I say. "And on and on."

His face goes stony. Does every villain believe he's actually the hero? "Well, I can't trust you now." Hugo's pupils become dark, dead circles. His eyes go as blank as all the ones at the bottom of the lake. I can almost feel it inside of him, how big this is, how unforgivable, for the deceiver to be deceived, and the big ego to be denied. He's going away, fast. Retreating, oh my God. Maybe gone for good already.

I panic. My anger collapses. My brave words do. "I'm so sorry." Tears roll down my face. I'm losing it, I'm losing everything. "I'm so sorry I wrecked this. A chance to know you . . ." I'm sweating. Even in that house that is kept the perfect temperature for the perfect people at every moment, my palms are wet and my heart is beating wildly, and I'm a regular mess of a human being, heated enough to pass out. I remember something about William Moulton Marston and the polygraph test, the lie detector, how he supposedly loved, *relished,* the idea that we could determine who was trustworthy and who was not. But it was Elizabeth who actually noticed the way her own blood pressure rose when she was upset.

Hugo's silent. Arlo twists his body to escape Hugo's grasp. His legs dangle down, the little fighter.

"Please," I say. I mean *Please don't shut me out,* and *Please don't leave me,* and *Please see what you're doing to Arlo, right this minute.* "I'm sorry. What can I do to fix this? You cared about us, right? You maybe loved us? You kept those photos of us. . . ."

"What are you talking about? What photos?"

"On a chip. In your dresser drawer."

"You were in my dresser drawer? Jesus Christ!"

"I'm sorry. I . . . I just saw us . . . on this computer chip. Pictures of Ros and me when we were babies. With you. Images of us together." When I say it, the word *images,* I realize it: how meaningless an image is, how disconnected it can be from what it appears to represent. It seems like proof of something, but it's only a split-second pose in pixels. One-dimensional, when we're never that.

"I have hundreds of those things. I don't even know what you're talking about. I've got thousands of photos."

I look at him. Uncanny valley—well, there's a human equivalent, isn't there? That very moment when a person goes from cool and interesting to creepy and disturbing? When our curiosity and openheartedness switch to distaste, unease, alarm, and even horror? I stop crying and pleading. My heart . . . It goes still and quiet. A wall unfolds around it.

"You can stay through the party, to help Aurora, and then you need to go," he says.

I think of every employee he's fired. But I also think of Susan, and Phoenix, and my mom, and the dog walker. This right here, this horrible feeling in my stomach, it's what Aurora is avoiding, I'm sure, by staying, by trying so hard and ignoring so much.

"Okay," I say.

"Leno!" Arlo cries.

But Hugo only heaves Arlo back up into his arms and heads out the door. Hugo will always be the more powerful one. He takes Arlo to . . . his office, probably. To rehearse with that robot. Inhuman man, with inhuman machine. Soulless, soulless. We've been maybe building creatures like that for centuries: self-centered, focused only on their own program, so very, very unseeing. Don't be fooled by the machine, but don't be fooled by the human, either. We've had robots making other robots for eons.

It's hard to leave Arlo's room. His moon night-light, his dino, his rumpled sheets with the clouds on them. He's all skin and breath and beating heart. I pick up *All the World*. I hold it close to me, I hug it hard, because . . . Well, I don't know what the because is. Just, I hope this book, all books, all art, even, have some kind of power bigger than this other power, but that's probably not true, and too much to ask.

When I go back to my room, I'm too stunned to feel much of anything besides that deep and forever hole. The yellow dress is on my bed. I will wear it, of course. I know what to do. I know what's expected. I won't be the smudge in this family, too. And I wouldn't want to ruin the pictures.

I feel inside the zippered pouch of my bag until my fingers hit that chip. At first I think I want to destroy it, toss it into the lake with those eyes, but instead I hold it in my palm. Those babies on there—they're precious. They're worth protecting. I don't need anyone to confirm that truth.

chapter
Thirty-Seven

THAT NIGHT I'M TOO DISTRAUGHT TO CALL NINO OR to reach out to my friends. And I'm way too upset to sleep. I just lie awake, wondering how this is going to end, asteroid, comet, robot apocalypse. I wonder when Hugo will call Mom, or tell Aurora about me, if he hasn't already. I wonder, really wonder, if tomorrow will be the last time I see Arlo. I listen to the waves slap against the *Hugo Naut* and *Theos,* but I don't want to look outside and see that sign, Psyckē, so large and powerful, a distressing neon pink in our beautiful, sparkling night sky.

In the morning I pack. I wish I could go into Arlo's room and give him a million kisses of appreciation for what a light he is. My heart is breaking for him, too. I want him to have an *All the World* world, not this one. *Please,* I silently pray. *Please, may he have the truck and the birds and the old and new and the me and you.*

In order to make Miss Fury mine, I have to do more than change the characters. I need to *see* the characters, and then change the plot. The story should be about kids who come up against stuff way bigger than they are and win. Or, at least, survive and come out whole. A book is a wish, too, a lot of times. A fictional wish we stare right at with our eyes open, participating in it with our full willingness, a wish that will glow and glow and stay lit for us, anytime it's dark and we need it.

The lace on the top of the dress is scratchy. Whoever made this—they thought about what it would look like, but not about who might wear it, what it would actually be like to have this against your skin. I'm already pulling on the neckline at my throat.

Something about this dress . . . It reminds me of . . . What? A dress I wore as a kid? A dress my mom had? The answer nags but doesn't come.

Downstairs, I hear the trucks arriving. The house is full of voices and motion, too. I see them out on the lawn, Hugo and Aurora and Arlo in their matching clothes. It's strange, because today Laura is wearing green, not yellow, not this squiggle design that reappears in Arlo's suspenders and in Hugo's bow tie and in Aurora's dress and in mine. She doesn't belong, but somehow even watching through this window, wearing this dress, I do. I'm *not* an employee. I'm not someone you can fire. My DNA can't be silenced.

The balloons are here. Jak made a breakfast spread for the family. I watch Greta snag a homemade cinnamon roll, and Aurora carefully pop a bit of muffin into Arlo's mouth. Has Hugo told them about me? My stomach roils with nerves. The actual party food arrives next. The waitstaff is here, and tray after tray comes in. A sound system is set up, and there's the sudden screech-blast of a microphone, *Testing, testing!* The theme is hard to understand—everything kids are supposed to like but probably don't really. Clowns arrive, and kids hate clowns. The little Ferris wheel begins to spin, and there's no way in hell Arlo will get on that. I see a snow-cone machine, and okay, okay. Lots of kids like those. I do. I like them a lot.

Someone's yelling, angry. Mathew? Or the party planner? Both. They're shouting something about a pony. It's hard to tell. There's a trailer, yeah, and that ring for the pony rides, not that Arlo will get on one of those, either.

Wait, wait. Oh my God, it's hilarious! The pony isn't a pony. It's supposed to be a pony, but it's a donkey. Perfect. The donkey made an ass of the situation, nice.

Hugo, in his question-mark-squiggly bow tie, strides over to the center of the dispute. There are hand gestures. His are dismissive. *Whatever,* his arms say. I hear his voice rise up. "Not the star of the show, anyway."

I think he means Arlo. I should have known better.

I'M SO NERVOUS WHEN IT'S TIME TO JOIN THEM THAT my hands shake on the stairwell banister. My feet in the new yellow shoes that came with the dress don't even look like my own. I'm so scared to see Aurora, to face her anger and disappointment about being lied to. I bump smack into her in the kitchen. I expect a wall of ice, but instead she beams at me.

"You look beautiful!" she says.

She *doesn't* know about me yet, clearly. "*You* do," I say. She does. She always does.

"We match." She holds her arm up.

I place my arm up to hers. My voice wobbles. God, I'm going to miss her. "We do. I love it."

Arlo saves me, the way I want to save him. He starts to cry. I don't even know where he is, but I hear his wail. This is such a mistake, all of it, beginning with the fact that we are approaching his nap time, and the guests will be arriving any second.

"Oh shit," Aurora says. "Can you . . . ?"

"Of course," I say.

OH MY GOD, LAURA'S HOLDING ARLO, BUT HE'S smacking her face. Oh man, I want to laugh, but he's losing it.

"Here," Laura says, as if she's handing off an unpleasant package.

"Hey, hey," I say to him.

There's so much activity and noise, so much stimulus

everywhere. I carry him to the quietest place I can find, out on the dock. We sit at the end, him in my lap, and I rub his back. *All the world is old and new,* I tell him, ever so quietly. I imagine us getting in one of those boats and sailing off together. We could do it, too. The little boat, *Theos,* has the key in the ignition, as always. What could they do to me, huh, if I took Arlo away from here, away from the fine event he's about to be used for, the reveal of this robot? I know stuff, a lot of stuff, stuff about Aurora and Frame, and about me and Rosalind. I never signed that DNA, NDE, whatever, and I'm his daughter, anyway. Arlo's body gets heavy and drowses in my arms. It would be easy. That's the ignition, that's the accelerator.

Yeah, like that would ever happen. I'm so dutiful that I'm still carrying my work phone. It buzzes and buzzes, and when I look toward the shore, she's waving her arms at me. Guests have arrived, I see, families with children, and people with cameras, too, big news cameras, the press. Hugo's voice begins to boom into the microphone.

It's time for Arlo to perform, and he's asleep. I'm at the end of that dock, and I've got two choices: forward toward them, or into that boat.

I go forward. I bring Arlo to his parents. It's their job to decide what's right for him.

Aurora takes him from me. "Eleanor!" She's breathless. In a flash Arlo is gone, swept up. They disappear behind a large screen that's been set up on the lawn. I wind my way through the crowd that's now here. No, not a crowd, an audience. I look around for

Nino, but I don't see him. I see his dad, though. Leo looks so alone, just standing near that fenced ring where the donkey waits to carry the little children around in a circle.

The show is beginning, or has begun. I can't even concentrate on Hugo's words. It's just a big wave of sound because something weird is happening in my body. It's happening in that hole I thought was forever. A hole seeks to be filled, and that's what it's doing. Filling, with some loud *thump thump thump*. A sound that gets louder in my head as Hugo emerges from that screen, holding sleepy Arlo's little hand. His other hand—it's being held by that robot. She smiles at the crowd, and then down at Arlo. She doesn't seem real to me, or else she seems too real. It's uncanny valley and uncanny valley.

There's applause. And then shutter-clicks, and the *thump thump thump* in my body.

"Happy birthday, Arlo," the robot says. She blinks. She smiles. Her hand ruffles his hair.

Hugo's introducing Mary. He's explaining the name—a mix of the most iconic mother of all, plus Mary Poppins, he jokes, and the crowd laughs. Hugo beams. I have that deep desire to take something of his again, more important than those eyes or that chip. That *thump* is getting so loud and strong. Yeah, that's what fury does. It builds. It's a fire, it's a blazing light.

Hugo whispers a reminder to Arlo. "Dank you," he says, just as he's supposed to.

"You must be so proud to be two and a half," the robot says. And then she kneels down and holds her arms out, and, oh my

God, oh my God, he goes in. There's a moment when we all see it, the connection. He gives a small, shy smile.

I meet the eyes of Leo Gemini, who just shakes his head sadly.

Hugo says more stuff. His big, loud genius voice blares around the lake and the city and the everywhere, the same way that pink neon from the sign blasts whether you want to see it or not. Arlo's behind the screen again, and people are clapping, and this is supposed to be a celebration for him, and I have never been more furious in my life.

There's a jumble of people and noise. I watch Mathew carry the robot into the house, and then he reappears to chat with a reporter. Little kids are lining up to ride the donkey. Hugo, looking expansive, carries Arlo on his shoulders as a small crowd waits to speak with him.

The dress. This yellow dress, the squiggles . . . I remember. I swear, it's nearly identical to one that Marla Drake has, I'm sure of it. She wears it just after she discovers the vials of Acrothorium, a substance that disintegrates metal on contact. She can use it, she realizes, to wipe out Nazi guns and tanks and destroy the enemy.

Well, I don't have any Acrothorium, but I'm in the yellow dress, and I have this fury, all right. Now *I* am that headline I saw years ago: *Protective Husky Defends Kitten Against Adult Cat.* But Arlo and me, we're the same, aren't we? I've worried about poor Arlo, growing up believing he should never have splotches and mistakes and imperfections, but this is who I am already. Face it—*I* try hard to be perfect. *I* am cultivating someone untrue. How can I see anyone else if I don't see myself first? I'm done with this game. I'm not anyone's robot. News flash! I'm going to be disappointing, so what. I'm going to be disappointing, hooray.

I stalk back into the house. Stalk—not passively watch, but aggressively walk. Where is she, that fake human? Probably locked in his office, that's my guess. I'm picturing—I don't know. If I have to go through a window, scale a wall in this outfit, I will, but I don't have a plan yet.

I run up the stairs. And—shit, she scares me. No, not Greta, not Aurora, that robot. She's sitting there right on the steps where I always watch the family. But she's all weird and quiet and rigid. She's turned off.

"I fucking hate you," I say to her. "You're a manipulative liar."

I grab her. I try to lift and, man, she's heavy. But anger has made me strong. Anger and my protectiveness for Arlo, and for all us kids. I might not like to use that word—*kid*—for myself, but that's what I am, that's what Clementine is, trying to keep her and Apple's world together, and that's what Arden Lee is, trying to keep himself together. I see why Marla Drake doesn't need special powers. Why she only needs fashion and fury. I reach for her, Mary, *it*, and I heave that thing over my shoulder. Let's not be fooled, it *is* an it, a machine, no spirit, no soul, so it shouldn't get the best things in life that we have to struggle and suffer for. It definitely shouldn't get a child's love.

Her skin is cold and rubbery, lacking the warmth of being alive. There are a lot of people right nearby, right in the kitchen and the living room. But I know this house now. I head upstairs, walk across the long hall toward the second staircase. I pass Hugo's gym.

"Your body isn't the thing that needs fixing," I say to an

imaginary Hugo when I weave my way to the exit and push open the door.

Oh, I must be a strange, strange sight. Uncanny valley—me. The robot is over my shoulder, like I'm a lifeguard saving a drowned swimmer, but I'd prefer to go in the other direction. I run toward that dock. It's wild because I'm totally getting away with it. No one even sees me, no one stops me, I'm unseen, Miss Fury in the shadows.

Well, I'm unseen because something else is happening. There's been a new development out here since I've been inside. It's clearly unexpected, a commanding voice in the microphone, gathering the crowd's attention. Is that Aurora? Is she on the stage, talking? Well, I can't stop to find out, as this thing weighs a ton, and I'm in a bit of a rush. Now the crowd roars at an announcement, something shocking, something going very wrong, or very right.

Shit, shit—I've been spotted, the girl in the question-mark dress, running as fast as possible (not all that fast, okay, okay) with a robot over her shoulder. I hear yelling, and someone is racing toward me. It's Mathew. And, man, is he ever going to be in trouble, not locking this robot up in the office, or whatever. She's probably worth . . . No idea. And I'm not kidding myself, all right? They'll make another and another and another. But this one, *happy fucking birthday,* no. No, no, no.

I am so angry. So furious, I am *fuchsteufelswild,* fox-devil-wild, the most extreme fury.

My yellow flats *slap-slap* against the dock. I could just toss her off the end, same as those eyes, but they'd fish her out, fast. She could be saved, maybe. I want Arlo saved. I want all the children saved. Every one of us—Clementine and Apple and Arden Lee and me and Arlo, and anyone else who needs it. See us, please. Truly see us, that's all, that's enough for right now.

Thank goodness I'm here, I've made it, because she's so very, very heavy. Wow, I've had to summon my superhuman strength, which has been there all along. I toss her, it, into *Theos*. I lean down, untie the rope, and toss that into the boat, too. I turn that key. Footsteps are coming closer; Mathew is. He's shouting at me. People are racing after him, shit, shit, shit, someone is filming this. People are going to see. Lots of people. Any hiding I've been doing, it's over. I'm doomed. Well, let me be doomed, if that's what it takes. Any hero in any comic knows you've got to do stuff that might wreck you if you want to crush the evil shit around you. The boat roars to life.

I give the boat a shove. It shoots off into the lake, see ya! *Theos,* with its oddest passenger ever, her legs up high in the air. Whoa—she looks like she's at a wild party, having one of those experiences that's supposed to be trained out of her. She's clearly out of control, feeling a moment of uncharacteristic unruliness or bravery, having too much fun, even, fun that she'll later regret. Oh, that's me. See? Even I'm getting us confused. That boat is spinning in circles. She's shooting from side to side. The boat is off-kilter, with that heavy metal human, all off-balance. Oh, she's going over. Yes, she is. Her hips are over the side right now, like it's a superhot day and she's decided to go for a little dip. Hey, I did that once, when Arden Lee's uncle visited and rented a boat, and let me tell you, getting back in is pretty much impossible.

Plop.

I'd love to see it, the sinking, but I've got to get out of here. Mathew's face is contorted, and he's coming after me, and Hugo's back there, too, running down the dock. There's only one direction to go, so I dive in.

When I come up for air, I hear it. The great groan of the crowd. I have no doubt that Fake-Human Metal Mary just went under. I have no regrets, not right then. I mean, instead of teaching that thing how to trick and manipulate little kids, they should have taught her how to drive a boat.

chapter
Thirty-Eight

I'M A GOOD SWIMMER, EVEN IN A QUESTION-MARK dress, and I don't have to go far. I loop around the next few houses, then haul my dripping self out of the water. I walk right up to the street, though I have no idea what to do now. I don't have a phone. Mine is still with my stuff at the Frame House, and my work phone went into the water with me.

But I'm not doing this alone, see? That's part of the point. Oh my God, there isn't only one magnificent hero in a costume; there are lots of regular ones in all kinds of outfits, just fighting the bad stuff together. I almost don't believe my eyes. I actually rub them, thinking it's a wish. But it's the truth: Nino's truck, Bowie, is coming my way. Seriously, it's driving right toward me. I stick my thumb out, like I'm an ordinary hitchhiker. He leans over and opens the door.

"What the hell? Get in."

"What are you doing here?"

"I think *I'm* the one with all the questions? I was just in my, uh, usual spot. Um, *watching*, okay? *What* is going on? I just saw a donk—"

"Hit it," I say, though no one is coming after me. No, it's that robot they're worried about. At this moment, anyway.

Now there's an equally unbelievable sight. At the end of the road, by the stop sign, stands a donkey. God, he looks casual, like he's waiting for a bus.

"Oh no."

"That's what I was just about to tell you! I was sitting there, and this donkey comes running out of nowhere, and there was all this chaos at the house, and then you—"

"We can't let him just stroll around," I say. "I don't want him getting hurt."

"That's what I'm trying to say! I was just coming after him. I didn't want him to get hit by a car or something. We can put him in the truck? Bring him back? Why are you all wet?"

"Hurry," I say. "I just sank that robot in the lake."

"You did *what*?" Nino starts giggling madly. The kind of wild, nervous laughter you can't control. "And what was all that with Aurora? I heard her on the microphone, all the commotion . . ."

"Aurora?"

"The donkey! He's trotting off!"

We both get out. That's when I realize that the yellow flats are gone, lost while swimming. I'm barefoot. I'm not in heels, okay? That's one difference. But Nino hauls the donkey by the reins as I say encouraging things, and he actually hops up into the truck bed like he's done it a million times.

And this is how, most inexplicably, miraculously, and disastrously, I finally become my own Miss Fury. Yes, there I am, I'm her, in a version of this exact frame from August 1942. Marla Drake is wearing a yellow question-mark dress, and she's in a car with a donkey. I have imagined myself in so many Miss Fury comics—hanging from ropes, jumping from planes, kissing Gary Hale, and fighting all the enemies. But oh, life, you devious fucker, you big meanie with your twisted sense of humor—I never ever imagined myself in *this* scene. In it Marla is an agent of her own disaster when she accidentally jabs the vial of Acrothorium with her high heel. What a mess! She has disintegrated the metal of her own vehicle while trying to save a donkey from the Nazis. Now she sits in the car's devastating pieces, the animal in the back, wondering what on earth just happened.

In real life *I* am in devastating pieces, wondering the same.

NINO'S MOM KNOWS WHAT TO DO WITH THE DON-
key. Let me tell you, if you ever have to even *think* a sentence like
that, you are likely in deep, deep trouble.

But she does. Somehow. I'm at their house, surrounded by
Gwen Geary's art, paintings that came from her own talent and
vision, descending from the work of the artists that came before her.
She faced the history; she looked and took it in. She learned from
them, the good and the bad, and then she made something better,
something new and uniquely hers. The women in her paintings—
they aren't objects. They're seen, and they say what's true. I want to
talk to her about this. I want to learn and be inspired by her.

Right now, though, Gwen's just out in front of her house,
watching a donkey being led up a ramp into a trailer.

"I feel like I'm dreaming," I say to Nino.

"Same," he says.

When Gwen comes back inside, we don't talk about her art.
Not yet. She's more than this thing called an artist. She's a woman,
and a mom, and a friend, at least to me, right then.

"You must be starving," she says, because real women, real
people, eat. I am, I realize. "Do you like enchiladas?"

"I love them," I say.

In the kitchen she makes efficient moves involving plates and
Saran wrap and the beeping of a microwave. And then there they
are, two mounds of cheesy deliciousness. Stupid robots really do
miss out on the best stuff, and how can you try to be human
without knowing *all* of these things—melted cheese and fear and
devastation?

"I've messed up so bad," I say. "I'm afraid to go home." Nino and Gwen just look at me with kind eyes. Nino passes me a tub of sour cream. I wonder if Aurora is thinking the same thing. Nino's dad called, and Aurora, Arlo, and Boolean are apparently stowed away at a luxury lakeside rental. Her carefully planned campaign is hitting the press. Nino showed me one of the articles. *Psyckēd Out: Aurora Harrison Battles Hubby with New AI Watchdog Group, Have I.* Wow, how I misjudged her. She's so brave. I feel a blaze of gladness at her courage.

"I'm scared," I say. I try to explain how impossible this feels, to go back to our house, where Rosalind is so golden and perfect and amazing, and where I'm just so wrong. Rosalind would never have messed up this big.

"You don't have to be perfect to be amazing," Nino says. "You don't even have to be amazing to be amazing."

I press my palms to my eyes to stop the tears. I've wrecked things with Hugo forever, and I'm probably in some legal trouble for destroying that robot, and my mother is going to *kill* me. Aurora, though . . . she's the true genius of this story.

"It's going to be okay," Gwen Geary says. She seems sure, but it's hard to believe her.

When we leave, she gives me a pair of her flip-flops to walk in.

───────────────

I WANT TO GO TO ARDEN LEE'S OR CLEMENTINE'S INstead of home. My stuff—it's still at the Frame House, my clothes, my art, my vintage *Miss Fury, Summer Issue, No. 2.* I wish Nino would just keep on driving us, going wherever we might end up. But we don't know each other well enough for that yet. He's never even been to my house until now.

"Left after the chocolate factory," I tell him, but he pulls over instead.

"Before we get there, I just wanted to play you something." He turns off the engine, pulls out his phone. "I told you the name of this truck?"

"Bowie. I was going to look him up, but I completely forgot."

"You and Miss Fury . . . I think you're going to like my dad's favorite Bowie song."

Nino presses play. He holds my hand. It's an anthem of pure emotion and triumph. *We can be heroes,* Bowie cries. *Just for one day.* It makes me think of Arden Lee's song, about *not* needing heroes. Needing, not needing, longing for, discarding . . . It makes me realize what a struggle they are, what a complicated desire, those people who seem so much bigger than us.

"Wow," I say when it's over.

"He put quotation marks around the title, though. Around the word *heroes.* To make sure we knew, right, that he meant an everyday sort? We could be . . . nothing grand, nothing huge, nothing world-changing. Ordinary."

He squeezes my hand when we reach my house. We don't even have time for a goodbye because my mom comes running out, as furious as a tornado, and he's just a dude behind a steering wheel.

My very unplanned campaign has also hit the press. *Shock Waves at Robot Reveal.* I'm still wearing that yellow dress.

"HOW COULD YOU *DO* THIS TO ME?" MOM YELLS. Nothing in my imagination can save me now. I slip off Gwen Geary's flip-flops, but I hold them close. Mom's eyes are cyclones of rage. It feels like objects are flying off our shelves, swirling around my head, but it's only her words. Her face is too close to me. I have to fight so hard not to shove her away.

"People have been *calling*," Rosalind says. She looks like she's been crying. "Reporters."

"Imagine hearing about this from *Karen*? I had to pretend to know what you've been doing all this time!"

I might be blacking out. For a second I can't even remember who Karen is, but then it comes to me: Venicenne's mom. The one who's so boring, according to Brandi Diamond. I realize that there's something worse than my betrayal: being publicly embarrassed about my betrayal.

"You *lied* to me!" she says. "How could you lie to me, after everything I've done for you?"

I want to try to explain, about Aurora at the pool, and falling in love with Arlo, and wanting to be close to my brother. About being desperate to know Hugo, the man; about longing for something that wasn't even there. But I realize that she won't hear me, not right now, if ever. I realize something else, too, that I'll never be able to explain to her: The hard thing isn't just no father; it's too much mother.

"I'm sorry," I say. "It's unforgivable, and I've been awful and selfish and the worst brat in the world." I know what to say, but it's also true.

"All these weeks, with *her*!" she says. "In Mexico, with *her*!" Worse than my betrayal, worse than being publicly embarrassed about my betrayal, is that I've betrayed her with Aurora, our family enemy number one.

I HAVE NO IDEA WHAT TIME IT EVEN IS. I JUST HEAR Mom and Rosalind eating dinner in the kitchen. They're so furious with me that I'm alone, maybe forever. I try to remind myself that it's a place I know already, my familiar place, just so I don't panic at how cold and lonely it is. I wonder about Aurora, if she's cold right now, too. I find a new article already online at *PCMag*. For once she's not described as a lifestyle influencer but as founder and chair of Have I, a global AI watchdog group. It mentions Stanford, and the prestigious award she received for her PhD thesis on the ethics of artificial intelligence. It talks about her work on Frame, and how her passion, anger, and worry have fueled this new endeavor. *I respect the tech and the talent involved,* Harrison said. *But we have a responsibility for what we create. We have a responsibility for* who *we create, too—our children and their future.*

My throat tightens with tears. Aurora has an *All the World* hope. Maybe she's not cold at all; maybe she's burning with her own light.

I'm scared for her, though, going up against Hugo. Her

relationship with him is likely done, same as mine. Her bravery—it gives me the courage to go into the kitchen, at least, to take my place at the table. When I do, Mom and Ros go silent. The silence is an enormous wall, with them on one side and me on the other. I reach toward the dish of broccoli, feeling consumed with guilt. I shouldn't even be allowed to feed myself, that's what it seems like.

Rosalind pushes her chair back. She retrieves a stack of Post-its and slips of paper. Now she drops them all over my head, and they rain down. *Bill Jasper, Wired,* one says. *Shaun Shrupti, Esquire,* reads another. There are phone numbers beside the names.

"Ta-da," she says.

"Ros . . . ," Mom says. "You don't need to answer those, Eleanor. Allison's sister-in-law's friend—she's a publicist for *Seattle Parent.* I just talked to her, and she said we should ignore them. Unless, you know, you want *me* to speak with them."

"No. No one talks. I signed an NDA," I lie. It feels like I signed a DNA NDE. My life, my own self, wrecked and ruined and gone. No home anywhere.

"Show her the video," Mom says to Ros.

"What?" I say. "There's a video? No. I don't want to see."

"Do you know how many cameras were at that event? The video was on King 5 News! Just super, Eleanor. Super. Even Niles just texted me." Rosalind shakes her head. Man, she's pissed. She shoves her phone in my face so that I have no choice but to watch that robot flinging herself into the water. I plug my ears after *Seattle billionaire Hugo Harrison's newest project had an unexpected "launch" today, into the waters of Lake Washington, in an apparent protest by a nanny for using AI on children. . . .*

Mom snickers. "It's kind of funny. Look at her legs, haha!"

Rosalind rolls her eyes. "Oh, *real* funny. And how hilarious is it going to be if she has to, like, *pay him back* for it?"

"Don't be ridiculous, Ros," Mom says, though she looks worried.

This isn't even an NDE. It's a DE.

"Eleanor?" Mom's voice changes. "The lying, the nannying, staying at their house, going on *vacation* with them, all of it . . . It was horribly wrong. Horribly. You've hurt me, and I have so many questions. But the robot thing . . . The way you *stuck it* to him? *Thank you.* I mean, *I* know why you really did this. For *us.* For *me.*"

That fury fills every part of my body again, right to the edges of my fingers. But I don't say a word. I don't see the point. I just dig my nails into my skin. I remember what Clementine said, how some people never evolve. You can't wait around for that, can you, for other people to be different? I'm the one who will have to evolve. My anger will. Maybe I can use it to fuel what matters to me, my art, same as Gwen, and Aurora, even. No idea. Not right now. Now I can only do one Eleanor-saving thing: I have to remember, in some deep and permanent way, that some eyes, like those ones at the bottom of the lake, they can't see, they just can't.

chapter
Thirty-Nine

THE NEXT MORNING MOM AND ROS GO TO THE GYM, to *work off some of this stress,* Mom says. I curl up in bed. I'm a ball of self-hatred and exhaustion and confusion. So much for Miss Fury. I'm back to the beginning, *Summer Issue, No. 2,* when she slips right off that roof, but we never see her land. I've wrecked my chances to belong anywhere.

I wish I could talk to Aurora, but I don't have a phone, and she probably hates me, too. By now she must know who I am and how

I tricked her. I want my stuff back, my drawings especially, and I miss Arlo, and Boolean, but I'll probably never see them again. I wanted to help Arlo, but I've 100 percent *verschlimmbessern*-ed, or however you past-tense that. *Worsen-bettered,* made a mess of what you were trying to improve. And it's *Weltschmerz* again, world pain. Weariness and suffering for the world and its inadequacies.

There's an annoying blast of honking outside. *Beep-beep-beep! Beep-beep-beep!* But I'm too tired to look.

Now our doorbell rings.

Ugh, ugh, ugh.

What if it's one of those reporters or something? What will I do? What if they find out that I'm Hugo's daughter? What kind of disaster will this be then?

I peek.

"Let us in," Arden Lee says.

"Emergency meeting of the Soggy Pages Book Club!" Clementine says.

"Get your book," Arden Lee says. "And for God's sake, put on some pants."

"THERE'S SOMETHING YOU NEED TO SEE FIRST." Arden Lee's driving Jackie's crappy Ford Fiesta. Its name makes it sound like a party, but the car is brown and dull, and it's always in the shop getting fixed. They make me sit in the front. Clementine might as well be up here, too. She leans forward, her head between us.

I groan.

"It's actually amazing, Eleanor," Clementine says. Her teeth look bright and her eyes shiny, even more since she fell in love.

"No, no, no," I say when I see where we're headed.

They ignore me. And now I see why. Protestors surround the front of the Psyckē building. People are marching and chanting. Lots of people. Signs bob up and down. *AI Regulation Now! AI Is Not for Kids! Keep Humanity Human!*

"The thing I most don't get?" Clementine says. "Why we'd even *want* to make a perfect fake human."

"Money, duh," Arden Lee says.

"He said he wasn't trying to make a human. He's trying to make something *better* than a human. More perfect."

"Okay," Clementine says. Her face is sad. "But wow, way to miss the point. Look at us right here, our imperfect selves, loving each other."

"Who are you calling imperfect?" Arden Lee says, and she swats him.

I watch the people chant and march as we just sit there, parked. "This all feels really bad. Like, really, really bad," I say. "Like, *I don't know how I'll recover* bad." Clementine hands me a stick of Big Red cinnamon gum, something she thinks can be as good as dessert when you don't have dessert. She gives one to Arden Lee, too, and then folds one into her own mouth.

"Très cinnamony," Arden Lee says with a flourish.

"Tell her your thing," Clementine says. "Your secret family thing."

"You have a secret family thing you never told me?" I ask.

"I was saving it for an emergency," he says.

"It seems like we've had plenty of those already, but I'm honored, I guess."

"It's a bit of sage advice," Arden Lee says.

"Which is way better than parsley advice," Clementine says.

"It's the *best* advice," Arden Lee says. "At least, it's helped me so much. You know, when I had my really bad time last year with my dad?"

"Yup."

"It's not really advice, just something to remember," he says.

"Okay."

"Most birds get up."

"Most birds get up? That's it?"

"What do you mean, 'That's it?'" Arden Lee says to me in mock horror. "This is one of our family mottos! Something my mom told me and her dad told her and so on. Something we *live* by, something we hold close to our hearts, that I am finally, finally, in your hour of need, letting you in on! A life *truth*. Because when those little suckers are flying around, doing bird life, and they make a terrible miscalculation, or just run into a moment of bad luck, i.e., someone's living room window, BAM! You hear the crash or the sickening thump—"

"*Sickening thump* is a cliché in every book," Clementine interrupts.

Arden Lee not only ignores her but also doubles down. "You hear the SICKENING THUMP, and you go out there to look. And you see the bird, right? And it looks dead, for sure. Absolutely one hundred percent a goner. Fuck! But . . . you've got to wait.

Because after a while, the little guy sorta sits up. It seriously looks dazed, like a cartoon dazed bird, like *tweet-tweet-tweet*." Arden Lee does a cartoon dazed bird impression.

"Well, first of all, I'm always too chicken to look after I hear that sound," I say.

"Me too." Clementine shivers.

"Would you guys pay attention? The point is, you think it's dead. But it gets up. It takes a while sometimes, but there it is, looking around. And after a while it flies off. It actually flies off. And, according to my mom, and to her dad before her, *most birds get up*. Most birds get up, El, and so will you."

———————

WE GO BACK TO CLEMENTINE'S AND HAVE OUR EMER-gency meeting of the Soggy Pages. Xavier Chen isn't here—apparently he's also a camp counselor for troubled kids, sigh, and he's hiking with them today. Jackie has sent over a bunch of groceries and a giant box of Otter Pops. Arden Lee's tongue and teeth are purple, and Clementine's are blue, and I'm guessing mine are orange, as we discuss the last of *The Agony and the Ecstasy*. Michelangelo—after delay upon delay, through struggle and political upheaval and even war—finally finishes the statues for the pope's tomb, and then the *Last Judgment* painting for the Sistine Chapel. When he dies, he leaves an astonishing body of work that still affects—Arden Lee looks this up—*millions* of people every year. The chapel alone gets twenty-five thousand visitors a day. *Twenty-five thousand visitors a day* who gaze upward in awe at his creation about creation, those two fingers touching. You can try to take that image, you know, in ways small and large. You can tattoo it on your own body, even, but it will never be yours.

"He still wanted to make stuff even when he was *dying*. Damn," Arden Lee says.

"Can you believe they were going to whitewash the entire *Last Judgment* painting? Ughhh!" Clementine moans.

"It *kills* me, how he had to paint on leaf bikinis so it wouldn't get destroyed by the censors. All that work, and it never got to look the way he wanted." Arden Lee opens the painting on his phone and shows it to us. "But wow. I mean, just *wow*."

Arden Lee's eyes are as sparkly as his tank top, his favorite vintage attire now, glam rock 1970s plus fedora. Me, I'm back to my Creamsicle attire. It's so wild that the three of us are sitting here in Clementine's ragged backyard, staring at Michelangelo's work some five hundred years later, just filled with . . . *something*. Some big feeling about life and humanity, as we look at what one person created through his own sweat and vision and talent.

It hits me, you know, how Michelangelo wasn't perfect, and his story didn't end perfectly—he never got what he deserved. It hits me how Clementine and Apple won't get what they deserve, either, and neither will Arden Lee, and neither will I, probably.

But we get this: the three of us, huddled over Michelangelo's heaven, Arden Lee smelling of grape, and Clementine smelling of whatever blue is supposed to be. We get summer on a scratchy lawn, friends forever. We get togetherness through hard times, through all times, and Arden Lee removing his fedora so we can choose the next book. We get ink on paper, words on a page, paint on a ceiling, music in our soul. Us, right here—it's not some manufactured heaven seen through a set of goggles; it's real. Real and beautiful, with leaf bikinis and wrong notes and the terrible mistakes and the accidental surprises, the falls and the triumphs, the splash, the sink, the swim, the wrecking, and the making. And it's perfect, you know, this moment is. Thanks to every single imperfection, including the mosquito bite on my leg and the knot in my throat, and the way Apple is here now, interrupting us, trying to squirt us with the hose as she runs around the yard yelling, "I'm home! I'm home!"

chapter
Forty

AFTER A WEEK OR SO, THE RUSH OF MEDIA STORIES
about the Psyckē party has died down, and so have those pro-
tests. Other news is appearing: the announcement of the separation of Hugo and Aurora Harrison. Her Rate Me score plummets
further, in spite of the good work she's doing, because the world
loves creative geniuses like Hugo, and William Moulton Marston.
I have no idea how I'm going to get my stuff now. It's upsetting
that my drawings are there, in that glass house.

We're having a separation, too—me and Mom and Ros. At least, they're barely speaking to me. One night, though, after I'm sure Mom and Ros are asleep, there's a tap at my door, and Ros pokes her head in.

"Um?" she says.

"Yeah?"

"So, what was it like? You know, *him*. His house."

I want to say a bunch of sarcastic things. But the Soggy Pages just picked Clementine's choice, *The Sovereignty of Good,* essays by Iris Murdoch. Xavier Chen's mom recommended it, and Clementine thought some challenging nonfiction would be good for us. It's challenging, all right. It makes me want to scream sometimes, it's so hard, and why can't we just read something for fun for once, huh? But the point is, the author talks about how true seeing means giving attention to the people and things in our world. Not the kind of attention Hugo wanted the robot to give, not the admiring kind. But attention as just a loving gaze on another person. So, with Ros, I only nod and keep my mouth shut. When I place my loving gaze on her, I see something surprising. Something we share.

"Tell me everything," Ros says.

I'M BEGINNING TO THINK THEY'RE GONE FOR GOOD, not just my things but Aurora and Arlo and Boolean, when my mom comes into my room one morning. "She just called," she says. I know who *she* is. The *she* to the *he*. My heart starts thumping hard. "Can you believe she actually had the nerve?"

"I'm the one in the wrong! I deceived them, and then I ruined, like, a jillion-dollar machine at the highest-profile moment ever. What did she want?"

"Don't be ridiculous," Mom says, gritting her teeth. "God, her voice! It's so annoying. How did you stand it for all those weeks? You can just tell she thinks she's hot shit. She wants to meet you at Green Lake to give you your bags. She said there was some stuff that was pretty important. I assume she means your *phone*."

I can't believe it. In the middle of all these important changes, she remembered. Somehow she got my things out of there. "When?"

"Today. She said you'd know the time and place? Wow. How intimate of the two of you. I told her I'd text yes or no. Good thing this is happening. I can't afford a new phone right now. But you don't have to jump because she says jump! Bossing you around, snapping her fingers. This is how she treats people, huh? She is *such* a bitch."

"Today is fine. I'll be glad to have my stuff back."

"I'll come with you," Mom says. "I'm sure I can take time off for a family crisis."

"I'm not a family crisis." I want to say a lot more, how they've always treated me like I'm the one with some problem that needs to be fixed. How I actually wonder about some of those problems now, like my rashes and my asthma. *It all doesn't have to be solved this minute,* I tell me. Loving attention can go toward your own self, too.

Mom looks like she has a lot more to say but decides against it. She's already asked me ten thousand questions, about Hugo, and Aurora, and their house, and their lives. Everything from the color of their bathroom towels to if Hugo still loves blue cheese to if Hugo ever cheated on Aurora. I told her about Sierra, then regretted it immediately. Mom seemed so happy about it when it caused Aurora a lot of pain. There were ten thousand more questions afterward, too, about that fight in Mexico, and about Sierra herself. If she looked more like her and Susan or Aurora.

"Ooo-kay," she says, and makes that motion, fingers across lips like she's zipping them.

I do know the time and place. Today is Wednesday. I say a silent prayer, but it's only one word: *Arlo*.

I'M WAITING ON THE BENCH OUTSIDE THE POOL when Aurora walks up. She's wearing a pair of cargo shorts and a T-shirt that reads *Web Summit, Lisbon* and the kind of clunky, natural sandals that Ros hates. This is how she should look, you know. The way she just plain likes. I wonder if she's even found a new nanny yet. She's hauling Arlo on her hip, bags slung over her other arm. My heart twists when I see him. She sets him down, and I kneel with my arms out.

He comes running. "Leno!"

"Boo boo, my little boo boo." I smooch him all over his cheeks. He rests his head on my chest in the longest hug ever. If

I never see him again, he probably won't even remember this, our summer together.

"Hey," Aurora says.

"Hey," I say.

"Your stuff." She lets my bags slip from her shoulder. "I had to get your art back to you, especially. That's the one thing that can't be replaced."

Oh God. I might cry already. A knot forms in my throat. "Thank you," I manage. "Thank you so much."

And then she does something entirely unexpected. She hugs me. She puts her arms around me, and it's the three of us and my stuff in an oversized and wobbly huddle on the Green Lake grass. A tear rolls down my nose, and another, and I'm a snuffly mess. I wipe my eyes and get it together because I don't want to upset Arlo.

"I'm sorry I lied to you." I can barely speak.

"Oh, Eleanor," she says. "I *always* knew who you were. I mean, *come on.*"

"Wait, what? You *knew*?"

"Hugo told me about you and your sister when we first met. I couldn't understand it, letting you guys fade off into his personal history, like you were his ex-girlfriends or something. So when a girl your age named Eleanor appeared at the pool, looking *just* like him, and like Arlo, too . . . You guys did this thing, where you touched each other's nose, and I just thought, *Here she is.*" I remember it, of course I do. Me and Arlo, the beep and the boop, the look on Aurora's face. "Well, I knew your dad didn't work at

Boeing. Plus, do you realize how many times you used your actual last name? Lots. I don't think you're meant for tricky subterfuge."

Right then I fall from all clouds, and I think my pig is whistling, and I'm shining like a honey-cake horse. Smoosh them together to make one glorious word, *aus allen Wolken fallen–ich glaub mein Schwein pfeift–strahlen wie ein Honigkuchenpferd,* because I'm shocked, and I can't believe it, and I'm so happy. In my mind right then, I peel off the Miss Fury disguise forever. It was never mine, Aurora's right, it's not who I am. "I used my own name?"

"So many times!"

"Did *he* know?"

"Not until you came to the office. And I didn't say anything because I was waiting until you were ready to tell us. I thought he'd recognize you immediately. I mean, all the time he spends in front of a mirror . . ." She gives me a *yikes* expression. "You and Arlo . . . You both look *exactly* like your dad."

My dad. How does this feel? I check around in my insides for rainbows or their opposite, but nope. A truth just sits there. The reality of the complicated man he is. Sadness, too, because hope can be so much nicer than truth. No wonder we cling to it. Fiction, too.

"Is he going to sue me or something? Or have me arrested or whatever?"

"What? Of course not. You're his daughter."

It's startling to hear it said right out there like that. I still don't even know what that means. "If a daughter falls in the forest but no one hears, does she still make a sound?"

Aurora snort-laughs. "Do you see why we're a pair, Eleanor? I just like the way your mind works. But I never did understand that whole tree-falling-and-making-a-sound thing. It's their quiet that makes trees so majestic, whether anyone sees or not. The way they stand there, being what they are, even if no one notices. They're wondrous. But oh my God, Eleanor! You sure weren't unnoticed when you went running down that dock with that robot."

She starts to chuckle at the memory. It becomes full-on laughter, slightly hysterical, and it makes *me* laugh, and Arlo gets amped up and pats me on the head too hard. Joy is doing its fountain-like burbling, but it's that other thing she said, too, filling me, lifting me: *Do you see why we're a pair?*

"The way the boat—" she manages to say, bending in half in hilarity. Oh God, it *is* funny. People are starting to stare at us. We're the two friends in yoga class again. "Her legs—" Another snort-laugh. We grab each other's arms until we're somewhat calm again. "You upstaged my upstaging!" Her eyes glitter.

"What you're doing is amazing," I say. "Wow. And people will finally give you credit for how brilliant you are."

"Whatever, you know?" She shrugs. "The work is the thing. I prefer to be a tree."

"Wait. I have a question." I have a hundred questions, about her and Hugo and what the future will bring for all of us, but it's too much for right now. "Did Greta know about me? She seemed to suspect something."

"She *always* suspects something of *everyone*. When she heard who you were, she told Hugo, *I'd take a DNA test, if I were you*. Eleanor, do you know that song, 'You Can't Always Get What You Want'?"

"No."

"Well, you can't, not with people like that. Believe me, I've tried. You should hear about the time we went to Europe." I make a face, showing support for whatever happened on that trip. There's so much more to learn about her, I realize. Her and Arlo both. "Greta barely tolerates Arlo. Now, Trevor, Hailey, and Jennifer . . . They walk on water. Like they're—"

"Golden."

"Exactly."

"I can't believe you knew who I was the whole time."

"I wanted to get to know *you,* too! And I just really like you, Eleanor. I like who you are. You're kind and good-hearted and so funny, and I *love* your style." I smile, blushing like mad. I turn scarlet, 100 percent.

"I love *your* style." I'm such a dweeb. Her T-shirt has a toothpaste splotch, but I do love it. I love her.

"I don't know what's going to happen with you and Hugo, you know, in the long run. I hope he figures out that you can't just turn people on and off like machines at your convenience. But I really want you and Arlo to be a part of each other's lives. I want you to be a part of *our* lives. Plus, Boolean insists."

"I want that, too. So much." It's all the world, that's what it is.

"This is a total long shot, but did you bring your suit?"

My heart is hammering with gladness. I put hope in the right place this time. I pull a corner of the bathing suit from my bag to show her. An ironic sea creature waves.

"Oh hooray! Let's get this stuff to your car," she says.

WHEN I GET BACK HOME, I EMPTY THE BAGS AURORA brought. My clothes are there, and my phone, and my artwork, even my shampoo. But *Miss Fury, Summer Issue, No. 2* isn't. Maybe Aurora doesn't even know about the sleek hidden drawer in that desk.

I could ask her to retrieve it, but I'm not going to. I'm done with it. I'm not canceling Miss Fury exactly; I'm just not renewing. I found out the history, as Arden Lee said, all those origin stories, and I've looked hard at it: the good and the bad, the feminism and fierceness of the comic and creating the comic, the racism and homophobia. I've looked at Miss Fury's villains and heroes, and Tarpé Mills's, too—the censors and the rivals like William Moulton Marston—and there just aren't reasonable explanations for some things. Not for making people into images or caricatures or objects to be used, not for depriving human beings of their dignity. I'm ready to make something better. It seems right that *Miss Fury, Summer Issue, No. 2* is there in the Frame House, a place of brilliant scientist billionaires, ego and danger, extravagance and fashion and adventure. A place where people don't see each other. Where even *I* thought I was seeing people, but I wasn't. It occurs to me, you know, that this is much of our job in general: figuring out what to carry forward, and what to leave behind.

chapter
Forty-One

THE BIRD, SHE'S GETTING UP.

After the sickening thump, I rise. I'm seriously dazed, like a cartoon dazed bird. But I shake my head. It's not a *tweet-tweet-tweet*, but a *no, no, no.*

I go back onto Rate Me that next morning. I delete all of my fake names, and then the account, because the truth is important. This is real life, and in real life people are not stars, one to five. They are not objects, judged by us.

It's still summer, and I'm newly without a job. The afternoon stretches ahead. I take out my drawings. I've got my Nino, and my Clementine, my Arden Lee, and my me, my Miss Fury. I know what she's missing. She doesn't have any actual powers or special skills? Bullshit! She has the light we all have, the fire, the glow; the real one, the one that no robot will ever have. It's hers and has always been hers, from the moment two fingers touch, and boom. In her hand I draw a pen. Its tip is a flame. The pen looks small, but are you kidding me? It's a fury, a force. I create a setting, a place called Flammarion, in danger from robots that look human but aren't, robots that make other robots. They attack with blinding blue lasers and neon pink sabers, and a glaring gold that isn't true gold.

Nino calls. He wants to meet me tonight. He wants to show me something. I hope he wants to show me him, under some sheets, but nope, not yet. He suggests meeting at the Ship Canal under the Fremont Bridge after dark.

Just after I agree, like, I swear, two seconds after, I get a group text from Arden Lee and Clementine. They want to get together tonight, too. It's the wildest thing, because they suggest meeting under the Fremont Bridge after dark.

Did you talk to Nino? I ask. I think that maybe they're all planning some surprise.

Nino? Arden Lee texts back.

Cute coffee dude who's your almost-boyfriend? We wish, Clementine answers.

Well, it's too great of a coincidence not to listen. Coincidences like that feel like fate, even if they turn out to be something else, something like the people who love you all giving you the same kind of message, telling you (or showing you) something you need to hear.

Can he come? I ask.

ARE YOU KIDDING?! Arden Lee answers. *OF COURSE!*

PARTY! I'll bring Xavier, says Clementine.

Want to meet my best friends? I text Nino.

If he wants to get to know me, well, here's where you really start.

I would love that. Shit, I'm nervous? But yeah.

That evening Rosalind and Mom are staying in and watching some wedding movie they like. They're already in their matching leopard shortie pajamas, like a slumber party, and I smell the start of a bowl of popcorn. I could borrow the car, but I decide to walk. I'm anxious about how it's going to go, the most important people of my life meeting each other. I carry my flashlight, letting the circle of white bounce as I walk, hitting the rocket ship, and the Theo Chocolates building with its smokestack billowing chocolate smoke, and the houses of my neighbors, our own metropolis. I arrive at the slice of the Ship Canal shimmering in what is now moonlight. I can't see it yet—the headquarters of Hugo Harrison's Psyckē.

I hear them before I see them, my friends and this guy I might love. I hear laughing and talking, Arden Lee giving a screech of delight. All the awkward stuff has happened without me, and they're already just fine, joking and getting to know each other. There's Clementine, in her cute plaid overalls with her orange braids, carrying a little camping lantern, and Arden

Lee in iridescent shorts and a chain-mail top, sporting those lit-up bracelets kids wear on Halloween, and there's Xavier Chen, too, looking shy, and my Nino, his glasses reflecting the moon.

I am so happy, with their joyful voices around me, so filled with what seems ordinary but is wondrous, the quiet, unique people you love, all in one place, that I don't even notice it at first. Far, far up on that building, the big pink Psyckē sign—someone has changed it. I have no idea how, but the *P* is burned out, and so is the tail of the *y,* and the *ē* has been ever so slightly altered. So now shouting in that night sky is a protest, and the protest says *sucks.*

Oh my God, oh my God! I laugh. I laugh with glee and surprise and the joy of something good prevailing. Genius robots, whatever, they could never have the creativity and wild imagination and fury and will to create *this.* What should we do with those all-powerful people we call heroes? No idea. But look around, look at us, we are heroes, everyday ones, aren't we? Oh man, Arden Lee will groan at that, but it's true. It's undeniable. Maybe we can't dangle from a roof on a rope, or disintegrate tanks, but we can protest and vote and make art and change a sign to shout the truth in the darkness.

"Hey, guys!" I shout. *"Sucks!"*

"Sucks!" everyone shouts back with giddy victory.

Now Arden Lee runs toward me. "ELEANOR!" he shrieks. "I GOT YOU A PRESENT!" He tosses me a battered *Happy Birthday* gift bag. "We had extras from when my grandma broke her hip. Mom made them, and we wore them to the hospital." I push aside the tissue paper, pull out a T-shirt. It's plain white, but on the back it features a big drawing of a dazed bird, standing off-balance on one foot, and underneath it reads, *Most Birds Get Up.*

I'm going to cry again, I am. I put that shirt on, right over my tank top. "I love it. I love it so much," I say.

"I brought drinks," Xavier says when I arrive in their circle. He means Mountain Dew. He passes around the bottles. He's someone who takes care of people, I see.

"I brought cookies," Nino says, and he and Xavier both shrug, grinning. He takes care of people, too.

"I guess we *all* wanted to show you," Clementine says, nodding toward the building. But then more quietly she asks, "Are you okay with this? He's still . . . your dad?"

"*So* okay. It *does* suck. It sucks so bad."

"Chocolate chip or snickerdoodle?" Nino says. He kisses me, right in front of everyone. Arden Lee puts two fingers in his mouth to whistle, but Clementine knocks him with her elbow. Nino tastes good. Really good.

"Snickerdoodles are my favorite," I say, but he knows that already. "Both is never a wrong answer," I tell my friends. It's my turn to whisper now. "Ralph?" I ask Nino. I nod my head toward the sign.

"He hated the part about the kids," Nino says. *"Hated."*

"Me too," I say.

"Same. And he's so right."

Nino passes around the rest of the cookies. He entwines his fingers with mine. Xavier brought a big blue blanket. He spreads it on the grass. I notice them now—Xavier's light-up tennis shoes, cool, who knew they made those for older people. They zigzag lightning bolts in the dark as he walks.

"Is it too late for music?" Arden Lee says, because he thinks about other people.

"It's probably okay if we play it soft," Clementine says, because so does she.

"I've got a great song that would fit this moment perfectly," Nino says. He's brought a little speaker, a glowing cube of brightness.

Well, I know what that song is, and it involves heroes, everyday ones, like the people who are adjusting themselves on this blue blanket on this summer night for a great view of the shimmering water and the moon and a towering neon sign that shouts something necessary. *Sucks,* yes it does. *Do something,* that sign also implores. You adults, you people who can do more than this act of high-wire courage, *please.*

The chords begin, and Arden Lee's face brightens. "Hey!" he says in recognition. It's glam-rock 1970s, and now there's a different spark, the flash of new friendship.

And right there, under the fake pink and under the real moon, I'm drawing this in my head, and, suddenly, it looks completely original—it looks like *mine.* I see it, the people and the story both. It's electrifying, and I'm *in* this particular party, not just watching it. I'm in all this light. I *am* this light. Those robots might attack with blue lasers, but we'll fight back with soul light and old starlight, light that inspires compassion and empathy and the creation of art. We'll shine it so we can see each other, really see, and see ourselves, too. So what if we're messy and imperfect, okay? We're real.

Pretend you're opening some *new* comic book, one with really cool lettering and bold, vivid images, colored in rainbow shades. It needs a villain, of course; every story has one, so add in the charming bad guy, the conniving-inventor billionaire. Imagine his headquarters, a building stretching to the stratosphere with a pink neon sign on top, a shade not found anywhere in nature, glaring to the point of burning your eyes. It's the extravagant lair of a titan in Gotham or Metropolis or Coast City, or name-the-place-you-live, yes, that one.

But now . . . picture your most unexpected hero, someone who looks a lot like your own self. Someone courageous and clear and other things, too—stylish and sexy, but living a regular old life of good and evil. She's wearing her faded denim shorts and a white T-shirt, one with a bird on the back, and it smells like a grandma's perfume, but you won't know that part. The bird looks a little dazed, and underneath him it says *Most Birds Get Up.* Yep, that's what she's wearing, for sure, and she's got a super-amazing flame pen, along with a flashlight. Her signature move will be the unexpected tackle, and in a few pages or many, she'll defeat a robot and emerge—triumphant *and* terrified—from a lake. The thing, the coolest thing, the best part, is that she isn't as lonely as she always felt and always feared, and she isn't as invisible, either, or as scared.

Pretend there's another everyday hero, too. She's got orange braids. Origin story: abandoned, though she definitely has the gift of sight and kindness and strength, and her light comes from a candle *and* a camping lantern, the more the better.

Now picture yet *another* superhero joining them. He burns with knowledge and shines via sequins and a new addition, glow-in-the-dark wrist bracelets. He's got too many gifts to mention, even if his backstory involves cruelty. Add in another kid, with glasses that are two discs of bright reflection and a true-gold heart; picture another, with a blue blanket cape and lightning-bolt tennis shoes; picture a Ralph, who we haven't even met yet. Origin story: abuse, triumph; let him scale tall buildings. Light plus light plus light: add a child named Apple holding fire-flowers, and a toddler in a dino shirt; give them the oldest light of universe eyes. Let all of them gather in the sphere where the villains work and live, let my pen see them and shower flame-light on them, let *art* see them—kids, each with their own story already.

See them, okay? Driven by need. See them, under the pure light of the moon, ready to face so much hard stuff, stuff no one can even imagine yet, with the special abilities they already have, their sight, their voices, their creativity, their fury. That pink glow doesn't have a chance. That pink glow sucks, all right. See them, taking back everything that should have always been theirs.

Acknowledgments

Huge love and gratitude, as always, to my cherished duo: my agent and friend, Michael Bourret, and my editor and friend, Liesa Abrams. Oh, I appreciate you both so very much. Special, heartfelt thanks as well to Emily Shapiro, Rebecca Vitkus, Barbara Bakowski, Angela Carlino, Liz Dresner, Megan Shortt, Shannon Pender, and Sarah Lawrenson, for all the thoughtfulness and care you give to our books. To my entire team at Random House Children's Books, including the RHCB marketing group, the school and library team, our sales force, and the entire supply and production chain, all led by Barbara Marcus: you have my deep appreciation.

To my dear family—enormous love: Evie Caletti, Paul and Jan Caletti, and Sue Rath. Renata Moran—*you* are family. Thank you for all our treasured years together. My beloveds: my husband, John; Sam and Nick and Erin and Pat—there are no adequate words for what you precious people mean to me. You are love and foundation, humor and support and the reason for being. Myla—I'm so proud to call you my granddaughter. You inspire me with your creativity and spirit and good heart. And to our littlest ones, Charlie and Theo and Riley, who are *so* seen, and so very, very loved—you are my pure heart-overflowing joy, that's what you are. Thank you for filling every day with purpose and light. I love all of you so much.

Miss Fury Image Source List

Chapter 1: From Miss Fury #2 by Tarpé Mills, published by Timely Comics, Inc., in Summer 1943. Licensed from Grand Comics Database (https://www.comics.org/issue/3017/) under Creative Commons Attribution-ShareAlike 4.0 International (CC BY-SA 4.0) License (https://creativecommons.org/licenses/by-sa/4.0/).

Chapter 2: From Miss Fury #1 by Tarpé Mills, published by Timely Comics, Inc., in Winter 1942. Licensed from Grand Comics Database (https://www.comics.org/issue/2577/) under Creative Commons Attribution-ShareAlike 4.0 International (CC BY-SA 4.0) License (https://creativecommons.org/licenses/by-sa/4.0/).

Chapter 3: From Miss Fury #3 by Tarpé Mills, published by Timely Comics, Inc., in Winter 1943. Licensed from Grand Comics Database (https://www.comics.org/issue/3392/) under Creative Commons Attribution-ShareAlike 4.0 International (CC BY-SA 4.0) License (https://creativecommons.org/licenses/by-sa/4.0/).

Chapter 4: From Miss Fury by Tarpé Mills, distributed by the Bell Syndicate, in November 1942.

Chapter 5: From Miss Fury #6 by Tarpé Mills, published by Timely Comics, Inc., in Winter 1945. Licensed from Grand Comics Database (https://www.comics.org/issue/4139/) under Creative Commons Attribution-ShareAlike 4.0 International (CC BY-SA 4.0) License (https://creativecommons.org/licenses/by-sa/4.0/).

Chapter 6: From Miss Fury #2 by Tarpé Mills, published by Timely Comics, Inc., in Summer 1943. Licensed from Grand Comics Database (https://www.comics.org/issue/3017/) under Creative Commons Attribution-ShareAlike 4.0 International (CC BY-SA 4.0) License (https://creativecommons.org/licenses/by-sa/4.0/).

Chapter 7: From Miss Fury #2 by Tarpé Mills, published by Timely Comics, Inc., in Summer 1943. Licensed from Grand Comics Database (https://www.comics.org/issue/3017/) under Creative Commons Attribution-ShareAlike 4.0 International (CC BY-SA 4.0) License (https://creativecommons.org/licenses/by-sa/4.0/).

Chapter 8: From Miss Fury #4 by Tarpé Mills, published by Timely Comics, Inc., in Summer 1944. Licensed from Grand Comics Database (https://www.comics.org/issue/3723/) under Creative Commons Attribution-ShareAlike 4.0 International (CC BY-SA 4.0) License (https://creativecommons.org/licenses/by-sa/4.0/).